Selected Professional Reviews

Flaherty's Crossing

A well-written book dealing with difficult issues of love, loss, healing, and faith, and never slipping into maudlin territory. A great debut novel!
—*SACRAMENTO BOOK REVIEW*

Severed Threads—Book #1, Threads Series

With plenty at stake—erotic chemistry, dastardly villains, a lost relic, an unusual setting, and a touch of the supernatural—this indie novel could stand on any romance publisher's shelf. The full package of thrills and romance.
—*KIRKUS REVIEWS*

Buried Threads—Book #2, Threads Series

Buried Threads, an erotic thriller, combines the action and adventure found in a Clive Cussler novel, the plotting and romance of Danielle Steel's books, and the erotic energy and supernatural elements of a work by Shayla Black.
—Lee Gooden, *FOREWORD REVIEW/ CLARION REVIEWS*

Banished Threads—Book #3, Threads Series

Family secrets, engaging characters, the heat of romance, and a standout suspense plot with a twisty, surprise ending make

Banished Threads a must-read addition to McFarren's popular Threads series.
                    —*CHANTICLEER BOOK REVIEWS*

Twisted Threads—Book #4, Threads Series

A tantalizing glimpse into a secret world of desire. Dive deep into the layers of this intoxicating blend of twisted pleasure and intricate mystery. Edgy, fierce, and undeniably stimulating.
—Alicia Tomelloso, *SAN FRANCISCO BOOK REVIEW*

High Flying

Kaylin McFarren's High Flying keeps the reader hooked from chapter to chapter, not only creating an exciting story premise and characters but also subverting the reader's expectations. Just when the story feels as if it's going to end up in one direction, it takes a sharp corner and veers off unexpectedly; this is done flawlessly, a true testament to Kaylin's writing skill that keeps the reader engaged till the very last words.
                    —Rachel Smith, *ENTRADA PUBLISHING*

Soul Seeker—Book #1, Gehenna Series

Soul Seeker by Kaylin McFarren is a riveting, supernatural thriller reminiscent of a Stephen King novel.
                    —Tammy Ruggles, *READERS VIEWS*

Kaylin McFarren Books

Annihilation

Kaylin Mcfarren

Distributed by:
Creative Edge Publishing LLC, 8440 NE Alderwood Road, Suite A Portland,
OR 97220

Copyright: December 2021 - Linda Yoshida
Cover Artist: Amanda Tomo Yoshida
Editors: Aimee Long & Jodi Henley

ISBN-13: 9781685640569
Printed in the United States of America

For the little devil
in all of us

"Destroy the seed of evil,
or it will grow up in your ruin."
—*Aesop*

CONTENTS

BEWARE THE DEVIL

Crighton and Ariel were strange soulmates.
They fought daily, made love, had unified fates.
Lucinda intruded, increasing their chide,
Her life filled with envy, the sin she denied.

In Hell, Crighton's body fulfilled her great need,
Creating winged armies from Nephilim seed.
Deception in battle would pull Castiel down,
Ensure the Queen's rule and secure the Lord's crown.

Crighton's young daughter found allies on Earth,
But their secrets and lies gave doubt to their worth.
With strong bow and arrows, she fought common foes,
Found compassion and strength among the Black Crows.

Satan took Legend's skin with revenge in mind,
Unaware he possessed deep feelings that bind.
His longing for Sam disrupted his purpose.
With singular thoughts, his body proved worthless.

Anxious for victory in the looming wars,
He replaced his skin with a deviant bore's.
He grounded his ash into a villain's eye,
After prophecy claims were shared by this spy.

Doom is imminent with a threat on the rise.
Satan's stolen Queen may have found her disguise.
A new prince is growing with ram horns and tail.
Leader or rebel, can he balance the scale?

Though death be random for the strong, calm, and meek,
It dies in the afterlife that others seek.
And when the end comes, complaint has no voice,
It arrives as promised, providing no choice.

So, latch windows, lock doors, turn on every light,
Horned demons are coming in the dark of night.
Beware of the shadows in long corridors,
Satan consumes souls and is coming for yours.

—*Kaylin McFarren*

PROLOGUE

The nightmare rushed back into Samara Daemonium's thoughts, leaving her gasping for air. Tangled up in her sweat-soaked sheets, she stared down at the demon-killing knife half-hidden in her nightstand drawer. A twist of darkness remained tightly coiled around the blade, concealing any trace of blood still clinging to it, but the horrifying memory of how it was used would be seared in her mind forever.

Was it only two months ago when it happened? When her world came crashing down?

Samara had always hated gossip, especially at school. She was never up to date on quarrels or disagreements between students. But even so, she couldn't help but hear about the latest Black Crow and Blue Jay skirmish. Apparently, an argument of words between gang members had escalated into a physical altercation that moved from inside the school out to the parking lot. Teachers were called in to stop it, resulting in several students being expelled. As the day wore on, everyone was speculating on the cause, but of course, no one really knew the circumstances surrounding the fight. For the most part, gang members kept their personal matters private. However, as the weekend drew near, the tension in the hallways began increasing and scuffles were breaking out on a regular basis. Debate was rampant about the cause, but Samara couldn't care less about anything that didn't directly affect her. She found herself oddly grateful for this latest round of Middle Earth drama, spilling into the hallways and outside the doors. The fact of the matter was the tension between these two testosterone-driven groups distracted the gossip-hounds from her own turmoil.

After weeks of obliviousness, or perhaps shyness on Legend Hunter's part, everyone had been waiting on tenterhooks for him to make his move, and Samara had been overwhelmed by all the gushiness and attention she was receiving from her friends. When he finally asked her to go steady, they went to extraordinary lengths to be together. In the three-minute interval between classes, Legend would meet her in the hallway, sneak a kiss, and carry her books to her next class. For the next two months, they were the perfect couple, doting on one another while walking to school. However, two weeks later, the honeymoon was over. Tension grew between them, and everything had rapidly spiraled downhill, ending in a spectacular break-up. Samara had thought it was temporary, until Legend arrived in the dining hall with Dainis the next morning. To say she was hurt would be a mammoth understatement. After five minutes of watching them grope each other at a nearby table, Samara had fled to the safety of the girls' bathroom and didn't come out for almost an hour.

All weekend, she remained in her bedroom, faking a severe headache, and refusing to take calls. Monday, however, was inevitable and she had to go to school. Legend and Dainis were walking the hallways twined around each other like vines, and Samara felt sick inside. Rumor had it that he had broken up with her because she wouldn't sleep with him, and everyone knew Dainis would. They were making no effort to hide their disgusting public displays, and Samara's lack of response over the weekend had allowed stories to grow unchecked. More than anything, she wanted to bury her head in Adison's shoulder to avoid the sympathetic, pitying looks directed her way.

Adison was a well-known member of the Blue Jays who shared classes and common interests with her. He was also a loyal friend and had shown up at her shoulder first thing Monday morning, refusing to mention one word about the whole embarrassing incident. After three days and six classes together, they walked into the library and sat down at a table.

"I'll be fine if you want to hang out with your buddies," Samara told him. "You don't need you to worry about me...not anymore."

Adison frowned and the wrinkle between his brows deepened, letting her know he was about to get serious. "I don't want to be with anyone except you, Sam. To tell you the truth, I never understood what you saw in that guy. You're too good for Legend, and everyone knows it. He's a fool for letting you go. On the other hand, I know how lucky I am to be with you." He flashed a sweet, slightly nervous smile. "Now tell me...how do you feel about seeing a movie at the Cineplex tonight?"

Samara looked down at her hands resting in her lap. "I don't know. Ask me tomorrow."

"I will. But if you say no, I'll ask you the next day and the next day, and the day after that." Adison's brown eyes twinkled, and his smile grew. Although he had recently turned eighteen in Earth years, he had the look of a mischievous child. "I read somewhere that if you're persistent, you will get whatever you're after. If you are consistent, you will keep it."

"*It?* Is that a reference to me?" Samara giggled. In the last two days, she had laughed more than she ever thought possible.

But something was holding her back from opening her heart up again—from fully trusting another demon.

Looking over his shoulder, she spotted Legend at the reception desk talking to an attractive file clerk. "He's here," she said quietly, looking back at Adison.

"As long as you both go to this school, he's going to be popping up from time to time. Don't let seeing him bother you, Sam. I'm meeting a few Blue Jays to discuss an urgent matter, but I won't be long." He stood up and kissed the top of her head, surprising her. "I'll look for you at the assembly. Be sure to save me a seat next to you."

When Adison was gone, Samara hurried out of the library with her head down, clutching her books to her chest. She headed down the long hallway towards the double doors at the main entrance, planning to escape before any of her teachers noticed her missing. However, it was a complete shock when she smashed into a stone wall and hit her butt on the ground, sending her books flying. Horror washed over her as her eyes locked onto a pair of black polished shoes and a long black robe.

Samara gathered her books and scrambled to her feet, apologizing blindly for her clumsiness. Then she looked up at Lestat Gorgon, her high school counselor. He regarded her silently with his green intense eyes and raked his fingers through his shiny black hair. In that moment, she would have given anything to know what he was thinking.

"Well, well...if it isn't Samara Daemonium? Seems it's my good fortune that you happened to drop here," he said. He chuckled while taking a step toward her, and she had to fight the impulse not to step back. "I've been looking all over for you. Do you mind?" He held the door next to him open and gestured inside. "This won't take long, I promise."

His politeness told her something was up. He was only six years older than her, and a good portion of the young female demons in the school had crushes on this guy, calling themselves *Gorgon Girls*. Samara realized the smart thing to do would be to walk away—just turn about face and dismiss him completely. His fury would be seen by anyone standing nearby and would undoubtedly dismiss her from whatever project he had in mind. However, her curiosity took over, and she followed him into the empty classroom with her head held high.

Turning around, she faced him and asked, "What can I do for you, sir?" She held her books against her chest in a protective embrace and noticed that the door had been closed behind him.

Lestat let out a snort. "What can you do for *me*?" He crossed his arms over his chest and asked in his deep, silky voice, "The real question is what can I do for *you*?"

Something about his tone wasn't quite right. If she didn't know better, she would think he was hitting on her. But that wasn't possible, was it? This was her counselor—the respected school advisor that encouraged her to become an astronomer. Yet, oddly enough, he continued to rake his eyes over her face and body, stirring her anger.

Samara decided right then and there she'd had enough. There was too much on her plate to deal with as it was, and this sick, twisted puppy was making her skin crawl. "Why were you searching for me, Mr. Gorgon? What do you want?"

He stepped away from her and returned to the back of his desk. She hated that she didn't take the opportunity to leave before something more disturbing was said.

"It has come to my attention that you've been on the receiving end of some very nasty gossip. Your former boyfriend stomped on your heart publicly and is currently parading his new girlfriend around. Have you considered that it's all a ploy to make you jealous?"

Color suffused her face, and she felt new waves of humiliation wash over her. If Lestat knew the dirty details, then the gossip was more widespread than she had thought.

"Is there a point to this conversation, sir? Because I really don't see how any of this is your business."

"Well, I'm making it my business because I know I can help you."

Samara huffed. This creature was bringing out her unladylike qualities. The woman who claimed to be her mother would be appalled by her negativity and rude behavior. But she couldn't help herself. "What could *you* possibly do to help me?" she asked rudely.

"It's obvious that you want Legend back, despite the lousy way he has treated you. That self-absorbed demon is enjoying all the attention he's getting from his friends and is willing to let you suffer to continue receiving it. The best plan to rectify this situation is to draw attention to yourself and away from him. Make yourself irresistibly attractive by dating someone else and make Legend incredibly jealous at the same time. The best way to do this is to give another demon free rein. You will have that weasel begging on his knees to have you back. In which case, you can forgive him or dismiss him. But either way, your reputation and pride will be restored."

Samara considered his plan. Legend *did* have it coming. He had been cruel and heartless—an embarrassment in front of her friends. However, she didn't have the desire or resources to pull off Lestat's plan. And as for Adison, he would always be a good friend but nothing more.

"Mr. Gorgon, I'm not going to pretend I'm in love with a makeshift boyfriend, and then dump him after using him. That's not how I operate. I'm not interested in using anyone to make Legend jealous. That would be selfish, harsh, and unfair."

"But what if the guy knew you were using him? If you made it perfectly clear that winning Legend back was your only motive for being with him?"

Samara looked up at Lestat. It was ridiculous to be discussing a personal matter like this with a school employee, and yet he had a valid point. Her ex-boyfriend needed to be taught a lesson, and she wouldn't mind being part of that plan.

"Just who do you have in mind?" she asked. "Who would be foolish enough to deceive Legend?"

"Why my brother Naburus, of course. He's a classmate of yours and has bumped heads with Legend a time or two. He would welcome the chance to make him jealous."

Samara swallowed hard. Naburus was a good-looking jock and member of the Blue Jays, enjoying the perks of popularity, romance, and inside information. But he also had a habit of sabotaging his relationships over jealousy issues, and Samara wasn't interested in making her life more complicated.

"My fear is that Naburus will believe in the lie and care too much," she said. "I don't want to be the cause of breaking hearts or destroying lives. Surely, you can understand that?"

"You're beautiful and alluring, Samara, but my brother isn't a fool. He knows when he needs to walk away and when it's time to stand up and deliver. But I'm leaving this all up to you. Whatever you choose to do, make sure you do it for the right reasons."

Samara nodded.

"Oh, and one more thing," he said. "Stay focused on your studies and try to maintain your interest in astronomy. I have a feeling that the stars are going to play an important role in your future."

Samara left Sutherlin's office feeling dazed and confused. In the hallway outside the gym, she saw Naburus gathering a stack of books from his locker. She hesitated before approaching him, telling herself it was foolish to involve another student in her ridiculous drama. Yet, surprisingly, he knew all about it and readily agreed to help her.

"I've always had a crush on you," he said.

"That's what I'm afraid of."

As she walked away, his laugh could be heard bouncing off the walls of the hallway.

The very next day, Naburus met her outside her first period class and planted a kiss on her mouth in front of her friends. It was a simple kiss that had no reason to quicken her pulse, but it did. Word spread rapidly, reaching Legend. According to friends, he didn't seem affected by the news, however, Adison was a whole different story. He walked by after seeing Naburus at her side, and the despairing expression on his face left her cringing inside.

Nothing is worth hurting a friend, she told herself. *So why am I doing this?*

Naburus went to rugby practice and Samara ducked into the bathroom to freshen up. As she hurried to her last class of the day, Legend walked by with Dainis on his arm, leaving her fuming again.

"Fucking idiots!" she blurted out. Several students turned to look at her outside their English Lit classroom. "Me, not them," she corrected.

Why were Legend and Dainis making it so hard to get on with her life? She was seeing them everywhere and was beginning to believe she was cursed.

"Hey there." A hand caught her arm, turning her around. It was Naburus, twisting a smile.

"What are you doing here?" she asked. "I thought you had practice."

"I don't mind being late, not for you."

When his lips met hers, she returned his kiss passionately. He pressed a warm hand to her cheek and gazed into her eyes, sending her pulse racing. Then he walked away, glancing back over his shoulder. When she walked into her classroom, a round of applause broke out, leaving her cringing.

This could get dangerous, she told herself. *Real dangerous. Try to remember why he's doing this, you fool.*

Two hours later, Samara arrived home and found Adison waiting on the front porch.

"If you wanted to make Legend jealous," he said, "why didn't you ask me? I thought we were friends. Maybe even a bit more than that."

"That's why I didn't ask. I want us to stay friends."

Adison shook his head. "Not possible."

"What do you mean?"

"I can't stand to watch your ridiculous shit show anymore. It's going to end badly for all of you. Don't you see that?" Adison shook his head. "I would have treated you right...the way you deserve." He looked down and lowered his voice. "I know you don't want to hear this, but I fell in love with you the moment we met. No one cares about you the way I do."

She held out a hand to him, but he stepped back beyond her reach.

"Goodbye, Sam," he said softly. "I'm done with being hurt."

He walked away, leaving her feeling frustrated and disappointed—angry that they couldn't stay friends. Why did it have to be so damn complicated?

I will never understand, she told herself. *Not for the life of me.*

The next morning, Samara arrived at school and saw Naburus standing at the bottom of the stairs leading to the main entry. He flashed a broad smile, and then he noticed the miserable look on her face.

"What's wrong?" he asked. "I thought it was going great. You've been enjoying my kisses...there's no doubt about that. And everyone, including Legend, is starting to notice. Maybe we should make a bigger show of it. Maybe I could *really* turn you on."

"Why bother?" she asked. "I'm not interested in having a relationship with you or anyone else. Not anymore."

He cocked his head to the side. "Wait a minute. We could turn this setback into a lover's spat. What do you think, sweet-meat? You could yell at me for making you jealous. Then we could kiss and makeup...give everyone something to talk about. Come on...what do you say? It might be fun to keep everyone guessing."

Samara looked down, shaking her head. *Loving Legend was the biggest mistake of my life,* she thought. *And kissing this fool was the second.*

Naburus stepped closer and lowered his voice. "You can't be serious. It's not over between us. Not until I say it is."

Samara's frown became fierce. "As far as I'm concerned, it never began."

"You're definitely right about that." He snorted and pulled up the collar of his shirt. "Jealousy isn't the only way to pierce a Black Crow's heart."

"What...what did you say?"

Naburus looked away, ignoring her. After spotting two *Gorgon Girls*, he roped his arms around their necks. "How about a foursome?" he asked, grinning. His voice was loud enough for everyone nearby to hear. "I can always ask my brother to join us. What do you say? Tonight at my place?"

Samara groaned. She walked past them and stood before her locker. Right then and there, she made up her mind to never allow a self-absorbed demon to touch her again. Better yet, not *any* demons.

Then it happened. While walking out of the cafeteria, Legend caught up with her. He asked her to meet him at the cabin in the woods—the same place they had pretended to be soulmates, before Dainis became entrenched in his life.

"We need to stop hurting one another," he told her. "I've always cared about you, and I know you still care about me. We just have to find a way to move past all this."

She mentally shook her head. "What about Dainis? I thought you two were an item."

"I ended it yesterday. Biggest mistake of my life...hooking up with her. That girl is sick, conniving, and spiteful. I was lucky to walk away with my life."

"So, now you come running back to me." Samara huffed. "I'm not interested in getting involved in your drama, Legend."

He took her hand and looked pleadingly into her eyes, seeking forgiveness.

She jerked her hand away. "I'm going to be late for my class. I'm already struggling in science because of you."

"Please...I'm begging you, Sam. Meet me at the cabin. I desperately need to talk to you." He hurried away, leaving her in a quandary. She could either fail the test she hadn't prepared for or meet up with the source of her ruin.

Ah, shit. Samara skipped her last class of the day and ran through the woods in the pouring rain. When she arrived at the cabin, Legend was standing before a crackling fire, rubbing his hands together. She brushed off her sweater before joining him, watching the flickering flames and the smoke go up the chimney.

"You're a good friend," he finally said.

"A better friend than *you* will ever be."

Legend smirked. "You're right about that, Sam. I was a terrible friend...and a horrible boyfriend."

"The worst kind."

For a long moment, they remained silent, staring straight ahead. Then Legend took her hand. "It was all a mistake," he said. "You were so serious, and I was afraid. I didn't know what real love was...not until I lost you. All I could think about was sex and pleasing myself. I was selfish, unkind, and—"

"A complete asshole," Samara added. She looked into his sorrowful eyes and kept her voice low. "This will be the last time I forgive you, Legend. I won't allow you to hurt me again. Not ever."

"Not in a million years. I promise."

He kissed her then, not gently, not tenderly. He took her mouth hungrily, almost savagely. Her throat caught on a whimper of protest as his mouth lifted from hers.

"There's something else you should know," he said. "Dainis is Naburus and Lestat Gorgon's sister. I used her and dumped her. I left her sobbing on her bedroom floor, and there's no forgiveness in that. The Gorgon family protects their own, so I'm sure they're looking for me. But you and I are together now, and that's all that matters to me."

"No! It can't be true! It can't!" Samara tried to push him away, but he stood still.

He gave her a slight, tight-lipped smile. "Unfortunately, it is," he said. "I fucked up *big* time, and there's no making it right. Not ever. I just need you to remember, Sam, no matter where you are, I'll be there. You will never be alone again. I promise."

"What are you saying, Legend? Are you telling me goodbye?"

"There's a good possibility I won't be around tomorrow."

Samara's heart was racing. "Then why don't you run while you still can?"

"I thought about that, but it's pointless, Sam. The Blue Jays have Trackers. They will find me...wherever I go."

"No! I won't allow it. I can't!"

His mouth opened wordlessly and for the space of six heart-beats they simply stared at one another.

Then Samara said softly, "Come with me." She held her hands out to him. "I can teleport us anywhere. We can disappear together."

"What about school? What about your *family*?"

She dropped her hands to her side. "They don't matter to me...not the way you do."

"You don't mean that, Sam. They love you and would do any-thing for you."

She looked down, refusing to meet his eyes. "I can't live with-out you," she murmured.

"Listen to me, Sam. I'm not going to spend the rest of my life looking over my shoulder. And I'll be damned if I let any-one harm you." He took her arms and wrapped them around his neck and wrapped his own tightly around her waist. "I still can't believe you're here," he whispered. "You're like a dream that came true."

Suddenly, there was the sound of powerful blows on the cabin door, leaving Samara staring wide-eyed at Legend.

"Hide in the closet and don't move until I tell you it's safe to come out." He picked up a baseball bat and nodded toward the bedroom.

Samara shook her head, refusing to move.

Knocks sounded on the door again.

"Damnit! Go now, or I'll skin you alive!" he yelled at her.

Samara ran into the bedroom. She crawled into the narrow closet, crouched down, and waited. Seconds later, the sounds of muffled voices and scuffles in the next room carried in the air. Three loud thuds soon followed and then complete silence.

After waiting for what seemed like an eternity, Samara realized Legend wasn't coming back for her, and she needed to know why. She slowly opened the bedroom door and what she witnessed next could only be described as ghastly. Three familiar bodies were lying face down on the floor. Blood was spreading beneath them at an alarming rate and spattered all over the walls. In the center of the room rested a 12-inch serrated-edge knife with a white elk-horn handle covered in blood.

Samara's mind was trapped in a fog of disbelief. She paused to look around again, caught in the surreal sense that everything that occurred over the past few months was destined to end in this mind-shattering catastrophe.

How could this happen? she asked herself. *Why am I the only survivor?*

Still in a state of shock, Samara stumbled out of the cabin and somehow managed to find her way home. She climbed up the back stairs to her room and sat on the edge of her bed, staring at the demon-destroying blade in her hand. For whatever reason, guilt was eating her alive, making her believe she was responsible for killing her best friend, a conniving slut, and the amber-eyed demon she wasn't supposed to love anymore.

CHAPTER 1

BEGINNING OF THE END

Two regiments of ram-horned, cloven-hoofed demons marched through the blazing corridors of Hell in preparation for the Red War against Heaven. Their stomping feet and thumping spears shook dust loose in the solid rock tunnels leading to twenty massive cellblocks, each identified by their cardinal direction: north, south, east, and west. Confined in one of the cells on the lowest level was Hecate, the Woodland Goddess and Queen Lucinda's loyal friend. Within a month of assuming control of Hell, word had reached her that Lucinda's new regime was responsible for numerous beheadings, boiling demons to death, and implementing monstrous atrocities against woodland creatures and outspoken opponents within her own council.

Believing their friendship would make a difference, Hecate arranged a meeting with Lucinda two weeks earlier and pleaded with her to abstain from cruel acts against mankind. "Think of your legacy...the positive impact you could make." The briskness she put into her voice was belied by the unshed tears glistening in her eyes. She shifted her position in the high-back chair and drew a deep breath. "Lucifer was brutal throughout his rein... up until the day he died. You've always made brilliant choices, Samara. I know that better than anyone. Lucifer made the worst decision of his life by sending Crighton to England, but only the Sovereign Sector is responsible for the consequences that followed. I'm just grateful that Lucifer didn't survive after that nasty battle with his brother, Castiel. If he had, who knows what would have happened?"

The Queen rested her chin on her fisted hands. "Indeed. But you need to remember that my name is now Lucinda. I changed it after meeting with the Knights of Darkness and taking control of Hell."

"Yes, of course. I'll never forget the day before that happened. I was in the old arena when Crighton's mother stabbed your father repeatedly," Hecate said somberly. "I understand she was welcomed into Heaven along with her soulmate, though I don't understand why..." She let her voice trail off, shaking her head. "I guess we should thank them for your justly-deserved position."

"I already have...thanked Crighton, I mean. I offered him a more substantial token of my gratitude as well, but he turned it down."

"Politely, I hope?"

"I was afraid to sit on the throne," she admitted. "That's why I waited so long to make changes. Tyrus helped Crighton escape from Hell, and Lilith played a large part in saving Ariel. But I was responsible for saving them all by agreeing to take my father's place."

"True enough, Lucinda." Hecate felt her eyes burn once more. She drew another deep breath before adding, "I'm sure your generosity will never be forgotten and will be celebrated for years to come."

"Since I managed to keep them alive, I suppose it's time for the three of us to assume our rightful responsibilities."

"Three of us?"

"That's right. Crighton, Tyrus and myself. We have a lot of unfinished business to resolve."

"Of course, Your Majesty." Hecate smiled at her, believing she was making progress.

"But first," Lucinda said, "I'd like to discuss your view on the way Tyrus' allies are likely to respond to our meeting. Especially with them opposing me at every turn. Then I'd like your personal impression on how the loyalists in my council will interpret your views on diplomacy in the woodlands. After that, there are a couple of treasury issues I promised to investigate. It's past time that my advisors and I established a tax structure and common currency. And now that we have the Imperial chambers remodeled and relaxed rules in place regarding horns, tails, and bat wings, we can start thinking about other things like enforcing appropriate punishment where it's due."

"Since you brought it up, don't you think it's a bit extreme... the way punishment is being handled? I thought you wanted to be a just ruler...the exact opposite of your father. If that's true, then why are you taking extreme measures with outcasts, human souls, and defenseless creatures? They would sing your praises if you allowed them to—"

"—run rampant and refuse to obey my laws?" Lucinda growled. She stood up with her eyes blazing red hot and her thin lips frowning. "So, *that's* why you're here. Not to support me but to oppose me like the rest of the ingrates in my kingdom. Leave and never come back here again! Your deception will not be forgiven or forgotten. Is that understood? I want you out of here... NOW!!" she screamed.

Hecate realized she had no choice but to act quickly. She returned to the Woodland Forest and announced to her guards and military forces that staging a rebellion against Lucinda's rule was essential to their survival. "Get everything ready," she told her husband. "We march at daybreak."

Word about their plans reached Lucinda quickly. Within hours, soldiers from Hell charged into the woods with bows and arrows, spears, and swords, killing hundreds of trappers defending the Woodland Goddess and their families. Those that survived were driven back to the cliff line and surrounded on three sides. Refusing to witness more deaths, Hecate surrendered on the spot and was immediately taken away. The next day, Lucinda sat on her throne and sentenced her lifelong friend to death by Execution Wheel. The device was designed to torture a prisoner in the cruelest way possible by breaking every bone in their body and then bludgeoning them to death.

Hecate's execution would be viewed by 60,000 demons in the new arena, aptly named the Theater of Pain. Then the Feast of Plenty would take place, offering human souls to the general population. The remaining otherworldly creatures, skilled in the art of manipulation, had been caged by order of the Queen and their names had been listed on her fine dining menu. After consuming *their* souls, her powers would grow stronger, exceeding Lucifer's and the goblin witches that were secretly hiding in Hell. In a matter of days, she would be invincible in the Spirit Realm—in the world beyond her current plane of existence.

Lucinda was giddy over the prospect. Although she tried to remain silent, while standing outside the bars of Hecate's cell, she proudly divulged her plans. "In two more days, I'll be the most powerful ruler in the universe and, sadly, you won't live to see it happen. No one will be able to stop me from accomplishing my goals. Not even God himself."

Hecate cocked an eyebrow. "Really? Well, I suspect *He'll* have something to say about that."

Queen Lucinda laughed. "God is powerless in the under-world. You know that better than anyone, Hecate."

The Woodland Goddess turned her face to the wall, ignoring Lucinda.

"We will be parting ways very soon. Tell me...are you afraid to die?"

"No. I've been close to death so many times that I stopped counting."

"Then you're braver than I am." Lucinda studied her intently. "You *do* know there's no chance of escaping down here."

"Why would I even bother when you provide such lovely accommodations?" Hecate waved her hand at the stone walls.

"I don't know what you have planned, but by your tone of your voice, I suspect you're up to no good again."

Hecate glanced over her shoulder. "How so? Surely you don't believe I have the ability to teleport from this place?"

"Of course not. But you're way too calm for what I have planned."

Hecate stood abruptly and stepped toward the cell door. "What's wrong, Your Majesty? Don't you trust me?"

"I trust you every bit as much as you trust me."

"As well you should." Hecate cast her a sympathetic smile. "You look flustered, darling."

"No matter. You've become a confusing creature...obviously, not in your right mind."

"Well, I would hate to be considered boring."

The Queen laughed without humor. "You will never be boring...for as long as you live."

A slow smile spread across Hecate's face. "I think I've had enough of this little conversation. Would you mind moving along, Samara?"

Surprise colored her face, turning almost at once to appreciation. "Yes, of course. Have a good night, Hecate. Don't let the screams in this place keep you awake." She stepped away from the cell bars and made her way to the exit. After a moment's pause, she laughed aloud and walked on briskly.

When she was out of sight, two guards showed up and threw two childlike creatures into Hecate's cell, one after the other. As they huddled together at the far end of her cell, Hecate used her telepathic ability to view their inner thoughts, learning their names and species with very little effort. Onoskelis was the last of her kind—an Imperial Shapeshifter, capable of transforming into any creature known to mankind. Her best friend, Yokai, was an accomplished Changeling. With a mere touch of her hand, she could replicate a demon or assume a human's identity, causing all manner of mischief.

Interesting, Hecate thought. *Why are they here?*

They whispered to one another, obviously believing their voices couldn't be heard. "There's nothing we can do," Yokai said. "Even if we managed to escape, the Queen and her Hellhounds would track us down. She's going to devour our souls and burn our bodies like all the others."

Onoskelis whimpered. "I'm scared, Yokai. I don't want to die."

The Changeling wrapped her arms around her friend. "Stay close to me, Ono. I'll protect you as long as I can."

The Woodland Goddess smoothed her hand over her torn green gown and continued to eavesdrop. After a few minutes, she finally asked, "Why are you here? Is there something the Queen's hoping to gain by keeping us together?"

"We honestly don't know," Yokai answered. "We were put here without any explanation."

"Hmmm...I believe you *do* know." Hecate was testing them and at the same time she was hatching a plan. Their innate powers might be dormant but awakening them was of pivotal importance. By linking their powers with her own, she could create a positive charge, freeing all of them. But they had to be willing to go along with her plans.

"You would be wrong," Yokai said.

"Then you need to listen well. Lucinda is aiming to be the most powerful being in Hell. Your souls and skills will help make that possible."

Onoskelis took a step forward. "If that's true and it's her deepest wish, then we are powerless to deny her."

Hecate shook her head. "I don't understand you! You accept her greed so easily. Grow a backbone and resist!" Their deaths would be instantaneous while hers would be ultraviolent and incredibly painful. This was her only chance for escape, and she needed to snatch it. "You don't need to sacrifice yourselves to please Lucinda," she said. "Th Queen has no appreciation for who you are...only for what you can give her. Don't you want to live long lives together?"

Puzzled by her question, they simply looked at each other then back at Hecate.

"Have you no courage?" she continued. "No interest in freeing yourselves?"

"What...what do you mean?" Yokai stammered. "We're trapped. There is no way out of this place for any of us."

Now that she had their full attention, Hecate felt comfortable in sharing her plan. "Alone, we lack the power to escape. But if we unite our inherent energies, we could leave here in one fell swoop...without anyone being the wiser."

Onoskelis began pacing back and forth in her short green dress and bare feet, asking question after question. "No one would know? Are you sure? How would that even be possible?"

"Trust me, it's possible," Hecate told her. "But fear and doubt make possible things impossible. You need to believe in yourselves and your abilities. You need to believe in me."

The Shapeshifter halted in place and glanced at her friend. "What do you think, Yokai? Should we take a chance?"

"I don't know. Where could we go and not be found?" Yokai asked. "If we're tracked down after leaving here, we'll suffer a fate worse than death."

"Worse?" Hecate shook her head and heaved a heavy sigh. "Besides being ripped apart, I can't think of anything more painful than having your soul sucked out of your body. Are you willing to let that happen...to both of you?" Hecate stared at the Changeling. She was a slip of a creature with untidy brown hair, a round face, and naïve blue eyes.

In a nearby cell, sobs erupted and there was a sound of anger and fierce resolve in that weeping, rather than mere helpless despair.

Hecate became more determined than ever to leave this hellhole behind. "Listen to me, little ones. I sense your lack of trust, which is understandable since we've just met and know so little about one another. But let me assure you that I have allies willing to risk their lives to protect me. I just need to reach my most trusted one before our window of opportunity closes."

Yokai and Onoskelis huddled together, whispering to one another again, while Hecate walked around them. Twenty seconds later, they took a step back and looked up at her.

"So, what do you think?" Hecate asked. "Do you want to stay here and die, or join me on my journey to freedom?"

They rushed toward her and wrapped their arms around her waist, emulating children. "Join you," they said in unison. "Please..."

Finally. Hecate looked through the bars, confirming no guards were in sight. If all went according to plan, they would be out of here soon.

"Are we leaving now?" Onoskelis asked, converting her nervous energy into enthusiasm.

"Yes, little one. There's no time to lose. Listen carefully and memorize these words. Ut nos hinc auferat, ut nos hinc auferat. Take us away from here. Can you remember that?"

Yokai cocked her head and narrowed her eyes. "It can't be that simple. It just can't."

"A little faith goes a long way, and so will we if you just do as I say. The words I shared will open a vortex...a hidden escape route. But we need to chant them together beyond the point of boredom, beyond your physical and mental endurance. When you've reached a point where you believe you can't possibly chant them one more time, reach deep within yourselves and chant the words again...until your consciousness begins to change. That's when we'll find our path to freedom."

"But what if you're wrong?" Yokai asked. "What if nothing happens? What if someone hears us and comes running?"

Hecate's knees were shaking. She desperately needed them to believe in her so she could replenish her strength. "What have you got to lose...besides your lives, of course?"

Onoskelis looked at her friend. "She's right. We need to trust her. What other choice do we have?"

Hecate gathered her long auburn hair and knotted it at the back of her neck. "So, if we're all in agreement..."

"We are," Yokai said. "So, where are we going?"

"You'll find out soon enough." Hecate flashed a quick smile. "Now, we must hold hands and you need to repeat after me. And most important of all, don't stop until I tell you to, understand?"

They both nodded, crowded closer, and clasped hands. Then they began chanting over and over, "Ut nos hinc auferat, ut nos hinc auferat. Take us away from here. Ut nos hinc auferat, ut nos hinc auferat. Take us away from here." They continued for five minutes, until practically delirious. The vortex slowly opened around them, and a shrill, whirling sound began. The darkness became blinding light, followed by a rush of freezing cold air. They were moving through walls, through the gates of Hell, and into the Middle Earth atmosphere at an alarming rate. They traveled together over land, large bodies of water and above tree-covered hills.

"Stop!" Hecate yelled, bringing them down. They landed hard in the Gnarly Forest near Wales, Hecate on her feet and the two little ones tumbling on their backs. It was as far as away from Lucinda and her legion of demons as the Woodland Goddess could manage.

This was an ancient place filled with contorted trees and rotten timber felled by age and fierce lightning. The inky canopies overhead blocked out the sun, reducing the forest floor to leaves, branches, bark, and stems in various stages of decomposition above the soil surface. Although easier to navigate, the lack of undergrowth and cave dwellings left virtually no place to hide. Their only chance for survival in Hecate's former home rested on reaching Nellie Longarms. She was a legend of folklore in England and Hecate's closest ally.

Known to live at the bottom of the ponds, canals, rivers, and marshes nearby, Nellie was a hag and water spirit, preferring isolation after the death of her son. Her green hair and skin camouflaged her presence, while her sharp teeth provided protection, along with the swamp weeds covering her from head to toe. The gills in her neck fed her oxygen, and her long arms came in handy for dragging creatures underwater and holding them there to die.

"How much further?" Yokai asked, huffing her question.

"Not far now," Hecate called back to her companions. She felt a sense of relief that their long journey would be coming to an end soon. The gravel path was easy to navigate for the first three miles, but soon after, they entered the woods full of rocks, hills, mud patches, and sticks. The obstacles they incurred threatened to break Yokai's and Onoskelis' small ankles, jeopardizing their escape and risking Nelly's life in the process. Their pace was steady at first, but halfway into the deep forest, they slowed from exhaustion. For every step Hecate took, the Shapeshifter and Changeling had to take two.

"We have to keep moving," Hecate told them. "I messaged my friend that we were coming. She's waiting for us in a bog at the edge of the woods."

"Messaged?" Onoskelis huffed. "How did you do that?"

"Telepathy. It is how we have communicated for years."

Yokai pushed tall grass aside and climbed over a downed tree. "She's waiting inside a bog?"

"That's right, but I guess I should warn you both," Hecate said as she walked. "Nellie is rather frightening to look at, but she has a good heart and is willing to help us escape. However, when you approach her, be careful where you walk. She opened her veins and gave droplets of blood to some of the tree roots and vines in the forest. If she feels threatened, they will wrap around you like boa constrictors and squeeze the life right out of you."

Onoskelis and Yokai looked at each other, grimacing.

The three of them continued walking until they reached a clearing and marshy waterway. A large mound of reeds floated on the surface and Hecate rushed toward it. "Nellie! We're here!" The Woodland Goddess leaned over, attempting to get a closer look. "Nellie? Why aren't you answering? It's me, Hecate."

Still no sound or movement from her. She appeared to be asleep. But roots from the surrounding trees were lifting the ground and reaching toward them.

Yokai disappeared briefly and returned with a small, leafless branch. She handed it to Hecate. "Wake her up," the Changeling said. "What's the worst that could happen?"

"You'd be amazed." Hecate determined that she could handle Nellie's anger, even after a rude intrusion, although she wasn't so sure about her companions. Gingerly, she tapped the pile of reeds then gave it a sharp poke. The pile rolled over, exposing the dead, ogle-eyed creature beneath them. She'd been gutted like a fish and left there to rot. The sight turned Hecate's face as white as chalk and left Onoskelis gasping for air.

From out of nowhere, two hellhounds bounded toward the Goddess. She backed away, but the dogs were too fast, tackling her to the ground. Yokai called out to Hecate, "Stop moving!" It was too late. One of the hounds clawed her chest, ripping flesh and drawing blood. She screamed out in pain before falling silent. Her blue eyes went from life-filled to black and scared in a matter of seconds.

"Yokai," she called out, yet her voice was merely a whisper. She couldn't get another word out of her throat; she couldn't draw a breath. The Woodland Goddess was dying.

Onoskelis fell to her knees next to her, bringing her head to her chest. Tears fell down her cheeks, and sobs racked her small frame. "I'm sorry, Hecate. I'm so sorry."

"Get over it!" Yokai snapped at Onoskelis. Before her eyes, Yokai's petite little body stretched and transformed into Lucinda's tall, powerful shape. She ran her fingers through her long hair, straightened her back and glared down at the defenseless Shapeshifter. "Keep blubbering and I'll absorb you like I did your friend. Now, help me drag Hecate to the Wiccan circle. We need to return to Hades with my hounds before dark."

While the cold wind whirled around them, the Woodland Goddess realized her greatest mistake was not anticipating the Queen's treachery or her stupefying bouts of jealousy. As a result, her closest friend was murdered and the normal life she had enjoyed with her family no longer existed. For Hecate, death would be a welcome relief and couldn't come soon enough.

CHAPTER 2

TORMENTED

Hecate slowly opened her eyes, disoriented and unable to move. She tried to break free from whatever was holding her but stopped short when searing pain tore through her body. Hooks were piercing her legs, arms, and shoulders, dangling her from the rock-covered ceiling on a web of chains.

"Help me!" she cried out. "Please help me!" Her cries were weak, but she continued begging for release. Yet no one came. She was helpless, suffering alone. Well, not *completely* alone. She hadn't seen Lucinda until now.

The Queen laughed while holding a torch next to Hecate's calf, causing skin to slough off in large sheets of bubbling flesh. Her black eyes smirked at Hecate, watching as she flinched and pulled away in pain.

"AAAAH! No! Please don't!" Hecate couldn't stop screaming. There was so much pain, so much redness, swelling and blistering. All her nightmares had come true, hurting her brain as much as her body. She imagined Nellie Longarms being tortured in similar fashion before being gutted like a fish. Death would have been a relief, but that still didn't make it right.

"Why are you doing this, Lucinda?" Hecate begged to know. "Is it because I escaped from your prison? From the horrible death you had planned for me?"

Hecate was confident that she would never torture a creature like this, not even Lucinda. The rebellion she led killed thousands of Lucinda's soldiers, but she lost an equal number of woodsmen and trappers in the conflict. Conspiring with witches to end the brutality was the only way to erase Lucinda's malicious demons and to save herself from their onslaught. With machetes and swords swinging and arrows flying, shooting their devil trap bullets was done out of necessity. They would explode on impact, maiming soldiers if shot in a leg or other parts of the body. But with pentagrams carved onto the tips of the bullets, they also instantly killed a demon if shot into their head.

However, this—hanging from the ceiling by hooks and chains—was the highest form of torture known to demon kind.

Tears streamed down Hecate's face. The pain was excruciating and never ending. "Why can't I just die?" she screamed at Lucinda. "Everyone in Hell would be happier if I was dead...if the villagers were no longer a threat to you."

"They never will be, Hecate," she said in a snarky tone. "I'll make damn sure of it...beginning with your husband and daughter."

"Oh, please...no! I beg of you, Your Majesty. Don't harm them! They weren't involved in any of this. They don't deserve to die or suffer for my mistakes." Hecate's world was one of agony and blurred colors, growing redder by the second.

Lucinda glanced up at her face but gave no clue to her mood. "My generosity depends on how well you accept your punishment, Hecate. Stay strong through your pain and grow horns from it. You helped me grow six horns out of mine. So bloom loudly, softly, however you choose...or just shrivel up and die."

Stepping back, Lucinda allowed a yellow-eyed demon to take over. He had a sickening smile on his disgusting face if it could even be called that. It was as if sandpaper had rubbed against his skin, piranhas had fed on it, and a lit match had set it on fire. Without a doubt, she would probably look similar with Lucinda in charge.

"My dear friend, let me introduce you to Smite," Lucinda said. "He specializes in these matters, so I'm leaving you in his capable hands." After a few whispers were exchanged between them, she left with the fading clicks of her heels.

"Hello, Hecate. I'm honored to be your tormentor." The nasty-looking demon sneered. "Very few of us are given the opportunity to torture someone high ranking…and beautiful too. Well, beautiful for the time being anyway." He chuckled then continued, "But I'll give you a choice, dear heart. Something not everyone is entitled to. You see…you don't have to endure this if you're willing to torture someone for me." He caressed her right foot and smiled. Then he rubbed her sweat and blood between his fingers. "I get the distinct impression you'd be great at it."

Hecate set her jaw straight and looked down at the demon. "Rot in Hell," she growled.

The demon smirked. "I'm already here and so are you. But I won't be the one rotting." He jabbed the tip of his blade into Hecate's middle, earning a painful moan. "Smite is my name and you best not forget it. My offer stands but you won't be able to… unless you agree."

"I'll never agree…no matter what you do to me."

Brave words she would soon come to regret.

Days passed by, then weeks and months. The mental torment never stopped, but the pain became bearable. There was no food, no water, no chance to sleep or rest between sessions. It was constant taunting with a few knife slashes in-between. This was Hell after all.

The demon made the same offer every time he came to visit. "Be my apprentice and all this will end. I will teach you to be an excellent tormentor. You'll only have to answer to me."

Each time, Hecate said no. Then Smite would start with small cuts on her body and cover them with acid. They burned horribly, but still she stayed strong, rejecting his offer time and again. Her whole body ached; white hot flame pulsed through her. All she felt was pain, and it overwhelmed her. She forgot how to care, smile, laugh. All she knew was agony and despair. She wasn't merely broken; she was shattered into a million pieces. One more push and she would give in, hating herself for it.

"Hecate!" It was a woman's voice, so familiar yet impossible.

"Nellie?" Hecate's eyes widened in disbelief. *No, it can't be*, she told herself. But there she stood plain as day. "You're alive... but how?" The Goddess' voice was hoarse in her own ears, and as she spoke blood trickled from the corner of her mouth. What was left of her heart now had hope, something she believed impossible to hold onto. Yet, there she stood. *Nellie.* Was her spirit capable of coming here? Willing to save her from a fate worse than death?

"How disappointing," the green hag said. "I never imagined something like this."

The voice wasn't Nellie's. The hope that had risen within Hecate was dashed within seconds.

That's not my ally, not my protector. It's a demon in disguise, masking as my friend.

Hecate's anger flared, overtaking the pain. "You bastard! Don't you dare imitate Nellie. I'll rip your throat out!"

"I'm no demon, Hecate. It's me, Nellie. I just came here to say I hate you. I hated you when you rebelled against Lucinda and my sweet Amon died. You promised to bring him back to me, but you lied. For too long you've only thought of yourself and cared nothing about—"

"Stop!" She fell limp, hanging from the chains.

"—the others. You couldn't protect me—"

"Damnit! I said stop!"

"—much less anyone else. You didn't escape to help Yokai and Onoskelis. You escaped to save yourself. And all those lives were lost in the rebellion because of you."

"Please…stop this."

"I hate you more than anything in this world. Why do you think I hid from you? From your selfish concern? I couldn't stand you, Hecate. I never could. And now you're in Hell suffering the way you richly deserve. I don't care that you're in Hell. I just wish you would've gotten here sooner."

"No. It isn't true! You can't be, Nellie. She would never say that to me! We're family!" Tears streamed down Hecate's face. *It's all a lie. We were friends. She wouldn't want to see me dead. We loved each other, cared for each other…when no one else would.*

"Damnit!" Hecate couldn't stop the tears, or the choking sobs threatening to strangle her.

It can't be true…it just can't.

Nellie moved closer. "But it is, dear heart. It's all true."

This is Nellie? No, not Nellie. A demon…a vile, corrupt demon. But how could Hecate be sure? It was impossible to tell the difference, and she just wanted her friend back. Just wanted to know she was sane.

A telepathic message entered her brain. *Smile at me, Hecate. Open your heart. I'm the friend you cared about. Is that asking too much?*

Hecate shook her head. *I don't know what's real anymore.*

Nellie extended her hand and waited patiently for her to grab it. "I forgive you, Hecate. We can be friends again now and forever. Just take my hand, and it will all be forgotten."

Hecate couldn't resist the offer. The chance to make up for her terrible mistakes. For dismissing Nellie's feelings and risking her life to unseat a power-crazed Queen. For sacrificing the lives of over 1,000 die-hard followers, including Nellie's son in a pointless battle.

Hecate reached out her hand and the hooks in her skin vanished. The chains fell away, hitting the stone walls. The pain she'd endured disappeared, lifting her spirits and the corners of her lips. "Everything will only get better now. I know it."

Nellie smiled, and her yellow eyes shimmered. "I'm so glad you chose me, my forever friend. I believe it's the best decision you've ever made...or ever will."

CHAPTER 3

MATING SEASON

Ariel's angelic soul had been struggling for months, trying to accept the female demon's body she'd been given to save her life. Daily, she told herself that she needed to be grateful for Lilith's shocking suicide, that she was lucky to be able to take over her body, that it was a blessing to be alive. But any hope of dismissing the conflicts within her was fading fast, leaving her mentally drained and short-tempered. Her blonde hair, blue eyes and white wings had been restored thanks to the heavenly spirits protecting her. However, her voluptuous body belonged to Crighton's lover and the mother of his child. The idea of totally losing her identity had become a frightening reality, a disturbing nightmare she couldn't ignore. By expelling the host of virtues she'd been given as an angel, barbarous vices were invading her thoughts and behavior, transforming her into the irrational, self-absorbed creature staring back in the mirror.

To her dismay, Crighton came up behind her shirtless with a familiar gleam in his eyes. He reached for her hand, turning her around. With one finger, he lifted her chin and gazed into her blue eyes. Although his kisses started out playful, passion put an end to that quickly. He pulled her tight against his body, bringing attention to his bulging need. Once again, he was taking everything she had to offer, his lips probing hers for entrance, his hands roaming across her back, her buttocks, her upper thighs—anywhere he could reach. Mindlessly, she opened her mouth under the onslaught and instinctively wrapped her arms around his lower back, molding herself to his body.

"Mmm…" Crighton moaned. He seemed content kissing her, yet not entirely. He kept her body pressed firmly against him and told her, "I could do this forever, but not here." With a devious smile, he towed her from the living room to their bedroom with only one purpose in mind—demon sex and lots of it. He dropped his jeans to the floor, then slid her snug-fitting black dress over her shoulders and down her back. More than anything, she wanted to resist, but her body had a mind of its own, craving his predatory touch. According to Crighton, she was built the way a soulmate should be. Shapely, with large breasts, plump lips, tiny waist, and rounded hips and ass. He stood back admiring her, then he ran a hand through his long dark hair and smiled. "Sometimes I look at you and wonder how I got so damn lucky."

Even though originality wasn't his forte, Crighton's cheesy words curled her lips. She absent-mindedly traced a hand down his broad shoulder and large bicep to the roped muscles on his forearm. Misreading her sensual touch as sexual desire, he clamped his hands on her shoulders and opened his mouth over hers, aggressively kissing her.

For a moment, Ariel was too stunned to say anything. Then she growled in a deep, menacing voice, "If I didn't know better, I would *swear* a different demon was inside you, making you behave rude and unruly."

"Swear?" The expression on Crighton's face reflected both humor and interest. "Did you actually use the *swear* word?" He moved his hands over her body possessively. "I can think of some other choice words I'd love to hear from those lips."

"Get over it, Crighton. I'm not Lilith…I'm not me. I'm not anyone," she said sadly.

After a moment's pause, Crighton laughed loudly, unable to control himself. He swept Ariel off her feet and carried her to their bed, laying her down gently.

The angel sighed in exasperation. For some unknown reason, Crighton had developed an unslakable appetite that controlled their lives day and night, leaving her physically and mentally spent. Yet at the same time, she remained decidedly impressed by his sexual prowess. Without knowing it, he was providing a frequent distraction from her dark thoughts and nightmares, as well as her mundane existence in Middle Earth.

The black silk bedcover and matching canopy curtains were pushed aside, and Ariel's anxiety and nervousness returned. She longed to be held and to hold, to love and be loved, to experience a deep connection without walls. And yet, with real love staring her in the eyes—with her loving partner standing before her, Ariel had a disconcerting urge to withdraw, to put up walls, even to run.

Crighton looked at her reproachfully, shaking his head. "Are you afraid of me, Ariel? Mating is required for sexual bonding, especially for demons. Of course, you *do* have the right to refuse me, but then I'd have to find comfort elsewhere."

"Comfort?"

"Fucking, my dear."

"Unbelievable." There it was, that appalling word. Why did he insist on using it when there were so many ways to say love?

"Would you prefer *screwing*?" He sat down on the bed and studied her face with mocking green eyes, his mouth twisted into a humorless smile. "The more we do it, the closer we become. Surely you understand that?"

"Of course, I do. But four times a day?"

"Frequency isn't the issue, it's your attitude. Stop closing your eyes and look at me. I'm no different than any male on this planet. Demon, angel, or human. Basically, we're all the same."

For the first time in her life, she ventured a look at what Crighton had in store for her, taking her breath away. "Do they all look like *that*?"

"More or less. Although I've been told considerably more in my case." Determined to get on with it, he stood up and swung his big cock around like a piece of rope. "There's no need to be frightened, sweetheart. I'm not going to do anything I haven't done before."

Ariel's mind was racing along with her heart. *Demons don't bond with other demons like this, do they? What about angels? If they make love, is it the same way or is it prohibited, like our union?*

Crighton climbed onto the foot of the bed. "There's a blood moon tonight, which means its mating season in Hell...a time when female demons are the most fertile and males can't get enough." He crawled closer to her. Then he touched her face and trailed a finger down her neck, between her breasts, and rested his hand on her stomach. "I'm going to pump you full of my seed tonight, then maybe I'll get the son I've been wanting."

Ariel huffed. "Is that what this is about? Having a son?" She considered telling him that the lunar eclipse was also the beginning of the end of time as prophesied in the Bible. The dark visions and dreams she'd been having were occurring more often and had become more frightening than ever.

"Do you love me, Ariel? More than anything in this world?"

She didn't hesitate to answer. "Yes, of course, I do." He was her soulmate, so she *had* to love him, or spend the rest of her life resenting him.

"Forever and ever?" His strong hands were on her thighs, pushing them further apart.

She nodded, her gaze strolling over his face absently. "I'm sorry you were forced into this…partnership."

"You don't have to apologize to me, sweetheart. No one forced me to love you."

She reached for his hand, needing to touch him without sex, even for a short while. "Thank you for saying that."

His fingers entwined with hers when he noticed her reaching for him. She didn't want him to believe she was cold and distant. But why wouldn't he? Nerves did that to a demon—brought their temperature down to almost freezing. Although Ariel hated to admit it, she was more demon than she would like to believe.

"For once in your life, trust me. Tell me you love me. That you'll never stop caring." He braced his arms on either side of her body and they trembled from the tension he was forcing on them. He wanted her so badly that his body shook, but he had to hear it—had to know he wasn't alone in this crazy yearning that never seemed to go away.

Ariel ground her body against his and faked a moan, believing her actions spoke louder than words. But then he forced her to look at him.

He barked out a demand, taking her by surprise. "Tell me!"

"I…I want you, Crighton."

He pushed deeper inside her, causing her to cry out. Sweat beaded on his forehead, but he wouldn't go any further. No matter how much he wanted her, he refused to continue. Not unless she said the words. "I want to hear it, Ariel. I need to know how you feel."

"I love you," she whispered.

"Again. Say it again."

"I...I love you." The words felt forced, unnatural, and insincere. But they seemed to please him. At her admission, he slid halfway in and dug his fingers into either side of her spine. She whimpered and her face contorted, as the feeling of utter and complete terror took hold. Her body felt as though it was being defrosted from the inside out, slowly thawing from the warmth of their joining.

"Relax, sweetheart. I haven't tortured you yet."

Ariel continued to hold onto him tight, neither of them moving for endless seconds. As he had done numerous times before, he waited until she made the first move. She rocked in place slightly, indicating she was ready. Grasping her hips, he lifted her from the bed, pulled back and plunged into her deeper, until the tip of his cock bumped into her cervix.

Her right hand found the edge of the bedspread and held it fast in her fist. She squeezed her eyes shut, refusing to open them.

"Trust me, Ariel. I won't hurt you, not this time. I promise."

"I'm closing my eyes so I can feel you inside me." She placed her hand over his heart and rasped, "I've seen too many bad things with these eyes. This, I will feel in my heart."

"And in mine," Crighton told her.

The tension in her body eased, and they began rocking slowly against each other in a finely honed rhythm. His fingertips pressed into her hips as he held on to her, alternating his thrusts between long and deep, shallow, and quick, angling her body along his for what he believed was mutual pleasure.

Remembering her connection as his soulmate, Ariel delved into Crighton's consciousness and discovered that his awareness was being used to protect his family against external influences. She also got the impression that Crighton couldn't get enough of her. That the feel of her walls on his shaft was threatening his sanity. Instinctively, she wrapped her legs around his waist, digging her heels into his back. Her body took over, grounding her center against him.

Crighton growled low and she sensed that if she didn't stop, he would hurt her—so strong was his need for her.

"Harder," she said. "Faster." She panted, her nails scoring deep into his skin. She threw her head back and kept her eyes shut. It was as if Lilith had reclaimed her mind and body, turning Ariel into a wanton creature.

That was all Crighton needed to hear. He grabbed her legs, pushing them farther apart. Soon the sound of mutual groans echoed in the room, bouncing off the walls, as his strokes became harsher, more demanding than ever. Sweat poured off his body, yet he managed to hold on, willing himself to stay hard for as long as it took. He needed his angel to come before him, a dozen times, if necessary, to give his male sperm the best chance of survival.

Ariel's fingertips pressed into his biceps, as he drove his length deeper with each thrust. Instinctively, she arched her back and rocked her hips faster, meeting him halfway.

"Ahhh..." he moaned. "Yes...yes...that's it. Keep going, sweetheart. Keep going..." His moist lips and tongue trailed over her jaw and throat, testing her endurance. "So good," he breathed in her ear. "So fucking good."

As he continued thrusting inside her, Ariel's breathing grew ragged. Her thighs trembled and little moans escaped her lips, signaling to Crighton that she was close to the edge. He drove his full length into her, grinding his hips as he pressed harder, determined to fit every inch of himself inside.

Pent-up emotions began to surface, causing tears to leak from her eyes. Crighton felt wetness on his chest and stopped moving, realizing Ariel was crying. "Oh, shit. Am I hurting you?" he asked, the concern showing in his voice. "I can stop if you want me to."

Ariel shook her head and dashed the tears away. She looked up at him in dazed confusion. Lust and passion were swirling through her body—this creature comfort that didn't belong to her. "I'm fine. Honest," she said, feigning a smile. "Too emotional, I guess..."

"You're so beautiful," he whispered. "I want to stay inside you forever."

"Then do," she said. Meanwhile, Ariel's brain was spinning. It wasn't supposed to be like this, not between angels and demons, even if their bodies fit perfectly together. She had tried, goodness knows she had tried, but she couldn't hold off Crighton's passion.

"Are you sure you're okay?" he asked.

She nodded again.

"I want you to be happy." His fingers toyed with her stiff nipples; his hands roamed all over her body, from a gentle caress of his fingers across her lips to a rough grab of her hip, as he grounded himself against her, picking up where he left off. "There's nothing on Earth that could keep me from you..."

She met his gaze dead on and matched his tone. "Except me."

He chuckled, believing she was kidding, then continued thrusting his hips in wild abandonment, attempting to please her the only way he knew how. In all truth, she didn't have the strength to fight back or resist him. Her heart was so completely in his keeping that she couldn't think straight, especially with his cock deep inside her, pounding away.

Apparently, negative feelings cropped up on her face, or maybe it was their soulmate connection, allowing him to see into her world. Either way, Crighton became anxious and extremely dissatisfied with his performance. He slid off the bed and disappeared through the open doorway. She considered following him, but then he returned quickly, carrying an oversized pillow. After placing it under her butt and spreading her legs wider, he inserted two fingers up to the knuckle and began searching diligently for her G-spot. Finding it, he stroked the rough surface repeatedly, leaving her body vibrating and her heart racing. A warm sensation spread throughout her limbs, growing more intense by the second. He pushed another finger into her, adding to her delicious turmoil and nearly ending it for her. As his other hand clamped around the side of her neck, his thumb held her jaw tightly. He made a move to kiss her. But then he jerked his head back and shot her a dark look. His green eyes were blazing as he glanced down at his fingers buried inside her. When his eyes flitted back up to her face, a smirk covered his features, irritating her to no end.

Despite the insane antics, his fingers never stopped moving. Her breathing was heaving, and by the look on his face, he relished the effect he was having on her.

Ariel tried to return his gaze but found it difficult to keep her eyes open. With every flick of his fingers, the heat inside her cranked up a notch. A warm flush filled her face and chest, and she squeezed her eyes shut once more. She couldn't keep them open anyway, just as she was incapable of not bucking her hips against his fingers.

"That's right. You deserve this," he murmured, his voice so deep she could barely hear him over the hum in her brain. "Come for me, sweetheart. Yes, yes. Let yourself go." He gave one more flick of his thumb over her clit. Instantly, waves of ecstasy rolled over her, and she found herself in the middle of another orgasm, even more powerful than the first. She cried out as the storm broke, tossing her every which way, like a ship rocking on a stormy sea.

Crighton pulled his wet fingers from her and slid them into his mouth, his tongue licking them clean. She stared at him with wide eyes as she came down from her high, trying to absorb every detail from his face. His eyes were still dark with need, and from the side of the bed, she could feel him pressing into her thigh, hard and eager for action.

Crighton whispered in her ear. "I'm not done with you yet. I need to provide a climatic finale. Something to make those dreams go away." Spreading her legs again, he jammed his cock inside her and began ardently pumping away. His hands—murderer's hands—were gripping her forcefully by the hips, exactly where it mattered, exactly where some infernal set of nerve receptors were waiting to be found. His speed and force doubled, causing the padded headboard to bang obtrusively against the wall, threatening to knock the large clock from its hook and destroy it all together.

Five minutes became ten, and despite all her efforts to hold back for Crighton, Ariel's body betrayed her, sending electrifying impulses from her ankles to her thighs before jolting her inner core over and over again. It was almost too much this time, and she tried to shrink back from it. But Crighton wouldn't allow her to do so. He kept on caressing her while pounding his cock into her, his hips jackhammering in time with his heartbeat. He looked savage, agitated and completely out of control as he moved faster and faster, resolute in reaching his goal.

"Crighton!" Ariel cried out, giving in to her mind-numbing orgasm a second time.

"I'm coming," he grounded out, his facial features twisting in pleasure. His back arched and his broad shoulders quaked as he climaxed with a loud groan, sending a final jolt through Ariel. Then he collapsed on top of her, crushing her body beneath him.

"Damnit," he said, righting himself quickly. His lips hovered over her eyelashes, and he was still breathing hard. "I'm sorry, Ariel…I wanted to go easy on you. But it felt *so* good. I just couldn't stop."

"I didn't want you to…stop that is." She nudged long strands of blonde hair away from her eyes and stared up at him—this muscle-bound, invincible, seductive creature. Despite her body aches and weariness, his obsession with pleasing her made her feel loved and desperately needed. But there was no satisfying this beast from Hell, despite her ardent attempts to do so. Tomorrow morning, they would be doing it all over again.

Slowly, Crighton withdrew from inside her, leaving warm seed seeping between her legs. He noticed her troubled expression and cursed out loud. "Damn it! I'm sorry, Ariel. I don't know how to handle this obsession. I'm afraid it's only going to get worse for you, until I can find another way to channel my energy."

"Worse?" She must have looked horrified. "You can't be serious…"

"I'm afraid so, but what can I do? Just looking at you excites me." There was no smugness in his boyish expression, only truth in his smoldering green eyes.

"I have no idea how your mind or body works. How could I, Crighton? I'm an angel inside a demon's body. Surely there's an answer…a remedy for this."

"I'm afraid we just have to let nature take its course. In the meantime, I'll try my best not to kill you." He smiled and stroked her cheek softly. "My destiny is tied to you, Ariel. I adore you… that much is certain. Despite your misgivings and disappointments in our little arrangement, nothing will change that."

Little arrangement? She pondered his carefully chosen words. The demon lying on his side next to her had not only taken her virginity, but he also owned half her soul as well. Though being a secular-minded demon, she was sure he didn't think of it that way. Of course, he didn't take her entire soul; that wouldn't have been possible. But he got such a significant piece that it felt as if all of it was gone. As soon as he had it, he not only forgot he'd taken it, but he also forgot that corrupt humans had helped him acquire it.

"So, shall we get at it?" He rose on his elbows and gazed into her eyes.

"What? Again? You can't be serious?"

"Only if you insist…" Crighton huffed a laugh. "Actually, I was referring to our morning schedule. We need to finish our chores soon because I'm meeting with Tyrus in a few hours. Unless you prefer staying in bed—"

"No, no…I'm up." She yanked at the sheet, gripping wads of it in her fists. "So, you're still going?"

He nodded. "In spite of him being a hybrid werewolf, Tyrus is my half-brother. He also saved our lives, which is remarkable when you think about it. I suppose meeting up with him to discuss his future isn't asking too much."

"Yes, of course. You're absolutely right."

"That's it? No argument? We are talking about Hell, Ariel."

She shrugged a shoulder. "I have no problem with Tyrus. I'm sure you know that. He cares about our family and looks after us. Now turn around, so I can get dressed."

"Really? Why can't I watch?" Crighton smiled. "Is there something you're hiding that I haven't seen before?"

Ariel pitched one of the pillows at him, smacking him in the chest. He picked it up and threatened to throw it back but carried it into the next room smiling instead.

For Crighton's angel, life was good for the most part on Middle Earth, despite giving birth in a borrowed body and raising his demonic child as her own. In his arms, she felt protected. She had built her home in his heart, and the roots of her soul were coiled inside his chest. They breathed together, thought alike, and finished each other's sentences. She belonged with him, though angels in Heaven denied it. So why couldn't she surrender herself completely? Why couldn't she appreciate the connection they had?

She raised herself up on one elbow and looked into his eyes. "What's the difference between the love of your life and me?"

He answered without hesitation, "One is a choice, and one wasn't. But that doesn't make me love you less."

Ariel hated the uncertainty she felt, and Crighton's words weren't helping. He had resigned himself to accept her by no choice of his own, and it seemed she was expected to do the same.

"I wish I could fly away and forget about all the worries and doubts," she murmured.

"Everyone has doubts, sweetheart. Instead of looking for problems in our relationship, we need to focus on living a full, productive life without regrets or remorse."

"Easier said than done," she murmured.

"What was that?"

"I said our dinner is done."

"Great. For a second there, I considered taking you over my knee, and we both know where that would lead."

"Unfortunately, I do."

Crighton walked away laughing, but Ariel didn't find the situation funny. She was accused on a daily basis of having no sense of humor, of not going with the flow, of not relishing their time together. But how could she be content with her own life when Crighton's happiness was all that mattered?

CHAPTER 4

RESIDUAL RESENTMENT

After Lucinda's ascension to the throne, Crighton had agreed to assist with the protection of the Outer Rim by eliminating the threat of Archangel invasions. Four months later, a fully trained demon battalion was in place, guarding the invisible barrier between Heaven and Hell. At this point, Crighton claimed his obligations and duties to the Queen were met. Yet for one reason or another, she continued to pull him back into her fold, demanding his undivided attention.

At the same time, Crighton's chores at home were keeping him extremely busy. Every morning, he and Ariel washed up, ate a hearty breakfast, and then set to work—chopping wood, stoking the fireplaces, cleaning the windows, sweeping the floors, and washing clothes. While working together, they casually chatted, discussing the possibility of traveling again. Yet there was one subject they couldn't broach without an argument ensuing, leaving Ariel bristling with anger.

Lucinda.

Crighton had insisted on maintaining his friendship with her, but Lucinda's presence in their lives had become a thorn in Ariel's side. For the last few months, whenever she asked about Crighton's past, Lucinda's name would inadvertently come up. He casually mentioned that years ago she had confessed her love for him. He cracked a smile and claimed he didn't reciprocate her feelings. However, for some unknown reason, the former soul seeker and current Queen remained deeply entrenched in their lives.

She's going to keep him in Hell, Ariel thought to herself. *I can sense it…even now.*

Crighton took the area rug outside for a thorough beating. Then he brought it back into the living room and covered the floor. Meanwhile, Ariel returned the broom to the closet and stood before the picture window, staring mindlessly at the trees bordering the edge of the forest.

"I assume you'll be seeing her again today." There, she had done it. Brought an end to the calm between them.

"It can hardly be avoided," Crighton said. "But no matter, you should be thankful. Lucinda did us a huge favor. If not for her generosity, I would be ruling alone in Hell right now, and our lives would be drastically different."

"Generosity? Isn't *greed* a better word?" Ariel turned away from the window and met his eyes. "The only thing missing from that creature's life is you."

"Are you kidding me? That *creature*, as you're so fond of calling her, is keeping us safe. She has forbidden demon attacks in DeVore and kept a mountain of twisted entities away from us. Just find a way to accept her, I beg of you, or we'll be fighting for the rest of our lives."

With Crighton and Lucinda both being demons, Ariel knew they had a natural chemistry between them and, unfortunately, similar personalities. On the other hand, Ariel was a guardian angel, struggling daily with her emotions, chronic nightmares, and her newly acquired responsibilities.

What am I supposed to do? she asked herself. Despite her feelings for Crighton, Lucinda had been a friend to their entire family. Truthfully, Ariel wouldn't mind if Crighton hung out with the Queen of Hell and caught up every now and then, but she selfishly wanted to be the most important female in Crighton's life.

Still steaming over their fight, Crighton stormed outside, slamming the door behind him. He stripped off his black shirt and tied it around his waist. Then he picked up a large ax and raised it high over his head. Ariel watched him from the bedroom window as he took out his hostilities on a huge stack of logs in the yard. *Whack! Whack! Whack!* He split them down the middle, with one mighty blow, log after log. Ten minutes later, he gathered up two armloads and carried them effortlessly inside. Then he restocked the metal racks in the living room and master bedroom before adding a few logs to the fireplaces. After washing up in the bathroom, he stretched out on their king-size bed, and silently watched her sort and fold a pile of freshly laundered clothes.

Are you kidding me? Ariel could no longer deny what she knew deep down inside. She would never get her life back. Even without some sadistic beast watching and controlling her every move, she would never be the same. Besides dealing with Crighton's antics, there was now a pre-teen daughter to worry about—the one Lilith's body had given birth to, and Ariel's soul and mind had struggled daily to accept as her own. Personally, she was amazed by Samara's rapid growth, from seven pounds to eighty in just four Middle Earth months. She had heard that demons mature at an alarming rate, but she wasn't prepared for this. On top of everything else, Crighton's daughter bore a striking resemblance to her mother. Simply put, with her strong jaw, pouty lips, olive complexion, hazel eyes and long auburn hair, Sam was remarkably striking and would only become more so with age.

But that was beside the point.

The internal connection between Crighton and the Queen had become unbearable, and Ariel had refused to accept it. "I don't understand. With every visit, you become more like her. You're not the dark angel I bonded with. You're...you're—"

"I'm the same soulmate you pledged to love. The same wicked demon you now refuse to recognize, refuse to believe exists. Leave if you must, Ariel, but just know there's nowhere you can hide where I won't find you. Even if you were foolish enough to follow me to Hell or attempt to enter Heaven, I would find you and bring you back. Despite what you believe, you belong to me." Crighton reached for her hand and jerked her down onto the bed beside him. He stared into her face with his glowing green eyes and ran a possessive hand over her thigh. "You. Are. Mine. Remember that Ariel, and we won't have a problem."

Her emotional dam suddenly broke, leaving her sobbing. She curled up on the bed and buried her face in her pillow.

Crighton growled. "So, now I'm a bad guy...for rightfully staking my claim?"

Ariel was weeping not only for the bizarre life she was leading, but from the realization that she could never return to her peaceful existence. The telepathic messages she had been receiving for the last three days and the horrible, gut-wrenching nightmares she'd been having left her frightened, exhausted, and on edge. But Crighton was impotent in his understanding. He was a Nephilim after all, the offspring of an angel and demon. With his black, feathery wings and sculpted body, he had the grace of an angel in the air. But demon blood coursed through his veins, warming his loins, and igniting his anger. He possessed a human soul made from the vessel of his angel and demon parents, and there was no escaping that fact.

Why did I agree to this? What does it all mean? Ariel asked herself time and again. Castiel was in Heaven with Acadia, where he belonged, but his warnings were a constant buzz in her head and impossible to ignore.

A war is rapidly approaching, and Crighton is the chosen one. The level of his power surpasses even Archangels; however, his loyalties will be divided. If he sides with angels, then he'll be declared an enemy of Hell. If he sides with Lucinda and her demons, then the Archangels will hunt him down and kill him. Crighton needs to remain neutral and only fight for himself. Above all else, your protection and Samara's training should be his primary concerns.

Ariel was fully aware of Crighton's predicament, and the pending battle between Heaven and Hell. But she wasn't prepared for his aggressive behavior, cruel indifference, and disturbing physical changes. With every visit to Hell, the bumps on his head grew larger, indicating horns were growing and soon a tail would follow—two physical features Lucifer had forbidden while ruling in Hell. But with his demise, it seemed his daughter Lucinda had ended normality in her hot, wicked chambers.

Ariel stared at the wall next to the bed, wondering if Lucinda had developed an insatiable appetite for the souls of angels and God-fearing humans the same way Lucifer had. Perhaps she was thrilled at the prospect of destroying the world and everything living on it. After all, without even trying, she was destroying Ariel's peaceful, metaphysical existence.

Crighton grumbled under his breath and rolled over, facing the angel's back. He placed a hand on her shoulder and said softly, "I'm sorry. I honestly don't know what's gotten into me lately. We were happy for a while there, weren't we? I mean… we didn't fight the way we do now. I know I've been difficult, but you're not innocent in all of this, Ariel. You know how to push my buttons and bring out the worst in me."

Ariel turned toward him. "Is there any way to pay Lucinda back, so we can get on with our lives? We have a daughter to think about and—"

Crighton placed his finger on Ariel's lips, silencing her. "I'm going to see her after my meeting with Tyrus and will ask her that very question…among others. Can you please be patient a while longer? That's all I'm asking for. Just your patience and understanding."

Ariel remained solemn and unyielding. "If things continue the way they're going, I don't know how long I can stay here."

The demon furrowed his brow. "What the Hell does that mean? Are you threatening to leave me? Because you know how that will end."

Suddenly, Ariel was braver and more brazen than she ever thought possible. "I'm saying if your attitude doesn't change in the next two weeks, I'm going to disappear, and there's nothing you can do to stop me." She fully expected him to throw a fit—scream at the top of his lungs and toss a chair or table against the wall. But he surprised her by looking down and silently nodding. "We are soulmates, equal in every way," she added. "You need to prove your loyalty and commitment without crushing me four times a day."

Crighton twisted a smile and made a move to kiss her, but Ariel quickly rolled away and rose to her feet. She picked up Samara's black dress from the pile of folded clothes on the foot of the bed and walked toward the open doorway. Then she paused a moment and glanced back at Crighton. Handsome and shirtless, this desirable, athletic demon was lying on their silk-covered bed looking longingly at her.

"Be careful today," Ariel said. "You claim that Tyrus is your protector, but you're walking into a lion's den. I guarantee that Lucinda wants more from you than your time. A powerful Queen can be dangerous, especially when she's lonely."

CHAPTER 5

FOOL'S ERRAND

"Three days in Hell! Three stinking days!" Crighton growled his discontent. This was obviously another attempt by Lucinda to humiliate him—to exercise her dominance over him. She was able to hear thoughts and manipulate minds with her newly acquired talents, but his brute strength allowed him to tear demons apart. With flaring tempers, they could easily regress from friends to foes and destroy one another. This thought and the underlying fear of what might follow weighed heavily on Crighton's mind. However, after being rudely ignored for three days, his patience had worn thin. For fear of what Lucinda would do to him, he couldn't allow himself to sleep, and fatigue made him more irritable than usual.

He approached the doorman stationed before Lucinda's private chambers, snarling. "Forget this game. You can tell Lucinda I'm out of here!" His tirade was so loud that demons up and down the halls could hear him.

The squirrel-like expression on the doorman's round face changed into a piteous look of dismay. "No! You are not allowed to leave without the Queen's permission. There's a formal gathering this evening and you're expected there."

"What the Hell?" Crighton shouted. "I've been stuck here for three days and now I'm expected to attend a cocktail party?

What if I refuse? I have no news to share that Lucinda isn't aware of, and I have no information the council hasn't already heard."

"That's beside the point. Lucinda is not in the mood for bullshit today. The underworld is shaking from her frustrations over disobedient souls, just like that church in Dallas, Texas. The one she's been toying with to frighten the new minister. Under her direction and supervision, the entire planet has become a Hellmouth."

"You could just say I didn't show up. What's the worst that could happen?"

"Are you crazy? My job as a doorman is bad enough. Being a messenger is totally out of the question. As it is, the hours are long, the pay is low, and Lucinda thinks the world revolves around her. She enjoys abusing everyone, especially low-level demons like me. Bring her a message with bad news, any bad news, and she'll fly into a rage and most likely strike out. And you might ask me why. Because you're within easy reach and expendable."

"Okay, I get it. I'll go to the Hall of Justice and wait there. But if Tyrus shows up—"

"I know, I know. Tell him you're pissed."

"Exactly."

Crighton traveled down a long corridor and sat down begrudgingly on a black stone bench outside the Chamber of Justice. He had no idea how long he was expected to stay there. Hours…days…weeks. There was no measure of time, no sense of day or night in this singular dimension, just a continuous cycle with no end in sight. Years ago, he had dreamed of escaping from this wretched place and finding a peaceful life in the outside world. He'd been assigned weekly missions to collect the souls of innocent angels and wicked humans to satisfy Lucifer's appetite. After disappointing him, Crighton had suffered skin-ripping lashes, scarring both his body and soul. But when he pleased him, his notoriety and position excelled, along with his visits to the Pleasure Quarters. He had spent endless hours there, reinforcing his idealized version of himself. Yet, as much as he enjoyed the attention, there was only one vixen he cared about and considered a true friend.

Vedas.

She was blonde-haired and blue-eyed, like Ariel, but that's where the similarities ended. She had an aggressive, temperamental personality and a wicked tongue that resulted in disputes even with her paying customers. When it came to lovers, she had no interest in developing real, meaningful relationships, especially with soul-catchers and barbarous soldiers. But then, one night after a villain named Sergei assaulted her, Vedas' opinion of Crighton drastically changed. He tracked down the vile creature that wounded her and beat him severely. Shortly after, Sergei left Hell half-blind, vowing his revenge. And as for Vedas, she became Crighton's number one fan and secret lover. But then fate intervened after his last mission to England. According to Tyrus, a powerful member of the Knights of Darkness became her sponsor and now her loyalty and body belonged solely to him.

As for Crighton, it had been a struggle after discovering his true identity. He buried his natural instincts and denied himself the pleasure of multiple partners—of seeing Vedas and the other sex-starved whores in Hell. He considered himself luckier than most demons, for they were damned here forever while he was able to freely come and go. He had a soulmate, a beautiful angel to satisfy his needs. And what's more, she bore him a child, risking her life and facing condemnation by other angels, all for the sake of love.

Looking around now, Crighton was reminded that there were no benefits, no amenities in this infernal place. There was nothing worth stealing or even salvaging. Yet Hell continued to exist between the realms of the living and eternally dammed. If someone were entirely forgotten, their contract in Hell would be diminished along with their value. Considering his current situation, Crighton wasn't sure which was more demoralizing: being forgotten by Lucinda the Queen of Hell or having experienced excruciating pain at the hands of her demented, now deceased, father.

"What's taking so long?" Crighton shouted to the ceiling. He listened and heard nothing but the echoes of his own voice in the blazing cavern. He had been confined to Lucinda's mansion with nothing to do but wander around inside the torch-lit hallways, worrying about Ariel and Samara back at home, who were waiting patiently for his return. Or were they? He felt alienated and disconnected in this terribly malevolent place. Even though it was swarming with demons, he had continued to think of and make plans to return to Ariel's warm embrace. His desire continued to find his way out of Hell and back to his home. However, it was hard to dismiss the drastic changes that had taken place during his absence.

The ancient law Lucifer had implemented forbidding horns, wings and tails had obviously been nullified. As Crighton sat in the hallway watching, most of the demons walking by were sporting all three. He gingerly touched the lumps high on his forehead. His head ached from the growing bumps he had sprouted weeks earlier. He suspected they would soon be full-fledged horns—the result of his frequent visits. The tail that would soon follow would make his altered appearance frightening to humans and perhaps Ariel too.

He continued walking a familiar path until he reached his former apartment—the space he shared with his mother until her untimely death. His curiosity drove him to open the door and step inside. Surprisingly, nothing had changed. Everything, even his bed and dresser, sat exactly where he'd left them. He opened his closet and discovered that dozens of black leather jackets with various cuts and matching custom-made pants had been added to the steel racks in his closet. But why? He had no intention of ever coming back here. At least, not permanently.

Crighton could hear rapid steps approaching, although not to be mistaken for mere demon steps. It was Serene, Lucinda's devoted servant. She was an anomaly of her own universe and represented the collision of everything he'd ever known or imagined. Her pink ears resembled a sprite—long and pointed on their tips and lobes. The green tendrils attached to her scalp resembled snakes, headless and in constant motion, and her horns were leaf-like in appearance. She wore a very short, very sheer black smock, tied off at the waist, and she seemed to have evolved into the age of seventeen or eighteen. But it was hard to tell because of her eyes. They were dark and old, filled with far too much knowledge to have been gathered in a short lifetime.

"The queen has requested your presence at your earliest convenience," she said in a soft, monotone voice.

In other words, now!

"I see," Crighton said. "Where did all the new clothes come from? Surely, they're not meant for me…"

Serene stood next to the massive door in his domicile. It was standing wide open, yet she remained in the hallway, not bothering to enter or answer his questions. "Are you coming?" Her curtness stung Crighton. He ran a hand through his coarse black hair, feeling a wave of heat furl from within its wavy confines.

He'd never witnessed sharp tones in Serene's voice before or her obvious impatience.

"Having a bad day, are we?" he asked.

"You have no idea."

He followed her quick steps through the halls.

Softening his tone he said, "Care to share?"

"I wouldn't know where to begin."

"Is it really that bad?"

"Lucinda squashed a rebellion, and now she's in a dreadful mood. If we don't hurry, I fear it's going to get far worse."

Crighton followed Serene through the open massive doors leading to the Chamber of Justice. Inside, Lucinda was resting her head against her gothic skull throne with her eyes closed and legs crossed at the ankle. Horned demon skulls accented the chair arms and the top of the throne had human skulls in each corner. Vertebrae and other bones formed the legs and sides, resulting in a chilling effect. But Lucinda's altered appearance was by far the most striking new development in the last 72 hours.

Five large horns had grown out of her skull and were adored with shimmering red rubies. In addition, short, black wings had sprouted on her back above her shoulders. She wore a tight, gray serpentine dress, specifically cut to show off her enticing cleavage and midriff. Around her neck was a solid gold collar, matching the shoulder armor and hammered cuffs on her upper forearms. Green lines were painted on her cheeks and chest bones, matching the one dividing her tense forehead. She looked up slowly, meeting Crighton's stare, setting him back on his heels. Her gold tiger eyes were framed in charcoal eyeshadow below severely drawn brows. Although her face held a sinister, troubled expression, an enigmatic smile played perpetually around her full blood-red lips.

"You're late, Crighton." Her crisp, icy voice sliced through eerie silence. "No one keeps me waiting. Not even you."

"I'm not late for anything. I don't have any duties, and I don't accept missions. I'm here because you requested my presence. You made me wait for three days, and for what? To test my loyalty...my endurance?" He looked down, shaking his head. "Tell me the truth, Lucinda. Have I ever neglected you?"

"Bullshit. You neglect me all the time." She spoke with such a heated tone that it threw him off.

"You never curse, Lucinda. There must be serious matters troubling you." He averted his eyes to Serene. She stood on the left side of Lucinda's throne with her head bowed and spoke quietly.

"Would you like me to leave, Your Majesty?"

"That's a peculiar question, Serene. When I'm alone is when I need your attention most."

"But you're not alone now, and I know you want to be," Serene pointed out. "There's an assignment you asked me to address. So, if you don't mind, I'll take my leave and attend to those preparations we discussed."

Lucinda nodded, and Serene disappeared through an open doorway.

Crighton wanted to say something to ease her tension. "You look beautiful, Your Majesty."

His words seemed to calm her, but she didn't acknowledge them. She simply nodded and stood. Then she began strolling down the hallway toward the refurbished ballroom with her long tail swishing back and forth and Crighton at her side.

"The Knights of Darkness will not be interested in your position as my protector," she told him. "They know you as Crighton, the Soul Seeker. They will most likely want you to tell them about the circumstances surrounding the upcoming war."

"And how am I to respond when they ask why I am not in the Outer Rim with the rest of our soldiers?"

"With the truth, naturally."

"I'm afraid the truth may not please them much."

She glanced over her shoulder. "And why is that?"

"Master Cletus told me that I needed to return to Hell due to your need for extra security."

"Extra security? Are you sure it was Cletus?"

"Yes. But there's no need to worry. I brought four soldiers with me to act as your personal guards."

"What about you? Are you here to protect me?"

"My commitment to service ended four days ago. After your reception, I'll be heading back home to be with my family." He cracked a slight smile. "I'm trying to make up with Ariel for being away, and now there's Samara to think about."

"I see." She seemed annoyed by his answer, so it was fortunate that they reached the ballroom when they did.

The guards stationed in the hallway bowed deeply, signifying their respect and gratitude. "Welcome, Your Majesty," they said in unison, opening the doors before her. Inside the ballroom, every head bowed as Lucinda entered. Then Crighton Daemonium was announced, and all eyes turned to him. He stood at the podium, controlling the shake in his knees as he welcomed the Knights of Darkness, council members and their guests. After giving a positive report on the front dividing Hell's army from Heavenly forces, he encouraged the continuation of their festivities. Then he went out of his way to personally greet the prominent political figures who could turn tides with their stamps of approval. It was all pomp and circumstance in this underworld game—a power play in the political arena that Crighton preferred to distance himself from, despite Lucinda's constant prodding. A demon of few words, he hadn't gotten used to the political side of his job and was relieved that his obligation was ending.

In the Outer Rim, he had accepted the responsibility of troop management, while Lucinda worked endless hours, assuming her role as Queen. According to her, there was no real feeling to any of it, including the demanding interactions with current and former Master Knights and political leaders. But after sitting on her father's throne, Lucinda experienced a powerful wave of emotion. Minutes later, she looked around her and there appeared to be an emptiness to it all. Crighton saw it, too. There were things she wanted to say to him, hollow promises that were as worthless as human fodder. If her father hadn't sent him to England on his last mission, things would have been different between them. But her position didn't allow for "what ifs," and the forced alliance to his soulmate had damaged any political aspirations, at least, where Crighton was concerned. Any plans for their future together were voided, but that didn't eliminate the heartfelt feelings between them.

Conversations about the pending war between Heaven and Hell continued throughout the room and, eventually, Lucinda and Crighton were separated by the crowd. As she had said, interest in the Outer Rim sieges involving Arch-demons and Archangels remained prevalent, and high-level demons flocked to Crighton to hear more about them. However, there were still a vast number of guests for Lucinda to entertain. Among them was Chancellor Milton Knox. His flowing locks of curly brown hair had been cut and styled in a respectable length and were now tinged with gray, making him appear dignified, although he was far from it. His goatee was neatly trimmed and showing streaks of white as well. With him being one of Lucifer's top contenders in the sports arena, he'd been rewarded with jewels from the mines and had spent a great deal of time in the Pleasure Quarters. Over the years, his elevated position made him one of the most outspoken voices on the council. Yet oddly enough, his remarks and objections often resulted in screaming matches among the harmonious members, proving irrationality was contagious in Hell.

Throughout the night, Crighton dodged questions from inquisitive guests and limited the scope of his answers. He stole a quick look in Lucinda's direction and openly frowned. Knox was standing before her, which meant trouble wasn't far away.

"It's a delight to be in your company, Your Majesty," he said, bowing respectfully. He stood a head taller than Crighton, but they were close in size across the chest. While rolling a cigar between his fingers, his lips held a flirtatious smile and his blue eyes a glint of humor.

"Put that smelly thing out!" Although Lucinda's face was twisted in a paroxysm of rage, the cause of her anger remained a mystery, as everyone knew she enjoyed an occasional cigar.

"What's the problem?"

"I said put that smelly thing out! It stinks to high Heavens."

The leather-clad charmer noticed Crighton staring at them. He held the cigar aloft so they could clearly see it. "I haven't lit it yet," he said, as reasonably as he could. "You can't possibly smell it. Besides, good cigars don't stink."

"I can smell it all right," she shouted back, "and I can smell you too. You both stink!"

He seemed convinced that she couldn't smell anything, except perhaps her own bile. But as much as he seemed to enjoy the banter, Crighton knew it was Knox's policy to never argue with fanatics on three subjects—religion, politics, and stogies.

He put his cigar back into its wooden case and slid it into his coat pocket, admitting defeat.

Lucinda leaned toward him with a devious smile on her face. She trailed her finger across his lower abdomen then snagged the cigar holder from his pocket. "Plotting war can be stressful, as I'm sure you're aware. A good smoke takes the edge off and is damn hard to find in Hell."

"If it takes war and a Davidoff cigar to provide this opportunity, then it's all worth it."

"Opportunity? I hope you're not being foolish again. Hitting on me is a waste of time for both of us."

Knox smiled the way females found winsome. "I've had time to consider options in your absence, Your Majesty. One that would greatly benefit both of us."

Crighton was half-listening a short distance away. *Oh, great.* No matter the subject, if Knox thought long and hard about something, his verbal vomit always resulted in offending somebody. Lucinda lowered her voice and told him to watch his tongue. But Knox had always been a stubborn, assertive demon. He never listened or heeded advice when it was given and saw everything in terms of power.

"I propose an alliance between our two families," he said. "I'm certain it will be advantageous for you. My term is not complete for another nine years, and your position in Hell would achieve true greatness with me at your side guiding you."

Crighton mouthed the words, *humor him.* Then he feigned interest in another conversation.

"What nature of alliance are you proposing?" Lucinda asked.

"Marital, naturally." he answered as though it was the most obvious thing in the world.

"I don't believe in—"

"Hear me out," he interrupted. "I've been observing your perseverance and am extremely impressed by your creative, original ideas. It's not just a marriage of politics that I speak of, but one of intellectual and sympathetic equals."

Crighton had always known Knox to be eccentric, but this was ridiculous.

"You must forgive me, sir," she pleaded. "I cannot see how your offer would be beneficial, though I assure you it's most flattering."

"In your distinguished position, it's obviously against protocol to publicly accept such a thing." Knox continued as though he hadn't heard her. "Perhaps you could use your solitude to consider it. But just know that I'm willing to wait for your response for however many years are necessary."

Crighton sensed Lucinda's simmering temper and read the impatience on her face. She would have repeated her rejection more forcefully, embarrassing Knox in front of his peers, if Crighton hadn't stepped closer.

"I believe her Majesty has heard enough," he informed Knox with the severity he was known for.

"Crighton…" she began.

"I believe the Queen can speak for herself, Soul Seeker," Knox bit back. "You can join the Hellhounds outside…where you belong."

Crighton took an offensive step forward. "Mess with the Queen and I'll do worse than kill you. I'll destroy your family as well."

"Crighton," she repeated more firmly than before.

Knox glared at him. "Why are you not with the protective forces in the Outer Rim? Is the Queen's chaperon and defender a hopeless craven or a dedicated warrior? That's what we'd like to know."

Crighton's right hand rested on the hilt of his sword. He alone rose to the height of the occasion and set his face against cowardly charges. And yet, he couldn't help feeling as if he bore the weight of this world while struggling to provide for his family. "I'm here to protect Queen Lucinda from outside threats," he announced. "But it now seems I'm shielding her from an inside one. You and your followers, Chancellor Knox."

"Stop it!" Lucinda snapped. Crighton turned to look at her. "This demon means me no harm, so I will thank you to stand down."

He threw one more glare at Knox before moving behind Lucinda.

"I was quite serious in my refusal," she said. "Marriage is not a goal I'm pursuing. However, I thank you for your generous offer."

Knox seemed to accept this. "Of course, Your Majesty. But if ever you change your mind, you know where to find me." With this, he left the room with dozens of eyes following him.

Once Knox was out of earshot, Lucinda spoke, keeping her back to Crighton. "Tell me, dear friend, do you think me so lacking in dignity to accept such a man?"

"With all due respect, Your Majesty, these days I can't be sure of what your intentions are or what the future holds for any of us."

"Well, I'm most certainly not interested in him. Rumor has it Knox favors men, and I've made it a point to avoid bearded relationships, especially for political gain."

Crighton suspected his preference six months ago after seeing Knox wrap his arm around the waist of a male escort. His failure to mention the incident seemed pointless now. "By the way," he said out of the corner of his mouth, "there are actions

I've noticed you've stopped taking, which is of great concern to me."

She turned her head slightly so she could see Crighton. "And what might I ask are these?"

"You used to smile and laugh, Your Majesty."

She disregarded his comment and turned back to face the crowd.

Crighton had been incapable of empathy or remorse before bonding with Ariel. Now these emotions seemed to come as natural as breathing, and at the worst possible moments. He could feel the heartbreak inside her—every shattered piece blaming him as it fell. The mess he had made of his life was his responsibility alone; there was no denying it. If Lucinda hadn't gotten carried away with her need for power, a romance might have bloomed between them years ago. But now, he had his family to think about. They were his priority, not Lucinda or her merchants of Hell.

"Excuse me," she said to the congregation, trying to hide the break in her voice. "Please continue to enjoy yourselves. You may seek a private audience with me to discuss your concerns and plans. Please make an appointment with my assistant, Serene."

There were grumbling voices all around them—disgruntled guests and Knights in the room.

Lucinda quietly spoke to Crighton without turning. "Say your goodnights to everyone. I need you to join me in the garden as soon as possible."

"Your Majesty, I'm sorry but I need to go home. I've been gone far too long and only came tonight out of obligation to you. Can't we discuss these matters another time?"

She turned abruptly; her glaring eyes burned white hot as she scowled. "You have no idea who you're fooling with, Crighton.

I've asked very little of you, yet you ask so much of me. This is not my chosen life, and I don't intend for it to be any longer than necessary."

"Understood. But it's the one you've got right now. I believe it's wise to make the most of it while you can."

"And you would know all about that, wouldn't you?" She laughed sarcastically and strode to the door. "We've got a war to fight, and you worry about inconveniences? Try explaining that to our soldiers, the Knights of Darkness, and our devoted commanders. I'm sure they'd love to hear how you're fucking an angel when the Red War is about to begin."

Crighton sighed. "Some demons don't care if you're telling the truth. They want to believe their own version of events, even if it's laced with lies. Please tell me you're not one of them, Lucinda. I make no apologies for how I choose to repair what you broke."

CHAPTER 6

SCORNED LOVER

Full of hatred and bitterness, Lucinda hurried along the winding stone path leading to her secret haven. The inner courtyard featured eight stainless steel torches mounted on black eight-foot-high posts, eternally lit from the fires of Hell. Within the circle of light, a stone bench rested next to an enormous three-tier fountain topped with an illuminated, rolling glass ball. This was the Queen's private sanctuary that no creature or spiritual being was allowed to enter. However, at that moment, she wanted Serene to be here to interpret the emotions she couldn't control. She wanted Crighton by her side, laughing like nothing had changed between them. But most of all, she wanted to be a normal demon again. Instead, the reflection of a dark-eyed, miserable demoness stared back at her from the surface of the water.

Well, I can change that, at least.

Lucinda threw water onto her face, washing the black eye makeup off, and rubbing it away with her hands. When she finished, she looked back at her reflection. That was the face she knew, though sadder and more tired than she appeared in earlier days when she'd been known as Samara, a soul seeker competitor obsessed with beating Crighton's record. After Lucifer gave him the power to teleport around the world, he also gave his daughter the ability to transform into a raven. But when she transformed back into a demon, she was left with black claws for hands. She foolishly approached her father, believing it was an oversight on his part.

"You ungrateful little bitch!" he screamed. "When you bring me more angel souls than Crighton, your grubby little hands will return."

The day her father died in the arena was the greatest day in Samara's life. After shoving his limp body into a blazing furnace, her hands were miraculously restored. The next day, she changed her name to Queen Lucinda and claimed Lucifer's throne as her own. Then two weeks later, while struggling with her responsibilities, an enemy of Crighton's showed up in her private chamber. Sergei offered to fill the void of loneliness in her life and Lucinda reluctantly accepted. This demon encouraged her to bend her father's oppressive rules by allowing the underworld population to grow horns, bat wings, and tails. The six horns that grew out of her own skull were a reminder of her demoralizing commitment to Sergei. In exchange for his nightly BDSM sessions in her soundproof bedroom and the loyalty of his well-trained army, she forced the Knights of Darkness to accept him as a member in their organization. She also promised a throne next to hers in the Hall of Justice, if his soldiers were successful in the upcoming Red War.

With Sergei's corrupt connections in the Outer World and Lucinda's newly acquired abilities, world domination remained within her reach, as well as the destruction of Heaven. What's more, they had bonded over their shared hatred for a common enemy.

Crighton.

Lucinda kept her eyes down, listening to his familiar footsteps in the courtyard. She sat down on the stone bench that curved with the shape of the fountain. As Crighton drew closer, she looked up and watched him sink his hands into his back pockets. He looked like a schoolboy, hoping for forgiveness from a friend.

"I'm sorry," he told her in all sincerity. "That was unfair and disrespectful of me. You have complicated issues to deal with, and we both agreed I'd stay out of them. I have no right to interfere in your life or judge your actions, even if I disagree. Please forgive me, Lucinda."

"No one is sorrier than me. I've destroyed our friendship. What's worse, I knew I was doing it, and did nothing to prevent it."

Crighton sat down next to her, close but not touching. "Our friendship was...well, it was never really much of a friendship, was it?"

"No," she admitted, staring at the slate-covered ground. "I'm still haunted with gloomy thoughts and sad memories I wish I could wipe away."

It was more, she realized. It had always been more, and they had both known it. She locked eyes with him and smiled sadly. "I'm thankful for everything you've done, Crighton. You've always been supportive. There's no one more loyal, despite what the council believes."

"You have to know..." Crighton began, pausing to look down at his hands. "It wasn't my decision to come here. When one of the Knights reached out to me and said you needed help, I...I couldn't stay away. I needed to make sure you were safe. But from what I've witnessed, everything is different now, including you, Lucinda. You don't need me. You've got more strength than your father ever had. More than I ever thought possible."

"I still love you, Crighton," she murmured and took his hand in hers. "I know that I shouldn't, but I never stopped. I gave up trying a long time ago. I'm helpless and hopeless, I fear."

"I'll always care about you, Lucinda, but my soul belongs to Ariel. I could never betray her, especially now. She gave birth to my child, and I owe her more than—"

She snatched her hand away. "When did you become so noble? So virtuous and moral?" Her gold eyes were boring into his brain, searching for who knows what. "Don't you think that I get lonely? It gets dark inside my head and in my heart. Check my pulse, Crighton. If there isn't one, you know why. I died when you left here…when you stopped caring."

"It's important to stay away from what might have been, Lucinda. You need to focus on what can be."

"Like what?" She was exasperated.

"When I look back at some of the most painful moments of my life, I see myself sitting alone, feeling either immense shame or regret. It's bizarre how we can get so offended and angry when other demons hurt us, and yet choose to torture ourselves far worse than they possibly could. For the longest time, my biggest regret revolved around missing out on life and the freedom I never had. But all that is gone now…because of Ariel."

Lucinda scoffed. "You owe me more than you'll ever know. More than that angel you profess to love."

"Owe you? I'm not a fool and I don't take things for granted. You insisted on taking over, remember? You provided a home for us and offered your protection. That's why I'm available whenever you need me. But Sergei? Of all the demons in Hell, why did you allow him to come back? You know full well he toys with humans and demons. His idea of playing with them is no different from killing." Crighton shook his head. "Frankly, I can't imagine being so hard up that you'd need a dildo delivered to your doorstep when there are ten other demons you could call on."

She looked down for a long moment then glanced up, meeting his questioning gaze. "What if I don't want you to leave?" She fiddled with her enormous ruby ring, turning it around on her finger.

Crighton furrowed his brows. "You can't be serious."

"I was cold and callous in so many ways. It was never my intention to challenge you…not when we were ten, or nineteen, or thirty. I wanted you to rule beside me. To offer your expertise and guidance. To teach me right from wrong—"

Crighton bit his lip to suppress a smile. "You know I can't stay. It simply isn't possible. Just keep your head on straight and stay away from Sergei. Believe me, that creature will trick you into doing his bidding."

She shook her head disapprovingly. "It hurts to know you'll never remember the things I'll never forget."

"I can't be sorrier than I am. I honestly wish I could make you feel better, but I need to go. I'll come back soon. I promise. Then we can discuss battle strategies and your future in greater detail." He reached out a hand to touch her shoulder and she grabbed it with both hands.

"Lucinda, this is ridiculous! Let me go!"

"Why?"

He jerked his hand away quickly, scratching his palm with her ring. "Ouch! You did that on purpose!"

Her hand flew up to her lips, and she pretended to look embarrassed. "Who, me? What can I say? It's not my fault that you excite me to no end. The idea that you're a dark angel, and I could have had you so easily…"

"I'm not an angel!" His eyes glowed bright green, displaying his temper.

"That's right. You're Nephilim…half-angel and half-demon. It takes balls for a half-breed to profess his devotion to the Queen of Hell. Especially when your loyalties lie elsewhere."

"Exactly." He looked down at the raised scratch on his hand and rubbed it hard. Within seconds, he felt a strange numbness in his palm, the back of hand, his fingers and right arm. The tingling sensation spread rapidly to the other side of his body and traveled down the muscles in his legs.

Lucinda leaned toward him, and the scent of her strong, musky perfume assaulted his senses. "That's it? After walking away and forcing me to rule alone, you've got nothing to add?"

"I…I don't know what else I can say." Crighton blinked, trying to clear his blurred vision.

Lucinda put her arms around his neck, pulling him closer. Her hungry lips found his within seconds, but there was something peculiar about this unexpected, mind-bending kiss. She grazed his lower lip with her teeth. Heat flared in his loins, and she brought her mouth down on his, harder and hungrier than before. She parted his mouth, thrusting her sharp serpent tongue inside with an eager, drawn-out moan. Then she pushed him away in a great show of disgust and abruptly stood up.

In Crighton's mind, there were questions to ask and riddles to solve. With an unspoken truth yelling in his brain, the space between them tilted. He tried to stand but dropped down again, feeling off-balance, confused, and disoriented.

"Confine him!" Lucinda yelled. Winding vines dashed out from under and around the bench. They encircled Crighton's arms and legs, holding him tightly in place.

"What's happening here? Why are you doing this, Lucinda?" His tongue felt thick as if he were drunk.

She smiled and waved a hand in the air. The flickering flames in the wall sconces grew into blazing torches. Crighton's body began to sweat profusely, triggered by the sudden rise in temperature. She sprayed her floral perfume under his nose, and he instinctively drew in another breath. He moaned like some horny, prowling beast. He wanted to sin with another member of his kind, to force another being to join him in wickedness. He felt a presence slide into his mind from the darkness—a presence subtle and insidious as a leaking vessel, slowly filling him, his mind. Its whispers besieged his ears, flooded his brain like the murmurs of a multitude of beings, and its subtle streams of perversion invaded his soul.

Surrender, Crighton. You have no strength to resist, no power to fight back. Your seeds will be sowed, multiplying the harvest of phantom warriors in Hell and the heavens tenfold. Surrender unto me, and your rapture will be boundless.

Crighton's fingers grappled with the vines, trying to tear free, and his teeth clenched as he suffered the agony of the conjured spirit's penetration. He wanted to stretch out his hands to choke the villain eluding him, inciting his blinding rage. The cry that Crighton had been holding in his throat issued from his lips. It broke from him like a wail of despair, a furious entreaty—a cry for iniquitous entrapment.

"NOOO!!"

"What's wrong, Crighton? Is there something you need? Perhaps a pent-up release? I kept you caged in this place for good reason. It was only a matter of time before your true demon took over and proved who you really are." Lucinda placed a hand on his face and gazed into his green glowing eyes. "By the way, do you like my new fragrance? I had it made especially for you."

Crighton shook her hand off. He tried to force his tongue to speak, but it was futile. *Let me go!* His mind cried out. *Let me go!*

Another woman approached…blonde-haired and blue-eyed. *Ariel? Is that you? What are you doing here?*

He watched her unzip her tight black dress and slide it off her shoulders. Like an adolescent fool, he stared at her nude body and noted the proud conscious movements of her head, adorned with two magnificent horns. He sat silent and immobile, as she unbuttoned his shirt and stripped away his pants. Then she knelt before him on a large pillow and leaned forward to embrace his waist, perhaps endearingly or gravely. He wasn't sure which. She sat back on her haunches and stared into his face, searching for recognition. But the demon inside him took over, preferring to watch the sensuous rise and fall of her breasts.

So beautiful. So tempting. His mouth parted, but no words were forthcoming. He drew in another deep breath, trying to clear his muddled thoughts, only to have them further clouded.

Lucinda stood behind him. She ran her fingers through his thick black hair and jerked his head back with one sharp pull. "Give Vedas a kiss," she demanded. "She's earned a dozen from you for what she's about to do…four times over."

Lucinda released her hold, and Vedas' round face came into view. She pressed her mouth against his, but it was pointless. Crighton's mind and lips would not relax, not long enough to kiss this mind-fucking illusion. He looked away, feeling sick to his stomach, feeling tricked and deceived by coming here.

"What's wrong, Crighton? I thought you liked this hellcat. So beautiful to look at, isn't she? I believe there was a time when you were willing to kill for her. Willing to subject yourself to Lucifer's punishment…rather than see her harmed."

Crighton's brain was in a fog, and he could hardly see straight. *If you're here, Vedas, don't do this. Don't give into Lucinda's twisted demands.*

"We're wasting energy and valuable time," Lucinda announced, leaning against the edge of the fountain across from him. "It's time to get down to business. Vedas, I want you to use that beautiful mouth of yours for something besides complaining. Do as you're told, or you'll die. It's that simple."

The beautiful courtesan gripped Crighton's hips firmly in her hands and took him with her mouth, like a demon possessed. After the longest minute of his life, he read the meaning of her bobbing movements in her sultry, uplifted eyes. It was too much for him. He closed his eyes and surrendered himself to her, body, and soul. He was conscious of nothing...just her soft, moist lips and swirling tongue, fueling his arousal. They stimulated his brain as though they were the vehicle of a secret language—something he was incapable of understanding, only feeling. The tension continued to build in his body at an alarming rate. He pulled against the vines so hard that they cracked. In his mind, a starving vampire had latched onto him, darker than the swoon of sin, softer than sound. Sucking the life out of him purely for Lucinda's enjoyment.

Crighton's legs began shaking, but still he refused to yield. All the while, jasmine perfume permeated the air, dulling his brain and ardent resistance. Five minutes became ten...then fifteen. *Slow down! You're killing me! Slow down!* Vedas had triggered a mixture of sadness, anger, humiliation, and heightened euphoria inside him. Her mouth became a powerful vacuum, switched on high speed. The constant hum in her throat vibrated throughout his body, and he felt his impedance crumbling. It seemed she was intent on draining every drop of semen out of him, and he was powerless to stop her.

Why are you doing this? Crighton wanted to scream. *What are you hoping to gain?* He was steadfast in his struggle, but this expert in submission and Lucinda's shackle-vines were equally determined.

"Faster!" Lucinda yelled. "Go faster! He's so close, I can feel it!"

There was no use. Crighton threw back his head and gritted his teeth, incapable of holding on any longer. His explosive release was more intense than he thought possible. It racked his body repeatedly, leaving him struggling to catch a breath.

Okay, you got what you came for, he wanted to yell. *Now, let me go!*

Still unable to move, Crighton looked down. Shockingly, it appeared that Vedas wasn't done with him yet. For the next ninety minutes, she kept her head between his legs and her demonic lips clamped firmly on him. She repeated her torturous withdraw three more times, leaving his mind wrecked and his body quaking. For all intents and purposes, his demon seed was spent and so was he.

Finally, Lucinda stood up and brushed herself off, seemingly satisfied. "You can let him go now." The vines relaxed their hold and slowly withdrew.

"You can go too," she told Vedas.

After retrieving her dress from the ground, the courtesan gave Crighton a mournful look.

"He'll recover...just as will you," Lucinda told her. "But it seems I need to reward Serene. She was right in her assessment. You *were* the perfect bait for our clever switch. Without your help, I don't believe any of this would have been possible."

Vedas looked down, shaking her head. She disappeared into the maze, leaving behind Crighton's exhausted body and broken spirit.

What was the point of that? He asked himself. *Did I deserve to be tortured...for not choosing Lucinda?* He pushed himself upright and tried to stand. His knees gave out, and he collapsed on the ground, practically boneless. He rolled onto his back and drew in another deep breath. His heart was still racing in his chest, and his swollen cock throbbed with every pulsating beat. He heard someone rapidly approaching and cracked his eyelids to view them.

It was Serene, openly starring down at him. "What a waste," she said.

"I know," Lucinda murmured. "If we only had more time..." She handed her assistant something that Crighton couldn't quite make out. Then his ears perked, and his eyes widened, as their deception began to register.

"What do think?" she asked Serene. "We can pump him again if need be. By the looks of him, I'm sure he could go another round."

Serene bent down and picked up the battery-charged pump and a clear plastic cylinder with an aperture at one end. She set them aside and held up four large semen-filled vials, giving them her smile of approval. "More than enough, I'd say. The concubines are ovulating right now. They've been injected with a multitude of hormones, along with your special elixir. In no time at all, you'll have an army of dark angels at your disposal."

"Will they all look like him? Every mouthwatering inch?"

"The doctors in the infirmary assured me that you'll have exact clones in less than two weeks."

Lucinda rubbed her hand between her legs and smiled. "Good. I need to keep one for myself....to make sure I'm fully protected." She started laughing maniacally with such force that it almost seemed funny, until she went on for such an uncomfortable amount of time that Serene began laughing for real.

"Enough!" Lucinda snapped, silencing her young apprentice. Reaching inside her dress, she pulled out a hand-held mirror. She smoothed the skin around her throat and studied her dark, maleficent reflection. "I'm going to need more souls before nightfall. My wrinkles are coming back. See to it, Serene."

Her assistant motioned her head toward Crighton. "So, what do we do with this one?"

"Help him get dressed and give him another whiff of my perfume. I've got two guards standing by. They'll escort him to the main gate. From there, I'm sure he'll find his way home... eventually."

"But what if he remembers? What if he tells his soulmate what happened?"

Lucinda set her mirror down and walked over to Crighton. Not so arrogant now, was he? She stroked his crotch and brought her face close to his, leering and laughing at him. "Crighton won't come to his senses for at least an hour," she told Serene. "When he does, he's going to think he got a hell of a blow job, but he won't remember anything else about today. In his depraved mind, he might even believe I serviced him, which is laughable now that I think about it. However, let me remind you, should *anyone* be foolish enough to tell him the truth, Crighton's retribution will be child's play compared to mine."

CHAPTER 7

DEMON DELIVERY

Onoskelis arrived at Lilith's house desperately seeking Crighton, and according to Ariel's daughter, her timing couldn't have been better. Her mother was lying on the sofa contemplating suicide, and the male creature growing inside her seemed to know all about it. Quite remarkably, he had been telepathically communicating his concern, consoling her when nothing else would. At the same time, her daughter had been reassuring Ariel of Crighton's devotion, but she refused to believe Samara, who was now at her wit's end.

"He's with her...that creature!" Ariel sobbed. "I can feel it in my soul...his guilt and betrayal are enormous, eating into his heart. While I'm here giving birth to his child, he's with a she-devil, plotting against me. Threatening to overthrow Heaven and destroy all our family members living there."

"That's not true," Onoskelis said, hovering over her. A long-time family friend, Onoskelis knew about Ariel's soulmate situation. "Crighton could never break his bond with you. If he tried, he would die...as would you, Ariel. Is that not so?"

She begrudgingly nodded. "It is, but that doesn't mean he hasn't cheated. My heart and soul ache, which tells me it's true."

"I don't believe it," Samara said. "Especially with Lucinda. From what I hear, she's a horrible, ugly creature. My father would never mate with her."

"That's right…he wouldn't," Onoskelis assured her. "Lucinda is a conniving bitch, but her interests lie elsewhere. Word has it she's building a Nephilim army in Hell and intends to take down Heaven with it, destroying the balance between them."

"Is there anything we can we do?" Samara asked. "Does my father know this?"

"He will soon enough," the little Shapeshifter said. "But right now, we need to keep your mother calm…until *he* arrives. That beautiful child growing inside her."

"And what then?" Ariel groaned. "I only see misery and heartbreak ahead of us." She let out a painful moan and doubled over, cradling her belly.

"Take hold of her arm," Onoskelis told Samara. "We need to move her." Together, they pulled Ariel from the sofa and half-carried her to her bed. Onoskelis rested her hand on Ariel's extended belly and smiled. The movement within the angel had stilled, alerting them that the birth of another demon was rapidly approaching.

"It won't be long now," the Shapeshifter said.

"What about Crighton?" Ariel asked.

"He'll be here soon."

Ariel remained doubtful. "He's been gone for two long months…with no explanation. Why would he return now?"

"Because he loves you," Onoskelis said. "He's not the fool you take him for, I assure you. Lucinda has been manipulating everyone. She's eaten the souls of dozens of mystics and absorbed all their powers. She's even threatened to eat mine…more than once."

The sound of rapidly approaching footsteps carried from outside, drawing their attention. The front door suddenly flew open and Crighton rushed inside, scouring the house for Ariel. He spotted his daughter standing in their bedroom doorway, watching a black cat climb through an unlatched window.

"What's going on here?" Crighton asked. "Why is Ariel in bed? What's wrong with her?"

Samara shrugged a shoulder. "She's having your baby."

Crighton pushed past his daughter and bent down over Ariel, concern etching his brow. "We're soulmates! We feel each other's pain. Why didn't I know? Why didn't I feel it?" His thumb crossed her lips, soft lips he had kissed dozens of times. His hand touched her fingers, soft and caring. Ariel had spent endless nights consoling him, holding him, surrendering beneath him. What a fool he'd been, leaving her without knowing, without seeing the obvious signs. His threat of impregnating her during mating season was done in jest—in the heat of the moment—not as a promise to disrupt her life more than he had already done.

From now on, he needed to be careful with her. The last thing Crighton wanted was a dozen Nephilim demons running around, flapping their wings, flexing their muscles, and screaming his name.

Samara joined him at Ariel's bedside. "There's something you need to know…about Lucinda."

Crighton's eyes rose to the wood paneled wall opposite him. He said words he didn't allow himself to use often. "I'm sorry. It was a mistake to leave you and your mother alone…to go to Hell when she begged me to stay."

Samara rested a hand on his arm. "Father, listen to me. Onoskelis was here. She said Lucinda is preparing for war. That she was building an army and—"

"That's not important right now. Your mother is our priority, and we need to keep her calm. I want you to find some towels and hot water. A new baby is about to arrive, and we have to be ready." Crighton untied Ariel's wrapped gown and draped a bed sheet over her to make the birth go smoothly without creating more laundry. Then he told her about his stay in Hell and how Lucinda refused to let him leave. "She had a gathering in the ballroom and some of the Knights of Darkness were there. They were discussing battle plans and the leadership in Hell. And then...she drugged me. For what reason, I have no idea. When I woke up, I was at the main gate, dazed, sore and confused. I don't know what she did to me or why, but I'm determined to find out...after everything settles down and you're back on your feet."

Ariel laid a hand on his thigh, and he instinctively backed up, allowing it to fall away. Her brow puzzled. "What's wrong? Why can't I touch you? Why are you acting so strange?"

"I'm sorry. There, I said it again. I'm just jumpy...after what happened. Of course, you can touch me. Although I'm not sure you'd want to right now. I'm kind of sweaty from running. But my hands are clean. See!" He held them before her and tested a smile, but it fell short. He struggled with meeting her blue eyes and told himself, *If I'm not careful, she'll see into my thoughts and never speak to me again.*

"So, what have you been up to," he asked, "besides growing a baby?"

Ariel moaned and gritted her teeth. The sweat on her brow increased, along with each painful contraction. Samara returned with a stack of towels and a pan of hot water. "Is there anything else I can do?"

"I'll let you know," Crighton told her. "Just stand by in case I need you."

Ariel was thankful to have Crighton there, although she could hardly think through her pain. Even so, she had considered asking for help from a neighboring demon. But she hadn't, even when she realized she was full term at two months. If there was anything unnatural about this delivery, she didn't want word to get out.

Another pain shot through her body. She could feel the child coming, as the contractions increased. Crying out, she grabbed Crighton's hand and squeezed tight. "It hurts so bad! Make it stop...please..."

He gave her a sympathetic look and gently stroked the back of her hand. "Be patient, Ariel. You're stronger than you know."

It was now dark outside. She could see that much from the bedroom window. There was no moon that night, which meant her child would be an angel, not a demon. Perhaps she saw some irony in that fact before another wave of pain took hold. She wondered if Crighton knew, would he still be here, witnessing the beginning of new life.

Samara was in the room, watching them, clearly in awe. Although Ariel preferred that she not witness the birth, there was hardly anything she could do to prevent it. She was in too much agony to care.

"Is that...the baby?" she heard her daughter ask. Shock was evident in her tone. "Is that how...I was born?"

Ariel gasped, tightening her grip on Crighton's hand. "Yes, Sam." She groaned then gave her a forced smile. "That's right." She cried out again, pressing her other hand tight against her swollen belly.

Crighton released her hand for only a moment—no doubt planning to shoo Samara out of the room. However, it was at that exact moment when Ariel felt the child leave her loins. With it came a huge sense of relief, making it impossible to speak. She waited eagerly to hear the baby cry, to announce its presence to the world. But there was only silence.

Tears welled up in Ariel's eyes, though she tried to convince herself that it meant nothing. As she watched, Crighton cut the cord and cleaned the baby gently. And yet he didn't offer even once for his soulmate to see their offspring. His expression was far too sad for a demon that had become a father for a second time.

"W—well…" Ariel whispered. "What's wrong?"

Crighton gazed at her with a look of anguish, as he held the silent newborn to his chest. "I'm so sorry, Ariel." He wiped his eyes with one hand, attempting to hide his tears. "Our son…he didn't make it."

Ariel's eyes grew wide. Her hands were trembling, and her tears began to fall. *Dead? Our son is dead?* She had wished it was so out of anger, but never meant it to be true. After all she'd gone through to give birth to this child, he hadn't lived long enough to take a single breath? How was it possible? How could God be so cruel?

She had heard him talking in her thoughts, begging to be born. Was this cruel punishment rightly deserved? "It's all my fault!" she yelled. "I made this happen!" Her despair was so deeply felt that the pain was consuming her, as long-lasting and excruciating as the child's birth.

"No…you didn't," Crighton assured her, holding her hand tight. "This was God's will. Not yours."

"But why?" Ariel asked. She pressed her hand to her belly and took a stuttered breath, as she realized what was happening. She was still in labor! "Crighton…" she gasped, looking up at him in disbelief. "A twin…he has a twin…"

Alarm registered on Crighton's face. There was no way to prepare for this…no way to know it was even possible. He handed the stillborn child to Samara and told her softly, "It will be easier on all of us if Ariel doesn't see him." By the time he sat down again, Ariel was far along in the next birth.

She began sobbing. "Crighton…I can't do this. Not again…"

"Of course you can, sweetheart. You're halfway there already." As heartbreaking as the situation was, Crighton wouldn't let her give in to her pain or her sorrow. He grasped her hand and continued to stroke it. He wrapped his arm around her back and helped her lean forward, just as another contraction took hold.

"Push! Come on, Ariel. Push! You've got this! Keep going, keep pushing! Don't stop!"

Moments later, a baby's cry sounded throughout their house.

"Thank you," Crighton whispered. After a quick cleaning and examination, he announced, "It's a boy! A beautiful boy!"

Ariel was almost too tired to hold him when Crighton placed him in her arms. But the moment she felt the baby snuggle close to her body, her entire life took on a fresh, new meaning. She looked down at the bundle of joy in her arms, her eyes still moist with tears. Everything would be okay now…if she relaxed and allowed it to be that way.

Crighton's little boy wailed. He had impressive lungs for such a small baby and a strong disposition too. Even when Samara held him, he continued to squirm and wiggle against her hold. However, she was so in awe of the child's beauty, that his cries fell on deaf ears. His green eyes shimmered, and his tiny pink mouth pouted. "He's adorable," Samara said, handing him back to his mother. At first, Ariel thought his thick hair was a light shade of pink, but after Crighton cleaned all the blood from his head, she realized this wasn't the case. The child's hair was stark white, a peculiar color for a demon, but according to Ariel it was a miracle. A sign from God.

"What are you going to name my son?" Crighton asked proudly. "It should be noble, powerful and enduring--like me," he chuckled.

At first, Ariel had no answer. She looked at the baby for a long moment, passing her hand over his soft, unusual hair. "He will be Cassius Daemonium," she said. "Cass for short. To honor your father, Castile." She held the small child close to her, only then allowing herself to cry. There were too many things happening too quickly. The joy of motherhood for a second time, and the sudden death of a twin. How could she be happy and sad at the same time?

"Crighton…" She looked up at him then, controlling her tears. "Will you ever forgive me?"

He gave her a look of surprise, and then gentleness. "What are you talking about? There's nothing to forgive, Ariel. You gave me a wonderful son…and a fine daughter too." He wrapped an arm around Samara's shoulder and drew her close. "What more could a father ask for?"

"Peace would be nice," Ariel said, offering one of her breasts to her new baby. It latched hold immediately and began feeding—accepting growth hormones and the nutrients it would need for the rest of his life.

Samara and her father exchanged knowing looks. Peace would be a long time coming if Lucinda had her way. "We can only hope, Ariel," Crighton said. "And perhaps you could pray…"

Samara bumped him with her elbow and smiled. "I've been practicing archery, while you were away. In fact, Tyrus told me that I'm better than you are, Father. We should have a contest tomorrow…to see if he's right."

"Tyrus? He was here? When exactly was that?"

"Four days ago. He said you never showed up for your meeting. That he searched high and low and couldn't find you anywhere. But how can that be…if you were there at the same time?"

"I don't know, but I suspect Lucinda does." Crighton's mouth tightened, and his stance spread into a more relaxed position. "Every nerve and muscle in my body tells me she's been up to no good. I'm planning to get to the bottom of this mystery as soon as I can, even if it's the last thing I do."

CHAPTER 8

UNHOLY GROUND

It was snowing when they buried Cassius' twin brother under the tree of ages, but Crighton was thankful for the cold weather. The bitter ice seemed to subdue the misery in his family, if only for a day. He was the one to place the covered basket in the small hole in the ground. But Ariel was troubled over leaving their child outside in the cold.

"Can we keep him with us a while longer?"

"For what purpose?" Crighton asked.

"So I can gaze upon his face. I don't want to forget him."

"You won't, Ariel. But if we wait, the separation will only be harder, and the snow will be deeper." He picked up the shovel and completed the difficult task of burying his son, while Ariel, held their sleeping baby and silently watched. Standing next to her, Samara stared at the small mound of dirt in forlorn silence. Then she spoke quietly to no one in particular.

"I didn't know demons could die," she said. "Not entirely."

"Without a soul, nothing survives," Ariel told her. "Not even human babies."

"Or my friend Legend," Samara added.

Crighton looked down at the stone marker he had created for his son, rubbing the back of his neck. "Caleb Daemonium. You chose a fine name, Ariel."

"I think so too. It means faithful...and brave," she said in a choked voice. "He would have been a wonderful young man. I'm sure of it..."

"Unfortunately, we'll never know. I'll never be able to teach him right from wrong. He might have made a few mistakes, but I'll never be able to correct him. I'm sorry for being selfish, Ariel, but I wanted Caleb to survive...to need me and know me...to grow up with his brother and look after him."

The temperature suddenly dropped. Ice began forming on and around the burial site.

"Coming?" Crighton asked Ariel.

"Soon."

Crighton nodded and adjusted Cassius' hat over his ears then followed Samara into the house, freeing themselves from the chill. But Ariel lingered a bit longer, mourning the loss of her first-born son.

"Although we never met, you will always be in my heart, Caleb." She bent down and laid a wreath of winter pansies on his grave with his twin brother still cradled in her arms. His soft cry reminded her that she had much to live for. It seemed he was disturbed by the melancholy air that surrounded them. In fact, the weight of it must have awaken him. She wrapped his blanket more securely around him and shushed his whine with her finger. "You miss your brother, don't you?" she whispered. "We both will...for a very long time."

Cassius continued to cry softly, despite his mother's gentle words. She soon realized that she would have to take him inside to calm him. Bouncing him gently in her arms, she made her way back to their snow-covered home. Then she stopped and glanced over her shoulder, viewing Caleb's grave a final time. "Goodbye, sweet baby," she said. "I promise to pray for you every day and to take good care of your brother."

As she reached for the doorknob, she heard a branch crack. Her heart leaped to her throat. She turned around quickly, eyeing the dense forest surrounding them. Heavy ice and snow covered the tree limbs, weighing them down. It wasn't unusual for branches to snap in the dead of winter, dumping their loads, but it was still unnerving.

Then another crack sounded, louder this time. Ariel's breath caught as thousands of crows suddenly rose above the fir trees and circled the air, noisily flapping their wings. More than a dozen flew above Caleb's grave, scenting blood. They landed on nearby trees and began cawing, attracting more birds, like vultures to a kill.

"Shoo!" Ariel yelled. "Get out of here!" The crows circled back and flew startlingly low, right over her head. Then they began disappearing into thin air one by one, like a magic trick. This went on for ten minutes until the entire flock was gone. Ariel shook her head, disbelieving what she had just witnessed. Was it a blessing from God or a curse from the Devil? The only thing she knew for certain was no one ever told her grief would feel so much like fear.

Turning back around, she noticed two large, white feathers on the snow-covered ground. She stooped to pick them up and smiled. How could she ever forget? Angels from Heaven were always nearby, bringing God's children into his fold.

"Thank you for caring," she whispered into the night air. "I've been away far too long."

Cassius whimpered again. The mild fussing sounded more like a request than complaining, like a neighbor asking to borrow sugar. "Patience, young man," she told him. "You'll be fed and put to bed soon." She stomped her feet before the threshold and stepped inside the house, closing the door behind her. Crighton's somber gaze met hers then drifted back to the crackling fire. He was prodding it with an iron tool to make it burn hotter. Nearby, Samara was curled up on the sofa, sound asleep under a blanket.

"I love the smell of a wood fire," Ariel whispered softly. She dropped down on the leather settee with her newborn still in her arms. It would be a sad night in their household, but at least they had one another to mourn their loss. Mindful of Samara's presence, Ariel lifted the corner of her blouse and brought Cassius to her breast. He started to suckle, but he also slept off and on, and had to be awakened to eat. Despite her dwindling patience, Ariel valued the loving and exclusive bond breastfeeding brought. However, tonight was different. Waiting for Cassius to finish was excruciating. Burying his brother was excruciating. Not knowing how to move on was the worst kind of suffering she could ever imagine. Eventually, Cassius' hands were no longer fisted, and he appeared to be sleepy, full, and content. Ariel set him down in his Moses basket and tucked a second receiving blanket around him.

As she stared down at him, an invisible Guardian angel leaned over, whispering in her ear, "Stay strong, Ariel. We're all trapped in our fates but acting as if we're not keeps us from dying from pain and despair."

Ariel blinked back tears and tried to swallow the lump in her throat. *It'll be okay*, she told herself. *I'll be fine*. But the guilt she felt over dreading the possibility of twins convinced her that God had punished her by taking her first born. And for that she couldn't forgive herself.

"Oh, Crighton, if I could only take it all back, believe me I would." Her shoulders slumped and he turned around. Her greatest fear was that disappointment would be carved in his face, yet surprisingly, it wasn't. As if sensing her remorse, his eyes searched her face for an answer—a reason to justify self-hatred.

"What did you do, Ariel? Why would you say that?" he asked.

While she sat motionless, refusing to say more, his gaze became more intense, and his concentration grew. He pegged her soulmate thoughts like a dart to a board, discovering her hidden secret. Turning away from her, he held a steady gaze out the window. "You have no fault in any of this," he told her. "But if you deny the pain you feel, you'll invite madness. And no one wants to live with a crazy angel."

Ariel huffed. "Sometimes the appropriate response to reality is to go a little insane." She looked down at her hands, resting in her lap. "If you don't want to forgive me or can't, I understand," she started. "Of all the things I've done, I'll never be able to forgive myself for sacrificing the life of our child."

"What are you talking about? That sad event was beyond our control…beyond our understanding. It was a cruel disappointment for both of us, and believe or not, I know how you feel."

"Don't call Caleb's death the event, that sad thing, or our disappointment. Caleb is our baby. He died and is buried outside in the snow. I find it upsetting that you can't say his name. And don't assume that you know how I feel, because to be perfectly honest, you don't."

Crighton looked down at Samara, still sound asleep, and kept his voice low. "What makes you think I have no feelings? Is it because I'm a demon, a Cambion by no choice of my own?"

Ariel had no answer for him. No compromise or even a sign of sympathy.

For a moment, Crighton simply stared into her eyes and then he drew a deep breath. "No parent should have to bury a child. No father should have to bury his son. It's not the natural order of things. Today, I buried our son under the snow-covered ground. There was no funeral, no friends, or visitors to mourn his passing.

I dug his grave under a tree, while you and Sam stood watching. I placed his tiny body in a hole and covered him with dirt and rock. I wasn't able to finish burying him before sundown, though I doubt that will affect his fate." Crighton shook his head. "I begrudge none of this to God. I don't curse Him or bemoan my lot in life. And although my heart keeps beating only to keep breaking, I don't question why it happened." A single tear rolled down Crighton's cheek. He made no move to wipe it away. "The world tells me that God is in Heaven and that my son is in Hell. I'm telling the world the one true thing I know. If my son is in Hell, then there is no Heaven, because if my son sits in Hell, there is no God."

Ariel laid her head back on the sofa. She rested her wrist on her forehead and blinked back a tear. But it escaped anyway and slid down her cheek.

Sensing her pain, Crighton stepped away from the fireplace and dropped down beside her. He wrapped an arm around Ariel's shoulder and drew her close. "I know your heart is broken, but we are fortunate…you and I. Cass is a handsome, healthy baby, and we have a beautiful, intelligent, and caring daughter. They need you to stay strong as much as I do. We will get past this one day and others like it, I promise."

Ariel felt sheltered and serene sitting there enveloped in the security of Crighton's embrace, but she was troubled by his secret meetings and devotion to duty. If only he could stay with her like this, assuring her that his love would never end—that their heartache would fade over time, and she would once again be the center of his universe.

"Are you hungry?" he asked.

"No, I'm okay," she said, though she hadn't eaten since morning. Sensing his separation from deeply felt emotions, she snuggled closer. *Don't go, please don't go,* she mentally begged.

"Should we move to our bedroom? It will be cold before morning."

Nodding against him, she held on tighter, unwilling to be the first to break contact. *Don't stop loving me. Oh, please…don't stop.*

"Are you alright? Do you need anything?" he asked, growing impatient over her odd behavior.

"Only you." She bit her lip and shivered from the cold air, seeping under her skirt.

Crighton's expression became ardent. "Your body disagrees." Unwinding himself from her, he pulled her back onto her feet. "Into bed and under the covers with you."

After asking Samara to watch her baby brother, he walked Ariel into their bedroom and tucked her in for the night.

"Now you," she said, reaching for his hand but finding only emptiness. He would leave her now, and she couldn't stop him. Not when his heart longed for Lucinda, miles away in the pit of Hell. Not when she couldn't break through the barrier between a demon's and an angel's soul, drawing him back where he belonged.

The table light was switched off, leaving Ariel in darkness. "Where are you?" she called out.

"Here, over here. I need to dress for my meeting."

"If you go now, I'm afraid you'll never come back." She could hear him in their closet, dropping clothes and shoes on the floor.

"How can you say that? I'm your soulmate. I'll always come back. But I have no choice in leaving tonight, not with the Red War about to break out and soldiers marching everywhere."

Heart in her throat, Ariel whispered in the night, "You above of all others have a choice. Please stay with me. Stay with your family. We need you more than Lucinda does."

"You know I can't desert her. Not right now, at least…"

"The war will happen whether you go or stay. Can't you see that? Lucinda will sink her claws into you and never let go. She'll make it impossible for us to be together, and I don't want to lose you, Crighton. I would shrivel up and die."

He walked to the bed, sat on its edge, and found her hand resting on the cover. "Ariel, you'll never lose me, and I won't allow you to die. Not without me at your side." He pressed her palm against his warm cheek. "Just between us, I'm meeting members of the Knights of Darkness in their secret chamber. We're planning to end the war before it begins. So, there's no need to worry about Lucinda, unless I arrive late, and she finds me wandering around lost."

In the flickering firelight, Crighton's emerald eyes glowed like radiant gemstones, warming Ariel's heart. She was sorry she had doubted his loyalty, his honesty, his undying love. Above all else, she was sorry she didn't believe him when he told her she was wrong. Crighton was her person, her soulmate—the only demon capable of telling an angel the truth, even when she was lying to herself. So why in the world did she find it so hard to believe him? He was predictable, reliable, and trustworthy. Wasn't he?

"I'll only be a few hours." He kissed her forehead and patted her hand. "While I'm away, get some rest. You're going to need it when Cass wakes up and our grown daughter wants fed."

All at once, Ariel sprang up and grabbed him around his neck with both arms. Her kiss was so sudden and fierce that he seemed shocked.

Crighton came to his senses and took a step back, grinning. "You're a bit of a wildcat tonight, aren't you? I guess I should leave you alone more often…or spend more time in our bed."

Ariel let out a nervous laugh. "Just hurry home."

"Don't worry...I won't be long."

She tried to push her psychotic behavior to the back of her mind by watching Crighton cross the living room floor, making as little sound as possible. After pulling on his boots and heavy winter jacket, he gently closed the front door and stepped into the powdery snow covering the entryway. From the bedroom window, Ariel watched him hurry off into the night. Then she climbed back into bed, pulled up the covers, and prayed for his safe return.

Meanwhile, outside their home, a vision of white swirled thought the sky, soon covering everything in its path in silent drifting snow. But there was no one outside to witness it. This place was neither here nor there—a perpetual stillness now bathed in pure white lit by a full, glowing moon. And yet, a baby's haunting cry echoed through the desolate air, piercing the stillness. There, cradled in the roots of a lone cherry tree under the freshly turned soil, lay a newborn babe, wrapped in a receiving blanket inside a woven basket. The high frostbitten branches of that tree were his shelter and comfort, and yet, strangely, he continued to cry.

However, it wasn't long before another presence stepped into the white snowfall. The Shapeshifter stared down at the small mound where a child had been buried. She noted the name on the headstone before scooping up the dirt with her hands and setting it aside. When she reached the cover of the basket, she lifted it carefully and stared curiously at the discarded infant. Even as the falling ice laced its way into her brown ponytail, the Shapeshifter remained motionless, intrigued by the disarming reveal. Her height, as well as her leather armor, cast a dark shadow over the baby. For only this reason, it began to sob harder. But the shapeshifter remained unaffected by this troubling scene. Before long, she knelt in front of the misplaced newborn and took him up into her arms.

"What are you doing here, little one?" Onoskelis asked. She looked down with soft brown eyes, chuckling when she saw the dark-haired baby smile. "You don't belong in this place. Not even close."

The child yawned softly, stretching, and wiggling in his admirer's arms. His eyelids suddenly lifted, revealing his coal black eyes. To anyone else, they might have been shocking—terrifying to some degree, but not to the Shapeshifter. In them, she saw remarkable depth and experience that surprised even her. "Such intrigue and knowledge for someone so young," she said. "And so clever, speaking to your mother while still in her womb. You protected your angelic brother in a brilliant, remarkable way…until you're old enough to slit his throat."

Onoskelis stood slowly, careful to keep Caleb close to her cold armor. At last, she gave the baby a knowing smile. "Perhaps I should give you a second chance in a better place. What do you think, little demon? Should I use my magic to make it happen?"

The baby's soft gurgle was ample response. The Shapeshifter reached out to the massive tree, carefully placing her hand on its rough bark. All at once, the snow fell from its branches and green leaves sprouted forth, as new life surged through its inner core and deep, twisted roots. Only then, did she kiss the child's forehead and set him back into his basket on the cold, icy ground. She pulled a knife from her pocket and cut off the end of a root. Then she encouraged the demon baby to suckle on the tree sap, filled with the nutrients he would need to survive. "Nature will protect you, little one. Feed on it and grow strong and confident. I will come again to visit you, Caleb…as soon as I'm able."

A quiet yawn from the infant stifled the falling snow. As he closed his eyes and nestled into the tree's warm base, everything around him fell silent. Onoskelis stayed to watch him for only a moment longer, sharing a bright smile. "Good boy," she whispered. "One day soon, you will be the most impressive entity in the world…the soulless angel chosen to replace Lucinda on the throne of Hell. A day of reckoning is coming when God will proclaim the end of time. With my guidance and protection, you will control all the bodies and souls remaining on Earth. Sleep well and rejoice, dark prince. Your powerful future awaits."

The Shapeshifter covered the basket with the lid she removed. She placed broken branches and young leaves over the top, then she restored the mound of soil and stood back. The only way to protect Caleb's future and implement her revenge was by infiltrating the Queen's organization and destroying her army from within.

Onoskelis smiled. "Ah, Lucinda. Your day of reckoning is coming," she said to the night air. "You might have eaten Yokai's soul, but you'll never take her completely away from me." The Shapeshifter sniffed and wiped her face and nose on her arm and, in a move that seemed to take all her effort, she retraced her steps to the scorched Middle Earth circle, half-covered in ice and snow. Whispering the words she'd learned from Hecate, she transported herself back to the underworld to begin her transformation from a recruit to a confident soldier in Lucinda's army.

Upon her arrival, a quick look around confirmed excitement was brewing everywhere. Demons were scrambling to collect their battle armor. Shouts echoed in the cavernous hallways, indicating archery training was underway in the newly converted ballroom. With the battle against Heaven only weeks away, a new batch of half-breeds were being delivered every hour in the pleasure quarters and had been growing at remarkable rates. During Onoskelis' short absence, flyers had been posted on every wall proclaiming a triple bounty on Imperial angels with the most prized soul belonging to Caleb's grandfather—the new Legion General, Castiel.

Yes, the Red War was coming and was predicted to be the deadliest conflict in biblical history. Archangels, with their powerful swords and shields, would be pitted against ram-horned flying demons, using every soul-collecting device in their arsenal. Unfortunately, human beings would experience a multitude of natural disasters due to the unseen battles occurring everywhere.

Onoskelis joined a large group of demons witnessing a speech by Lucinda, as she stood on a balcony in a gold sequin dress, shimmering in the glow of a hundred lit torches.

"There is nothing God can do to end the carnage," she said, "aside from demolishing his own creation and every living creature on it. According to my last count, the number of evil creatures thriving on Earth and in Hell has grown to epic proportions, outnumbering heavenly beings, angels, and religious souls of every faith one hundred to one. Earth is a priceless gem in God's jewelry box, and I intend to pluck it from the universe and claim it as my own. Are you ready to join me in this great endeavor? In the new world I'm creating for you?"

Lucinda's sea of followers cheered, and their stomps became thunder, sending ash high into the air. Onoskelis was joined by her commander, sending her heart racing. He cleared his throat and proudly told her, "It's only a matter of weeks now before our soldiers march to the surface with their guns, spears, and bows. When God sends his Archangels and Guardians down from Heaven to rescue the humans he promised to protect, we'll use all our weapons and our sword-wielding winged army to destroy them. How does that sound to you, soldier?"

After considering the sheer number of lives that would be lost, the Shapeshifter swallowed hard and answered with only one word. "Unbelievable."

CHAPTER 9

HUNTERS

S amara awoke at dusk to the sound of a blackbird squawk-ing, howling winds in the naked tree branches, and streaming sunbeams slowly but surely fighting their way through cracks in the clouds. Her eyes drifted open, immediately spotting a crowd of pine trees in the distance. Apparently, she had been astra projecting again and left the house some time during the night. But where was she? The air was cool and there was no snow on the ground, only soft, fresh-smelling grass. Though it was unexpected, it wasn't unsettling. In fact, it felt so soothing that she decided to close her eyes again and keep them that way for a while longer. She took another deep breath to fully return to the present. After the nightmare she had involving her friend, her heart was still pounding hard in her chest. She attempted to move her legs but came to the quick realization that they had gone numb. As she continued to lie still, the horrifying sensation of a thousand needles prickling every nerve in her legs forced her to sit up. Whether or not her head was prepared for this quick action was a whole different matter, and obviously that wasn't the case. The strong, dizzy sensation persisted, turning her stomach and world upside down. She held her head with both hands, attempting to bring balance to the whirling vortex inside her skull.

The blackbird's call grew louder, and for a moment, it almost sounded as if it were sitting mere inches away. She planted a cool palm on her forehead before slowly opening her eyes again. The sun made its way through the thick carpet of gray clouds in the sky, blinding her with its brightness.

"Miss, are you alright?" An unfamiliar voice broke the silence and pulled her out of her thoughts in an instant, startling her so much that her breath caught. Her eyes drifted upward to meet those of a tall blond man, most likely in his early twenties, analyzing her beneath stern, worried eyes. "My sincerest apologies," he said. "I didn't mean to startle you, Miss."

Samara blinked several times. Her vision grew clearer as her eyes adjusted to the sun's brightness, as well as the crisp, cool breeze blowing across her face. The stranger squatted down next to her, obviously to reassure himself that she wasn't hurt. This action provided her a better view of the man's light green eyes, nice facial features, and buff upper body. She couldn't help but notice how familiar he seemed, despite her inability to place him.

Is it possible that he's related to someone I know?

"Are you not feeling well?" he asked. His breath was surprisingly minty, and his body emitted a musky scent—strong, warm, and sweet. So unlike the demons she had encountered in Hell, radiating with sulfur and ash.

"I…I'm honestly not sure," she muttered. Despite the clarity of her vision, her mind remained foggy after her baby brother's death. The last thing she remembered was reading about funerals in a strange book she'd found on her parent's bookshelf. But she couldn't remember the name of the place she'd been reading about or where it was located. And now, she was here in this bizarre *human* place. Or was it? Were there demons here as well?

"I must've passed out...or something," Samara said. "I don't remember much of anything, let alone how I got here."

The man seemed to be visually scanning her for injuries from head to foot, at least that's what she assumed. Otherwise, it was a perverse, inappropriate act. According to her father, humans were wicked, deplorable creatures, unfit for existence on Earth, or anywhere else. However, for the most part, this one seemed harmless enough.

"I figured as much," he said. "You'd have to be out of your mind to take a nap in a graveyard."

"Graveyard?" Samara sat up quickly, despite the vertigo it caused. She gazed around her only to see hundreds of tombstones as far as the eye could see. Some were made of gray stone, others were shiny marble, and some were huge monuments that had fallen into disrepair.

Where am I? How did I get here?

At the edge of a nearby forest, a flock of blackbirds burst into the patchy sky, crossed over the cemetery, and circled it before heading south towards the darkening horizon. Judging by the overwhelming scent of flowers, freshly mowed grass, and turned soil, she was seated near someone's grave. The mere thought filled her with dread. She sprang to her feet quickly, much to her body's chagrin. Only two seconds in an upright position brought her back down to her knees. The world was spinning violently before her eyes.

"Easy there, ma'am! Easy."

The man's strong arms came to her rescue, intertwining with hers to soften the fall.

"Maybe you should sit here a bit longer," he said. "Wait, I'll get you some water."

"No, that's not necessary," she said. "I'm fine. I'm—"

As her knees grazed the grass below her once again, she managed to catch a glimpse of the tombstone protruding from the grave she had fallen asleep on. She quite literally stopped breathing the second she realized whose name was carved on the gray marble—the all too familiar name issuing an immediate flashback, including all the images, conversations, and sensations from their last encounter.

Legend Hunter.

"He's buried here. But how can that be? Isn't this a *human* cemetery?" She was stunned and confused by everything she was witnessing.

"I'm sorry…what did you say?"

The man raised a concerned brow when she said Legend's name once again. However, this time it was more quiet, too quiet for a human to hear.

"Stay here," he said. "I'll be right back." And with that, he took off without giving Samara a chance to protest. But she was stuck in the morass of thoughts, questions upon questions falling like rain. While she stared at the name carved in the tombstone, as if hoping to find answers there, a strong tempest from the north arose, causing withered leaves to wildly dance around her friend's tombstone.

"Is all of this a dream?" she asked aloud. "If so, why does it feel so real? Why am I here, Legend?"

Samara's eyes drifted away from his name and spotted what appeared to be a snow-white lily on top of the tombstone. She immediately recognized it as her own…even remembered the small flower shop down the road she had visited before coming here. But that was two weeks ago, wasn't it? And yet, the lily was still there, fresh in all its beauty, the white petals gently swaying in the wind. It was Legend's favorite flower—the beauty in nature he had eagerly shared with her. But now he was gone and never coming back.

Was it because of her? Because he had refused to walk away from a fight?

Samara touched a tear on her cheek and stared down at it. "What is this? Sadness on my fingertips? Does this come from the pain in my heart?"

She closed her eyes and took another deep breath. Dropping back down into her mind, she relived each moment from her faded dream. The black door in front of her inner eye opened, giving birth to images as colors and patterns transmogrified into contours and shapes. Mere seconds later, she was back inside the cabin in the woods. The familiar scent of old timber, pine and soil were numbing her senses once again. The sound of thunder had trailed off as the pitter-patter of rain fell. What was left was the taste of clean air and the soothing whisper of whirling winds rattling tree branches. A single sunbeam, fragile yet radiating, created a cone of light on the floor only inches away from her.

She could feel it again—that sweet, tender sensation of two arms closing around her waist from behind, pulling her back against a strong, masculine chest. She felt Legend's lips against her neck, warm and soft. Unlike any demon she had known before.

"I'm sorry about the fight and for hurting you," he half-whispered. "I was stupid for letting you go. I'll always be jealous of any guy that looks at you the way I do."

A series of knocks at the door stole their attention. Releasing his hold, he told her, "Hide in the bedroom closet, and I'll let you know when it's safe to come out."

Her memory was filled with holes—dark passages of time. And yet small pieces of the puzzle were slowly coming together, giving her a glimpse of what was to come.

Legend was face down in a pool of blood. She knelt down and gently turned him over. His brown eyes were black as coal, and his beautiful face was half-covered in blood. His throat had been cut with a knife, robbing her of her only chance to say goodbye.

Why did it happen? Was she responsible for this? Three bodies were face down and lifeless on the floor. As she rocked back and forth on the ground crying, a whiff of cold air tickled her neck. An invisible entity wrapped around her, grazing the surface of her skin, and softly whispered in her ear, "Don't blame yourself, Sam. It was all my fault. All of it..."

A chill ran down her spine, and before she was able to respond, the embrace fell away. Legend's spirit retreated into the shadows and disappeared behind the pitch-black door in her mind. Another voice broke through the veil, bringing her back to an ominous place—to her best friend's final resting place.

"Here, take this," the human said. "I'm sorry it's medium temp, but it's the only one I could find."

Samara's eyes latched onto the bottle of water then lifted to the man standing above her. He seemed to be out of breath from running his errand, for whatever reason, she hadn't a clue.

Her lips twitched for a second before curving into a smile of gratitude. "Thank you so much, but you really didn't have to do that. I don't make a habit of drinking water…not the way you might."

"Really? I don't drink as much water as I should either. By the way, I'm Damian. And what might I ask is your name?"

She looked down, feeling suddenly shy. "Names are like clothes," she murmured. "I have many options but stick to my favorites."

"And which ones are you wearing today?"

Clever question. She could sense that he liked her words, but after discovering she was a demon, he would no doubt change his mind.

"My name is Samara Daemonium," she volunteered. "But my friends and parents call me Sam."

"A lovely name for a beautiful lady," he replied with a smile. He nodded nonchalantly as he attempted to lower himself onto the grass, though not without seeking her approval first. "If you don't mind…"

While taking a small sip of water, she responded with a subtle nod of her own. "Of course not. Take a seat."

Once the stranger had settled down, he turned to face her. His mesmerizing eyes were an unusual color—a pale shade of green with the faintest touch of gray. She noticed that his perfect lips were moving, but she couldn't hear a single word he was saying.

A gentle nudge to the shoulder was all it took to regain her attention. "Are you feeling dizzy again?" he asked.

"I…uhm…I…"

"I'm sorry if I'm annoying you, Sam. It's just that you seemed to be drifting off…"

She felt a warm wave of embarrassment rush across her features. "Trust me, I'm fine. There's just a lot of craziness going on in my head right now."

A lot, indeed.

Once more her gaze was drawn to the tombstone in front of her, almost as if it was calling her name. With Damian sitting so close, something was off. She could feel it in every fiber of her being. But at the same time, she couldn't determine the reason behind the ache in her stomach.

A puff of freezing air blew against the back of her neck, causing her to shiver.

"You still seem on edge," Damian said. "If you need me to call a doctor or anything like that, please let me know. Okay?"

The way he looked at her was so caring, so heartwarming. It was hard to believe he was a human, after reading about their history. "I appreciate that," she said, "but it won't be necessary. I'm perfectly fine now."

As she spoke, a beam of sunlight illuminated her feet and the grass surrounding them, turning the coneflowers covering Legend's grave to gold.

"I'll take your word for it," Damian said. "But I insist that you allow me to escort you home. Do you live in Alturas?"

"Where?"

"Alturas. You know…California?"

"Oh, no. I don't live here. Actually, I'm just…visiting." The beam of sunlight began to expand, making its way towards them.

"That's nice," he said, inching a tad closer. "Visiting friends or exploring the countryside?"

"To be perfectly honest, neither. The only reason I came here was to say goodbye…" her voice trailed off, "…to someone special."

Samara began to worry. *Was it wise to share personal information with this stranger?* As trustworthy as Damian might be, the thought of him knowing so much about her left her feeling exposed and ill at ease. She could literally feel his eyes on her, genuine curiosity as well as bewilderment in his gaze.

"So, I'm assuming you were one of Legend's friends?"

The sun had broken through the carpet of gray clouds at last and was now warming her face. She didn't avert her eyes from the grave, although she was somewhat puzzled by the subtle shift in the tone of Damian's voice.

"I'd like to think so. He was very special to me."

"Lots of visitors have come here to pay their respects to him. Some leave flowers and even gifts…a few take photos and sit for a while. But you are definitely the first one to fall asleep on top of him." He released a low chuckle, capturing her attention. He was smiling now, drowning out her unwanted feelings of guilt and shame. "No offense taken, by the way."

"Offense? Why would you be offended, unless you—"

"I didn't know him, but I know *who* he is."

A moment of silence followed, as the sun slowly retreated behind the cloud. "He's my brother."

"What? What did you say?"

Samara had been called an Astral Wanderer. She'd been called a Soul Whisperer when it was discovered that she could walk between worlds. She had also been called a Channeler, although she had no idea what the term meant, or if it had any meaning at all. She had always thought she was dreaming—sometimes during the night, sometimes throughout the day—and occasionally, she shared her dreams with her parents. But this dream, if that's what it was, changed her life and her entire perception of humans in the blink of an eye.

"Legend is my brother…two years younger than me."

"But how can that be? He never mentioned you. And he was…a demon." A wave of what felt like a hundred different emotions hit all at once, overwhelming her and causing her to tremble. Although she knew there was something familiar about him, the fact that he alluded to being human brought enough discomfort to Samara that she got up and took a step back.

"Just as I am," he said. "But there's no need to be nervous or scared, Sam. I'm also a human being…more or less."

"You're a Cambion? But how is that possible?" The realization of whom she'd been talking to settled in Samara's brain and flooded it with dozens of questions. Some of them were impossible to express with words alone; moreover, the significance of this meeting felt divinely guided, as surreal as that might seem. "I…I apologize, Damian. I sincerely do. This is just so unexpected and…confusing. Part of me was convinced that this was just—"

"A dream?"

"Exactly. But if it's true, and your half-human and demon, how can you be related to Legend?"

Damian's verdant eyes rested on her face. "He asked that same question all the time and was convinced he'd been lied to. He called me an abomination…and maybe he was right, though our mother would beg to differ. She loved my human father until he died, despite what others thought." He lowered his gaze to the grass and released a deep sigh. Whether he was expressing self-pity or deep sorrow, she couldn't tell. Although the half-hearted smile that followed almost spoke for itself. "Please sit down again. I enjoy your company and will be happy to answer any questions you have."

A harsh gust of wind blew against her back, sending her a clear sign to accept his invitation. For a moment, there was doubt and reluctance on her part. Despite Damian's sincere and tranquil presence, something about this entire situation bothered her deeply. Yet even with the constant nagging in her brain, she felt neither alarmed nor worried. In fact, her whole being was strongly drawn towards him and opening up about her reasons for being here seemed perfectly natural.

"Look, I don't really know how to make this right," she said. "I'm terribly ashamed and embarrassed."

"About what?"

A weak nod in the direction of his half-brother's grave was all she could manage. "Because I…you know…fell asleep on

Legend's grave. I mean…that must have been a weird thing to see. I just hope that you believe me when I say how sorry I am and that I still have no explanation as to why or how it could have happened."

The river of words and excuses came to a halt when Damian raised his hand, silencing her in an instant. "Normally, I come here once a week. Occasionally two times, if my schedule allows. What I'm saying is that for some strange reason, I felt drawn to come here today. It almost felt as if my bother demanded it."

"So, you feel as though Legend wanted us to meet?"

The corners of Damian's mouth curled. "Yes, I believe so. He brought us together…there's no doubt in my mind. While he was alive, he told me about your special friendship and how you shared so many interests. When I walked up to his grave, I heard you talking to him, like he was still here."

"What?" Samara's eyes met the Cambion's stare. She found herself wondering if his mother was an incubus, succubus, or some other kind of mystical being. His instincts about her and intuitive flashes were obvious, perhaps inherited traits. But oddly, Legend had never mentioned a sibling. Yet here he sat, eager to know more about her.

"You said his name while you were sleeping…along with a few other things I couldn't make out. In fact, it sounded as if you two were having a regular conversation."

"I…I—"

"It's alright, Sam. I talk to him all the time. But he never answers me. Perhaps he's still mad at me for not protecting him from our mother."

"Your mother?"

"Verity. She's the Grand Master in Hell and thirteenth member of the Knights of Darkness. Maybe you've heard of them?

Anyway, she forbade him from seeing you…from having a demoness relationship that she hadn't approved. But after our conversation today, I'll never understand why. I mean, you seem normal enough to me."

Silence engulfed Samara and a frown settled on her face. *His mother? Would his mother kill him because of me? Because of our love for one another?*

"I don't understand why he was buried here…in this human cemetery."

"My mother insisted. She believed that burying him next to my father was the right thing to do. She's convinced Earth is the safest place for his body. You see, members of the Sovereign Sector are always on the lookout for trapped souls. They visit demon cemeteries and experiment with body swapping."

Samara cocked her head to the side. "Legend has a trapped soul?"

Damian nodded. "An Archangel's knife was acquired by an Arch-demon, elevating his status within his faction. After my brother humiliated him in front of his peers, he cut Legend's throat with that knife, tearing his soul from his body and ending the possibility of him ever coming back."

"I…I had no idea…"

It felt like an eternity before either of them would do anything—not make a move nor a sound. The exchange of bewildered looks was the only form of communication. Then, with all the courage she could gather, Samara inched closer to Damian. With a soft expression of empathy on her face, she placed her hand over his. "I'm so sorry, I truly am. I don't know what else I can say…or do."

"It wasn't your fault," he said. "You have to believe that. My brother's responsible for his own actions, not you. He was wild and played around a lot, as I'm sure you're aware. His biggest mistake was trusting a flirtatious young female demon—"

Samara held up her hand, silencing him. "I need to go," she said, coming to her feet. "If my father discovers I'm missing…"

Damian jumped upright, and his arms shot around her, squeezing her tight yet gently. She closed her eyes, relishing his smell, his rapid heartbeat, his warm breath on her skin—so much like Legend, yet wonderfully different. Then she thought about Verity and her uncompromising rules—how her father was jeopardizing his life with every visit to Hell. Lucinda might be a conniving she-devil, but Grand Master Verity was behind the scenes, pulling all the strings.

Damian's arms fell away but his eyes remained on hers. "Can I tell you something before you leave? Something personal?" He smiled shyly. "I don't want you to think I'm crazy, but I can't leave here without saying this."

"Saying what?"

"You're one of the most beautiful women I've ever met. And your brown eyes are striking, truly unforgettable. Has anyone ever told you that?" Damian's arms fell away and everything within Samara's line of vision blurred. The cemetery was turning dark, and she was struggling to stay upright. Within seconds, everything went black and when she opened her eyes again, she was in her oversized bed, safe and sound. But she must have fallen before arriving there, because her right wrist hurt, and pain was shooting through her fingertips.

The sound of a gasp caught her ear, and she realized she wasn't alone. Someone was sitting in the dark corner in her room, waiting for her.

"Sam! Where have you been?" Ariel breathlessly asked, rising from her chair. She stepped closer and leaned over. "You've been gone all night!" Unshed tears filled her green eyes. "You can't just up and disappear like that."

A look toward the open doorway confirmed her father was standing there, silently observing.

"Apparently, I went to visit my friend," Samara said. "The one I told you about."

"Who?" Ariel incredulously asked.

"Legend. Remember? He died a few weeks ago." Samara spoke to her father, walking toward her bed. "I'm sorry if I frightened you, I wasn't planning to go to the cemetery. It just happened…while I was dreaming."

Crighton towered over her. "We're glad you're safe, but you're not a child anymore, Sam. You need to find a way to control your gift. It isn't safe for you to make random trips without supervision. There are threats everywhere, especially when it comes to male demons. All of them would like you to believe they're your friends. But I assure you, they're not. They want your innocence, and once it's gone, you'll never get it back."

"I understand all that, Father. We've discussed it many times. But there's something important I need to share…something you should know. You see, while Legend was alive, he refused to talk about his family, so I never them. I didn't even know who his mother was… …not until today."

"Hmm…I see. And the point of all this is…"

"I believe she intends to kill me."

Ariel sucked in a quick breath and met her gaze steadily. "Why would she do that?"

"Because she forbade her son from seeing me. He defied her order, and now he's buried in a human cemetery."

Crighton crossed his arms and shook his head. "That's crazy. You can't blame yourself for the actions of some sick, demented demon. In due time, I'm sure she'll get what she deserves."

"I sure hope you're right."

Crighton quirked a brow. "She hasn't threatened you, has she?"

"No. At least, not that I'm aware of."

"Good. Then there's nothing further to do or say about this. Just keep your distance from her and everyone else in her family."

Samara sighed. "I know you don't want to hear this, Father, but I recommend you do the same."

Crighton lowered his arms and glared down at her. "What's that supposed to mean?"

"Legend's mother rules the underworld in Hell."

"Oh, really?" He gave a harsh, derisive laugh. "And just who might she be? Lucinda?"

Samara swallowed hard. For a few endless seconds, she debated on how to answer. Finally, she looked up, meeting her father's stare. "Verity. The Grand Master of the Knights of Darkness."

Crighton gasped. "What? That can't be true! Verity's position prohibits intimate relationships. She would never violate the steadfast rules of the governing body. Not ever!"

"Her eldest son is living proof of her defiance."

"That's impossible. I'd like to speak to him. What's his name? Where can I find him?"

Samara glanced at Ariel before answering. "Damian is a Cambion, and I know how you feel about them. But hear me out, Father. Verity is his mother, and although his father is dead, he was a human and he has no reason to lie."

"Humans lie for the sake of it. Even if they have no reason, they do it. Sometimes to make their life sound more interesting or because they lack self-esteem. You can't trust them because they're incapable of telling the truth. The same applies to half-breeds like him," Crighton growled. "The fact that you were in that creature's company angers me to no end. Where's your commonsense, Sam? I thought I taught you better than that." He turned to Ariel and continued his tirade. "She's not to leave this house under any circumstance. Is that clear?"

The angel nodded and wrapped her arms around Samara, trying to protect her from her father's rage.

"I'm going to get to the bottom of this!" Crighton shouted. "And I don't want interference from either of you. Is that clear?" He stormed out of the room and, within seconds, out of the house, slamming the door behind him.

Thankfully, Samara had no idea where Damian Hunter lived, and even if she did, telling her father was out of the question. If he approached Verity in the Knight's Hall, she would no doubt deny his accusations, avoiding ridicule and discipline from her comrades. Samara would be branded a liar, adding to her father's humiliation, and no justice would ever be served for Legend. Sadly enough, there were no laws against killing one of your own, denying their existence, or even threatening a demon's life—not in the bowels of Hell.

CHAPTER 10

RE-EDUCATION

Hecate cracked the dense tresses of the cat-o'-nine-tails across a naked demon's back with practiced precision. Every heavy-handed lash caused his screams to grow louder, but sadly, his pleas for mercy fell on deaf ears. Even if she wanted to release him, Hecate was incapable of doing so. It was now her job to punish the evil creatures entrusted to her, and from the records she'd received, this one deserved every scar on his body.

"Only ninety-nine more to go," she told him. "If you last that long."

The sound of pain and suffering had become music to Hecate, even after experiencing her own torture. It was especially pleasant when she heard it from the very souls that abandoned her on the battlefield months earlier. Her rebellion against Lucinda might have failed, but it could be said that Hecate had become one of the most feared tormentors in Hell because of it. In fact, she had been so well trained in the art of affliction that even the most stubborn souls would cry out for the Lake of Fire rather than face her abuse. In many ways, it was as if she was born for it.

Years ago, Hecate had read in a book, acquired through a black-market exchange, that human philosophers and psychologists had long argued whether the main reason people punish others for bad behavior was to enact retribution or to impart a moral lesson. The answer, in this case, was obviously both. But what about the young female demons that her trainer, Smite, had personally handled? They were less steeped in societal values, so the corrections in his private quarters, that he performed daily, were less deserving yet far more deprived as evidenced by the sound of their repetitive moans echoing down the hallway.

All torture aside, Hecate was different from your average demon. She'd been born to incubus parents and was proclaimed the Woodland Goddess in Middle Earth six months before their shocking disappearances. While growing up, she avoided inflicting pain on others. If she did hurt someone, she typically experienced guilt, remorse, and distress. But after her confinement in Hell's prison, cruelty became pleasurable, and at times even exciting. The more time she spent at her job, the more sadistic she'd become and denying her dark side was becoming increasingly difficult. But she had a soft side too—a side she avoided showing to anyone.

As a child, Hecate had secretly visited a botanical garden, where humans thrived in great numbers. It was there that she discovered her appreciation for sunflowers. Their color stood out from the other flowers on Earth, filling her with warmth and happiness. Of course, she'd never tell anyone about her secret obsession, especially the demons residing in the penal colonies. Blood was often shed when she was laughed at or humiliated because of her unconventional upbringing, so her love of nature would never be appreciated or shared. Others only needed to know her name, rank, and career in Hell. The rest of her life would remain a secret forever.

The sound of pounding footsteps turned her around. Smite was back from his walk and attempting a smile on his hideous face. "You seem to be enjoying yourself, Hecate. I knew you'd excel at this. So much talent in that body of yours…and so damn tempting too."

Rarely did she engage in idle conversation, especially with Smite. As lonely as she might be, she would never respond to his sexual innuendoes or allow him to touch her in any manner. After all, this creature had forced her into accepting her position. He tortured her into compliance. For that alone, she would never forgive him. In fact, not a day went by when she didn't imagine disemboweling him and feeding his innards to the Hellhounds caged nearby.

"Would you like me to take over, so you can visit the lower cells?" he asked sweetly. "I need to inflict some serious pain any-way…before my naughty females arrive."

Without as much as a word spoken, Hecate handled over the whip and pulled off the tight-fitting heat-resistant gloves cover-ing her hands and arms. She smoothed her palms over her black PVC corset that squeezed her body into a shape that accentuated the sensuality of her curves, pushing up and exposing most of her breasts. Her clothing had been designed specifically for her by Smite. Same as all her outfits, they also included metal rings and ties for various accoutrement, and a garter belt to hold up her black fishnet stockings. With stiletto high heels completing her outfit, Hecate resembled a dominatrix with one singular pur-pose in mind: torment the disobedient demons to the maximum degree after sentencing from Lucinda.

Hecate tucked her gloves into her cleavage and strolled through one of the many blistering, gas-filled chambers. Screams of panic and pain filled the air along with cries begging for relief. As the flames around her grew hotter, she became more and more aware that her only link to the outside tunnels was the elevator at the far end of the cavern. As she passed by open doorways, the sound of whips cracking against skin and the laughs of the maniacs using them became louder. The smell of copper, sulfur and burning flesh wafted through the air—odors and sounds she'd become accustomed to after Smite's re-education program.

Hecate entered the elevator and exited two floors below. She halted her steps in front of a large black door covered with metal studs. On both sides of it, screaming demons had been cast in molten bronze and were positioned there as a stark reminder of Lucinda's final judgment in all things. After pushing the iron door handle down, Hecate entered the dark, shadowy room lit only by flickering torches on the surrounding walls. She was met with a yelp of fear from the occupying soul, cowering pitifully in the far corner. As was her practice, Hecate visited the new inductees on a weekly basis, interrogating them for Smite and his band of tormentors. However, the fate of this deplorable man's soul had been left to her discretion. Ultimately, she would be judged by her actions today and punished or rewarded accordingly.

Where should I begin? Hecate estimated the man's age at sixty human years old. He was extremely overweight and experiencing hair loss. After being stripped of his clothes, he was shivering like crazy, but whether it was purely out of fear or the extreme drop in temperature mattered little to her. She was there to do her job and nothing more.

Having done her homework, Hecate fully appreciated his jaw-dropping reaction upon seeing her. According to his file, Vincent Prescod had been a mafia boss and was solely responsible for the deaths of more than thirty men. Ultimately, he died from a gunshot wound to the head, while attempting an escape to Argentina—the same place Hitler's SS officers had gone.

The irony of his actions wasn't missed on her, and it wouldn't be missed by Smite either.

Hecate slipped her hand behind her back and withdrew his file. After scanning it for a few seconds, she began a round of mandatory questions with a final sentence already in mind. "Vincent Aldo Prescod. Am I saying your name correctly?"

The man nodded quickly, and Hecate smiled. "We don't want to make any mistakes here, now do we?"

He just stared at her not realizing she was waiting for a response. He quickly shook his head.

"Excellent." She began walking slowly around him while reviewing his list of sins. "You lived in Palos Verdes in a lovely estate overlooking the valley." She glanced up smiling. "How nice that must have been."

"Yes…it was."

"I see here that you also owned a structural engineering company. Is that correct?"

"That's right. It was a profitable venture…left to my children."

"Well, it seems your successful business was responsible for faulty construction, which resulted in the failure of five levels of an exterior bay. Ten workers died because of your fraudulent practices and twenty more were severely injured. But that didn't slow you down, Mr. Prescod. You paid people off to look the other way, and the ones who wouldn't were murdered."

The mob boss was now standing ten feet away, sweating profusely. "It's all lies, I tell you. I didn't hurt anyone. I'm an outstanding citizen and have a plaque on my wall to prove it. Just ask around. I have a great reputation among the people I do business with."

"Hmm…that's odd," Hecate said, pursing her lips. "According to the notes I have here, you raped and strangled two women with your bare hands and ordered the murder of eight men who were threatening to sue you."

"Oh, that wasn't my doing," Prescod said. "Some of my guys acted on their own. I knew absolutely nothing about any of it. I'm really a good guy at heart, just…misunderstood. I gave thousands of dollars to charities and dozens of blankets to the homeless. I even set up a scholarship fund for abused kids. Clearly don't belong here!"

"Well, from what I see, you definitely do." Hecate smirked and closed the book. "Guilty in Hell." She tossed the file against the wall. They watched it to burn to ash. Then she reached into the top of her laced corset and pulled out her gloves. While Prescod kept his eyes planted on her, she slowly slipped them on while crossing the room. After opening a small metal door set into the wall, she withdrew two sets of glowing, red chains that had been resting in a bed of hot coals. Without hesitation, she threw the chains across the floor towards Prescod. They wrapped around his ankles and gripped his legs. He screamed in agony at the top of his lungs while the flesh below his knees melted.

"You have a lot of blood on your hands, Mr. Prescod!" Hecate shouted. "Your punishment is well deserved and final."

Within seconds, flesh and muscle had burned away, leaving only bare bones behind. Despite her gentle upbringing, Hecate laughed uproariously, unable to contain the emotion bubbling within her. It was her job after all, and one measly villain within the realm of humankind would never be missed by a generation of corrupt beings. Or would he?

CHAPTER 11

DIVERSION

After another sleepless night, Samara woke up tired and ill prepared for the day ahead. Her head pounded with a mind-splitting headache and her throat was rubbed raw, like she'd been screaming in her sleep. She cracked her eyes open painfully and realized they had somehow crusted together overnight. The world beyond her eyelids was no better. Her ceiling was swirling and curving into itself.

Even she knew this wasn't right. *What's happening here?*

Her heart started to pound several beats a second, so fast that she could feel the veins in her temple raise. The air reverberated like a rush of water in her ears. Her palms and forehead were covered with a sheen of cold sweat. There was a weird jittery sensation dancing in her brain, and she wondered if she might have caught something from the half-human she'd met.

Do Cambions spread diseases? Did Verity cast a hex on her?

Samara sat up, groggy. Her arms were threatening to give out. Her hand flew to her mouth, blocking down nausea. A voice was echoing from the kitchen below, and Samara's could see bursts of light with every clink and clank coming from downstairs.

"Samara!" Ariel called from the kitchen. Samara gasped as the syllables ricocheted and slammed themselves into her eardrums. Her pulse was going too fast, and she could barely think straight. She wiped her sweaty palms on her blankets and took a few deep breaths, allowing her heart to slow down. After a few seconds, her eyes became fuzzy, but at least they stopped inverting images. She began to feel better as the nausea passed and her ears quieted down. But her head continued to pound.

"Sam, are you up yet?"

She reached for her phone sitting on the bedside table, fingers shaking. Her hand whacked a notebook in the process. It flew into her lamp, which then fell onto the floor. Sighing, her throat rasped painfully, "Damn it!" She'd worry about the lamp later. Meanwhile, she found one lone text from her girlfriend wishing her a happy eighteenth birthday, despite it being four days away. She replied that she would call later, and they would celebrate all week, like they did on her seventeenth birthday.

"Sam!" Ariel shouted again. For some ridiculous reason, the angel downstairs, pretending to be her mother, hated it when she slept in, even on weekends.

"I'm up! I'm up!" Samara yelled back. She immediately regretted it, but surprisingly her throat felt better. She stood up, hunching her back, immediately missing the warmth of her blankets. She pulled on the first pair of jeans she could find, along with a blue crumpled -p t-shirt, and staggered out of her room like a mindless zombie. The world was a cotton ball of fuzz. Her muscles ached from cross-training before Astral Wandering in the cemetery, along with the rest of her body. One might think that being around for so long would make her act less like a 17-year-old, but somehow, she managed to behave like any rebellious teen would without even trying.

Four more days and I get another candle on my cake. Oh, goodie.

Samara stumbled a little in the hallway, feeling cookie crumbs in the carpet. Oops, she was supposed to vacuum yesterday and fix the garden fence outside. Where was her head anyway? Without warning, her foot caught on something, and she was jolted forward. Her shin banged into the door frame, her hip followed, and she planted her hands on the floor, quickly catching herself before doing a face plant.

"What's wrong with me?" she muttered, shaking her shaggy bangs out of her eyes. She twisted around to squint at the thing that had tripped her. It looked like a tree limb, thick and covered in a slimy green moss with dangling vines searching for space to spread out. Strangely, it seemed to be coming straight out of the floorboards in the hallway.

Is it normal for trees and vines to grow through the floor of a house?

Samara got up carefully, half-expecting the mutant thing to attack her. She made a mental note to ask her dad to chop it down before anyone else tripped over it. Even with semi-blurred vision, she could see the dark bruises forming on her knees.

Half-limping, she made it to the bathroom and flipped on the light switch. Using her hip, she nudged the door shut, not bothering to lock it since anyone who was supposed to be there was already downstairs. Absent-mindedly, she picked up a toothbrush that she hoped was hers and started brushing her teeth. Peculiarly, the reflection in the mirror looked unfamiliar—as if another face was staring back at her from somewhere beyond the glass. Blinking and bringing her eyes closer only confirmed her suspicion. She could see her own face in there too, and it wasn't looking very good. She was going to need a make-up fix to cover the damage her tossing and turning had caused. On closer inspection, she looked like a creepy doll in the bathroom lighting with gray half-moons under her eyes, especially with her olive skin tone. It was the strangest mix. You would never see a complexion that matched hers on Middle Earth. Not that she went around comparing her skin with other young demons. That would be weird. Like the strange birthmark on her shoulder resembling a phoenix, growing darker and more defined with age. She wondered if other young demons had unique birthmarks as well.

Oddly enough, Samara didn't consider herself eye-catching like Ariel with her ice-blue eyes and platinum blonde hair. Also, she was nothing compared to her majorly handsome dad with his intense green eyes and black shoulder-length hair. For some reason, she was right in the middle, neither blending in nor standing out. In her mind, she believed she was remarkable enough to look at once, but not exceptional enough to notice twice, although she'd been told quite the opposite by male demons. The older she got, the more she resembled Lilith's picture—the one with long auburn hair and sparkling eyes. But that would be normal, considering she'd been born inside her body. Ariel was simply a surrogate—a sad replacement for her mother.

Samara rubbed the back of her neck. Something didn't feel quite right today. It was the same feeling she got in dreams when the universe dropped out from under her feet. The room would spin around like a carousel. The tiles on the floor would shift color with the yellow and red patterns twisting together in giant orange blob. For a moment, she thought maybe she'd slammed her head against her bedpost during the night, causing strange visions to appear. Behind her was a dark, freaky shadow, reflecting in the mirror, watching every movement she made. She spun around to an empty bathroom, bewildered. She couldn't focus on anything more than two seconds. The world inside her brain was going nuts.

Again.

"You're just growing up," her father had said. "You're going through major changes, mentally and physically. In two months from now, you'll be older and wiser. You won't even recognize yourself." He had laughed, obviously thinking it was funny.

Dragging herself down the stairs and into the kitchen, she headed towards the sink to finish getting ready before being stopped by an energetic, cheerful angel. "Someone got to bed late last night," Ariel said. "We have a lot to do today, Sam. While your father's away, you need to start listening to me when I give you chores to do…and when I tell you to go to bed early." Ariel continued lecturing her on her attitude and responsibilities in their household, but Samara's scrambled brain tuned her out. Her thoughts circled back to Damian and her father's order to never see him again. He didn't know all the facts, and that wasn't fair. They'd only just met, and she wanted more than anything to see him again.

"Do you know where the soap is?" she grumbled. "I brushed my teeth upstairs but didn't find any in the dish."

"There's extra soap in the bathroom drawer. Honestly, Sam, I don't know why you can't get ready upstairs. Maybe drag a brush through that tangled mop of yours while you're at it…"

"Why bother? I'm not going anywhere. Not even outside this house." She dropped down into a kitchen chair, glowering and pouting like a child half her age.

"Your father and I just want you to be safe. There's a great deal of negativity floating around in the air, and if you're not careful, it will stick to you."

"What's that supposed to mean?"

"Sometimes you have nothing to worry about yet feel edgy or tense. Or perhaps you feel tired when you have no reason to. Other times, you might have sneezing fits. These are all signs that you've accumulated stagnant energy and need to get rid of it."

"So, sitting around here is going to make me feel better? Is that what you seriously think?"

"No, but this will." Ariel threw what looked like a newspaper into Samara's lap, but a quick look told her it wasn't press-related. It was her list of duties and chores for the day—everything from wet mopping to emptying trash. There was also a notation at the bottom of one page regarding the two heavenly beings Ariel had invited to stop by.

"Angels?" Samara looked up in stunned disbelief. "God-fearing angels?"

"I received a message this morning from a special friend. Vera is a Guardian of the White Wing Arclight, and her daughter Kaiya was an angel in training the last time I saw her. I'm looking forward to seeing how much she's grown and hearing the latest news about Heaven."

"You're kidding, right? Angels in a demon's house?" Samara couldn't help but cringe at the thought of feathery creatures walking around, possibly touching everything.

"I know it sounds absurd, but they met your father shortly after we became soulmates. I'd love for them to meet you…and your brother."

Samara sighed in mock frustration and shook her head. "I can't imagine why *anyone* would approve of them being here, especially my father. And just how is it legal anyway? If Lucinda found out—"

Ariel took a step forward, meeting her eyes. "It's not about that creature, it's about me. We live in Middle Earth, not Heaven or Hell. The rules of the universe don't apply here. At least, not for the time being. And as far as your father goes, he doesn't need to know. In fact, it would be better if he didn't."

Unreal. As a demon, it seemed natural for Samara to have a low regard for angels—to resist the idea of mingling with them. She'd spent most of her adolescent life believing demons were superior beings. Yet never once did she intentionally set out to hurt Ariel with her prejudice, simply because of her celestial roots.

At least, not until now.

"Father told me that your body was given to you by my mother…a beautiful, brilliant demon, and that your angel wings and face were miraculously restored, making you a Nephilim. If that's true, Ariel, then why would God allow his perfect creatures to come here?"

Surprisingly, the angel's temper was controlled by her calm disposition and the gentle soul within her. "I really wish you'd stop calling me by my first name, Sam. I gave birth to you after all, which I feel deserves some respect. And just so you know, my body doesn't define me. The souls inside all of us are how we're defined…along with our actions." Taking a deep ragged breath, Ariel turned away from her. "Please try to keep that in mind while our guests are here."

"I can't believe you're doing this. It's crazy…which makes me wonder if you are too." Samara smiled disdainfully, hoping her insult and contempt for angels would irritate her further.

"I know you're upset about being restricted," Ariel said, taking a broom and dustpan from the closet. "But there's a big difference between expressing your opinion and being outright rude. All I'm asking for is good manners and civility in our household. Certainly, that's not too much to ask for."

"So, you want me to pretend to be nice?" Samara replied with enough irreverent sarcasm that Ariel was taken aback.

The angel remained silent for a long moment, and then she began sweeping the wood floors with concentrated effort. "You've pretended to care your whole life, and I've accepted that. In fact, I've learned to be good at it too. I say one thing when I'm thinking another. I act like I'm listening when I'm not. I even pretend to be calm and happy when I'm scared and crying inside. It's one of the many skills you perfect as you get older, along with patience, tolerance, and acceptance."

Samara's cruel words weighed heavily on her conscience, but she refused to feel guilty. She rose from her seat and removed a bucket from under the sink. While filling it with hot water, she turned toward Ariel. "What about love?" She asked. "Is that pretend too?"

"No, sweetheart. It feels like everything you've lost has returned, making you whole again."

Samara regarded her with a puzzled expression. "Whole? Does that mean we're incomplete without someone in our lives, filling it up and taking it over? I'd hate to think *that* was the case."

Suddenly, there was a knock at the door, interrupting their conversation.

"One minute!" Ariel called out in reply. She returned the broom and dustpan to the closet and gestured at her daughter to do the same with the mop and bucket.

"I thought we had two hours. What gives?"

"I don't know. It's so early…"

Several impatient knocks rang out, as Samara ran towards her room. "I need to freshen up," she called over her shoulder. "I'll be back in a flash."

"Not literally, I hope!"

Ariel smoothed her hands over her black fitted dress and put on a sweet smile. Then she slowly opened the door. In front of her stood Tyrus, a demon werewolf and Crighton's soft-spoken half-brother. He was dressed in his usual attire: white shirt, tight black jeans, and ankle-high boots. With his curly brown hair and long sideburns, he could easily pass for a handsome human. But months earlier, on a dark, starry night, she'd witnessed him hunting for woodland creatures near their home, practically scaring the life out of her.

Upon seeing his glowing red eyes, razor-sharp teeth, and the devil wings on his fur-covered back, she screamed at the top of her lungs and ran for help inside the house. "There's a beast outside! A BEAST!!"

When Crighton discovered the cause of her alarm, he collapsed on the sofa and rolled around hysterically laughing, adding insult to her sullen humiliation.

"Hello," Tyrus mumbled. He was a foot taller than Ariel, but she refused to let that bother her. However, the impatient expression on his face urged her sensibility. "We need to get going," he said. "Is she ready?" His loaded backpack was slung over his right arm, and he readjusted it in front of her.

"That's all you have to say?" Ariel shrugged a shoulder. "No good morning…how are you?" She tried to sound as friendly as possible, despite being annoyed. "My soulmate has gone to Hell, and I don't—"

Tyrus cut her off. "Yeah, I know all about that. He asked me last week to work with Sam. You know…archery lessons? He said there shouldn't be problem if I l arrived early and asked you first."

Samara came up from behind her, grinning from ear to ear. "Uncle Tyrus! It's so good to see you! I'm ready to go whenever you are." She met Ariel's blue eyes and tested a smile. "It's okay, isn't it? I won't be wandering off, meeting strange boys or anything like that. My father told me that I need to be confident to take care of our family, if the need should ever arise."

Ariel glanced at them then reluctantly agreed. "I suppose it's all right. Just be back before dark."

"Thank you!" Samara gave Ariel a quick squeeze then hurried out the door, following behind Tyrus.

After a long walk through the outskirts of Hell, they turned down a stone path that took them between thorny hedgerows and Manchineel trees. Uncle Tyrus was quiet as usual, being more of a get-things-done kind of guy, then a storyteller. But she always tried her best to get him to tell her about her dad, when he was a young demon. Samara was enjoying the respite from being grounded at home and took in the new surroundings. On their left was a building with rows of thick posts. It also had several stories, tall but not ridiculous, like some of the towers she could see in the distance. From this side, she couldn't detect any obvious entrances or see the telltale banners of the four-demon fortresses. But it vaguely fit her recollection of the games taking place on the reclaimed monastery grounds.

Tyrus cleared his throat. "We're finally here...Beothorn. This is where young soldiers receive their basic instructions."

Samara hadn't met any of the young demons engaged in combat training and doubted they would be out and about this early in the day. While walking with Tyrus, they had encountered only a handful of guards and groundskeepers. Still, it was scary to think that she could meet some of the main participants in the Sword and Arrow Knights Game. Exciting to some degree, but unnerving at the same time.

The silence between her and Tyrus became a bit awkward, so she looked up at him and asked the first question that came to mind. "What's on our to-do list?"

"We're going to head to the training grounds and organize weapons and supplies before students begin training for the day."

"Sounds great. What kind of supplies are they?"

"Oh, you know...practice swords, arrows, training dummies. That sort of stuff. We get deliveries every other day and I usually go through them before issuing supplies to the students."

"Do they break weapons that often?" she wondered out loud.

"Sometimes. The equipment goes through a lot of wear and tear, so it's my job to keep it all in tip-top shape and have plenty of back-ups on reserve."

"Got it," she replied. "But I think you mean *our* job, right?"

Tyrus took a few long strides in front of her then turned around. "Look," he began, folding his arms. "I get that you're trying to be friendly and all, but I'm used to working alone. Crighton asked me to bring you along to get you out of the house. So, just observe while I do my job. Okay?"

Yeah, Samara wasn't going to have that. "What about this?" she suggested. "Why don't you teach me how to do things? I'll follow your lead, listen to your instructions, try my best not to screw up, and defer to you for everything. How does that sound?"

Tyrus furrowed his brows, and his amber eyes bore into her. "Fine," he replied. "You better not screw up though."

"Of course not. I'm here to learn."

After a little more walking, they reached the training arena, but all she could see of it was a stone wall. Tyrus pushed open the wood gate and ushered her inside. It was a wide, open space filled with rows of training dummies and targets. The perimeter was covered with grand arches and columns—unnecessary touches for the most part, but Samara had no interest in knowing the architectural decisions of a repurposed monastery or the history of this place.

"They usually keep the supplies out back," Tyrus said, pointing to one of the far corners. Samara followed him, and as they got closer, she spotted a handful of crates stacked in the corner. In her mind, the pickings were slim—a wood sword, two worn lances, four bows and a few bundles of arrows.

Tyrus stopped in front of them and picked up a single bow, thoroughly examining it.

"So, what's the plan?" Samara asked. "These can't be everything, right? To be perfectly honest, they're a little underwhelming."

"The new supplies get dropped off next to Knights' Hall," he said. "I'm just checking to see what needs to be replaced."

"I see." Samara began wondering if she should have stayed home. With her chores done and Ariel's guests gone, she could have gotten back into the Hobbit, a book she had recently started reading. The one about the battle of five armies. Now *there* was something to get excited about. Intense warfare between mystical woodland creatures, giants, and warlocks.

Tyrus seemed to know what she was thinking, as he pulled back on the bowstring and cast a look in her direction. "What do you think? Want to give this overused weapon a shot?"

She took a seat on one of the empty crates and quietly watched Tyrus restring the bow. Then he took aim at a target on the wall and released an arrow. The string vibrated with an audible *thrum* as the arrow soared through the air and landed outside the bullseye.

"Close. At least you hit the target," Samara said, smiling. "Wait a minute, I thought this was your thing?"

He tried again, but this time his shot landed near the outer rim of the target, leaving him grumbling.

"Hey, it's not that bad," she said. "You're just warming up, right?"

"Are you saying you can do better? Get up here and prove it."

"I don't think you want me to embarrass you in your workplace."

"Is that right? It seems you've gotten a bit cocky since our last session. If you're so sure of yourself, let's see what you can do." Tyrus handed the bow to her and plucked three arrows from the quiver.

She nicked one of them, pulled back as far as she could, and released it without taking precise aim. It sailed straight towards the center of the target and stuck fast. "Yes!" she yelled.

Perfection.

"Okay. Let's see you do that again. Two more times…dead center."

With each pull, the arrows flew with speed and precision until they were practically on top of each other. "I won't shoot another, putting another one in the bullseye will only damage your arrows." Samara's smile grew even wider. "Want to challenge me? I bet I can beat you, Uncle…"

As if on cue, the gate to the inner courtyard opened and two guys walked in. The first one had dark, short hair and wore an embossed teal shirt and metal shoulder plates. The taller of the two had blond hair and wore impressive Great Sun armor chest pieces that made a clinking sound as he approached.

Fuck.

"Hey there!" Tyrus called out to them.

With her promise to stay clear of Damian, there was no one more threatening to her security and wellbeing than this half-human creature. If word reached her father, he would be furious, believing she had deliberately defied him. She wanted to run away and hide, yet at the same time, she realized it was best to play it cool—show virtually no sign of concern. After all, Tyrus got permission to bring her to work, and there was no way of knowing Damian would be here.

Wait a minute! Tyrus knows Damian?

"Tyrus!" Damian called back with a bright, captivating smile. "It's good to see you!"

"We were just getting in some bow practice," he said. "Look…perfect bullseyes!"

The dark-haired young man pushed in front of Damian and glanced at their handiwork. "Not bad," he said, smirking.

"Three perfect strikes," Tyrus replied. "That's far better than I've witnessed from you two."

"You're right," Damian said. "But enemies don't stand still on the battlefield. Not for long, at least."

Damian's companion put his hand on his hip. "Aw, come on, Pal. Don't beat up our old friend. He's trying his best to serve our Queen…same as us."

Samara's mind was spinning. *Serve Lucinda? A half-human serving the Queen of Hell? How is that possible?*

"Thanks a lot, Warwick," Tyrus said, unstringing the training bow. "I've never thought of myself as old."

Samara couldn't tell if they had even noticed her. "Friends of yours?" she asked Tyrus.

"Sort of," he replied, shrugging with his load.

"Who's this?" Damian asked, gesturing at Samara. "I don't believe we've officially met."

She narrowed her eyes. *You're kidding, right?*

"Samara," Tyrus said, before turning to her. "This is Warwick and Damian. Warwick and Damian, this is my niece Samara."

"I train here on a weekly basis," she said, rising from the crate. "But I'm just helping Tyrus today."

Damian laughed. "That doesn't sound like the almighty Tyrus we know. The Hybrid who doesn't accept help from anyone. The same guy who glares at the poor new acolytes trying to give him a hand. Just how did this happen?"

"Sam asked if she could be my assistant a few weeks ago. She has an interest in archery and a natural talent for it...something I've never witnessed before. Those bullseyes over there just happen to be her handiwork, not mine. But of course, you would never believe me. With her being a female demon and all..."

"Sam, huh?" Warwick said, sending a dour glare in her direction. "You're in for quite a time. I don't know any demons outside of the Knights of Darkness that work as hard as Tyrus does."

"I'm becoming well aware of that," she said, casting Damian a curious look.

Her reply earned a slight smirk from him, but it quickly faded.

As she stood there watching them, she began to wonder how well these three knew each other. Since Damian was half-human and Tyrus was half-werewolf, what exactly did that make Warwick? In the light of day, they could all pass for demons, so there was no telling who or what he might be, aside from Damian's friend.

"Don't you think it's a little strange though?" Warwick asked Damian. "I mean...a female demon working directly with Tyrus. I wonder if Queen Lucinda knows about this."

Samara heaved a heavy sigh. *Lucinda again. How often are these demons going to talk about her* "Does it really matter?" Samara asked. "I'm new here, like Tyrus said. Today is my first day on the job. I haven't officially met the Queen, just heard her name thrown around a lot at my house…mostly in heated arguments."

Warwick shoved his brown hair out of his eyes. "Oh, really? Heated, huh? Well, I'm sure you'll get to meet her soon enough. She's an endlessly kind person, you know."

Tyrus twisted a smile. "Unfortunately, I wouldn't know about that. My only experience with her has been in the presence of others, but that was months ago. Since then, I've been to Hell several times, but she's always too busy for visitors. However, she seems to make an exception for Sam's father."

Everyone was nervously glancing at Samara, as though they weren't sure if making eye contact would help or hurt their respective causes.

"By the way," Warwick said, "My uncle kept it a secret for years, so not many people know that Queen Lucinda is my mother."

Mother? Like…blood related? Samara began choking and had to look away. Feeling three sets of eyes on her, she quickly turned back. "Sorry, sorry. Must've swallowed a bug or something."

"I wasn't aware of that, Warwick," Tyrus said. "I'm sure your respect and devotion to service are greatly appreciated by her."

Warwick smiled and nodded his head. "Anyway, my mother never talks about Crighton. But she seems to be impressed by his extraordinary ability to father children. Quite a few of them, I understand."

Samara blinked and bit her lip. There were only three siblings in her family that she was aware of, and one of them happened to be her. However, before meeting Ariel and becoming her soulmate, it was widely rumored that her father was a frequent visitor in the Pleasure Quarters. She wondered if perhaps there were little demons running around that he was responsible for—siblings that Warwick seemed to know about.

Damian adjusted a strap on his armor. "I understand Queen Lucinda is extremely busy and gives her staff plenty of space to work. I'm sure Samara's presence isn't a problem for Tyrus."

A faint smile was the only indication that she was amused by this. *Thank you, Sir Damian. You're a real asshole, you know that?*

Tyrus cleared his throat. "Speaking of work, we'd better get moving. Maybe we'll see you guys later."

"Oh, wait!" Warwick said. "You know our names, Sam, but Damian and I haven't officially introduced ourselves."

"This is pointless," Damian muttered. "She's already been told who we are. Weren't you listening?"

"From what I've seen, it's not your style, but would it kill you to be polite now and then?"

Damian smiled. "I agree. It's quite a bit harder to kill me than that."

"Anyway, the name's Warwick De'Mon. I'm the Commander of Queen Lucinda's Honor Guard. And Lieutenant Damian Hunter is technically my subordinate."

Damian scoffed. "You won't *always* rule over me."

"Well, I was going to say that we're more like partners." Warwick gave Damian a hard slap on the back. "We've bailed each other out of enough jams to call each other that by now, right?"

"I stopped keeping count of the times I've saved you. Almost as much as my brother," Damian replied dryly.

Samara shook her head. "Yeah, right. I think Tyrus and I need to finish up here. I'm sure my mother is missing me by now… not to mention my father. He's fond of saying that sometimes you have to accept the truth and stop wasting time, especially on the wrong people."

Tyrus smiled. "A wise man, your father. And a great brother too."

"I'm sure he is," Damian added, his eyes pleading for understanding.

As they walked away, Samara glanced back at him, wondering what she saw in this fool in the first place. He tricked her into caring…into talking openly about herself, and no one would ever do that again. *Not ever.*

After checking in the new equipment and making notes on reorders, it seemed Tyrus' duties were complete. But then the doors opened on an adjacent building and dozens of demons poured out, all wearing metal armor. They lined up and nodded at Samara before accepting the new weapons she held out. When everyone was fully armed, they joined their instructors on the practice field.

Samara spotted Damian in the distance, enthusiastically waving a sword around. She looked away and when she glanced back, he held her stare for a long moment before dropping his eyes.

"Time to go!" Tyrus announced. "If you don't want to come back here, I'll understand."

Samara pursed her lips. "Yeah, I'll let you know."

Together, they began their journey once more. When they reached the familiar stone-covered path leading to her home. Samara turned to Tyrus. "Before we go our separate ways, I need to know more about Warwick. Is he half-human like Damian? And just how did you hook up with those two anyway?"

Tyrus smiled and resumed their walk. "You have an inquisitive mind, Sam…just like your father."

She grabbed his forearm, halting their steps once more. "You can't tell him about Damian, or anything about Warwick, for that matter. If he finds out I was socializing with them, I'll never be able to leave the house again."

"Of course not. Don't worry. Your secret is safe with me. And as to your questions, both are the result of verboten intercourse. You know…demons mating with humans?" Tyrus ran his hand over the back of his neck and wiped the sweat on his shirt. "To tell you the truth, I had no idea we'd run into them today. I received an order from Lucinda to assist the Cambions the only way I know how. For the most part, she doesn't trust any of them because of their shifting loyalties."

"Really? All of them? Cambions?"

Tyrus nodded. "Despite giving birth to one of them, she'd end Warwick's life without a second thought. Especially if he refused to fight in her war against Heaven."

"Wow, just like Verity. I didn't know demons could be so twisted. Mating with humans, of all things."

Tyrus mopped his brow. "Actually, it's pleasurable…if both parties agree."

"How do you know?" Samara investigated his face. "Have you ever tried it?"

Tyrus huffed a laugh. "No, I haven't personally, but humans are not so different from us. In fact, I've been told that fallen angels have sex with them quite often. So it's not as far-fetched as some might believe."

"Huh…I had no idea. I hope you don't mind my asking. Talking to my father about this stuff would be kind of weird."

Tyrus smiled. "Well, I'm sure your friends are a better source than I am."

Samara turned toward her uncle and asked, "How do you feel about Lucinda? Wasn't she your friend?"

"Lucinda is obsessed with power. She's not the same demon your father and I knew years ago."

"Then why does he continue to see her?"

"That's a question you might consider asking him. And one more thing, Sam. I wouldn't repeat that tidbit about Verity having sons. The fact that her secret was publicly shared surprises me greatly."

They resumed their walk, both absorbed in their thoughts. Before long, they arrived at the black iron gate in front of Samara's house. "I still can't believe it's happening…the Red War, I mean," she said. "I don't know how anyone can pick sides, especially Ariel. She's more angel than demon in so many ways."

The front door flew open, and Crighton stood before them. His green eyes were clouded with concern and his deep voice boomed. "The front door was wide open when I got here. I looked everywhere for Ariel and Cass. Do you have any idea where they might be?"

Samara swallowed hard, not wanting to show weakness in front of them. "Early this morning, Ariel received a telepathic message from an angel, a close friend of hers. She was coming here with her daughter for a visit. I honestly didn't think—"

"You're right! You didn't! Angels would *never* come here!" Crighton bellowed. "With the Red War approaching, they've been called back to Heaven. Everyone knows that!"

"Well, obviously, Ariel didn't!" Samara snapped. "And neither did I!"

Tyrus stepped closer and placed a hand on his brother's shoulder. "This isn't Sam's fault. If you want to blame someone, blame me…"

Crighton drew his arm back and punched Tyrus in the jaw, knocking him to the ground. "You're right!" Crighton yelled. "If not for you, Ariel and my son wouldn't be missing. Instead, my daughter would have been home where she belongs…looking after them."

Samara jumped between them. "Why is it *my* responsibility to protect them and not yours?"

"Listen to me!" Tyrus yelled. He rolled up on one elbow, holding his jaw. "This isn't getting us anywhere. If they've been taken, there's a good chance Lucinda's involved. You just saw her, Crighton. Is it possible that she distracted you to get to them?"

Crighton shook his head, trying to make sense of it all. "What do you mean? Why would she do that?"

Samara reached out a hand to Tyrus, helping him back onto his feet. "They're valuable to her," Tyrus said. "I can almost guarantee that she brought you to Hell under false pretense, needing your advice on some trivial matter. Remember that your soulmate and son have connections in Heaven and are potential pawns in her war. In fact, it wouldn't surprise me at all if she was behind the message Ariel received."

Crighton stood before them, staring off into space, putting all the pieces together. "That fucking bitch!" He blasted. "Even if I have to die a thousand deaths, I'll do whatever it takes to get my family back."

Tyrus stepped up. "Not without me!"

"Or me!" Samara injected. "I *have* to go with you, Father. There's a reason why I'm an expert archer. I was trained to do this!"

For a long moment, Crighton looked down, saying nothing. She thought he was preparing to dismiss her, claiming she was too young, naive, and inexperienced. But then, with simple three words, he surprised her.

"I fully agree," he said. "We're *all* going to Hell."

Samara felt a rush of joy, followed by a crush of anxiety. "Really? I can go?"

"Yes, but only on two conditions. Stay close to Tyrus and avoid any unnecessary actions. We'll bypass the main gate by transporting into the main tunnel. If we're stopped and questioned, we are there to volunteer our services and need directions to the enlistment office. However, what I really need you to do is snoop around with Tyrus and report back your findings. But that doesn't mean doing anything we'll both regret. Is that clear?"

"Crystal clear. Thank you, Father."

"Right. Now let's get whatever weapons we need from the storage room and head out. The sooner we get this business over with the better."

All her life, Samara Daemonium dreamed of being a hero—that's all she ever wanted. Even if she didn't have the wisdom that came with age, even if the whole world seemed against her, this was the goal she had chosen. Yet it had remained completely out of reach.

Until now.

Samara rubbed her hands together, unable to stifle the biggest smile she'd ever had in her life. *Outstanding*, she said to herself. *Fucking outstanding.*

CHAPTER 12

TIGHT SPOT

Ariel awoke from a drug-induced sleep, blinking in the darkness surrounding her. She was confused and stiff, lying face down on something lumpy, hard, and warm. She lifted her head only to thud the back of it on something hard just inches above her. She winced then tried to get her bearings by assessing her surroundings with her other senses. The air was stuffy, humid, and warm—uncomfortably so. Ariel could feel sweat collecting on her forehead, upper lip, and lower back. She was lying face down, and under her was a silent female creature.

Oh, my God! Is she dead? Am I buried under the ground with a demon?

Ariel bit her lip to keep from screaming. Although her full weight was on this small creature, it sounded like she was breathing efficiently. *Who is she? Why is this happening to us?* Ariel raked her brain for information, then a familiar woodsy scent reached her nose. She recognized it and her anxiety lessened a notch. At least her fellow captive was a known entity.

"Onoskelis," the angel murmured. "I should have known you'd be here."

The Shapeshifter didn't move.

"Onoskelis," Ariel said louder, shaking her shoulders and silently cursing. "Do you know where we are? How we got here?"

A muffled metallic sound filled the small space. "Onoskelis! Wake up! We need to find a way out!"

The Shapeshifter was as immovable as an oversized bag of rice. She gave no response, and Ariel gave up trying to wake her and instead began gingerly exploring their surroundings. The space was long and narrow. The padded ceiling that she had bumped her head against wouldn't budge, and neither would the hard surfaces surrounding them. She discovered Onoskelis' arms were pulled above her head and handcuffed to a metal bar of some sort. She surmised that their movement must have been the metallic sound she heard. Within the confined space, there was a limited supply of air, smelling like leather. There was also a small object under Onoskelis' head, emitting the same nauseating smell.

Wait a minute! It finally came to her. "We're in a coffin!" she shouted. "A frigging coffin!"

Onoskelis shifted in place and released a low moan. "Whuuuh? Little one, is that you?" She muttered some indecipherable words in the darkness, leaving Ariel slightly puzzled.

"It's about time you woke up," she snapped. "Are you injured anywhere?" It was a question of taking stock of their situation rather than concern. "Do you have any idea how this happened? I opened the door thinking you were my angel friends."

"Where are we? What's going on?" The Shapeshifter seemed to be as mystified as Ariel.

"I don't know. I woke up a few minutes ago and can't move. What about you?"

"No, I can't move either. I can hardly breath with you on top of me."

"It seems you're handcuffed to a metal bar," Ariel confirmed. "I think we're in a casket or box of some sort. All I remember is answering knocks at my door and seeing you standing there with a young boy at your side. Then I felt a sting in my neck and pulled out a dart. It must have been dipped in a drug because I woke up here…stacked on top of you."

"What about the young boy? Did you see him?"

"Yes. He had long black hair and looked vaguely familiar. For a quick moment, I imagined he was my son. But, of course, that isn't possible. Caleb died and was buried six months ago. It must have been the drug causing me to hallucinate or something. There's no other explanation for what I witnessed."

"Do you remember anything else?"

"He reached out to me and asked why I had forsaken him. I'll never forget the hatred in his black eyes. The resentment in his voice."

"Caleb doesn't hate you. He's confused and empty…longing to get his soul back."

Ariel couldn't catch her breath. She was close to hyperventilating, overwhelmed by the image of him standing before her—by the revelation that her dead son was alive. "I can't believe it! I just can't!" She was ecstatic for only ten seconds before doubt left questioning logic. "How is that possible, Ono? How could Caleb be alive?"

The Shapeshifter didn't respond.

"What kind of deal did you make with Lucinda? Did she revive my soulless son to torment me? To punish me for taking Crighton away from her?"

The Shapeshifter drew a short breath before answering. "Three days ago, I received a telepathic message telling me that Caleb was the chosen one. 'Bring him to Ariel and she will guide him to his greater purpose,' the voice said."

"I don't understand," Ariel said, shifting her weight.

"There were dark forces at work the day Caleb was born... spectral beings invading your home. You couldn't stop them from stealing his soul even if you knew they were present. However, you can support your son now...if you're willing."

Ariel used her fist to bang against the inside of the coffin. "I don't understand! Why is this happening to my family?"

"There was a time when everyone thought your soulmate would lead us out of the darkness in Hell, but he's trapped in Lucinda's web. He's forgotten the demons her father killed and the gifted ones she's cruelly destroyed. The blood of your own kind was shed and more will soon follow. She must be stopped, Ariel. She's a heartless bitch and doesn't deserve mercy. With the power she now possesses, no one will be out of her reach. She'll demand allegiance from every living soul and destroy anyone who defies her."

"Did Lucinda create this illusion to kill us?"

Onoskelis snorted a laugh. "This is *real*, Ariel. We're trapped here together...but trust me. I think I know a way out."

"I don't understand. You knew my son was alive for six months and said nothing. Now you expect me to trust you?"

"I'm trying to be honest here, which isn't easy...being a demon and all. Lucinda kept me in a cell and bewitched me into doing her bidding. I had no control over my actions. She devoured the souls of all my friends and turned the Woodland Goddess into a vicious assassin. There's no telling what she has in store for your sons...or your soulmate, for that matter."

Ariel clenched her fists and gritted her teeth. "Like turning them into killers...capable of destroying angels."

"Listen to me! I know who was behind this. His reputation is well known. Believe it or not, Caleb warned me about Hecate's brother...the headhunter who lives in the forest. I should have paid attention when I had the chance. If I had, we wouldn't be here right now."

"Well, guess what?" Ariel said, exasperated. "We were both drugged, and as far as I can tell, we still have our heads."

"So it seems. He's obviously improvising."

"Really? And just how do you know so much about him?"

"I heard rumors from the demons in my legion."

"Are you kidding me? Rumors from soldiers?"

"Did I mention the headless skeletons we found in the forest?"

"Dear God in Heaven," Ariel murmured. "Does this head-hunter prefer angels or demons?"

"Actually, I'm not sure. Hecate's brother has been searching for her for months, but he'll never find her by killing everyone that comes near him."

"Hecate?"

"The Woodland Goddess. The one I told you about, remember? If your sons went with him willingly, there's no reason to believe he would harm them." Onoskelis blew out a quick breath to move Ariel's hair from her face. "I have a set of keys in my pants pocket. There's a handcuff key on the ring along with a little flashlight." She chuckled again. "I've been locked up more times than I can count, so I always keep a handcuff key tucked away... for special emergencies."

Ariel slid her hand into the closest pocket she could find. "This one?"

"No. *My* right."

"Okay...hold on." Ariel shifted to her left and slid her slender fingers into the Shapeshifter's pocket.

"If I was monkey, you wouldn't have any problem. But I can't change my form in this tight space."

"And I wouldn't want you to," Ariel said. Her fingers closed over the key ring, and she withdrew it from Onoskelis' pocket. Metal jingled as she felt her way through the key ring, discovering the penlight. "Here we go."

"Just get my hands loose. I'll figure it out from there."

"Got it," Ariel said triumphantly. The little flashlight came on. She smiled briefly then felt up the Shapeshifter's arms to reach her wrists. After a few unsuccessful tries, Ariel managed to free her hands.

"Okay," Onoskelis said. "Let's get out of here."

Ariel pressed her back against the top of the casket. "The lid is stuck or bolted. Something might be holding it down. We're getting air from somewhere, so I don't think we're buried."

"No, that's not his style. We're probably just somewhere remote, like his other victims. Surrounded by woodland mementos, honoring his dead friends and missing sister."

"Why did he take both of us?"

"Well..." Onoskelis began, "he has this thing about mothers and Shapeshifters that I—"

Ariel cut her off. "Never mind. Let's just get out of here."

"I'm going to try to open the lid."

"I tried that. Believe me, it doesn't work."

"Can we just remember who has animal brawn here? If we need this casket analyzed for kryptonite, you'll be in charge. I promise."

"Krypton is actually a noble gas. It doesn't fragment into unrecognizable pieces to protect itself."

"Thanks for that. I'll file it away somewhere." The flashlight caught Onoskelis rolling her eyes. "Now, here's what I think we should do. You need to go down toward my feet and I'll brace my feet against the lid. We'll push up together."

"Okay. I can do that."

They shuffled awkwardly in the small space with the tiny flashlight, providing a small amount of light. Once in position, Onoskelis' feet braced wide against one end of the lid and Ariel pressed her body against the opposite side. Wood screeched in protest and one end of the lid lurched upward several inches, letting in dim light and little bit of fresh air.

"Wow!" Ariel said. "You're stronger than you look."

"Right. Let's stay focused. The lid feels like its nailed in a few more places. If we can turn around, we can do the same to the other side and get the lid open."

Ariel nodded. "I'll flatten myself against the side and give you the space you need."

Onoskelis agreed. It took a few minutes to awkwardly shift and shimmy in the confined space. Thank goodness the Shapeshifter was small.

Once she got into position she asked, "Ready?"

"Yes. Let's do this."

With a grunt, the Shapeshifter heaved upward, and the other end of the casket lid creaked free, they were nearly out. With one more grunting push, Onoskelis broke through the final pair of nails securing the lid. The lid crashed to the floor. Both occupants disentangled themselves and sat up, stretching out cramped arms, legs, and backs. A crack of light shone under the door and illuminated the walls of a storage unit. The metal walls were covered with shovels, picks and axes of every size and shape. Onoskelis snatched the flashlight from Ariel's fingers and crawled out of the casket. Ariel followed behind her, drawing a deep breath.

"I wouldn't have had the strength to force that lid open," she whispered. "Thank you for saving us."

"Of course, Ariel." She said her name gently, almost reverently. "I would've found you. I would've saved you, despite how you feel about me."

The angel lifted her face and looked into the demon's eyes. "Maybe."

"I'll always find you. I'll always save you….and your sons," Onoskelis said fiercely. Her eyes met Ariel's with dark intensity. "Always."

Ariel didn't realize Onoskelis was a gender-shifting Shapeshifter until that very moment—that there was more to this pint-size demon than a creature longing to run wild and free. Ariel sensed the mental struggle going on inside her. In a strange way, both of them were internal Shapeshifters, trying to figure out their purposes for living and where they belonged in their separate worlds.

"That's admirable and extremely kind," Ariel said, "but you *do* realize that Crighton is my soulmate. He looks after me and—"

"Really? Then where is he now?"

Ariel looked down, feeling alone and exposed.

"Ah, let me guess. In Hell, of course…taking care of Lucinda's needs." Onoskelis met Ariel's troubled eyes and instantly changed her tune. "That was cruel. I didn't mean that. I never want to hurt you. Not ever." She stretched up on her toes and leaned forward, resting her forehead against Ariel's chest. What came next might have been a verboten kiss—could have been if Ariel's knees hadn't chosen that moment to collapse. She dragged Onoskelis down with her, leaving them both sprawled out on the uneven ground.

"Woh. That's embarrassing. Must've gotten a bigger dose of that drug than I thought." Ariel stood up quickly and brushed her dress off. Then she watched Onoskelis push herself back onto her feet. "Are you okay?"

Surprisingly, what might have seemed misguided and clumsy didn't result in any sign of embarrassment. "Yeah, I'm fine." The Shapeshifter brushed her hands off.

"So, what happens now?" Ariel asked.

"I'm going to get that storage door open, locate Cass, and make sure you get home. Then I need to return to Hell before I'm missed."

"What about Caleb?"

"He's a survivor. I'm sure he'll turn up when the time is right."

The arduous tasks the Shapeshifter set for herself seemed impossible, but Ariel trusted her confidence. "Do you think the Trapper has Cass?"

"Most likely. Your son is a great bargaining tool for freeing his sister, Hecate."

Ariel's eyes clouded. Her voice lost its brave edge. "He's growing up fast, but he's still young and innocent. I'd hate for him to witness the horrible things corrupt demons are capable of doing."

Onoskelis looked over at Ariel. "Yes, of course." Because it suited her deep purpose, she agreed, though obviously distracted. She chose that moment to close her eyes and utter incoherent words in a sing-song voice. The sound of them left Ariel imagining solemn covens chanting, straggling torchlight processions winding up mountain-tops, stone circles, sacred trees, and springs. However, the effect of Onoskelis' mantra was drastically different. Within a matter of seconds, she transformed into a huge gorilla. With a large head, broad chest and long powerful arms, an animal like this would normally present a huge threat, but Ariel sensed its peaceful nature and specific intent. She also knew this creature would fight to the point of death to protect the females and young demons in their group—a reassuring thought, even for Ariel.

After knuckle-walking toward the metal door, Onoskelis ripped it off its hinges, and hurled it through the air using pure animal power. The door bounced off a tree, coming to rest twenty yards away, stuck into the ground like a spear. Then she tipped her head back and sniffed the air above them. Demons emitted an odd odor when fear controlled their actions, like raw meat with a hint of papaya. Apparently, the Trapper was reeking of it, because Onoskelis picked up his scent within seconds. She motioned a large hairy hand, directing Ariel to follow, and walked upright into the nearby forest with a determined stride.

As Ariel hurried to keep up, she kept telling herself to trust this creature—to believe in her ability to fight back and, most of all, her selfless devotion. But the voice in Ariel's head that talked to her at night was growing louder by the second, reminding her to remain vigilant and wary. If offered a significant prize in exchange for Ariel's offspring, Onoskelis could change her allegiance as quickly as changing her skin.

TRUE EVIL

The tension in the dark cavern leading to Lucinda's throne room was so intense that it seemed almost tangible. Samara trailed behind Tyrus and Crighton, keeping her black hoodie pulled over her head, while hiding her purple tank top beneath it. Her arrow-filled quiver was tightly secured to her back and her bow was looped over one shoulder—all within easy reach should a threat to their safety arise. As they slowly advanced, she remained silent, while Tyrus bared his teeth and hissed, looking ready to kill. Crighton, was lost in his thoughts, wondering about the significance of the winged and horned demons marching through the intersecting tunnel ahead of them. As they drew closer to this intersection, he got a better look at the individual demons walking by. They all resembled each other, as if they were siblings. Each had long dark hair, strong chins, and green eyes. They were familiar because Crighton saw those same features every day in the mirror. Each of these creatures had an uncanny resemblance to himself.

He couldn't think straight. What was happening here? Where did these clones come from?

Meanwhile, Tyrus seemed relatively unaffected, as if he'd seen this phenomena dozens of times before. Looking down the tunnels lit with wall-mounted torches into the maze of bisecting corridors, He kept his focus on moving forward, not allowing for distraction. His long sword was close to his chest, anticipating a potential battle on this mission to save Ariel.

Samara's range of emotions were displayed on her face, troubling Crighton. She rarely shared any feelings with him, least of all disappointment. This situation was no different. Although he knew how to approach his strong and fierce daughter, he had no idea how to deal with this unfamiliar side. Or, for that matter, how to explain the strange development she was witnessing.

Samara went through a range of emotions. When she had her first glimpse of the marching army, she looked confused and quickly progressed to concern then finally anger.

"I don't know what's going on here," Crighton claimed.

Samara just glared.

"I can understand what you must be thinking. That these demons are my children. I'd think the same thing too. But I honestly don't know what's happening here. They can't be mine." Crighton whispered emphatically. "I would never break my vow to Ariel. I never did. You *must* believe me, Sam. I had no part in any of this." He held his breath, afraid to hear her response—to see the hatred in her eyes.

"How can you say that? Of course, you did." Samara avoided looking at him and continued to stare at the soldiers marching by, each of them an exact replica of her father. She shook her head and huffed. "Unbelievable."

Crighton looked down, feeling the weight of the world on his shoulders. "I would never betray Ariel. Not ever," he said.

Samara hissed. "Don't you see the problem here? Whether you did this consciously or not, you have no control over what happens in Hell. You're just a pawn, Father, controlled by Lucinda and her minions."

She looked angry, extremely angry. And fierce too.

Good, Crighton thought. He needed her to be angry. She needed be fully engaged. After all, they had come there to save Ariel and Cass, not to determine Lucinda's maniacal plans and her means of achieving them. That would come next. After Ariel and his son were safe.

Tyrus shook his head and kept his voice low. "I should be thrilled by the idea of bringing destruction and death to these demons...reveling in my basic instincts. But I'm not and that worries me. I don't recognize myself here."

Crighton realized he was right. After Lucinda and Tyrus disposed of Lucifer's body and she replaced him on the throne, he volunteered to establish a military post in the Outer Rim and oversee the development of a communication system before settling down with Ariel. Tyrus took over the training of young soldiers at Beothorn, climbed mountains, and offered free advice to anyone who would listen. Each of them chose their own paths in life, but none of them anticipated the effect power would have on Lucinda or the wicked creature she would ultimately become.

"You're not alone, Uncle Tyrus," Samara said. "I don't know how I'm feeling either."

Crighton tightened his lips and glanced at them. "What do your guts tell you?"

She hesitated for only a second. "To save our family and stop these demons from doing whatever Lucinda is demanding of them."

Crighton was vibrating with tension. "Okay, that's a start. Now, let's do what we came here to do. I'm going down to the prison cell level to look for Ariel. While I'm gone, I need both of you to stay together and find out what's happening here. We need to know why these clones were created."

Tyrus nodded. "We'll figure it out. Don 't worry. We'll do whatever we can to help find Ariel and Cass."

As soon as Crighton was out of sight, Samara turned to Tyrus and whispered, "Did you notice the horns sprouting from the top of my father's head? They started growing after his last trip to Hell, but now they seem to be growing faster by the minute. You have horns growing out of your scalp too. I'm just hoping I'm not next."

Tyrus touched one of the small bumps on the top of his head. "I'm afraid the longer we stay here, the more animal-like we become. Before we know it, we won't recognize ourselves or be able to leave."

"Then we need to find out what's happening and get out of here as soon as possible," Samara told him.

Soft voices floated down the tunnel. Both Samara and Tyrus quieted and flattened their bodies against the wall. They inched along, out of sight, until they could see the creatures who were whispering. Both Samara and Tyrus were shocked to see familiar faces.

"I can't believe it. Damian and Warwick," Samara whispered. "What are they doing here?"

"That's a good question," Tyrus whispered back. "Lucinda must be desperate for soldiers to trust Cambions in her army. But then again, a legion of Cambions could easily blend in with humans. Their interference in world affairs could led to a disastrous aftermath, possibility annihilating the human population."

Samara winced. "Do you really think that's possible?"

"Of course I do. But there's only one way to find out for sure. Stay here." Tyrus stepped out from the shadowy alcove and walked into Warwick's line of vision. "I sure wasn't expecting to see you two here," he said, approaching them. "Seems the Queen wasted no time in recruiting talented soldiers for her front-line division."

Warwick's brown eyes widened. "How…how did you get here? Where…where did you come from?"

Tyrus smiled. "From Middle Earth, of course. I hope you're ready to fight. Those feisty Archangels are vicious creatures, and their weapons are deadly, you know."

Damian looked around them, verifying they were alone. "We've been told not to associate with anyone from Middle Earth. There are traitors living there that could jeopardize our mission."

"Really?" Tyrus said. "Good to know. I wasn't aware of that."

"He's right," Warwick confirmed. "How do we know you're not one of them? You show up everywhere we are and are quick to ask questions. By the way, weren't you banned from Hell? From ever seeing my mother again?"

"I haven't seen your mother in months. But even so, we have been on the best of terms for years. We have a dark history together…a history that unites us in more ways than one."

"You don't say." Warwick chuckled. "Well, I have it on good authority that you and Crighton are no longer allowed in Hell."

"That's not true. We have every right to be here. Even more than you."

"Wait. Are you saying Crighton is here? We've been told to report his movements to our superiors if he shows up and—"

Samara stepped out from the shadows, flipped her hood off her head and pointed an arrow at Warwick's chest. "What are you going to do about it?" she snapped. "Go crawling back to your horny-toed mother?"

Damian smiled at her. Then he said very quietly, so that she almost didn't catch it, "Sam…it's great to see you again."

"You're unbelievable," she grumbled.

"You're definitely a breath of fresh air in this place."

"Is that right? I've never met anyone so two-faced. You were sweet and charming when we met at the cemetery. Then at the practice arena, you acted like we'd never met before. What's up with that, Lieutenant Hunter?"

"It's complicated." He glanced at Warwick. "I was being stupid, acting like a tough guy to impress my team."

"Cemetery?" Warwick asked. "*What* cemetery?"

"Well, you got the stupid part right," Samara said. "That's for sure."

Firm, stern and merciless. Her father's cautionary words came to mind. *Demons must always keep a cold heart. Do not cower or back down from anything. You are in power, in control. Never show weakness, and most important of all, ignore your emotions. They will imprison you and weaken you physically and mentally. Take advantage when you find demons willing to dedicate themselves to you. But keep in mind that male demons aren't capable of love and will only break your heart.*

Samara narrowed her brow. Numbness was better than caring. "Get the hell out of here before I shoot both of you. Now!"

Damian bowed his head. "I didn't mean to hurt you, Sam. You must believe me. I've never stopped thinking about—"

"Beat it!" She yelled, refusing to look at him. "GO!"

Warwick hightailed it out of there, while Damian veered off in the opposite direction. Seconds later, the sound of pounding footsteps grew louder, echoing from both sides of the tunnel. Eight growling guardsmen surrounded them in seconds flat, providing no avenue for escape. Then six of them jumped on Tyrus, wrestling him to the ground. Two more grabbed Samara's arms, jerking the bow and quiver from her body.

The Queen and her entourage arrived on the scene, and she was towing Warwick behind her. "Coward! Pathetic ingrate!" she yelled. "You don't deserve to be called my son." She continued to berate him, disregarding anyone watching or listening.

Nearby, a demon with four short horns held a large ax above Tyrus' head, snarling and threatening to kill him.

"You again!" Lucinda yelled. "Unbelievable! Take Tyrus below and lock him in Crighton's prison cell. I'll deal with them later."

A group of one-horned demons arrived shortly after, eager to see blood and gore. Their snake-like eyes gleamed and their long serpent tongues flickered. Lucinda was obviously in the mindset to deliver cruel punishment and, somehow, they knew it. She let go of her son's arm and shoved him roughly to the ground.

"Please...don't turn me into one of them," Warwick begged. He looked at the scrawny demons behind him and shuddered in disgust.

"To tell you the truth, I'm feeling rather generous today," Lucinda said, mocking empathy. "But calling you my son is a discredit to my good name. Ah, Warwick. You continue to disappoint me in every way possible and always will, I fear."

"Please, Mother...give me another chance. I would never deliberately defy you—" Warwick was startled by a red mist-like cloud, thick and looming, which appeared with the snap of her fingers. He franticly looked around himself trying to brush off the fog as it raised up and over his head. It surrounded him and obscured him from sight. Seconds later, the red mist dissipated leaving Warwick cowering in front of his mother. Samara and Tyrus gasped. Warwick had been shrunken to at least half his size. He looked up at everyone around him who just seconds before were shorter than him. He glanced down at his body and turned his hands over, staring in disbelief. Then he looked up at his mother with terror-stricken eyes. He was unrecognizable in his green gelatinous form.

Lucinda smiled. "You *do* understand that not following orders is a serious offense?" It was a statement not a question. "You will be punished in accordance with our laws. Until I decide otherwise, you shall remain in this primitive form. Pray in my name, dear boy, that I'll forgive you one day. Then perhaps I'll be generous and kind to you again."

Warwick, who may have lost his ability to speak, nodded his understanding instead.

"Serene, tell the guards to put this *thing* in the newcomer's pen," Lucinda said.

One of the guards leaned down and explained to Samara that the newcomer's pen was a place where new demons were housed. "They're taught discipline and to obey the rules in Hell," he said. "If they behave, they will be restored to their original selves in thirty days. But if they rebel against the Queen and her rules or try to escape, they will suffer the consequences with a lifetime of torture."

"That's right, Samara," Lucinda said. "As long as you serve a purpose and behave yourself, you will be treated fairly. You'll be rewarded with my kindness and given the chance to enjoy a rewarding life in Hell. However, if you deliberately break my laws or issue blatant disregard for my authority, your body will be torn limb from limb and thrown into a furnace. It is the same fate my father endured when I took Hell as my own."

The Queen's servant rested her hand on Samara's shoulder. "Whatever you do," she whispered, "don't upset Her Majesty."

Lucinda pointed her finger in her servant's face and snarled. "Serene! Do exactly as I instructed, or you'll be next. Remember that!"

"Yes, Mistress." Serene turned away from her. "Guards, bring that thing to the newcomer's pen and clean up the mess it made. If you leave a stain on the Queen's floor, she'll have your heads."

Two guards rushed up to Warwick, green, slimy, and slug-like, attempting to crawl away. "I hate cleaning up after Briones," one of them said. He picked Warwick up by the back of his neck and carried him off, while the other guard cleaned up an ugly trail of green slime.

Serene stood by, gnawing on her bottom lip, watching the nasty display. Then she turned back to Lucinda. "Is there anything else, Mistress?"

"No, that's all for now. You may leave," she said, pinching the bridge of her nose and closing her eyes.

"Yes, Mistress, of course. Please let me know if you need anything else." Serene bowed and disappeared quickly, leaving behind a dark, misty fog.

Lucinda directed her bodyguards to take Samara into her throne room. Then she demanded they guard the doors to prevent her from leaving.

"If you value your life, keep your eyes down," one of the guards told Samara. Then the doors slammed shut behind her, trapping her inside.

The Queen climbed onto her ominous throne. It was created from demon skin, spines, and blackened skulls. She looked down at Samara, while resting her head on her fist, contemplating what to do with her. "Demons think my position is an honor and privilege. But being Hell's ruler is truly a pain in the ass," she said. "Sure, it has it perks, like having full control of everything. All gods of the underworld bow before you, and everyone is willing to fight to prove their loyalty. But sometimes, the all-controlling part can be overwhelming. It can make even a sane demon snap. You see, I've been ruling this place since my father's death, and not a month goes by when I haven't felt the need to verbally explode over my disappointments with idiot beings, terrifying every demon within earshot. Today is one of those days that tempts me to throw a table at every soul in this place. That might surprise you, but it's acceptable in Hell. Almost everything is, but I need to maintain my inner Zen and calm demeanor to ensure a healthy mind and body. After all, I have about four centuries to rule, until I reach the ripe old age of six hundred and sixty-six. So, it's important to stay focused on my good side and kind nature, ironic as that might be."

Samara kept her eyes down, but her ears remained open.

"My subjects are bitching more these days. It's all about head-turning exorcisms, backstabbing vendettas, and tormenting demon souls. Things aren't going as smoothly as I had hoped, and it seems all the problems in Hell are left for me to solve. Every single day I hear the same complaints and demands. Sign here, Mistress. We're running low on blood stock. The underlings are escaping their pens. So on and so forth. I really need a reliable assistant, a right hand other than Serene. Someone I can trust before I make clouds rain daggers all over this place." Lucinda chuckled. "Actually, that might be entertaining to watch."

Samara stole a quick look at the Queen, decorated in her fearsome glory. The six ram horns protruding from her scalp where thick and long, divided by a green and gold crown centered on her head. Two more horns curved downward on either side of her face, replacing the hair she must have had prior to her transformation. Her shoulders were capped in pure gold with matching bands cinched around her biceps. The green serpentine dress she wore was open all the way to her navel, barely covering her nipples. It hugged her body tight, resembling snakeskin. But it was also open at the back, freeing her short demon wings and long lizard like tail.

It was easy to understand why her father could be captivated by this nefarious creature. With her sultry voice, glowing eyes framed in black eyeliner, and her perfect rose-colored lips, it was obviously impossible to ignore her.

Lucinda continued to ramble despite Samara's lack of interest. It was impossible to stop thinking about her family. If the Queen could change her son into a green slimy thing for being a coward, what kind of "punishment" did she have in store for them?

"I have plenty of volunteers for that spot I mentioned," Lucinda said. "They claim to be loyal, to clean up after themselves and help everyone thrive. But it's Hell, is all I'm saying. If you live here as long as I have, you see through their motives. They all want power, and the stuff they say is pure shit. Believe me, no one can be trusted in this place. Not even your father, Samara. I honestly thought his last visit would dissuade him from ever coming back. But, oh no. He just can't stay away. And now he's lowered himself by bringing you and Tyrus here under a false pretense, claiming I stole his soulmate and her do-nothing child. What kind of nonsense is that anyway?" Her voice grew louder, and her eyes were now red. "I'm not the monster you all make me out to be. But with this vile accusation throbbing in my brain, I have no choice but to be one."

There was a shout behind Samara as the door to the throne room flew open. A small, shapely demon marched up to Lucinda with sandy blonde hair draping over her sun-kissed shoulders. She was biting down on her full bottom lip, and her eyes were the color of sky. Correction…eyes the color of the sky on Earth. As far as Samara could tell, the sky was always dark here in Hell, which left her wondering how anyone could tell the difference between day and night.

"Well…aren't you going to say something?" The female demon tilted her body sideways, showing more of her chest. "Not even hello?" She was eyeing Lucinda expectantly, as if waiting for her to make a move. All the while, she kept licking her bottom lip and touching Lucinda's arm.

Who is she? Samara was anxious to know.

There was something vaguely familiar about her. Perhaps she'd seen her while internet shopping, in a Middle Earth boutique or on a late-night television show. No matter how hard Samara tried, she just couldn't place her. Meanwhile, Lucinda remained emotionless. She rolled her eyes, then she glanced back at Samara, obviously aware of her interest.

The nympho sighed in frustration, realizing that she had failed to grab Lucinda's attention. She bent even lower, keeping her butt high in the air. "You couldn't have forgotten me already. Not after our last two-hour session. Say I need you, Clio. I want you *so* bad…"

"You're crazy. I don't know what you're talking about," Lucinda growled, clearly annoyed.

"Of course, you do," Clio said. She lifted the Queen's chin up, so that their faces were inches apart. "It's been *way* too long. A little one-on-one would do us both good. Don't you agree?"

"Hell, no!" Lucinda jerked her head away from the succubus and attempted to look beyond her—to focus solely on Samara.

Clio positioned her face closer to Lucinda, her left cheek pressed against her shoulder. "Come on now. You know you want it. You deserve it…for all your hard work."

"Fuck off, Clio."

"Aw, you're no fun at all."

The succubus stepped back, and a dark mist surrounded her. When it cleared up, her true form was revealed. Her blonde hair turned black, and her blue eyes turned red. The white bandage dress she was wearing transformed into a black bikini-like outfit with a matching dark cloak that hung from a chain around her neck. She held out a hand and a staff appeared in it, silver, and glinting. Large demonic horns protruded out of her head and what were delicate fingers quickly morphed into claws.

"Can't you see I'm busy?" Lucinda snapped. "What in the name of my father are you doing here anyway?"

"I figured I'd stop by and maybe, you know…we could have a little fun." She trailed her claws down Lucinda's exposed cleavage, all the way down to her waist. Then she tugged on her dress, indicating she wanted what was hidden beneath.

The Queen pushed her hand away in disgust, and a look of surprise instantly appeared on Clio's face. She was the premier temptress, after all. No one, not even Lucifer, had ever rejected her, according to underworld rumor. In fact, a story regarding her qualifications had appeared in the Hellhound News. To the Devil's delight, she'd been featured in a full-page spread, quite literally. "It's stigmatizing, degrading, extremely hard, and the best thing I've ever done with my life," she was quoted as saying.

Although Ariel had been forbidden to bring the tabloid paper home, some of friends had been circulating it on the school grounds in Middle Earth, causing quite a stir.

"Piss off, Clio," Lucinda said. "How many times do I have to tell you? I don't want or need your special attention. NOT NOW!" Lucinda snarled at her, exposing her fangs.

The succubus brought her hand down to her waist, appearing to be thoroughly offended yet intrigued at the same time. "Playing hard to get, are we? You know how much I enjoy a challenge…and a captive audience too." She smiled over her shoulder then moved her face closer to Lucinda. While Samara stared in disbelief, she started nibbling the Queen's bottom lip. There was simply no controlling this creature.

After pushing her away forcefully, Lucinda's lower lip was bit in the process, drawing blood. At this point, she was shaking in anger and done with degrading theatrics. With a flick of one hand, the chandelier hanging from the center of the room came crashing down, scattering lit candles in all directions. "Get out before you start regretting your fucking decision to come here!" she screamed.

"Sounds good, babe," Clio said, licking the blood on her fingertips. "You'll come crawling to me like you always do. And then you'll see how badly you're treated. By the way," she said, smiling, "would you prefer the long pink feather or horsehair whip tonight? You know, on second thought, let's just make it ice cream for two." Clio licked her lips provocatively and smiled.

Lucinda closed her eyes and pinched the bridge of her nose. "SERENE!"

Her loyal servant appeared in an instant. "Yes, Mistress?"

"Get this skank out of here. I cannot be disturbed while I'm working. Is that clear?"

"Yes, Mistress, of course. Right away." Serene turned to Clio and grabbed her by the arm. "Dead or alive, you're coming with me."

Clio jerked her arm away and growled at Lucinda. "No need for bullying, thank you very much. I know my way out." She turned on her heel and started making her way toward the door. But then she stopped midway and glanced back over her shoulder. "See you tonight, Babe."

Lucinda groaned and banged her head with her fist.

"Are you alright, Mistress?" Serene asked, concern lining her face.

"Everything's just peachy," the Queen mumbled.

"If it will ease your stress, the lost souls are being punished in the Chasm."

A grin crept across Lucinda's face. "They are, are they?"

"Yes, Mistress. Hecate asked if you would like to stop by."

"Good, good. I could use a nice distraction."

"Also, the two invaders will be brought to her for discipline, just as you requested."

Lucinda cleared her throat and stood up. "Alrighty then. Enough work for today." She stepped down gingerly from her throne in her five-inch stiletto heels, arriving next to Samara. Then she clapped her hands, bringing her bodyguards inside. "Serene, do you mind taking care of this matter while I'm gone? Eliza is waiting in the Pleasure Quarters with Bram. I want them to implement hard-core training immediately. No kid gloves here."

Serene kept her eyes down. "Yes, Mistress."

Lucinda leaned in close to Samara. "If a female demon threatens one of my soldiers or disrupts his training in any manner, they pay the price a thousand times over. Who knows, my dear, you might even enjoy all the attention you'll be receiving... from every horny demon in Hell." A devilish grin split her face, teeth gleaming in the flickering torchlight.

The guards immediately grabbed Samara's arms, giving her no time to react. "NO! NO! NO!" She screamed. "LET ME GO!"

"Consider yourself lucky," Lucinda said. "My assassin has been known to whip a demon to death for less."

"I HATE YOU! DO YOU HEAR ME? I HATE YOU!!!"

Lucinda pursed her lips. "What's the worst possible thing you can call me? Now, don't hold back, Sam. You're probably thinking of words like slut, whore, bitch, cunt, skank. Notice anything? The worst thing you can call a girl is a girl. Being a female is the ultimate insult. Now tell me that's not royally fucked up." Her sinister laugh echoed in the room and continued to ring in Samara's ears.

"You're going to regret this! I PROMISE YOU!" Samara shrieked, kicking and wriggling—trying everything to break free from the hands restraining her.

"My only regret is not doing this sooner. Get her out of here…NOW!!"

Samara was thrown face down on the floor. Her hands and feet were tied together, and a gag was stuffed in her mouth while a needle went into her arm, dulling her senses. Then one of the guards slung her limp body over his shoulder. Serene opened the door and together they began walking through a dark tunnel toward the evilest place in Hell. But little did they know that someone was trailing close behind, hiding in the shadows—waiting for the opportunity to strike.

CHAPTER 14

DISCIPLINE

"**M**ove, you worthless souls!" Hecate shouted, cracking her whip in the air. "Out of the tunnel and into the Chasm!" The demonic beings began moving faster, albeit still rather slow due to their leg manacles. "You don't want to be turned into slimmy Briones, do you?" She hissed, impatient as always. "I want a fully functioning vortex between Hell and Earth in the next three days. Let's not keep our soldiers waiting."

"You might want to listen to her," Lucinda shouted from the top of the cliff line.

"Queen Lucinda! How nice of you to join us. You gave me a hard-working crew this time. They moved twenty yards of rock in two days. I can't wait for you to see the spot I picked out for your rip in the atmosphere." Hecate bowed deeply before turning back to the pit. "Behold, our leader! Show your respect, all of you!"

At once, the lost souls stopped dead in their tracks and lowered their heads, lifting the corners of Lucinda's lips. "I see that you're having fun here. Mind if I join in?"

"No, of course not, Mistress. Have at it..."

Finally, some entertainment. Lucinda teleported to the floor of the pit, where dozens of lost souls were waiting. "Hello, everyone. How are you finding your new home?"

One of the spirit entities made his way toward her, just a shapeless form floating aimlessly in the air. "Please, Queen Lucinda…please, let me go back. I need to resume my form."

"You'd like to return to the mines? To be a hardworking demon again?" She cocked an eyebrow. "To bring me sky blue sapphires to add to my collection?"

He vigorously nodded. Hope seemed to be glinting in the abyss of his eye.

"Ah, let me see what I can do." She opened her palms and the entity started squirming in pain, howling like a banshee, as she drew energy from its soul.

"You don't seem to like the home I've provided you with," she said. "So, tell me…does this ease your suffering?"

He stuttered a couple of times then began screaming again.

"What's that?" She asked. "I didn't catch what you said. Was that a thank you?" She feigned concern and sympathy. "You know, not everyone gets a home like this. But then I could always lock you in the darkest place in Hell…or leave you freezing for all eternity."

"Pa…please. Ma-ma-make it…stop…" He sputtered with a barely audible voice.

"Again? I couldn't quite make that out."

"I DO NOT WISH TO GO BACK! JUST PLEASE MAKE IT STOP!" the soul shrieked.

Lucinda fisted her hands, and he dropped to the ground.

"Thank…you," he said, breathing hard.

Hecate threatened him with her eyes. "That will teach you not to defy us. All of you, in fact." Her laugh echoed through the whole place, leaving Lucinda quietly grinning.

"Uh…Mistress? So sorry to interrupt," a deep voice said. Lucinda turned around to see Ramón back in his demon form.

"WHAT?!?" she bellowed. "Who turned you back? I gave no such order!"

Ramón kept his eyes down. "Hecate did, Mistress. She...she needed me to unlock the Pit of Souls."

Lucinda heaved a heavy sigh. "So, what's your problem, Ramón?"

"S-someone is requesting your presence, Mistress."

"My presence? Who has the nerve to ask for me here? I'm busy punishing lost souls. Have they no eyes?" Lucinda growled.

"Uh, I'm not sure, Mistress..." He trailed off, fear obviously clouding his vision. "We picked up a child's voice in the air, and he's...well...not exactly from here."

She narrowed her eyes and snarled. "What are you talking about? A child's voice? Ah, forget it. Let me see for myself." She created a translucent orb on the surface of her palm using magic from the hundreds of beings she'd ingested. As she stared into it, her insides began churning. Thoughts of the mysterious boy came to mind—the child she'd been dreaming about for days. Sure enough, the orb zoomed in on him. He was sitting in a dark, vine-covered place, reading something out loud from an ancient, leather-bound book. The book that had been stolen from her library!

"Unbelievable. So, you want to meet me, do you?" Lucinda muttered to herself. "Your wish is my command." A huge grin crept across her face. "Tell Hecate to proceed with punishing the unworthy souls," she told Ramón. "I'm going to Middle Earth to meet a child that's craving my attention. A little, dark-haired boy to replace the slimy buffoon I foolishly brought into this world."

"Yes, Mistress." He bowed and hobbled away, disappearing into the room where Hecate had gone only moments earlier.

Lucinda wiped her hands together quickly and brushed off her black dress in preparation for her departure. Then the sound of a whip cracking and a screaming soul hit the air, halting her actions. It seemed that her old friend was exceeding her expectations as Chief Tormentor. In fact, she was torturing souls in record numbers, exceeding her mentor's count, and ending his usefulness. Lucinda would have to reassign Smite or dispose of him as soon as possible. She really had no choice. After all, he'd been fucking and brutalizing more than his allotted share of young demons and whores, and she hated to be taken advantage of, especially by an ugly, sharp-tongued demon.

Then a delightful thought occurred to her. After Samara's novelty wore off in the Pleasure Quarters, as it most surely would, Crighton's daughter could take out her anger and hostility on the wicked souls backlisted for punishment, making her a great apprentice for Hecate. But what about Crighton and his beast of a brother, Tyrus?

Ah, what to do? What to do?

Surprisingly, the solution became clear. The more time they spent in Hell, the more they would change—growing horns, long tails, and more submissive to their Queen—eager to accommodate and please her in every way possible. It had been years since she had a strong, virile, horny demon between her legs. The idea of them screwing her for endless hours dampened her black v-string panty and left her sighing.

Ah, yes. It won't be long now. I'm going to have two sexy creatures in bed with me at the same time. Is that fucking hot, or what?

The guard at her door adjusted his stance, snagging Lucinda's attention. Could he see into her thoughts? Was he reading them now? Naw, it wasn't possible. She would never allow that. But all the same, she needed to down-shift her thoughts.

"Enough of that," she murmured. "On to the matter at hand. It's time to say hello to my new little helper…Caleb Daemonium."

She'd never been a fan of Crighton's family after Ariel stole him away. But what could she do with them being soulmates and all? By killing the angel, she would've ended her dream lover's life as well. But now, with Onoskelis' help and the witches' black arts handbook in her possession, everything was going to change for the better. Ariel's death at the hands of her own child would break the soulmate bond the Sovereign Sector had created, freeing Crighton from his obligations and domestic drudgery.

Lucinda chuckled softly and smiled. *Oh, yes, yes, yes.* With the war against Heaven and upcoming attractions, there would be much to celebrate soon. She raised her right arm, concentrated on the dark cavern in her head, and vanished into thin air.

CHAPTER 15

CALEB'S REVENGE

A blinding light appeared, but it was gone quickly, leaving the eight-year-old boy undeniably disappointed. He threw the heavy book into the corner of his cave, knocking over a pile of well-read books. Then he let out a frustrated sigh and began complaining to his circle of candles, flickering in the dark. "Stupid shit. I should have known it was fake. Nothing is worth anything in this place."

"So, you want to be Satan's Little Helper?" Lucinda asked. Her voice came from behind him and had apparently caught him unaware, as his shoulders instantly stiffened. "Unfortunately, My Father is indisposed at the moment," she said. "But I heard your call and am more than happy to assist you."

"Maybe I do and maybe I don't," he calmly replied. "Who are you anyway?" He turned his face towards the sound of her voice, only to see just blood-red mist in the air.

"You're a brave one, aren't you?" she replied.

He turned around and witnessed her materializing before him in an unoffendable form—minus horns and provocative attire. His coal black eyes never left her face, watching her rosy lips move. "My father was known by many names," she added. "The Devil, Fallen Angel, Ruler of Hell, the King of Demons and of course, Lucifer. I am his ruling daughter...his replacement per se. My name is Queen Lucinda, but I'm often referred to as Satan, despite being female."

Her petitioner was a splendid-looking young boy, naked except for a black cloak covering his left shoulder. He had a fine head of hair, long, black, and wavy, and a trim body with two black wings protruding from his shoulders. The only flaw Lucinda could detect were his soulless eyes, making her wonder if they were sensitive to light.

He continued to stare with his jaw agape. "You're so...young."
And beautiful, a voice in the back of his brain added.

"As are you, squire," Lucinda said. "And telepathic too. I never expected that."

"And you're what? Six hundred and sixty-six?" He deadpanned his question, cocking an eyebrow. "Is it strange that I'm comfortable enough with who I am that I can insult you, knowing that you can destroy me in a heartbeat? Is it also weird that I don't give a shit?"

"As much as I despise how rude you are by making fun of Hell's ruler, I must admit that I admire your cavalier attitude. So unexpected." She smiled wickedly for a few seconds, and it fell away just as quickly. "And no, I'm not that old. I'm only 134 by human years. I have a long life ahead of me."

"Still old," he muttered.

"I would suggest caution, young man."

"Yeah, right."

Lucinda opened a small black book and ran her finger over her list. "Just double checking my facts. You're Caleb Daemonium, a still born, buried shortly after your birth. Thanks to my helper, you were miraculously brought back to life. You're also incredibly smart and intuitive for your age. With no one here to answer your questions, it seems you decided to summon a demon who will. Not My Father mind you, but his daughter instead. So, here I am, Caleb. You should feel honored by my presence."

"I'm the one offering my services as Satan's Little Helper. You're the one who should feel honored."

"Feisty and bold." She nodded her approval and snapped her fingers, vanishing her book. "I've got a feeling that you'll do great things as my right hand...more than I ever deemed possible."

"So, that's it? I'm your right hand already? That quick? But you know nothing about me or my talents. I can make vines come to life, wrap them around demons and strangle them. Doesn't that scare you?"

"Very little does, I'm afraid." Lucinda laughed at her unintended quip. "So, what do you think? It would be fun, would it not? Since I'm here and you have no one to miss you or ask for your whereabouts, I might as well give you a shot. As far as I can tell, I've got nothing to lose. Do you?"

Caleb seemed surprised and mystified by her answer.

"What did you expect?" she asked. "A blood oath and back breaking tests in Hell?"

The boy reluctantly nodded.

"You read too many fantasy books, Caleb. And speaking of your name..." She pointed at him accusingly. "We really should work on that, if you're going to be my Little Helper."

He frowned. "What's wrong with my name? I was buried with it."

"Yes, I know. It's a fine name and all," she said, half-shrugging. "But unfortunately, it means devotion to God. Now, do you understand how ironic that is...I mean, a follower of God in your line of work? That's actually laughable—"

Caleb cut her off with a wide grin. "How about Yama?"

"The God of Death? That's very ambitious, don't you think? Yama is the King of all ancestors, King of Ghosts, and the King of Justice. He was the very first human to die and found his way to the Underworld where he became Ruler of the Dead. Now that I think about it, I actually find this name fitting." She smiled mischievously. "But unfortunately, I need you to prove yourself worthy of it...*and* your new position."

The young boy groaned. "But you said—"

"I know what I said. But things change. I want you to complete one small task. Kill your mother as a sacrifice to me. Nothing will make me happier than that. I assure you.

"You want me to kill my mother?"

Lucinda smiled. "That's what I said, didn't I? Besides, she's never cared for you anyway. You were written off years ago... right after your birth. It should be the easiest job in the world," she said, dismissively. Then she took a step back. "Don't tell me you've already changed your mind?"

"No, I..." He clenched his fists and look down for a moment. "Fine. I'll do it."

"Splendid! Since this will be your first official kill, I'll be extra generous. I will give you two days to complete your task. An earlier completion would be much appreciated, otherwise, meet your deadline. By the way, I will be watching. So, don't try anything funny or you'll pay a costly price for breaking your bargain with the devil."

"Yeah, sure...thanks." He rolled his eyes again. "So, what now? Do you just disappear into thin air and like...go back?"

Amusement flickered in her eyes. "Actually, yes. But before I leave..." She took a step forward so that they were only inches apart. Then she leaned down and whispered in his ear, "I bet you'll love the taste of lost souls as much as I do. You might even keep one for yourself, filling that void in your life." With that, she gripped his head with both hands and brought their foreheads together. While he continued to watch her, Lucinda closed her eyes and began chanting ancient words, stirring the air and dust around them. She pushed him away a minute later and gave him a beguiling smile. "There we go. Now you're a *real* demon."

"What did you do to me?" he asked, surprisingly calm.

"Nothing much really. Just a taste of my powers to inspire you."

He raised a brow. "Powers?"

"That's right. Special abilities if you prefer."

"What will I able to with them? Grow fangs and have horns sticking out of my head?" He stifled a laugh. "Will I have a tail and turn beet red too?"

She punched him in the arm, and he feigned a look of pain. "You're such a smart ass, Caleb. I like that about you. But there's one thing you did get right…growing fangs. Try to be patient, young man. Until you reach puberty in four days or so, you won't be receiving the benefits of adulthood." Lucinda shook her head. "Geez, I really need to burn your book collection. You have the strangest ideas."

"No! You wouldn't dare!" He sneered at her, and fangs immediately replaced his canines. He ran an index finger over them, testing their sharpness. "What's going on? What did you do to me?"

"My, my, my. How about that? Aren't *you* a quick learner?" She smirked, mockingly applauding his quick development. "Well, it's time for me to go now. Hell awaits…along with my rulings."

"Hold up. How do I retract these things?"

She sighed, her impatience not withholding. "You'll be needing some training, I suppose. I'll send two of my agents to teach you our ways. Just know that your fangs will only appear when you're irritated or hungry, and for blood, of course. To retract them, you need to calm down or feed yourself something raw and juicy. Simple as that. Oh, and one more thing. In Middle Earth, you'll be known as Caleb, like you already are, but when you set foot in Hell, you will be Yama, my loyal, devoted right hand." She moved closer to him and kissed his forehead. "But with me, and strictly me only, you will be My Little Man. And when the time is right and your training is complete, you'll be much more than that." A wry smile twisted her lips. "Now, don't forget. I'll be listening. And just so you know, patience has never been my forte. So, don't waste time."

With one swoosh, she was gone, leaving Caleb's life in complete chaos. In less than two days, he would be a murderer with his mother's blood on his hands, and the only one celebrating his monstrous deed would be Lucinda, the Queen Bitch of Hell. However, if he played her game right and kept his secrets and talents hidden, he had every reason to believe that the tide would turn in his favor. In just a matter of months, he would unseat her in Hell and become the true Satan—beet red, horn covered, and hungry for blood.

CHAPTER 16

DOWN TO BUSINESS

A male demon appeared in Caleb's cave, dusting himself off from head to foot. He had black shoulder-length hair, a grizzly beard, deep scars on both cheeks and two stubby horns on his forehead, reminding Caleb of the Little Goat picture book he had received a month earlier. He was the equivalent of only three years old at that time and still struggling to read the books he'd been given. But with each passing day, he could feel himself growing older and taller—far wiser than his years.

Caleb took a few steps closer to his teacher, but before there was time to make introductions, a female demon arrived. She was small, not much taller than him, and her long brown hair reached clear to her waist. To his amazement, she was wearing a black tight-fitting jumpsuit, showing off her interesting curves. Her gold tiger eyes met his and he smiled shyly. He had never been this close to a female demon.

"I'm Junius and this is Loki," his teacher said. "She's here to assist me and should not pose a distraction in your training. Is that clear?'

Caleb paused before nodding. The petite brunette was cute by human standards, but he had no interest in females after hearing how manipulative they could be.

"Good. Now, let's get started, shall we?" Junius continued. "We have a lot to cover in a short time."

During the next four hours, Junius attempted to educate Caleb about Hell: the daily rituals, demon responsibilities, human soul-eating practices, and the history of rulers before Lucinda. The works, you might say. He began teaching him the demonic alphabet as well, but strangely enough, the ancient symbols were already imbedded in Caleb's mind. So, that made his ability to remember spells and commands much easier. For the most part, his training was boring, but it became far more interesting when the spell book came out—the same book he used to reach Lucinda.

"Don't be afraid to ask questions," Loki said. "We're both here to help you."

"Afraid?" Caleb snapped. "Why would I be afraid?"

Loki flashed a weak smile. "Of course you're not. No one is saying that."

Caleb snorted his disapproval. *Why is this demon here?*

For good reason, Junius telepathically answered. *You'll see soon enough.*

Right. He would have to censor his thoughts from now on. There was no telling who might be listening.

His next lesson involved gaslighting, perhaps one of the cruelest, most insidious forms of trickery and torture. "A skilled demon can flip a human's reality and sense of understanding, leaving them questioning their own sanity."

"Cool," Caleb said. "Tell me more."

"Gaslighting can take many forms. Yet it all comes down to the conscious and psychological manipulation of another being for the purpose of power and control. This involves making someone doubt their judgment and perception of reality by giving them false memories and information. They become confused, anxious, and distrustful. All in all, any mechanism that is used to overpower, manipulate, and control another soul is insidious, but this is common practice in Hell and on Earth, mainly by corrupt human beings."

"You don't say..." Caleb was enjoying this part of his lesson. Manipulation was his greatest talent. But the only person he was able to test it on was Onoskelis, and she knew how to turn his gift against him.

The next session involved physical training, and it seemed Junius lived up to his name as Lucinda's brightest star. Nothing got past him. Although Caleb tried hard to wrestle him to the ground, he couldn't overpower him or even lay a single finger on him.

"Just keep practicing what I taught you," Junius said. "You'll get better, I promise."

"But I don't have time to learn. I don't even know where to find my target, let alone how to kill her."

"Wait! I have an idea!" Junius said. "Let's have you practice on Loki. Just pretend that she's Ariel and you've come up behind her."

"I can't do that! She looks nothing like my mother. How am I supposed to practice on *her*?"

"I can remedy that," Junius said. "With a little black magic, I can change Loki into your greatest enemy."

Before Caleb had time to respond, Junius began chanting indecipherable words. A dark cloud of smoke covered the female demon and when it parted, a mirror image of Ariel was standing before him.

"That's not her...is it?" Caleb asked.

"Of course, not," Junius answered. "Now, let's try this again. Come up behind her...like you would in the forest. Wrap your hands around her throat and squeeze tight. And don't worry, Caleb. Loki's had lots of experience with this in the Pleasure Quarters. If I remember right, she actually enjoys it during her sexual encounters." Junius gave her a wry smile then he nodded at Caleb.

The young demon did as he was told. He saw the tiny twitches of neck muscles in his hands, tightening and adjusting to make sure she couldn't wriggle free. He watched the pulsing vein in her neck slow and then disappear. Her face turned red then pale white. Her golden eyes stared up at the ceiling, first with blatant disregard then with true fear. He hated that look. Hated the idea that she feared him, even if she had every reason to.

"Stop! You need to let go!" Junius shouted. "You proved your point. You can do this."

Loki was panicking, struggling to pull his hands from her throat. "That's...enough," she managed to choke out. "I'm not... your mother."

He released his hold and looked down at his hands, stunned by what he had done.

Loki transformed back into herself. "Look at me, Caleb." She turned to face him, but he avoided her eyes for as long as he could. He looked at her cheeks, her forehead, her nose, and her chin.

Ah, shit! There was a ring of bruises around her throat. He wanted to throw up and would have if he'd eaten anything in the last two days. But her expression only softened more, until she looked downright sad.

"Look me in the eyes," she said. "There's nothing to fear but fear itself, I assure you."

Caleb sighed. He didn't have a choice. Besides, after the pain he'd put her through, she deserved a little cooperation, right? So, he met her halfway and melted a little inside. There was so much trust and understanding in those spectacular tiger eyes— eyes that he would never forget. She looked at him like he meant the world to her, like he could do no wrong.

Doesn't she remember what I did to her? How I almost killed her?

"Caleb, you did nothing wrong," she said. "You didn't hurt me, Lucinda did. You didn't almost kill me, Lucinda did. You didn't do anything…it was Lucinda, okay? It was all Lucinda. You couldn't have stopped her, regardless of what you did…or what you're about to do."

Junius growled. "What did you say? You know it's forbidden to speak ill of her. To say anything hateful about our Queen."

"But it doesn't make sense. I don't understand any of this," she said. "Why would anyone want to kill their own mother? Especially an angel?"

"It's not important for you to know." Junius picked up a wicked-looking knife from the crudely made table and balanced it in his hand. Then he tensed up and glared at Loki, the restraint on his powers rippling. "Or for you to live!" With a quick snap of his wrist, he slashed her throat from ear to ear, dropping her on all fours. When she finally collapsed, her body was surrounded by a pool of blood, spreading rapidly across the ground.

Caleb stared in disbelief, not trusting his eyes.

"Relax," Junius said. "It's no big deal. Just one less demon is all. There are plenty more like her in Hell. Believe me."

Junius snapped his fingers. A gray shimmering light appeared, blanketing the dead demon and blood on the ground. It vanished as quickly as it came, taking all evidence of Loki and her death with it.

The teacher showed no emotion. He pursed his lips and remained silent for a few seconds before turning back to Caleb. "I just received word that your mother is in the Bangor Forest with Onoskelis. As I'm sure you're aware, the last Shapeshifter in Hell is also in the Queen's army and capable of changing into any animal she chooses. She became a gorilla to protect your mother from the Trapper—the demon that stole your twin brother. This delusional fool is planning to use Cassius to free his sister from Hell, but things aren't as simple as they seem. You see, the gorilla is leading Ariel on a wild chase and very soon straight into your hands."

The furrow between Caleb's eyes deepened as his brows drew down further. "What about my brother? The twin I didn't know I had?"

"He'll be captured along with the Trapper and disposed of by the Queen's assassin. You must remember, Caleb, she's all-controlling and nothing, I mean *nothing* gets past her."

"Yes, I understand." Though he really didn't. His head was beginning to itch, and he had no idea why. Was this the sign of another gift Lucinda had forgotten to tell him about?

"By the way," Junius added, "there's a bag on the floor for you. Inside, you'll find a black shirt, jeans, leather jacket, sunglasses, and boots. The Queen has impeccable taste and is brilliant at determining the sizes of her disciples, as well as her helpers."

"Disciples?"

"That's what you'll be one day…if you follow her rules and continue to please her."

"No kidding?" Caleb emptied the bag on top of his make-shift bed. While Junius stood back watching, he pulled on his new clothes and approached the reflective glass in his cave. *Not bad looking for a murderer,* he said to himself.

"Okay. I need to transport you to Ariel's location. The rest will be up to you."

"Sheeze…you don't mess around, do you?"

Whether he heard him or not, Caleb couldn't be certain. His teacher remained silent as he gathered his gear, preparing to leave. He pulled on his armor in the visible darkness—the darkness Caleb had become accustomed to since birth. After setting a disgusting helm on his head, Junius tugged the leather straps attached to it, locking it firmly in place. Then he fixed his attention on Caleb.

"Put on your sunglasses and stand perfectly still. Don't move from the circle I drew on the ground. Is that clear?"

Caleb centered himself before nodding. "Okay. I'm ready."

"Oh, and one more thing. Take this with you." Junius handed him the knife he had used on Loki. "That weapon belongs to Lucinda. She's lending it to you for this mission. You should know it's efficient for destroying most demons and will kill their human hosts at the same time unless their bodies are already dead. However, if you stab one of them in a less vital area, they'll experience intense agony but will still survive and come after you. So, whatever you do, don't miss."

Caleb's brows came down into a barely perceptible frown. "Ariel is an angel, isn't she? How will this knife work on her?"

"Her host body belonged to Lilith, a warrior demon. When her body dies, so will Ariel."

"I see. And what about my father?"

"Time is fleeting, Caleb. You need to perform your duty." Junius held his left hand above the boy's head and began chanting Latin words. "Hoc daemonium! Hoc daemonium! Hoc daemonium!" The cave floor rumbled, and a crack spread open behind them. Stones began tumbling from the walls, threatening to bury them alive.

"What's going on?" Caleb yelled. "Are you trying to kill us?"

"Sorry. Wrong incantation." Junius flashed a quick smile then he began again. "Incipio! Angelus enim inveniet! Incipio! Angelus enim inveniet!"

A soft hum came out of nowhere, growing steadily louder, until it reached an ear-piercing decibel. It was joined by a powerful whirlwind, leaving Caleb's throat dry and his mouth gasping for air. He couldn't shout at Junius or scream out of fear. He had to distract himself, concentrate on something more painful, more threatening than death.

Empathy. An innate weakness in humans and angels, impossible to be experienced by demons, he recalled from his dictionary. He would never know this sentiment. As a soulless demon, he was incapable of feeling any emotions, unless he allowed himself to, and Loki's death was bothering him more than he let on.

"Incipio!" Junius shouted again. "Angelus enim inveniet!"

While choking on dust and evading small pebbles, Caleb miraculously slipped into another dimension, arriving in a dense, misty forest. There were no creatures stirring in this place, not even a band of ravens he could frighten away. But he wasn't completely alone, at least, not in his brain.

"You've got to be kidding," Caleb grumbled. Shouts, curses, and screams from Lucinda were making his head throb, even though they weren't directed at him.

No mercy, Junius! I'm going to belt whip you to a pulp! YOU HEAR ME? To a bloody pulp!

Obviously, Lucinda was furious over Junius' teleporting ineptness, making him the laughingstock of the underworld. Just the thought of her assaulting him would have left Caleb laughing, if not for the dust in his throat.

Okay, Caleb, she said, no doubt realizing he was listening. *You're on your own. SO, GET BUSY!*

A quick look around confirmed he was standing at the edge of the woods, a short distance from where Ariel would soon appear. It was all a matter of timing and limited skills on his part. "I can do this…I can do this," he said, adjusting the knife in his belt. "I have to…for my own sake."

CHAPTER 17

HEARTLESS

A small log cabin sat at the edge of a clearing in the Bangor Forest and was bellowing smoke from its chimney. It had a sloping, moss-covered roof and looked as if it were trying to crawl into the thick woods nearby. As Caleb stepped closer to investigate, he noticed the front window had been braced open, allowing fresh air to circulate. He ducked under it, hoping to capture a sound from inside and was rewarded by his effort. A man's voice carried in the air—breathy, raspy, and strained. "When I tell you to listen, I mean it," he snapped. "If you disappear like that again, I'll tear your wings off and make sure you never make it out of here alive. You got me?"

It was the Trapper, the demon hunter Caleb was told about. And, unless his intuition was wrong, the kid on the couch was his brother Cassius. He was perfect in every way, according to Onoskelis, even with his freaky white hair and piercing blue eyes. "He's strong, forthright, and ambitious," she said. However, as Caleb raised his head a few inches higher to peer through the windowpane, he witnessed a very different side to his sibling. The fear on Cassius' pale, tear-stained face was undeniable, giving Caleb immense satisfaction.

"What a loser," he whispered. "And you call yourself my brother? What a joke." Caleb's eyes continued to roam freely, surveying the cabin's interior. The Trapper was standing before the fire with his back to Cassius, warming himself. A large knife was tucked into the leather sheath strapped to his thigh. On the wall above the fireplace rested a rifle and a shotgun. In addition to this arsenal, two handguns were sitting on a round table where he'd been cleaning them, and a box of demon bullets was resting beside them.

Caleb sighed heavily, realizing this was an ambitious mission considering the number of weapons involved. Unexpected trepidation crept into his mind over the possible outcome. But there was no denying it. If he didn't complete the task Lucinda had sent him on, he would lose his chance of receiving a soul in Hell and any positions he'd been promised. His throat would be slashed like Loki's, or he might be tossed into the Lake of Fire, putting an end to his life and all his hope filled plans.

What am I supposed to do? There are too many weapons. Do you hear me? Too many! And my mother is nowhere around. Isn't that why I'm here? To kill her?

He was still second-guessing himself when the sound of approaching footsteps came from the woods, forcing him to hide on the left side of the cabin.

"He's in there," Ariel said, pointing. "I'm sure of it. I can feel him." She was standing next to Onoskelis in her gorilla form. But that didn't pose a threat for Caleb since she'd been this caregiver from birth. What he wasn't prepared for was their undeniable affection for one another. The way the Shapeshifter held up a protective arm and looked down at Ariel, obviously concerned for her safety, and how his mother smiled up at her. The line had been crossed between demon and angel, leaving no room for third-party loyalty.

Does Lucinda know about this? Caleb wondered, gritting his teeth.

Onoskelis walked on all fours with the fingers on her hands folded inward. As she neared the cabin, her intent became instantly clear. She had come to rescue Cassius from the Trapper—to return his self-centered brother to Ariel. In Caleb's mind the act was an insult to the Queen, the ultimate sin. The Shapeshifter had broken all trust and deserved to die far more than his mother did.

Caleb growled and charged at the gorilla with the knife firmly held in his hand.

Ariel jumped in front of the Shapeshifter and opened her wings, using her body and invisible shield to protect them.

Caleb halted and stared in disbelief behind his dark sunglasses.

Disappointment filled the air, bringing tears to Ariel's eyes. "Dear God," she called out, "why is this happening?"

"Is your revenge aimed solely at me?" Onoskelis asked, stepping out from behind the angel.

"You know it isn't," Caleb snapped. "At least, not until now. Why are you helping her, Ono? You knew I was coming here today. I'm sure of it!"

"Well, I suspected as much. But you must understand, Caleb, I have no choice here. We haven't talked since you ran off, and a great deal has happened that you know nothing about."

"Oh, really? And why should I listen? Oh, that's right. It's because you're all-knowing." Caleb gave an angry snort. "A great deal has changed with me too, Ono. I have powers now and someone in my corner. Someone who isn't afraid to stand up to you."

"Unfortunately, I'm well aware of that," the Shapeshifter said. "You may be Lucinda's weapon of choice, but that doesn't make it right." Her eyes never left the knife, even as she spoke.

"Why should I care?" Caleb asked. "No one's ever thought about me. Not even my mother."

Ariel took a step forward. "That's not true," she said. "I think about you constantly. I just didn't know..."

Caleb snarled. "So you say."

Onoskelis transformed back into herself, clothes, and all. "Ariel's telling you the truth," she told the young demon. "She didn't know you even existed. No one in your family did. How could they? I kept you a secret. I protected you for as long as I could from the dark side...from Lucinda getting her hands on you."

"But you didn't. Not really."

It seemed Onoskelis still trusted him, but he didn't trust himself. It wasn't easy to extinguish the spark in his chest that made him want to eliminate Ariel, the same way Junius had erased Loki. He looked down at the vines edging closer, eager to squeeze the life out of anyone threatening his safety. Only he had the power to stop them, and at that moment, he had no desire to do so.

"Listen to me," Ariel said, stepping toward him. "I'm here with you Caleb. I'm not going anywhere. Understand?" One of the vines wrapped around her ankle and she ignored it. She reached out, taking his hand in hers. He tried his hardest not to flinch, but he still tensed, afraid of the physical contact. She pressed his open palm against her chest, just under the neckline of her shirt. Her skin was so warm, so soft. Beneath his hand, her heartbeat maintained a steady rhythm that said she was alive and there for him. He relaxed a bit, if only enough to ease the tension in his shoulders. But she didn't let him pull away, and clearly, she had no intention of allowing him to escape.

"I never stopped thinking about you. I'm with you now, my son. Are you with me?"

He hesitated. Even though she'd taken his hand and held it in place, he still wavered. It seemed every time he remained still for too long, he was taken back to the grave and became terrified again. It was as if one of these days he would wake up and try to move only to have his body stay exactly where it was, under a heavy mountain of dirt. Then Ariel squeezed his hand where she held it to her chest, snapping him out of his dark thoughts and reminding him that she was waiting for his response.

"Yeah, I'm here." It wasn't much of an answer, but he spoke without effort. He was relieved, but not very. His other hand clutched the knife at his side, while he debated on what to do with it. Then he noticed the vines wrapping around his mother's legs, crawling higher and squeezing tighter with each passing second.

"Dimittis!" He yelled. "Release!" The vines loosened their hold. They fell to the ground and slowly retreated into the forest.

Meanwhile, Onoskelis tried to reach him the only way she knew how. "Caleb, trust me. You can let go of the knife now. Lucinda is back in Hell with her minions. She won't harm you… not with us here."

"That's right," Ariel said. "There's no reason to kill anyone to please her. Not any longer."

Caleb gave her a wry smile. "Your death isn't for Lucinda."

His inference silenced his mother, but she remained physically unfazed by his words. She lifted her other hand to cup his cheek and made him face her again. However, he refused to meet her eyes. He was terrified to see the same fear he had caused Loki. He never wanted to see that look in anyone's eyes again.

Ariel continued to touch him, running her thumb along his cheek bone until he let out a sigh. "Will my death satisfy you?" she asked. "Is that what you long for?"

"Yes…no. I don't know any more." He sensed her tension when she tightened her grip on his hand. He heard her let out a ragged breath and sniff a few times, trying to compose herself.

"Why do you hate me so much?" She finally asked.

It was an honest question, but it was clear from her tone she didn't want to hear the answer. He stayed quiet, but his thoughts said it all. *I hate you more than you'll ever know.*

"Why, Caleb?"

He still couldn't bring himself to look at her. "Because you left me in the ground to rot."

Ariel sighed. "Ah, Caleb, you have to understand. We all thought you were gone. That we'd never see you again. But I never stopped caring. I never stopped thinking about you."

"It doesn't matter now. If Lucinda comes back into my head, she'll know I failed. She'll know I didn't do what she asked of me. I'll have no choice but to act."

"Then act now."

"What?"

"Act now, if you must." Ariel wasn't asking questions anymore. She was daring him to take her life. *Shit!* The angel that mourned his loss was welcoming her death beneath his cold, insensitive hands.

"I think you know what's supposed to happen here," he murmured.

She nodded. The answer was evident in her eyes, in the way she clutched his hand in hers, like a life preserver, trusting him to do the right thing. If Lucinda showed up, or if he felt his anger return, he'd only have seconds to act. And not much could be done in seconds with his mother sharing her heart and guilt circulating in the air.

There were no warnings from Lucinda, no calls for help from him, but there was enough time to assume control over his own body before Lucinda claimed it in Hell. Right then and there, he made up his mind on how to proceed. He wasn't going to do the devil's bidding any longer, even if it meant burying the knife between his own ribs. He had mentally practiced the motion anyway. He could do it in under two seconds, which he hoped was fast enough to keep his mother and Onoskelis from stopping him.

Ariel's breath caught, after witnessing his dark thoughts. She lowered her hand from his face down to his chest, placing it over his heart like a shield. "Caleb don't do anything foolish," she said. "Give me the knife before someone gets hurt."

"No." He didn't move, didn't shake her off or walk away from her touch, but he didn't let go of the knife either.

"Sweetheart…please listen to me." Her voice was thick with emotion, but it wasn't enough to move him, not enough to stop him. The knife was his way out of this mess. It was his security, his backup plan. A way to stop his future from coming true—a future he never allowed himself to think about until Lucinda showed up. But even if he burned in Hell for all eternity, he wasn't going to hurt her. Not this angel. Not his mother.

"Caleb, I…I need you." Her voice cracked and tears filled her eyes. She wrapped her arms around him, drawing him close. It was an instinct to snuggle against her, but he didn't loosen his grip on the knife at his side. Even though she shook with sobs, he refused to let go of it.

"Listen to me, Caleb. You have no idea how much I need you. How much I want you in my life." Ariel closed her hand over his, where it touched the handle of the blade. Yet still he remained silent. She tried to pry his fingers from it, but he wouldn't let her. He simply couldn't. It was now a battle of wills, and he wasn't about to let her win.

"Caleb, please!" she begged. "I love you!"

Her words made him falter enough for her to get beneath one of his fingers and pry it off the knife handle. Just one, but he wanted to cry regardless. She didn't seem to understand his dilemma. Why was she taking his only ticket to Hell away from him? It was all so confusing.

"Honey, let go. I'm not going to ask again." At the same time, she didn't let go of him. She didn't even move or hesitate, which he loved and hated at the same time. For some unknown reason, she trusted that he wouldn't hurt her. But she wasn't going to let him keep the knife.

"I love you," she whispered again, still tear-filled and choked up. "I love you…and can't imagine this world without you. Not when I just found you again. Not when I have the chance to be the mother you truly deserve."

She earned another finger for that, which he cursed himself for. She was not going to be the one who talked him into giving up his only way out. But she was tempting him to hurt her again— for weaving her way into his conscience and making him care. Her persistence was exhausting and pointless in his mind. Everything would be so much easier if she wasn't here.

"Just let me have it, Caleb."

His name again.

"I'll always love you and need you, no matter what." Another finger fell away. "You mean the world to me, sweetheart. If you went away now that I've found you, I don't know what I would do." Another finger relaxed. "Please, I beg of you. Do this for me." Finally, she pried his thumb off the handle of the knife. She took it from his open hand and slid it into her waistband. Then she grabbed hold of his hand, refusing to let go. Once again, he felt like he couldn't breathe. He wanted to throw up. If Lucinda were to hear about any of this, there was no telling what she would do. She might even force him to kill his whole family as retribution for his disobedience, and that would be unbearable. Yet despite his apprehension and growing doubts, Caleb couldn't get the thought of making Ariel suffer out of his head. He knew how much Onoskelis cared about her and that alone was unforgivable.

"Honey, please say something," Ariel pleaded.

What could he say? He couldn't yell at her for being afraid of him, for encouraging his obedience, or for exposing his vulnerability. Knowing how much he hated her, it was puzzling to hear how much she still loved him. How could anyone in their right mind love a soulless demon, especially an angel?

And yet, somehow, she did.

"If you need to hold onto something," she said, "hold onto me."

And that's exactly what he did. He grabbed her wrist so hard she would surely bruise. But she didn't wince or cry out. He could feel her pulse—the same pulse he felt inside her before he was born. The same pulse that kept his brother alive, while their mother contemplated suicide. He saved her life then and Cassius' as well with his telepathic messages, and now it was up him to save his brother again. He had nothing to lose anyway, except a life that never really existed.

"I'm so glad you're here," she said.

He kissed her temple because he couldn't help himself.

"I love you, Caleb."

He froze when he heard her words. For the first time that day, for the first time in his life, he gaped at her because he understood the weight of their meaning. It wasn't just I love you, it was I missed you. It was I'll do anything to protect you. It was I trust you with everything I am. The sincerity in her eyes was more than he could hope for—more than he ever dreamed possible. Despite his evil, vindictive intent, she said them anyway, and he relished every single word.

"I love you too, Mom. I always will."

Then Caleb released his hold. He grabbed the knife from her hand and flashed a smile before charging into the cabin to save his brother. Gunfire followed seconds later. With terror in her eyes, Ariel ran after him with Onoskelis trailing close behind. The front door stood wide open, and she stumbled inside. She stared down at her son, gasping in disbelief.

Cassius stood frozen in the center of the room with a pistol in his hands. The Trapper was on the ground only a few feet away with a bullet in his shoulder and a gun resting in his hand. And Caleb, sweet Caleb, was sprawled out on the floor with a demon bullet in his brain and smile on his face.

After taking the gun from Cassius, Ariel set it down on the table. Then she wrapped her arms around him. She held him tight, hardly breathing, never wanting to let go. Seconds later, she lifted his chin and looked down at his tear-filled eyes. "I know you shot The Trapper, but you did nothing wrong, sweetheart. You were simply protecting yourself...and your brother. I'm just glad you're alright. I would be lost for all eternity without you."

Onoskelis stepped closer and rested her hand on Cassius' shoulder. "Your mother was so worried about you," she said sweetly. "Both of us are relieved to know you're unharmed."

As if reading Ariel's mind, the Shapeshifter took Cassius by the hand, bringing him to a safe corner in the room. Then she nodded reassuringly at Ariel. "Take your time. We're fine here."

"Thank you." Ariel moved to Caleb's side next to the fireplace and dropped down on her knees. His sunglasses were on the ground, and his black eyes were wide open, staring at nothing. Tears rolled down her cheeks and her heart ached. The exchange between them was so short, so disturbing, so tragic, and yet tender and unforgettable. She couldn't imagine how to tell Crighton about any of this. Where would she begin? Who could she blame, if not herself?

Ariel took the knife out of Caleb's hand and set it aside. She crossed his arms over his chest, wiped tears from her face, and bowed her head to say a prayer. With all eyes still on her, she stood up and returned the knife to her waistband. She waved her hand over him and spoke in a near whisper. "Protect this innocent child. Take my son into your care, sanctum est." A white shimmering light magically appeared, blanketing him in a warm glow from head to foot. Then the luminous spirit lifted Caleb's body from the ground and vanished with him as quickly as it came, taking him to a kinder, more welcoming place.

"Aaaah…" the Trapper moaned. The gun he fired at Caleb was now in Onoskelis' possession, leveled confidently at his head. She picked up one of the devil-trap bullets from the table and ran her index finger over the pentagram carved into the tip. According to Crighton, these bullets were the best-known defense against demons. They could debilitate them—keep them from moving or using their powers. But they weren't deadly to any underworld creatures unless fired into their brains.

Ariel looked back at Cassius, now sensing his solace. The last thing she needed was for him to be traumatized by his quick-thinking actions and his twin brother's second death. But what about The Trapper? He was the director behind this frightening drama, setting everything in motion. There was only one question left to ask, and he was the only one with the answer.

Ariel stepped closer and stared down at him, bemoaning his fate. The jagged scar across his throat was hard to ignore but no doubt rightly deserved. "Why?" she asked. "Just tell me why."

His voice was barely a whisper. She had to lean closer to hear him. "Lucinda," he said. "She took my sister. She made her an assassin. I only wanted her freedom. That's why I took your son. It was all about Hecate's freedom."

"But why take my son? He's innocent and naive. He knows nothing about Hell. Nothing about the corruption and evil there. Why would Lucinda return your sister in exchange for *him*?"

"Because of his value."

"Value? I don't understand. What value?"

"Lucinda never wanted Caleb. She called him a stand-in. A deplorable freak of nature. But he was willing to do anything to please her…even kill you. And that was too tempting for her to refuse. The only pawn she's ever been interested in is Cassius. He's the key to the Red War, to destroying Heaven. If Lucinda threatens to kill your son, Crighton's father will lay down his arms. Castiel will sacrifice himself to save his only grandson, and the Queen of Hell knows that all too well."

Ariel shook her head. "How do you know all this? How do you know it's even true?"

"Because Lucinda's servant is my daughter. Serene was born with her dead mother's talents. Telepathy, telekinesis, teleportation, and other psionic abilities that set her apart from other demons. But she keeps them all secret. She fears the Queen's judgment and is always being watched. If she's no longer useful, her soul will be absorbed like all the other gifted beings."

"So, it's true. My son really is in danger."

"Yes, Ariel, he is."

She looked around in a panic, realizing Onoskelis and Cassius were gone. *Where in the world did they go?*

"You need to hurry," the Trapper said. "The Shapeshifter belongs to Lucinda. Her loyalty has never wavered."

"Oh, dear God! She has him!" Ariel charged through the open doorway just in time to see Onoskelis step into a circle at the edge of the forest. Cassius was holding her hand, looking up at her expectantly. Then his eyes shifted to Ariel who was running toward him as fast as she could.

"Mom!" he called out. "Hurry up! We're leaving!" He didn't understand that Ariel was not invited to go with them.

"Onoskelis!" Ariel screamed. "STOP! PLEASE STOP! I BEG OF YOU!"

The Shapeshifter mouthed the words, *I'm sorry*. Then they both vanished in a whirlwind. Ariel reached the empty circle and stood motionless, unable to process what she had just witnessed. How could she be so wrong about someone—the only being from Hell she thought she could trust? Why in the name of God did this happen? Why was He forcing her to endure so much pain?

Then Ariel realized she alone was responsible. She alone was to blame. Now, it was up to her to rescue her child from Lucinda. Turning on her heel, she walked back to the cabin. She looked down at the Trapper and realized she had no choice but to strike a bargain with him. "I'll remove the bullet from your chest and help you retrieve your sister in Hell, if you help me rescue my son." She pulled the knife from her waistband. "But as God is my witness, if you refuse to cooperate or find a way to trick me, I won't hesitate to kill you. Is that clear?"

CHAPTER 18

EARTH ANGELS

"**S**am? Can you hear me?" She didn't respond, but when Damian grabbed her shoulders and shook her, she turned her eyes instinctively toward him. Her gaze slowly focused after holding a vacant, detached stare. "Can you hear me?" he asked again. "Are you okay?" He glanced frantically over his shoulder and demanded an answer from the petite female demon standing behind him. "What happened to her? Is she hurt? I gave you specific instructions and told you to take care of her, Eliza."

The dark-haired beauty looked down at her fingers, pursing her lips and grumbling over a chip in her red polish. "She's probably in shock. I tried to wash her up before you got here. Far as I can tell, there's nothing physically wrong with her, but she hasn't said a word yet. At least, nothing I could make out."

With a little snort, Damian lifted one of Samara's lax arms and gestured at the gore splattered across her. "Does this look like she's okay?" He began checking her for any signs of injury, which was difficult, considering the amount of blood splattered on her. "Well, are you going to tell me, El? Where'd all this come from? And what did she look like before if you cleaned her up?" He lowered his voice to a half-whisper, "I'm going to kick that guard's ass. He said she'd be fine."

Eliza let out a nervous little laugh. "Oh, she's fine alright. Like I said, nothing happened to her physically. That's Cerberus. You know, the guard."

Damian's brow furrowed. "What's Cerberus?"

Eliza crouched down next to Damian. With her fingertips she warily analyzed the goo-splattered clothes covering Samara's unconscious form. "I might be wrong, but I think this is." She held Samara's arm and grimaced at the chunks of flesh and drying blood, covering her from shoulder to fingertip, not wanting to know what part of Cerberus they came from.

"What?" Damian repeated, staring at Samara and then down at his badly stained carpet. A look of dawning horror and understanding filled his face, as his sister dropped the lifeless arm she was holding.

Samara started to stir.

"Yeah, he's dead," she added, wiping her fingers on her jeans. "Or totally gone, you might say. When we transported Sam to Earth, an Archangel followed us and smote the crap out of him."

Damian shook his head, obviously in denial. "You're sure? I mean, maybe he just vanished or something

"Are you kidding? Look around, Bro. He was exploded with a wave of power and light. Like a water balloon filled with chunky soup." She leaned over the couch where Samara was regaining consciousness. "Oh good. She's waking up," Eliza said with feigned excitement.

Samara fought to keep from gagging when she saw what was covering her entire body.

"I thought we were goners for sure, but he just disappeared in a flash of light." She turned to Samara. "I'm El, by the way."

Sam nodded with wide eyes.

Eliza continued, "Didn't have a chance for intros while bashing Serene with a chamber pot and escaping with Cerberus. I turned in my resignation telepathically from the fuck me royal quarters and didn't wait for a reply. No doubt the Queen Bee is pissed off at me anyway…after grabbing her wholesome recruit." Eliza's smile was sardonic, yet her brown eyes had a glint of humor. "Don't get me wrong, sweet pea," she added. "You're pretty and all that. At least you were before Cerberus exploded. I just thought you should know that I don't make a habit of helping my baby brother, unless absolutely necessary."

"Then I guess I should thank you," Samara said.

Eliza waved her words away with a broad smile. "Ah, don't stress it. Lucinda gave me the lowdown on your family, and I'm really impressed. A demon angel for a mother? Now *that's* mega cool."

"Yeah, I suppose it is."

"And Crighton's your dad? I saw him bare chested once and nearly fell over. Talk about a powerhouse. Wow! That man is legendary."

Samara cringed.

"With looks like that, he could have any female he wants, which explains a lot about Lucinda's jealousy."

"What do you mean?" Samara asked.

"While Lucifer's body was burning and Ariel was dying in prison, she issued a proclamation giving Crighton equal power in Hell. But then your mother survived, and you were born. After helping Lilith rescue Ariel, he owned Lucinda a great deal. However, his devotion to Ariel never wavered. So, for years, he's endured the Queen's flirtations, though I know for a fact he's never acted on them. Now she's got your dad where she wants him and his clones are marching around Hell, which makes me wonder if she's planning to fuck all of them."

"It wouldn't surprise me," Samara said. "Although Clio might have something to say about that."

Eliza laughed. "She's a piece of work, isn't she? Lucinda's bitches are all idiots, and her guards are even dumber. For the promise of a blowjob, they'll do practically anything. Even escort my drugged-out pal to Earth."

Samara decided that she liked Eliza. She had a zany, imprudent way about her. It was interesting that Damian mourned his brother on a regular basis but hadn't mentioned his sister at all. Not even her gold twisted horns or sexy red outfit. The lace-topped, thigh-high nylons she wore were especially nice, and Samara found herself wondering what they would look like paired with her short plaid skirt.

Damian cleared his throat. "Would you like to get cleaned up, Sam?"

"Oh, yes. Definitely." She shuddered. "By the way, where exactly are we? I thought I heard something about Earth…"

"That's right. Woodsboro. I share this house with my sister, but I never know who's going to be here. I also have an apartment in Hollymead."

"Oh, I see." She tried to smile but felt a headache building behind her eyes. "Do you have a bathroom? I could really use a shower."

"Just up the stairs on the right."

Samara breathed a little easier after locking the door. Being alone and not in the company of Cambions helped. Having them stare at her like she was going to break any second was making her feel fragile, and she was anything but that. She figured a few minutes alone was all she needed to get herself together and acquire some sense of calm after being subjected to Lucinda's insanity.

As she stepped away from the door, Samara caught sight of her reflection in the mirror. *No wonder they're worried. What a mess!* She was only days away from reaching her eighteenth birthday and the vision staring back at her was shockingly real. Her long auburn hair was hanging in twisted sections, streaked with blood, and matted to her head. She could see where El had wiped her face with a wet towel, but bloody residue was still on her cheeks and neck. Her clothes were covered in foreign matter, which she assumed was brains and other disturbing body parts. It was disgusting, leaving her stomach churning. She lurched sideways from the mirror over the sink and heaved into the toilet.

After emptying her stomach, she felt a burning sensation in her throat. Her nerves were frayed, and her hands were shaking. She couldn't get over the fact that Lucinda's bodyguard had died during her rescue—a rescue she couldn't imagine Damian capable of, let alone his sister.

Samara dropped her gross hoodie on the floor and yanked her splattered tank top over her head. She shoved her blood-soaked jeans past her hips and down her legs, then she frantically toed her boots off. Looking down at herself, she felt a bit better, but she quickly realized from the smell of her body that a shower was mandatory.

Egad. Stripping out of her underwear, Samara glanced over her shoulder, catching her reflection in the mirror. The phoenix birthmark was still there—a cyclical symbol of constant renewal always present in her life. She stepped into Damian's hot shower and adjusted the faucet, desperate to get clean. After picking up the bottle of shampoo from the ceramic tile floor, she poured a capful in her hand and worked up a lather in her scalp. It wasn't even close to what she would've normally used but being manly and pine-scented seemed a great substitute for the metallic smell of blood.

While rinsing her hair, Samara remembered the tingling sensation she'd felt when Damian sat down next to her at the cemetery and touched her hand. It was hard to believe that this was the same demon—the same half-human creature that pretended not to know her at the practice range. Now she was here, in this house on Earth's crust, thanks to his sister and Lucinda's obliterated guard.

Who was Damian Hunter anyway? Could she trust him? Could he help rescue her father and uncle? Would it even be possible? She needed quick answers.

She allowed herself to stand under the hot stream of water until her muscles in her back and neck started to relax. But Samara knew she needed to get moving. She didn't have the luxury of wasting time. Not any longer. She wanted to vent about everything that had happened in Hell, but she wasn't prepared to cry in front of Damian and Eliza.

Stay strong, she told herself. *Find Lucinda's weaknesses and use them against her.*

When she stepped out of the shower, Samara was surprised to see a fresh towel and stack of clothes just inside the door. She would need to thank whoever had scrounged them up for her. There was no way of salvaging her own clothes, which still lay in a gory heap on the floor. She reveled in the clean t-shirt, sweatpants, and a pair of flip-flops. She could have used a pair of underwear and maybe a bra, but she wasn't going to complain.

After running a brush through her hair, a fresh wave of power rolled over her. It was time to get on with her life beginning with a teleported trip to Hell. But this time she needed to be better prepared and have a solid escape plan.

As she entered the hallway, an exchange on the main level drifted upstairs. She stepped softly on the stairs, eavesdropping on the conversation between Damian and his unseen guest.

"Zach," he said. "I should have known you'd show up eventually."

"Clearly, you're upset."

"Yeah…a little. Your brainless buddies jumpstarted Judgment Day."

"Maybe we *let* it happen, but we didn't start anything."

A broken picture frame near Samara's foot caught her eye, and she bent down to look at it. Behind the shattered glass was a photo of what looked like 10-year-old Damian holding a fish proudly for the camera.

"You had a chance to stop your brother and didn't," Zach lectured. "So, let's not quibble over who started what. Let's just say it wasn't anyone's fault and move on. Cause like it or not, it's Apocalypse now, and we're back on the same team again."

Sam leaned around the corner to get a better view and caught sight of white feathery wings. *Angels!* She flattened her back against the wall. *What are angels doing here? This is a demon's house, isn't it?*

"You think so?" Damian said, sounding unimpressed.

"We get it. You want to kill the new Devil in Hell. We want you to kill her too. It's…synergy."

"And I'm supposed to trust you? Get screwed, Zachariah."

"This isn't a game, son. Lucinda is powerful in ways that defy description. We need to strike now, hard and fast…before her father finds his vessel."

Eliza spoke up. "His vessel? Lucifer needs a meat suit?"

"His daughter foolishly thinks she destroyed him, but he's an angel, like us." Zach chuckled. "Those are the rules. And when he touches down, we're talking four horsemen, red oceans, fiery skies...all the greatest hits. You can stop him, Damian, but you need our help."

"After what you did...exploding that guard...leaving parts all over my house, I don't want jack squat from you!"

"Listen to me, boy!" the angel shouted back. "You think you can rebel against us? Like Lucifer did? Like Lucinda thinks she's going to?"

Samara shouldered around the edge of the wall and descended the stairs quietly. The angel was facing off with Damian and his sister stood next to him, backing him up. She exhaled a deep breath and told herself, *It's now or never.*

"Geez, Louise..." Samara casually said, walking into the room. "You can cut tension in here with a knife." She crossed her arms over her chest to hide her lack of bra, while attempting to diffuse the tension in the room.

Zachariah stepped back and sneered at her. "I know what you are."

"I think the word you're looking for is who. Am I right, or am I right?" She glanced at Eliza and forced a smile.

"You're Ariel's daughter," the angel said, pointing an imperious finger at her. "And your father is Crighton. I know all about you, Samara Daemonium. You have a part to play in this too."

"Oh, really?" She half-shrugged. "Isn't that nice. But I'm with Damian on this one. He's already told you that we don't want anything to do with you or any of your cohorts."

"You think what you want makes a difference?" he snidely asked. "You'll do exactly as you're told."

"Is that right? Hmm...I really don't think so."

Zachariah raised a finger in the air and brought it down quickly in a sharp angle. A trickle blood slipped down Samara's inner wrist and over her arm. "Would you look at that," he said. "You're bleeding."

She glanced down at her arms crossed over her chest. "So, I am," she agreed. She stepped away from the entry and dropped her arms. "For an angel, you don't play nice." She reached for the long spear leaning against the wall behind the partially open closet door. The angel couldn't see it, but he knew what she had in mind before she did.

He started towards her. "No! Don't be stupid!" he screamed. "You'll regret your actions!"

Her bloody palm connected with the shaft before the angel could reach her. Lifting it shoulder high, she drew her arm back, preparing to launch it.

In an explosion of light, the angel disappeared from Damian's living room.

"I learned that from watching my uncle, you asshole!" she yelled toward the ceiling.

Eliza released a deeply held breath. "Thanks for the backup. Looks like you found Damian's clothes."

He tore off a piece of the shirt he was wearing and tightly wrapped the slash on Samara's wrist, stemming the flow of blood. "Taking out the trash might be your new job in this house," he said.

Eliza grabbed her brother's arm and stared into his face. "Is what he said true? Is Lucifer back?"

"Yeah, that's the story. Lucinda has got to be worried. She threw his vessel into the main furnace. If you'll pardon the pun, him finding out must've burned."

Samara snickered, more out of nervousness than anything else.

Eliza narrowed her eyes. "This is serious, guys. We're not playing games here."

"Yeah...I'm sorry," Samara said. "I'm just trying to catch up with this...mystery. There's so much I don't know—"

Damian placed his finger to her lips, silencing her.

Stepping back, beyond his reach, she growled. "I don't get it. Why don't I deserve an explanation? According to that angel, I'm involved...even if I don't know how."

Damian sighed and reluctantly told her, "I'll explain it all in the car. But we should get out of here before that asshole comes back with his friends."

"What? You have a car?" Samara's curiosity became instantly aroused. "A *real* car? I've only seen pictures of them in magazines. Are we going to ride inside one? Who's going to drive? Can I?"

Damian snorted a laugh. "Ah, boy...this is going to be fun."

They walked outside together, and Eliza slid into the driver seat. She watched Samara run her hand over the hood of car and squeal in delight. "Open the rear door, sit in the back seat, and be quiet, Sam," she told her. "I need to concentrate on my driving." Then she turned to her brother beside her and kept her voice low. "Honestly, Damian, I'm not sure bringing this cute little demon here was such a good idea. You're going to have to sit on top of her to keep her quiet."

As the car rolled down the street, Samara rocked from side to side in the back seat, overwhelmed by what she was seeing. "I can't believe I'm really here. ON EARTH! None of my friends will ever believe this! A REAL CAR!"

Eliza glanced at Damian. "Yeah, good idea, Bro. She'll have no problem fitting in...if we're going to a sanitarium."

CHAPTER 19

HELL HATH NO FURY

A riel's feet slammed against the ground at the mouth of the cavern leading to Hell. She didn't realize she'd been shaking from the weight she was carrying until she almost lost her grip on the Trapper's waist. After releasing her hold, she closed her wings against her back and pulled her black-hooded cloak more tightly around her. She drew in a cold breath and turned to him.

"The east gates are open," she said. "There's a dense mist ahead of us. It's filled with tumult and confusion. I can sense it… standing here."

"Are you sure this the right place?" the Trapper asked.

"Please be patient. We'll be in Hell soon enough."

A whisper-soft movement in the dark alerted her, and she held her breath, straining her eyes in the blackness.

"What's that sound?" he nervously asked.

A flurry of wings erupted, filling the space above them. "Just bats."

Ariel lit a torch on the wall and carried it with her toward the back of the cave. She waited for the Trapper to take his position behind her. Then she followed a familiar path, allowing memories to creep out of the dark places in her mind—memories of Lucifer, the prison cell, hopelessness, and the isolation that nearly killed her. She was being guided on this worrisome journey by some otherworldly spirit. But because technically her whole species was otherworldly, she doubted any metaphysical support would be arriving. This was a place filled with pain, torment, and loss...oozing in misery. With each carefully placed step, Ariel was finding herself wholly consumed by it, being dragged down into the pit of despair.

I can't believe I'm here...in this horrible place.

A flash of white hair and light blue eyes appeared in her mind. *Cassius.* The guilt over letting him leave with Onoskelis hit her like a sledgehammer, threatening to bring her to her knees. Tears came to her eyes, blinding her, but she refused to turn around, refused to surrender the precious gift from God she'd been given.

Don't break...don't break, she mentally chanted. She questioned why she had come back here with a stranger—with the man who had shot her wayward son. He had no soul to speak of, but Caleb had a heart, desperate for love. Opening her heart to him had left a gaping hole, larger than before. And now with Cassius' safety consuming her thoughts, she found it hard to keep breathing. If he was taken from her forever, she could never exist with just a sliver of a heart to sustain her.

Ariel's guilt continued to grow over the next two hours, fed by the dark forces around them. Yet still she kept moving, determined to find her son and bring him home. Then something quite remarkable happened. She felt a fluttering in her chest—a lightness, increasing with each step she took. The heady sensation was undeniable. Crighton was here in this hellish place, somewhere nearby. He was her source of hope, her light in the dark, guiding her closer and closer. They could do this together! She wasn't alone. Together they would take back the son they had lost and leave this place, never to return.

"Is this the right way?" the Trapper asked, struggling to keep up. "We seem to be going downward."

"Where do you think Hell is?" Ariel asked. "On another planet? At the bottom of the sea? Let me tell you so it's very clear. Hell is in the center of the Earth...the city dump of all eternity. Its darker than darkness, deeper than any abyss, hotter than the sun. Hell is a place with more wailing and gnashing teeth than any writer or artist can portray. It's a place beyond the limits of our language and far worse that you could ever imagine. That is where your sister is...and my husband, and my son. Together, we'll find them, but it won't be easy, it won't be pleasant, and believe me, it won't be forgettable."

"That's a frightening thing to say. Is it really necessary?" *You've got to be kidding.*

Ariel halted irresolutely, not knowing whether to go on alone or stay put and argue. "Fear has two meanings," she said. "Forget everything and run away or face everything and rise to the occasion. The choice is yours. As for me, I intend to keep moving and finish what I came here to do."

"Alright. Let's keep going."

"And just to remind you, I've been in Hell before. Believe me, it's not a place where any angel wants to go. Not unless they're willing to lose their soul." She exhaled another deep breath and began walking again. "Try to keep up. We're going in the back way to avoid detection. It's going to be a little rough, going around the Lake of Fire, but then it's all downhill from there."

"Downhill?"

"That's right. Deeper than deep."

"There's an actual lake with fire and brimstone? I thought that was just a biblical reference. You know...a way to frighten sinners?"

"Yes, it's real. It's the final destination for sinners and disbelievers…the cast-offs in Hades. Cowards, abominable beings, murderers, sexual deviants, and chronic liars are tossed inside, never to be seen again." Ariel stumbled but caught herself before falling. "I've been dreaming about this place for months now, being pulled back by tormented souls…all reaching out to me. Sometimes, I cry out at night and wake up covered in sweat. After spending time there, it's like I have a foot in Hell and one in Middle Earth. Perhaps it's because my soul is trapped in a demon's body. But it was the only way to survive and be with my soulmate too."

Ariel glanced back at the Trapper. The puzzled look on his face was hard to miss. "And here I thought you were an angel all this time. It never dawned on me that you were a demon too. I'm sure that's a struggle for you. By the way, my name's Perseus. My mother Danae would never understand my being here. She believes we choose our own paths. But my sister was enslaved by Lucinda and forced to accept the life she now has. That's why I'm here…purely to save her."

"And my son and husband too," she reminded him.

"Yes, of course. By the way, thank you for allowing me to bring my sword and gun with me. I'm a bit rusty, but I've taken down some mighty foes in my time."

"I'm sure you have, Perseus. You might have to prove that here, but I have faith in you, and I trust your ability. Perhaps one day soon, you and your sister will make the world a better place for all of us."

She looked over her shoulder and noted his downcast eyes. "Is there something else?"

"When your demon son came at me with a knife, I reacted the only way I knew how. I'm sorry for what I did, Ariel. I would *never* deliberately kill a child. You have to believe me."

Ariel nodded and rested her hand on his shoulder. "I already forgave you, Perseus. Caleb is where he belongs now, but Cassius isn't. He's just an innocent young boy...sweet, naive, and impressionable. I don't want him hurt or damaged by any of this."

"I'll do whatever I can to help him...to help your soulmate and save my sister too. Even if I have to summon the Gods on Mount Olympus to make it happen."

"Well, hopefully, that won't be necessary. But we'll know soon enough. The Lake of Fire is just up ahead. Watch your step now. It's not an easy path. I might have only dreamed about this ghastly place, but I assure you it's real."

They continued their grueling journey stepping around jagged rocks and battling steep terrain until the trail leveled off. The soil beneath their feet had changed from shades of gray to blood red. Burning hot smoke, gas, sulfur, and steam filled the air. The red, opaque mist parted, and an enormous lake of fiery brimstone now loomed before them. The sight caused them to gasp. This was the place for second deaths—the end of the line for corrupt souls.

There was a sound of marching soldiers approaching and wretched screams in their pack. Ariel motioned for Perseus to join her, hiding behind an outcropping of rock. They watched in horror as two men were hoisted on shoulders and tossed into the lake. Arms reached up and hands grabbed hold of them, pulling them under the fiery waves. All the while, haunted screams of a thousand demons echoed against the cavernous walls.

Perseus cowered and covered his ears. The soldiers stood at attention, waiting for word from their commander. With no audible instruction, they did an about face and were gone as quickly as they came.

When it was quiet once again, Ariel stood up and motioned for Perseus to join her. The tunnels leading to the prison cells were just ahead, and she was being drawn toward them.

"We need to be more careful from now on. Demons are everywhere, and all of them are loyal to Lucinda. If we're found, we'll never leave here...not alive anyway."

Perseus kept his eyes down and nodded.

"I'm sure you've seen worse. You grew up among Gods after all."

"Nothing so brutal as that. Those voices...where did they come from?"

"From the souls of demons and humans...all of them tormented. This place is filled with anguish and cruelty. I know you're here to rescue your sister, but you need to be prepared, Perseus. She might not be the goddess or the sister you remember. Torture can change any creature into becoming something they're not."

He shook his head in denial. "She's stronger than you'll ever know. Hecate led an army against Lucinda. If need be, she'll do it again."

"Just heed my warning, Perseus. Please. I don't want to leave you behind if she refuses to go."

"There's no reason to worry about that," he said.

"I sure hope not. Now, let's find our loved ones and get everyone out of this horrible place, while we still can."

CHAPTER 20

DARK SECRETS

"The Ojai Motel in sunny California," Eliza announced. "I guess this is as good a place as any." She pulled between two cars in front of a pink two-story building and shut off the engine. Then she turned around in her seat. "I promised to give you the full story, Sam. So unbuckle, sit back, and most of all, don't interrupt."

"Story?"

"About Legend. I remember you asking, right?"

Samara nodded and glanced at Damian, looking depressed and gloomy. He was staring through the passenger window at a big black dog tied to a fence post.

"You know, you don't have to do this right now..." she told Eliza.

"I insist. Besides, I won't have to deal with you asking me again."

"Okay, you're right. I'm listening."

By sharing the full account of Legend's death, Samara was hoping to fill the holes in her memory. But surprisingly, that wasn't the case. In fact, she was left more perplexed than ever.

"I don't understand. Why was someone following us?"

"They were Blue Jays...raring for a fight," Eliza bitterly answered. "Like I said, Legend disrespected one of them. So he grabbed him from behind and cut his throat. Basically, my brother died for nothing."

For some weird reason, Eliza's account seemed completely off, but Samara wasn't prepared to correct her. "I don't get it," she said. "An insult? That's *all*? What kind of reason is that to kill someone?"

"The Black Crows and Blue Jays have been enemies for years. Legend never pulled punches, not where those guys are concerned. So, it comes as no surprise that he insulted one of them. But still, I've never known Blue Jay retaliation to go so far."

Samara shook her head and sighed. "I'm so sorry, El. Someone kept knocking on the cabin door. Legend told me to hide, and then everything went haywire. If I had only stayed..."

"It's a good thing you didn't, Sam. Otherwise, you wouldn't be here right now."

"Yeah, I suppose you're right. I'm just so...incredibly sorry."

Damian looked both uncomfortable and fed up with Samara and her apologies. He mumbled something about taking a walk, since they were already checked in. His sister climbed out of the car and trailed after him, while Samara rolled down the window, knowing it was best to stay put.

A short distance away, Damian crumpled to the ground next to a tree, folded his arms around his legs, and lowered his head. His sister approached him from behind and wrapped her arms around him. "We'll figure this out," she said. "I promise. He didn't die for nothing. That was a stupid thing to say."

Damian looked up at her. "It was over an angel. A goddamn angel. I just wish I knew who she was, El. I'd strangle her right now if I could."

Samara swallowed hard. After meeting Ariel, Legend told his friends and apparently a few family members that he was secretly dating an angel. Whether it was to impress them or to simply stir up trouble, she had no clue. "I know you don't want to hear this," Legend told her. "But you'll always be an angel to me. So sweet, beautiful, and innocent. I don't know how anyone could mistake you for a demon."

"But *that* is what I am," she snapped. "And I'm certainly not ashamed of it. So, why lie?"

Samara's stomach twisted over the memory. She suddenly felt sick again, sicker than she ever thought possible. She needed to leave this place right now. Go back to Middle Earth, find her family, and get on with her life. It was too dangerous staying here not knowing when her memory would return and the truth would come out. There was no doubt about that.

She knew in her heart that Adison wasn't to blame, but she didn't want to believe Naburus and Lestat were involved either. If they were, she might have played a big part in Legend's death and knowing of that would be unbearable.

Eliza stood next to the car, looking sideways at her. "Are you okay?"

She nodded and feigned a smile. "I'm great. Why wouldn't I be?"

The bright sunlight made Eliza squint. "We're going inside for a while, and Damian wants you to come too. With humans walking around, it's not safe for you to be out here by yourself."

"Right. Of course." Samara followed Eliza and jumped when the door slammed behind her. Then she dropped into the nearest seat.

Silence filled the room for a few minutes, but eventually Damian broke it. "I didn't mean to be rude, especially to you, Sam. So many bad things have been happening lately. I went to

Hell with Warwick to secretly get information. I honestly had no idea what would happen to him."

Samara looked up when his voice trailed off. Damian was looking down, clasping his hands, avoiding eye contact. The air in the room was oppressive, and she looked back to see Eliza scowling.

"What's wrong?" she asked.

Eliza tilted her head. "I've been trying to figure out why my brother would go after an angel when he had someone like you."

"I have no idea." Samara was sweating, feeling like she needed another shower. "Maybe he didn't think I was good enough."

Damian grabbed her wrist as she attempted to walk past him. "You were *too* good for him, Sam. You were the only female demon he ever talked about. But there's something going on here. I can feel it…I can smell it in your blood. What are you hiding? You can't keep lying about whatever it is. Someone could get hurt."

Samara yanked her arm away. "Like Legend? Too late, he's dead. Why are you asking these stupid questions? Are you afraid that I might be lying about knowing something? Or worse yet, ditching my duped friend? Oh, wait. You already did that."

Damian jerked back, reminding Samara that sometimes words were more effective than a slap. "Yeah, you're right about that," he muttered. "I know something about keeping secrets and the damage they can cause."

Samara shrugged off his words. She didn't know what she could say or do to heal the wound she had opened. After glancing at them, she decided it was best to just step away for a while. "I'm going to freshen up. Knock on the door if you need me." She started toward the bathroom, but then paused to add, "I didn't mean that, Damian. Sometimes I speak without thinking."

"No different that shooting without aiming," he said. "I've been known to do that too."

"Sure." Samara stepped inside the bathroom and closed the door. Then she stood before the mirror, taking long, deep breaths. *It's going to be okay. It wasn't your fault. You kissed Naburus, trying to make your cheating boyfriend jealous. Just like the school counselor told you to do. That's all you did, right? Then why do you feel so guilty? So damn responsible?*

Samara splashed water on her face and dried it with a towel. Then she counted to ten before walking back into the room.

Damian was alone now, loading a pistol at the table. "Feeling better?" He asked her.

She nodded and glanced around the room, focusing on the silver embossed wallpaper peeling slightly in the corner.

"Good." He loaded the magazine into his pistol. "I'm sorry about what happened to you."

She wasn't sure which incident he was referring to, but both were equally shocking. When she felt tears stinging her eyes again, she sat down on the edge of the bed and busied herself by thumbing through a magazine.

"I know that you took Legend's death hard," he said softly. "He was a good friend, but I'm wondering if he was more than that to you?"

She paused in the middle of the page and made direct eye contact. As smooth as Damian might think himself, the edge under his tone wasn't missed and neither was his comment about her blood. "Legend was my best friend. Do you expect me to have no reaction after witnessing his death? And what did you mean about smelling my blood? Are you a vampire too?"

After setting his gun aside, Damian turned his chair toward her. "You fell asleep on his grave. I get it! You obviously had feelings for him. I was just curious to know how deep they ran."

In that moment, she was certain she saw something in his eyes—something akin to longing. But she could've been wrong with having never witnessed it before.

"As far as your blood goes," he added, "It's just an instinct I was born with, Sam. I can sense anxiety, and I understand how worried you are about your family. Just know that part of the reason why we're preparing for battle is to help you. Try to relax for ten minutes, if that's even possible. And don't go doing any astral wandering. I had a hard time getting over your last disappearance." For a moment, he simply gazed into her eyes. Then he picked up a demon bullet and ran his finger over the carved tip.

"What do you mean…hard time? Did I offend you somehow? It seems that's all I'm capable of doing, Damian. Disappointing everyone in my life." She stood up and moved toward the window, looking outside at nothing. When he didn't respond, she turned back around.

His face and neck were flushed. He kept his eyes down and whispered something she couldn't hear.

"What did you say?"

"I need you, Sam. There, I said it. I can go days without talking to you, months without seeing you. But not a second goes by that I don't think about you."

The words sent a shiver down her spine. She closed her eyes and felt her heart skip a beat. When she looked up again, Damian was staring at her with undeniable yearning in his eyes. His lips curled in a sweet smile, sending her pulse racing. It was suddenly easy for her to imagine that her fears and anxieties were needless.

That he cared deeply for her despite their vast differences. He was the kind of demon that would love her forever no matter what others might think, including her father.

Damian stood up and walked toward her. He looked deep into her eyes and opened his heart with his words. "I'm learning that if I react a certain way, it won't change anything. It won't make anyone respect me more. It won't magically change their minds. Sometimes it's better to just let things be, to let feelings go and not fight for closure or explanations or answers. To not expect everyone to understand where you're coming from. I'm slowly learning that life is better lived when you don't center it on what's happening around you and just center it on what's happening inside you."

"Wow." Samara gave him a quick smile. "I wish I could be honest like that. I wish that I could trust my feelings and just—".

Without warning, he wrapped his arms around her and pressed his lips to hers in a warm, powerful kiss. Endless seconds later, she turned her face away, desperate to breath. He relaxed his hold and began taking his time, delivering soft, tantalizing kisses to her neck and throat. He breathed into her ear and slid his tongue across her bottom lip, drawing out a staggered breath in response. A wave of heat was building within her with each sensuous kiss, setting every nerve in her body on fire.

This is what longing feels like. What craving means...

Damian smiled at her again, then he swept his tongue between her lips, pressing his warm, soft lips to hers. He slid his hands up the sides of her body, molding every curve, and cradled her face in his hands. Then he brought their lips together in the most passionate kiss—deep, long, and potent. Her knees became weak, and she felt a growing urgency inside her. He was breathing heavier than before, waking her primal need.

"You have no idea what you do to me," he whispered against her cheek. "I've never felt like this with anyone before." His lips moved to hers again, and his kiss became more subtle, not demanding but more inquisitive. The tidal wave of lust coursing within her slowly calmed. He eased back and looked deep into her eyes. The intense passion she saw there left her struggling to breath. She rested her head against his chest and closed her eyes. *It's true*, she thought to herself, *demons don't revere their blood or their heartbeats. They don't appreciate the air they breathe.* When she looked up at Damian, she was reminded of all the things that kept this Cambion alive.

She smiled and wrapped her arms around his neck. He pulled her into a tighter embrace and this time when he kissed her there was no sense of restraint. It was like kissing an inferno. Hot, breathless, so overwhelming that her senses shattered. How could kisses from a human do this to her? She desperately wanted his lips on hers again and could think of nothing else more thrilling. With the press of his mouth on hers, all the things he could never say aloud were spoken.

Damian pulled her far enough away to see her face but still held her arms firmly in his grip. "Sam, there's something I need to tell you. Something you should know…"

"Go ahead," she beckoned. "You can tell me anything. I'm sure you realize that by now."

Eliza charged into the room and froze in her tracks, eyes wide open.

Damian unlocked Samara's hands from around his neck and stepped back beyond her reach. She was disconcerted by his actions then became keenly aware of Eliza's presence behind her.

"Well, well. Would you looky here? This is what happens with a lack of supervision in the room. Geez, Bro, it's about goddamn time." A wry smile crept onto her lips. "You can't keep your eyes off her, so you might as well drill her."

Samara looked down, feeling extremely awkward, which seemed to anger Damian.

"Damn it, El," he blasted. "Why do you have to be so crude all the time?"

"Just lucky, I guess. Get over it, lover boy," she said. "I have a gift for both of you." She tossed a sealed packet at them and waited for a reaction. When she didn't get one, she proudly announced, "Hex bags! No way any Archangels will find us with those. Demons either, for that matter."

Damian looked at the bag suspiciously and turned it over in his hand. "Where'd you get these?"

"From Ransom. What's the problem? We can use them, right?"

Before he could answer, a red-headed, shaggy-haired creature appeared in the open doorway. He strode into the room, seemingly without a care, and snorted. "Your brother's face says it all, El. You didn't tell him I was coming, did you? I'm truly hurt, babe."

Damian scowled. Clearly, Eliza's friend wasn't welcome. Yet despite the reaction he invoked, she remained visibly amused.

"He's a replacement for Cerberus," she said. "We needed one, you know…"

"No fucking way."

"Ransom was reassigned to Lucinda's army. He's risking his life to help us. How can you possibly say no? Besides, he's Cambion and would make a great addition to the Black Crows."

Samara stood back observing. It seemed Damian wasn't prepared to accept this nitwit or brief him on all that had happened—how his living room was covered in blood and his house had become a dangerous place.

"Hey, I know you." Ransom's dark eyes were fixed on Samara. "You're Crighton's kid...and Tyrus' little helper. I saw them both in prison. It was the damnedest thing ever. After they were brought in, Tyrus kept insisting his brother be tied up and gagged. And your father kept saying he wasn't Crighton. Guess they both snapped or something. Anyway, clearly there's no love lost there."

"What were you doing in the prison block? Is my dad still alive?"

"I was a security guard there. And the answer is yes...at least, he was alive four hours ago."

Damian snarled. "He's a notorious liar, Sam. You can't believe anything he says."

"But he saw him...he said so."

"Let's just hope he's right." Damian glared at Ransom. "Now go out the door you came in. We don't need help from a vampire hunter."

"They're beefing up security and are keeping an eye out for you. Face it, you won't get past the front gates or the Hell Hounds without me."

"You heard me! Walk out of here while you still can."

"This isn't about that psycho chick, is it?" He cocked his head to one side. "It wasn't my fault she offed herself. Tabitha had issues...lots of them."

"You know nothing!" Damian growled before taking a swing at him. Ransom ducked under his fist and knocked him back with an uppercut. Damian came back angrier than ever, grabbing his shoulders, and driving his knee into his face.

Ransom touched his bloody nose and looked down at this finger. "Mmm...that tingles in all the right places," he purred. Suddenly, he lunged forward, and Damian sidestepped his attack, letting his momentum carry him past the sofa. Then he delivered a low punch to his kidney. But unfortunately, the blow didn't even stun him, like it would have with a normal demon. He took advantage of their proximity to drive his elbow into Damian's face.

As her brother prepared to swing his fist again, Eliza stepped in, shouting, "Stop it! Both of you! You're wasting valuable time." Then she glared at Damian. "Grow up! Remember who we're fighting against. We need Ransom to get us into Hell. Don't you get it? When I took Samara, all our bridges were burned there. We can't create the chaos we promised without Ransom. He's the key to getting us inside."

Samara narrowed her eyes. "Chaos?"

"You don't need to know about that," Eliza said. "It doesn't concern you."

"Really? My family is locked up in Hell. I need to rescue them, including my baby brother."

Eliza snorted, her impatience showing. "Onoskelis has been directing us and is waiting for our return. She has been secretly guarding Cassius and didn't want you or your mother to know any more than necessary. She asked us to keep you away from Hell…to keep you safe."

"WHAT?? You knew that all this time and said nothing? I don't understand, Damian. Why would you do that? Why would you keep all of this a secret?"

"I was told the less you knew the better," Damian answered. "Tyrus was training the Cambion army. That's why I was surprised to see you there…at the mission. I was told to buddy up with Warwick to get close to Lucinda. If he knew about our personal relationship, he would've told her, risking the lives of faction members in the Cambion Crows Force. We're trying to end the war, not be part of it."

Samara looked down, shaking her head. "So, you've been plotting behind my back all this time, treating me like a child. You must've thought I was so stupid…both of you." Damian reached for her hand, and she slapped it away. "Don't even think about touching me," she warned. "I'm leaving and there's nothing you can do to stop me. NOTHING! Do you hear me?"

"Grab her!" Eliza shouted. "You can't let her go. She'll ruin everything!"

Samara shoved a chair at Eliza and tumbled over the sofa. She closed her eyes and concentrated on teleporting inside the Gates of Hell, vanishing in an instant. She arrived flat-footed on steaming, rocky ground. Even with the chained Hellhounds barking behind the gates, their red eyes glowing, and razor-sharp teeth bared, her plans remained solid and relatively simple. After finding the arsenal storage room, she would reclaim her bow and quiver. Then she would find her missing family and do whatever was necessary to get everyone out alive.

CHAPTER 21

HE'S BACK!

Lucifer watched Samara from the dark shadows inside Hell's Gate, keenly aware that this was Crighton's beloved daughter, returning to rescue him. The irony of her mission left him vaguely amused, knowing her efforts were pointless. Both he and her father had come full circle, back into the bowels of Hell—where torture and death were inevitable. There was no avenue for escape from this god-fearing place, except by permission from the Knights of Darkness or the mercenary Arch-demons hellbent on destroying their own.

In Lucifer's mind, Samara's appearance at the human cemetery was more than sheer coincidence. It was destiny, beyond the power of God. Seeing her lying on Legend Hunter's grave had piqued his interest and kept his spirit circling nearby. He was searching for a new vessel at the time—a young, attractive, well-endowed body, strong to enough to address his need for revenge. As it turned out, it was simply a matter of timing—kismet he liked to believe. The Cambion had been recently buried and was trapped in limbo, due to his half-demon origin. Slipping into his body required only a few alternations, nothing too drastic or distasteful. Hair just long enough to tie into a ponytail and, of course, an idiomatic speech pattern those closest to him would recognize. There was also the matter a sliced throat, which fortunately could be repaired with a little black magic. After witnessing Samara's grief, Lucifer was determined to keep the demon lying beneath her looking as authentic as possible. With the right strut and smirk, he might even trick her into believing Legend had been brought back to life all because of her undying love for him.

Lucifer snorted his delight. Selecting the Cambion as the replacement for his ruined skin was beyond perfect; it was a foolproof disguise, allowing him to regain his power and enact justice for the pain he had suffered. Distrust was already circulating in the air. He could smell it, especially on Earth. With a few well-chosen words whispered in the right ears, he could encourage revolutionary humans around the world to randomly kill their own kind. To push the red button, blowing everything to smithereens. Then, with all the winged creatures in Hell and Heaven rebelling against God and the self-serving leader of his army, complete annihilation would be imminent.

Yes…all in due time, Castiel. All in due time.

Lucifer smoothed his hand over his snug-fitting black leather pants, enjoying the feel of his new body. But what about his tangled-up thoughts? While Samara stealthily moved about behind stone-covered walls, avoiding guards and soldiers in training, memories from her interactions with Legend rushed into his brain. Fighting over music, discussing favorite books, relentlessly tickling one another. How she smiled whenever they met, how she nervously nibbled on her lower lip, how the sunlight danced in her auburn hair. The way she insisted they wait to have sex until the time was right. None of it was real, they weren't his thoughts, but Lucifer still enjoyed watching the scenes unfold in Legend's mind. Every vision featuring Samara left him more intrigued. He replayed the memories again and again, believing he was part of them now. Thinking about the way her sexy body looked in tight little shorts and black skinny jeans. The way the vest tops she chose to wear showed the best views of her chest. Most of all, he loved the look in her eyes—the spark he couldn't define. It was like an inner glow—pure innocence with a hint of rebellion.

So perfect in every way.

A beautiful, strong, feisty queen would make a wonderful addition to his kingdom, complete with his sex-starved harem. *We're going to have so much fun, Samara,* he thought to himself. *I can't wait to spread those shapely legs and introduce myself...the way you truly deserve.*

Lucifer felt a sense of heaviness between his legs, unlike anything he'd experienced before. He pulled his zipper down and slipped his hand inside his pants to confirm his suspicion. His testicles were full and enormous. He pulled out his cock and was stunned by his discovery. It was thick and hard, measuring over eight inches long. Never in his life had he seen anything like this, and he wasn't even fully erect! No doubt his new equipment would require frequent use to keep it in tip-top shape. With his ability to go deeper than ever before, every female demon he jammed his massive cock into would scream at the top of their lungs from the pleasure and pain he could deliver, one after the other, of course.

Ah, yes. There was so much to look forward to and to be proud of, it seemed. A smile of satisfaction lit up his eager face, but then it occurred to him that he would have to go easy on Samara. She was a virgin, after all, and seeing the size of his package could scare her half to death, if he was lucky.

"Work time," he murmured, forcing his cock back into his pants. Unfortunately, work in Hell always came before pleasure, unless he could combine the two. Just seeing the look on Lucinda's face, after realizing he was resuming control, was going to be worth more than all the blue sapphires in his vault.

Hmm…fifty lashes for her part in my demise seems reasonable. But what am I going to do with Crighton and Tyrus? If Lucinda agreed to end their lives in a spectacle of some sort, then he might consider lessening her punishment. Otherwise, it would be doubled, leaving her crawling on all fours.

Then there was Ariel to think about. He'd been craving her soul for some time now. After devouring it, he could focus on his tasty dessert, nibbling on her daughter's tantalizing breasts before ramming his impressive cock into her over and over again.

Holy shit! The pain in his package was excruciating. It was hard as a rock and growing harder by the second, making it difficult to concentrate on anything else. From his viewpoint in the dark corner, he could see Samara now approaching the tunnels, branching off in all directions. He would let her wander free for a while longer before having her brought to him. Meanwhile, there were changes to make, judgments to enact, and a blowjob badly needed. Otherwise, he'd never be able to zip his pants back up again. It was no wonder Legend had kept his hands to himself. Controlling his beast when Samara was around must have been a full-time job. *Egad!*

Then, to his surprise and delight, a shapely blonde succubus entered Hell through a secret passageway. After greeting the returning guard, she veered off in the direction of the Pleasure Quarters, sashaying her hips as she walked. Lucifer stepped out of the shadows and followed her, drooling in anticipation of the pleasure she could amply provide.

As if sensing his presence, she stopped in her tracks and turned around. "Well, hello there," she purred. "Such a handsome young man, sniffing around in Hell. Are you new here, sweetheart?"

Lucifer grabbed one of her hands and pressed it against his bulge. "I need your help with this."

"So impressive. If you'll just come with me, I'm sure we can take care of that *big* problem." She smiled coyly. "Actually, I'm a little tense myself and could use a good—"

He placed his hands on her shoulders and shoved her down to her knees. His viselike fingers grabbed hold of her jaw and forced her mouth open. Then he whipped out his throbbing member and guided it down her throat, revealing in the fear in her eyes. "Please me or die," he growled.

With his red eyes glowing, recognition instantly registered on her face. She held onto his thick shaft and frantically went to work, choking and straining to breathe.

His brow raised as he watched her struggle, watched her flesh grow damp and bright pink from her stilted breaths. Lucifer was enjoying this immensely. He liked to see the fear he invoked, to know he possessed that power.

Clio seemed to know it too.

Lucifer released his grip on her neck and looked down at her, sighing with satisfaction. After ten long minutes, his body jolted a few times, filling her mouth with cum. She swallowed hard, licked her lips, and looked up at him lovingly.

"Welcome home, Master," she said. "I almost didn't recognize you. If not for your voice…"

"Shut up and come with me." He grabbed her by the back of her neck and directed her down the hall toward the throne room's main entrance. Then he stood back watching as she opened the massive doors. Lucinda was seated on his throne, giving orders to four armor-suited guards. When she looked to the side and saw Clio, she growled her disapproval.

"I thought I told you to stay away from me. Are you on a death mission or something? Is that it? Because I'll be more than happy to accommodate you when I'm done here." She looked back at one of her guards and snorted. "That succubus can't get enough. Perhaps I should send her to the garrison to entertain *all* the soldiers."

Clio stepped away from the open doorway, leaving Lucifer in her stead. He stood with his feet slightly apart with his hands in the pockets of a black leather trench coat. It hung slightly open, revealing his impressive, toned abs and tight leather pants. Of course, Lucinda didn't recognize him at first and chuckled at the imposing presence, capturing everyone's attention. "Did you bring me a special gift, Clio?" she asked, smiling demurely. "Something to sink my teeth into?"

Lucifer's lips spread into a slow, devious smile. "You've been up to no good, my dear," he said. "Making alterations without a single thought for my feelings. Fortunately, I'm finding the improvements somewhat refreshing...especially mine."

Recognizing his voice, Lucinda stared in disbelief, incapable of uttering a single word.

"Well, what do you think of my new meat suit?" He rubbed the large bulge in his pants. "It beats the horns and tails in this place, that much is certain."

Two guards rushed toward Lucifer with their swords drawn, and Lucinda halted them with a shout. "STOP! You're looking at Satan, the ruler of Hell! We've been waiting for his return. It just took longer than we expected." She flashed a smile at her father, and then turned back to the large gathering in the room.

"Kneel down, all of you! Pledge your allegiance to our almighty king!"

Lucifer smirked. "That's not the way it works, dear child. I know all about you and your great ambitions. About your loyal friends here and their devious undertakings. I've been secretly visiting Hell for some time now, familiarizing myself with your changes and strange activities. It's just lucky for you that I'm equipped to deal with the problems you've created." He dropped his coat to the ground revealing his bare chest and muscular arms. Then he turned around slowly, providing her with a good look at his young, vastly improved body. "What do you think? Not bad for a discarded old man, right?"

"You look amazing, Dad. Even younger than me."

"I want you to stay exactly where you are, Lucinda. Our conversation is just beginning." He moved toward his throne and waited. An armor-clad guard rushed into the room carrying a red velvet robe. The guard draped the fabric over his shoulders then backed away, bowing his head.

"I really missed this," Lucifer murmured, feeling the fabric. He swung the robe around himself and sat down on his throne. Then he gazed at the large gathering, waiting for deliberations and monetary settlements.

Unbelievable!

Whatever patience Lucifer had was long gone. He had more important matters to worry about, and witnesses to his brutality were not going to be wanted or appreciated.

"OUT! EVERYONE!" his voice boomed. "NOW!"

Demons scrambled to get out of the room, pushing past one another. Within seconds, the room was cleared. Clio was the last demon standing by the door, preparing to follow them.

Lucifer cleared his throat. "Clio!" He called out. She glanced over her shoulder to see him beckoning her with one finger. "Ah, my lovely, attentive demon. Did I ask you to leave?"

"I'm sorry, Sir. You did say everyone..."

"But you're not everyone. You're my special succubus, and your presence is needed along with my guards. Now come back here and drop down on your knees before me." He opened his robe, unzipped his pants, and pulled out his sizable erection. "I don't understand why this keeps happening to me. As you can see, I'm hard as a rock again."

Clio audibly sighed and rubbed the back of her neck. "That *is* a problem, isn't it? I know a few vixens that could be here in no time at all. They wouldn't mind addressing this issue. In fact, they would consider it an honor to—"

"Take care of it! NOW!"

Clio did as she was told, taking the end of his cock into her mouth. But that didn't satisfy Lucifer. He shoved her head down, forcing her to take it all. While her head bobbed, and she struggled to breathe, he motioned for one of his guards to come closer.

"I want Hecate brought here," he demanded.

"Are you sure, Sir? It might be awkward for her to witness your pleasure..."

"NOW!" he yelled.

Lucinda watched the guard disappear. Then she stood by staring straight ahead, trying to ignore her father's beastly behavior. Within minutes, Hecate appeared. She was dressed in her usual working attire and brought a cat o' nine tails whip with her, anticipating the need for it. Clearly nervous, she glanced at Lucinda and then stared at the young man seated on the Ruler of Hell's throne, obviously enjoying himself thanks to Clio's capable mouth.

"I was informed of your return," Hecate said. "What can I do for you, Sire?"

"You can address my little problem, that's what."

Hecate watched Clio's head in perpetual motion and swallowed hard.

"Don't worry," he said. "It's nothing you haven't done before. I want you to deliver punishment to a disobedient rebel."

"A rebel? Are you planning to bring him to me, Sir?"

"The demon I was referring to is my daughter, Lucinda. I believe fifty lashes are justly deserved...for trying to kill me."

Lucinda dropped to her knees. "I beg of you, Father, don't do this. I deeply regret my actions and promise to stand by you. I will never act again in such cruel fashion. Not ever—"

Lucifer waved his hand, silencing her. "Your punishment stands. Chain her up!" He told the guards. Then he turned to Hecate. "Fifty lashes. After that, I'll decide if she requires more."

She compliantly nodded. "If I can borrow two guards, I'll escort her to the torture chamber to carry out her sentence."

"No, I want it done here...so I can watch." He was squeezing the top of Clio's shoulders, rocking back and forth in his seat, matching the rhythm of her movements. "In fact, I think all of your beatings...should be in my throne room...from now on. Perhaps seeing them...will help me calm down. Yes...yes...yes... proceed. Exactly...what I need..."

Two guards stood on either side of Lucinda. They tore her dress apart and jerked it down to her waist, exposing her bare back. Then cuffs were clamped on her wrists. Chains were dropped from the rafters and attached to the cuffs, stretching Lucinda's arms high over her head.

Braced in her stilettos on the black marble floor, Hecate turned to Lucifer and nodded. "Ready, Master. When you are."

"Yes, begin," Lucifer told her, practically panting. "I love…a good show…"

Lucinda was facing away from her father with her back fully exposed. Hecate brought the whip down with such force that it whistled through the air. Lucinda wilted from the contact, but remained silent, as if determined not to cry out. Hecate repeated the action more than a dozen times, increasing the power behind each strike.

"Faster!" Lucifer breathlessly demanded. "Faster! Faster! Faster!"

Hecate quirked a brow. "How soon do you want this to end?"

"No, not you, Clio." He was gripping the sides of his chair with both hands, arching his back, huffing his words. "That's it…that's it. Keep going…yes…yes…yes…" Even though he was panting hard, he kept his eyes leveled on the scene before him. "Aah…aah …" All the action in the room continued without interruption. Whip cracking, Lucinda's body slacking, Clio's lips smacking, as her head bobbed up and down.

The guards standing nearby registered no emotion, as if they had witnessed scenes like this a dozen times before. Eventually, Lucifer groaned and threw his head back, writhing in pleasure. The flames in wall torches shot higher, matching his explosive release.

A few seconds passed, and then Clio wiped her mouth on the back of her hand and started to stand.

"Not yet!" Lucifer yelled. "You're not finished yet."

"Really? I know you're excited about your new body, but how is that even possible? Surely, you must be tired, Master…"

"Drop down and keep your mouth where it belongs until I tell you otherwise."

"I can't do this anymore," she said. "You need professional help. Whores from the Pleasure Quarters, not me."

After sneering at her in disgust, Lucifer stood up and began hitting her, first with an open hand and then backhand, sending her head flailing from side to side. He snatched her cinched belt then grabbed one of her thrashing arms, growling his contempt. He swept her feet from beneath her, and she fell into a heap on the floor. Normally, a brutal exchange would calm him, but this only fed his excitement, making him more determined to have his way.

Standing upright again, he grabbed Clio by the wrist and forced her to turn around. Then he shoved her onto the ground on all fours, facing away from him. From where he stood, he could feel the heat and tension building between her legs. Now blind to what was happening, she whimpered, anticipating another brutal assault. Straddling his armless throne, he pulled her body closer to him. Then he pushed her panties aside and inserted three fingers, testing her moistness. "You want me, don't you, Clio? Come on, say it. Tell me how much you need me. How much you want me inside you."

Before she could answer, he rammed his nine-inch cock into her. As her body swallowed him in a tight, wet embrace, he groaned, and she did the same. "It's so…large," she muttered. "Please…go easy…go easy…"

Lucifer smiled, enjoying this new game. He rocked his hips from side to side, leaving her groaning. While holding his breath, he jerked her hips toward him, deepening his reach. Then he began slowly moving his hips again. He would show her repeatedly what a G-spot was when the time was right, until she was begging for him to stop.

As he continued pumping away, he found himself enjoying this new sensation, unlike anything he'd felt before. But after a few minutes, he grew bored. His mind and body were eager to delve deeper, to know what his weapon could do. Ignoring her pleas, he banged into her harder than ever, only to discover he was halfway inside.

What the hell is this?

He moved his hips a little faster, and as he did, her wetness increased. She began moaning repeatedly, but she had yet to experience him fully. He jammed her tighter against his body and rocked his hips from side to side, amplifying her screams. His deceivingly gentle hands spread her inner thighs further apart and his hips bent lower. Then he began pumping again, forcing his length deeper and deeper inside her.

"That's it…that's it…uhhhhh…so good," Lucifer murmured. "Almost there, almost there."

Her body relaxed and she annoyingly cooed, "Mmmm…yeeesss…yeeess…"

Damn it! Clio was enjoying herself. He wanted more drama, more pain, more excitement. He thought about Samara and felt himself growing harder, stretching the nympho's pleasure hold to maximum capacity.

"Take it all, Clio. That's it. Take all of me." He whispered vulgar words, while his manhood pumped in and out of her. Skin slapping against skin and the sounds of squelching flesh added to his furor. He reached down a hand and felt her up, as her breasts bounced in synchronized rhythm. Gritting his teeth, he dug his fingernails into her hip, while groping her breast at the same time. Her insides were wet and hot, clamping tight on his ever-expanding cock, driving him over the edge. He pumped faster and faster, ramming into her harder and harder, grunting louder and louder.

Clio tried to twist her hips away from him, but this only gave him leverage to enter her deeper in different angles. "Stop it!" she yelled. "You're hurting me! Stop it!"

"Mmmm…yes…yes…" He sighed hoarsely, enjoying her pain and helpless struggle. He continued his onslaught, gripping her waist more firmly. He felt her pull away and responded by pushing into her even harder. He was now fully invested, pounding mercilessly into her core.

"Aaah…aaah…aaah…" he moaned again and again. Beads of sweat formed on his body from his exertion. All his senses were fixed on his cock, begging for release. His speed switched into high gear, banging her like a racing rabbit, smacking skin against skin in a race against time. "Uhhh…uhhh…uhhh…"

Forced to remain on the ground and spread wide for him, Clio had no choice but to accept his brutal assault. Sweat was dripping down her face as she twisted in his grip, trying to escape his building climax. Fast and hard, deep, and wide, he continued his incursion until her body was uncontrollably shaking.

"Pleeease…" she begged. "I need…you…to….stop…."

"Nooo…" He could feel her inner walls tighten around him, and more than anything, he wanted to hold back his release. "Not yet…not yet…" Believing her pain was pleasurable, he continued thrusting wildly and kept his hand on her back, steadying himself. He growled in warning at the slight twist of her hips, not willing to accept any form of rejection from her. Sensing the building orgasm within her, he grabbed a fistful of hair and yanked hard. Still pumping away, he threatened in a near whisper, "Don't test me, Clio. I always come first." He slapped her butt for misbehaving, then held onto both hips and continued relentlessly pumping away.

Between her moans, his deep thrusts, and the cracking whip in the room, it was almost impossible not to explode. "More! Scream more!" He yelled at Clio. The sound of their slapping skin was louder than the whip in the room. The nympho's whole body shook in tremors as he continued to grind against her, desperate to fill every inch inside her.

Her back arched and she began chanting, "Oh, yes...yes....yes. That's it. Faster...go faster!"

Lucifer stopped moving and whispered in her ear, "Do you know why you're enjoying this so much, Clio? It's because you know deep down inside that no one can give you what I can." His hands tighten around her waist, and he became a wild beast, pounded viciously into her. "Cry out, Clio! Cry for me! Hurting you only makes me harder."

A whimper escaped her throat, and he cackled in reply. Sex now permeated the air, along with the smell of blood, hate and sweat, exciting him to no end.

"Yes! Yes! Yes!" he shouted with each pumping action. He could feel her hips tilting slightly, notwithstanding her resistance. Her inner walls pulsed, and she cried out, climaxing despite his abuse. But he wasn't done with her yet. Not by a long shot. Panting his pleasure shamelessly, he doubled his speed. Her groans filled the room, matching his tempo. Her pain and resistance only egged him on. He thought about Samara in her ass-hugging jeans and imagined her on all fours, enjoying his relentless banging.

"Almost there...almost there...get ready, Sam. I've been saving this for you," he murmured. Tightening his grip on Clio's hips, he let out a deep groan and blew his load inside her. His release sparked one more sinful contraction deep within her, adding to his mindless pleasure. As his manhood pulsated and twitched, he continued grinding his hips against her, relishing the electrifying sensation. When his body finally stilled, he withdrew his cock and stepped back, supporting himself on the arm of his throne. Then he appraised the damage he had caused. Clio was lying on the ground in front of him with her hands between her legs, pathetically moaning. It seemed his weapon of choice was more damaging and effective than he ever deemed possible.

"Outstanding!" he roared, proudly stroking his cock. If he was feeling merciless and not softening in another ten minutes, he would give this whore another shot. Or maybe he would venture down the hallway to the Pleasure Quarters and rip a few there. After all, he needed to be in tip-top shape before using his prized possession on his new virgin queen.

"Can I leave now?" Clio meekly asked, crawling back onto her feet.

"I suppose but keep yourself available. There's no telling when I'll need you again."

"Crack!" Lucinda's body jerked. Blood splattered from her back. She held onto the chains to keep herself upright.

Shit! Lucifer covered his mouth. What was the count? Had Hecate reached fifty or had she exceeded that number? During his engrossing exercise, Lucifer had completely lost sight of Lucinda's purpose for being there. Raised welts and strap marks were crisscrossing her back, extending from the top of her buttocks to her shoulders. On her right side, her skin was split open in several places, and blood was flowing from her wounds, pooling on the marble floor beneath her. None of this made up for the disappointment and aggravation Lucifer felt after discovering his daughter's involvement in his near death. Even if Hecate continued her masterful work, aside from killing Lucinda, he doubted he would ever be satisfied.

"Enough," he grumbled, halting the tormentor's actions. "Your work here is done, Hecate. Have Lucinda taken to her room and send for a doctor. After my session with Clio, I'm feeling rather generous. So much so that I think I'll pay a visit the

Pleasure Quarters and get reacquainted with the female demons working there. Who knows…by the time I get there, I might even drum up some extra work for them."

Lucifer smiled. He briefly considered trailing after Samara on her journey through Hell but figured he would have plenty of time to wrestle with her later. Right now, squelching his need was all he could think about. In fact, if he didn't know better, he might even believe Legend was behind this—controlling his mind and body, making it virtually impossible for him to focus on anything else. But damn, it felt good. He was addicted to the rush of endorphins flooding his brain and eager to find his next fix. He knew that *certain* demons might find it amusing—this uncontrollable need he now had—but he couldn't care less. His swollen member required his immediate attention and there were fifty sex-starved demons in the Pleasure Quarters eager to please him by whatever means necessary. Hell, he might even take on three succubus at the same time, or surprise everyone by setting a record at six.

CHAPTER 22

HOSTAGE SITUATION

Onoskelis had been watching Cassius for three weeks now, witnessing his rapid growth into a preadolescent teen. Born with snow-white hair, the only way to avoid attracting attention was to insist he wear the black knit hat she'd acquired during one of her outings. He was taller and stronger than most demons his age and had the unrestrained movements of a young colt. His perfect nose and mouth were envied by the female population living nearby, along with his expressive, mesmerizing eyes. They included a thousand shades of blue and a small touch of hazel radiating in soft swooping arcs. The emotion in them was fathoms deep, yet they reflected the warmth and life of the fire-lit torches lining the cavernous walls in Hell. Although he was shy and soft-spoken, which the Shapeshifter loved about him, Cassius was also inquisitive, clever, and highly intelligent. Not a day went by that he didn't ask questions about his mother, father, and sister. He simply couldn't understand why Onoskelis had been tasked with watching him, while everyone else in his family had returned to their Middle Earth home.

During the fourth week of his captivity, Cassius became more anxious than ever. As he paced back and forth, there was borderline resentment in the way he looked at the Shapeshifter, making her extremely uncomfortable. "If I stay here any longer,

I'll be climbing the walls," he forewarned. "You know I'm capable of taking care of myself, so why are you keeping me here?"

Onoskelis had to come up with an answer—a way to frighten him into staying. He was her bargaining chip, after all. The only way to get Yokai back from Lucinda. "It isn't safe for you on Middle Earth," she told him. "Not with the Red War breaking out. Your parents would be risking their lives to protect you from Archangels and demon-eating cannibals in the lowlands. You don't want to have their blood on your hands, do you?"

Cassius shook his head in defeat. He returned to the stone bench in the cavern and sat down, deep in thought. Serious and sad, his head tilted forward, and his shoulders slumped.

"Your mother asked me to protect you, and that's exactly what I'm doing. No one is going to harm you here," Onoskelis said, reminding Cassius of another promise, another time.

With his hopes crushed, she left him to mourn his predicament, disappearing into the long, dark tunnel to further her military training. After devouring whatever food was left, he retreated into his room and stayed there, sulking on his bed.

Daily life continued in similar fashion, leaving him bored, frustrated and extremely anxious. Another week went by and any patience he had evaporated, turning him into an angry, demanding teenager.

"If I can't leave here, then neither will you!" He blocked her exit, and she shoved him aside, bringing him to his knees.

"You're being ridiculous!" she shouted. "I have to put in more training before my commanders realize I'm gone. If I don't go back, they'll come looking for me and won't rest until they find you. Believe me, Queen Lucinda will torture and kill you without even blinking an eye."

Choking back his rage, he tried to speak calmly. "Why can't I come with you? I could fight in Lucinda's army too."

Onoskelis was quiet for a long moment, debating on how to answer. "I'm keeping you here for your own good, Cass. You just need to accept that."

Her arrogant manner had become irritating, and her habit of going into deep trances before answering him was incredibly annoying. Once again, she was disappearing for endless hours, leaving him isolated, desperate, and angry.

"Why are you torturing me like this? Why are you being so cruel?"

"First off, I don't have the words to tell you how grateful you should be for what I did for you and your family. Keeping you alive when everyone in Hell is determined to kill you is a huge accomplishment. And believe it or not, I'm proud of my heart. It's been played, stabbed, cheated, burned and broken, but somehow it still works…where you're concerned."

"Just barely."

Onoskelis chuckled. "When I get back, we'll take a walk. Maybe get some food in the mess hall and pitch rocks into the void. How's that sound?"

He didn't bother to answer.

After she left, his destructive nature took over. He chiseled violent pictures on his bedroom walls and ceiling. He became a possessed demon, testing evil smiles, his levitating skills, and an unnaturally deep voice. He even broke every mirror and glass he could find. Then he cut his hand and watched blood pool on the ground.

Eventually, Onoskelis returned. He expected her to blow up over the damage he had caused. But instead, she stood back appraising his handiwork, giving him kudos for originality. For the most part, she wasn't a melancholy Shapeshifter, but she seemed to be a quiet one. Even when she found something funny, she would simply nod her head and smile. Only when Cassius was slinging snarky comments about Lucinda did he hear her laugh aloud.

"I have a motherly lecture for you, and I'm not going to charge you admission."

A lecture? he thought, displaying a speculative glance. He sat down on the bench and an awkward silence followed, as he waited patiently for his lesson to begin.

Onoskelis' gaze turned to him. Not only had she given Cassius her solemn expression, but she also had the same penetrating stare when she was serious. "You seem to enjoy art a great deal."

"How do you know that?" He asked.

She nodded toward his bedroom. "A bit crude, but I get the theme you're going for. Death, Destruction, and Despair. The three Ds for a demon. You need to conquer your fears, Cass. Only then will you understand life in its entirety."

"Not as long as I stay here."

Onoskelis feigned a smile. "You depend on other demons too much," she told him. "Figure out the answers to the questions in your mind when you're by yourself. Throw all your frustrations away and concentrate on being stronger…both physically and mentally."

"So, that's what it takes to earn freedom? My strength?"

"We always have a choice to be free. At the right time and place, mind you. Never once, in those moments of perceived despair, did I point a finger at you and demand that you lose hope."

"All right. I'll do as you say. I'm going to better myself. Then you'll have no choice but to let me go."

"Have at it," Onoskelis told him. "I can't wait to see what you make of yourself."

During the next ten days, Cassius followed her instructions to the letter. He did calisthenics and a hundred pushups a day. He also read one book after another for hours on end. However, interacting with other demons was totally out of the question, despite his interest in making new friends. While around other demons in the mess hall, Onoskelis passed him off as her younger brother, however, she preferred keeping him to herself for the most part, until arrangements for his exchange were complete. She wanted her best friend Yokai back in her life, but meeting with Lucinda was dangerous, and she wasn't willing to risk her own life to make it happen. On top of everything else, if for any reason Onoskelis' plot became known, her shapeshifting ability would be absorbed by the Queen and her soul eaten, like all the other gifted beings that had mysteriously vanished from Hell.

Looking back now, she found herself troubled by sheer coincidence where Master Sergei was concerned. Shortly after Caleb's funeral, he discovered her roaming around Middle Earth, dressed in her leather armor. After telling her that he could retrieve Yokai's soul from Lucinda if she was willing to transform into his favorite whore, Onoskelis readily agreed. She foolishly convinced herself that generosity and kindness drove him to help her. But then he told her there was only one small condition. She had to bring Crighton's only living son to Hell to use as a bargaining tool in their trade deal. The Shapeshifter reminded herself that Ariel had a healthy daughter and Crighton to look after her. Like the fruit in her garden, he would give her more offspring, replacing the ones she had lost.

For the most part, Sergei's plan seemed reasonable enough. And it wasn't just that Onoskelis trusted him. She was beginning to have romantic feelings for him too. In a time when demons were self-centered and focused on their own issues and wellbeing, it was reassuring to know that he was willing to take risks for his closest friends. As he frequently told her, he ignored a troll that spit in his face because he understood the troll's motivations. He was someone who won't be heckled or stopped by hate; someone who continued to evolve, not perfectly, and was always open to new possibilities. Those were the reasons why Onoskelis trusted and adored Master Sergei. He would never do her wrong, never harm or deceive her. Or so she believed.

Before going to bed, Cassius once again asked the same question he'd been asking for months. The question that Onoskelis could never come up with an answer for. "Is it possible for you to contact my mother and ask if it's safe to come home? I miss them all so much."

The Shapeshifter feigned a smile. "I'll call and check tomorrow morning. But if the answer is still no, then you need to accept it. You need to continue living your life the way they would want you to...obedient, caring, and honest."

After Cassius went to sleep in his cavernous bedroom, Onoskelis closed the door and waited in her quarters for Master Sergei to show up for his weekly visit. He arrived right on time in his black tailored suit with his matching black patch over one eye, looking as handsome as ever.

"How's it going?" He asked her. "Is he still giving you grief?"

"Not more than usual. He's a growing boy and is driven by curiosity."

Master Sergei pursed his lips and nodded his head approvingly. "In two weeks from now, Cassius should be ready for sex education classes, and I can sense how eager you are to teach him."

"You have a sick mind," she hissed. "Has anyone ever told you that?"

"I believe that's what you enjoy most about me. How about you change into Clio, and I'll prove just how sick I am?"

"Later. Right now, I need to know how much longer I'm expected to keep Cass here? You promised to talk to Lucinda and help me get Yokai back. Why is it taking so long?"

"It's a rather complicated matter. Lucinda needs to trust me completely to let go of a soul with such talent as Yokai's. Especially when she enjoys it so much. Why only yesterday, I saw her change into Tyrus. She's got his physique down pat, even the way he walks. But she needs to work on his voice and—"

"I understand, Master Sergei. Honestly, I do. But I spoke to a shaman yesterday that knew all about reintegrating lost souls. He told me it was only possible if a body remained intact. So, I need to know what Lucinda did with the bodies of the beings she absorbed. Is there a place she stores them? Can I find Yokai's body in a storage room of some sort?"

"I'm still trying to find out, Ono. My meeting with Castiel…I mean Lucinda will bring this matter to an abrupt end. I'm working as hard as I can to finalize the correct time and place for our meeting."

"Please listen to me, Master Sergei. I can't stay here any longer. I'm being followed by soldiers, and Cassius has become inquisitive and demanding. There's no telling what would happen if he was left alone for an extended period."

Master Sergei snorted. "He's never alone in Hell. Where can he possibly go without someone leading the way?"

She glared at the Knight of Darkness in the flickering torch light. "You don't seem to understand. If his identity is discovered by members of Lucinda's army, he'll be dead within minutes. Or worse yet, if some bleeding-heart female finds him alone, she'll escape with Cass and bring his entire family back here to kill me...and possibly you as well."

He let loose a long impatient sigh. "My dear, sweet Ono, you need to learn how to relax. Believe it or not, there are reliable demons in Hell, individuals I can call upon. The fact that I'm here proves my loyalty to you, right?"

Loyalty? She leaned in and pressed him further. "I don't understand, Master Sergei. Why are you helping me? What's in it for you?"

He reached out his hand and stroked her back, as if he were soothing a neglected puppy. "Like I told you before, I'm an equal opportunity defender and my schedule fills up quickly. However, I've made a point of visiting you whenever I can. Isn't that true?"

Onoskelis reluctantly nodded.

"Tomorrow, I will be meeting with Queen Lucinda, just as I promised. Then the emotional and physical injury I suffered years ago will be addressed by handing over Cassius Daemonium. This will, of course, aggravate his father and bring him running to Hell. His father Castiel will be pulled into the situation, and both of their heads will be lopped off and delivered to Queen Lucinda, securing my position beside her."

"And what about Yokai? She's the reason for all of this, isn't she?"

"I believe we still need to discuss that matter in greater detail, which I plan to address. I just need a little encouragement that I believe you're capable of giving." Master Sergei rubbed the bulge in his pants and leered at the Shapeshifter in a provocative way. "Well, do I get to play with Clio or what? You do want your girlfriend back, don't you? I can't imagine how much she's missed you. Your reunion will be unlike anything I've witnessed before."

Onoskelis lowered her eyelids. She imagined Lucifer's favorite whore and changed into her before Master Sergei's eyes, bondage dress and all. However, she had taken on Clio true appearance with her long black and red piercing eyes.

"What the Hell? I don't like this look! I want the Clio you became before. The one with the blonde hair and blue eyes...and large sexy lips. Change into that incubus! I demand it!"

Onoskelis licked her lips and smiled. "You will have what you want when I have what I need...and not a second sooner, Master Sergei."

"What if I refuse to deliver Yokai? Then what choice will you have? Just think about that. You'll have no recourse but to please me or face your own death. Is that what you really want? Or are you willing to service me the way I wish and receive the reward I promised months ago?"

They looked at each other, neither of them willing to back down. "So, what's your decision, beautiful?" he asked. "Accommodate me or watch me walk away. Just remember every step brings us closer to the top of the mountain," he said. "The end will be worth it. Just try to remember what's at stake here."

Onoskelis narrowed her brow. "And what exactly does *that* mean?"

"Simple. Let me get my rocks off, Ono, the way we both want. When we're both satisfied, then our plans will continue."

"And they are?"

"Don't let that tadpole out of your sight. Just try to be strong a little while longer, Ono, and we'll get what we deserve...I promise."

He couldn't have said it better. Neither concession nor command. Just a statement, the best possibility for both of them.

"Patience," he said again. "Just until Crighton is dead and Castiel accepts his defeat."

"But that could take weeks. Cassius will run off if he finds out what I've done—"

Exasperation crossed Sergei's face. "He'll never know our plans, unless you reveal them." He shook his head, self-protection outweighing decency. "It won't be long now. I've done everything I can on my end. Either Lucinda cooperates or—"

"I'm done for." She had meant to reassure him that she would never challenge his authority, never question his carefully laid plans. But as he spoke, she heard his words as a slap against her cheek. Whimpering, she leaned into him, the first time in years that they had openly held each other. In the interest of getting all the wrongs right, he might forgive her for everything. Even her conflicting emotions where Ariel was concerned.

How could this have happened? How could I have been so wrong? Onoskelis asked herself. Like any demon who had been duped, she was saying very little. After emptying her home of every possession, she found temporary shelter in the woods. Perseus, the expert tracker who could hold still and disappear into thin air, helped her when no one was looking. His plot to capture Cassius after disposing of his soulless twin brother was perfect, until he discovered Master Sergei's involvement.

When all was said and done, Perseus promised to keep up the ruse if his sister was kept safe. In the meantime, Cassius was so vulnerable and naive that Onoskelis felt sorry for him. He followed her everywhere, hiding in the shadows, making sure their secret walks through Hell brought them back to their safe place. Her face brightened at seeing him smiling at the simplest things: a spider tangled in its own web, a dancing flame on the wall, a blind mouse running in circles. His blond, shoulder-length hair swayed as he walked, stirring twisted thoughts in her mind. She wanted to educate him in the black arts, to train him on how to please a female demon or a Shapeshifter, like herself. He was so beautiful, so flawless that it was hard to remember his purpose for being there. Although she wanted to keep him to herself for long as possible, she knew Master Sergei had other ideas in mind. His promise to restore Yokai to her former self was her sole reason for taking Cassius in the first place. She hated disappointing Ariel, but her own well-being had to come first, or she would never be happy. Besides, Ariel had Samara and Crighton in her life, and too much happiness could spoil a demon in an angel's body. At least, that's what she told herself.

"So?" Master Sergei asked. "Are you willing to deliver what I asked for? Or is this the end of our arrangement, Ono?"

Before he could say more, Onoskelis became the blonde bimbo he'd been asking for. She unzipped his pants and felt around for his cock. Finding him semi-erect, she dropped to her knees and took him into her mouth. He grew hard, but not as big or thick as usual. As he moaned, she felt a small amount of pre-cum on her tongue, surprisingly tasting like raspberry. She stroked him while licking his tip and teasing his crown, inhaling all of him as she sucked faster and faster. Onoskelis sensed that he wanted to tell her that he was about to come but thought better of it. After pleasing him for another minute, he exploded in her mouth in three quick squirts, and surprisingly, she climaxed at the same time.

"I'll stay in touch," Sergei said, zipping his pants up. "Just keep to the plan. Everything will work out great. You'll see."

The next day, Cassius was waiting outside her door. Making their way through an unusually crowded corridor, Onoskelis noticed two female succubus creatures sashaying toward them.

Word had it they were new additions in the Pleasure Quarters and were still being trained in the art of seduction.

One of them grabbed Cassius' arm and pulled him closer. "Hey there, Cutie. We could have a lot of fun together, you and me. There's this great spot I know where no one goes anymore. It's dark, quiet, and soundproof. The perfect place for a little one-on-one exploration if you know what I mean."

Cassius glanced at Onoskelis, and then back at the wanton creature. "I'm afraid the answer has to be no."

"Come on! Wouldn't you like to experience the joy of sex?" she taunted. "To know what *real* demons do behind closed doors?"

"I said no. Now move along. I don't know how much clearer I can make it."

"Wow...can you believe this guy?" the succubus said to her friend. "I just offered him a free double-header and he had the audacity to say no. It seems this one prefers men over women. Isn't that right, pretty boy?"

Cassius looked at her hard, while attempting to pry her hand from his muscular bicep. Then something drastically changed in his temperament. He became extremely angry, and his eyes began glowing pure white. Within seconds, they flashed with such intensity that the wanton creatures ran away, fearing for their lives.

Oh, shit! Onoskelis stared at Cassius, standing alone with adrenaline coursing through his veins and a scowl darkening his face. She quickly dismissed any sympathy she felt for him in an instant. True, he grabbed her only two days earlier and kissed her crudely and forcibly, but that kiss wasn't an insult. She believed her flirtatious behavior and his curiosity caused him to behave badly, plus he was practically oozing testosterone. As he tried to explain his bold actions, shame ruled his emotions. He sat quietly writing a note to her in terms of the most unmanly contrition, ascribing his wrong doings and imploring her forgiveness.

"Don't worry," she told him. "I've been kissed before. There's nothing to forgive."

Cassius looked down, shaking his head. "I don't know what's gotten into me lately. I'm so sorry."

"Don't beat yourself up. I forgot all about it and so should you." The matter was dropped, and their relationship became platonic once again.

Their daily routine now included walking through remote areas of Hell. However, occasionally, he shifted his gaze from the stone walls around them to one of the dark, winding tunnels ahead of them, and the questions would begin all over again.

"When can I go home? I miss my family, Ono. Why can't I leave here?" When he turned toward her, his face caught the glow of a wall-lit torch, and she noticed the piercing gleam in his blue eyes—so childlike, so innocent, so demanding.

"I keep reminding you that I was asked by your family to keep you safe. To keep you away from Queen Lucinda, and there's no better place than under her nose. She'd never think to look for you here. When the time is right and it's safe for us, we will leave here together. I promise."

It was becoming harder and harder to lie to Cassius. The Shapeshifter realized he'd been listening to the sounds around them, growing louder every day. She explained away the tumult of shouting and screaming on the other side of stone walls as military training, which seemed to satisfy him to some degree. But then she grew to hate him because of his unwavering trust.

One day, Onoskelis stepped away for a few minutes to receive an update from a fellow soldier. During her absence, Cassius walked into the mouth of a dark tunnel. But his confidence vanished as quick as it came. He returned to his familiar surroundings and sat down on the stone bench. Then he investigated the void, waiting for her to return.

Quite remarkably, Cassius confessed his temptation to leave and fully expected to be punished. Picking up a rock, he pitched it into the void. The sound of hitting the ground never came back. Sitting by himself, he looked like a sculpture carved in the stone of the Rim, giving the impression of complete isolation. Sadness, it seemed, was threatening to overwhelm him and Onoskelis was powerless to act.

After telling him endless war stories, she wondered if he was thinking about the death-defying battles his grandfather might have summoned him to lead—of the pain, hatred, and death that would have resulted in both Heaven and Hell. Lately, they had been so close that she seemed to divine his thoughts. In those moments, she found herself softening toward him. Her body quivered and stirred with an intangible feeling that was akin to pain, yet too deep for her full understanding. She felt sorry for Cassius, until her pride resurged. Failure wasn't in her vocabulary but there were glimmers of doubt in her mind.

What if Sergei couldn't convince Lucinda to restore Yokai? She remembered her passionate lover's interest in all things, the wonder and admiration, the glowing copper light in her eyes. Cassius had not been repugnant to her, until she thought about the Changeling again. He might be flawless, almost angelic in so many ways, but she had her heart set on Yokai.

Bah! He's not a miracle child, she told herself. *I'd hate him even more if he was.*

Suddenly, Onoskelis felt cold shivers steal over her body. Cassius' eyes were fixed on the hidden door leading to the closest exit from Hell. Her breath hitched and her mind raced. If he discovered a way out, she would meet her death the moment Crighton got hold of her.

"Is there something troubling you?" Onoskelis asked, hoping to capture the young boy's attention.

"It's been quiet lately, which makes me wonder if it's a good time to leave."

"That all depends on Lucinda and her army. Protecting you is still my priority, but I will ask Master Sergei on his next visit. Believe it or not, I'd like to know too."

He turned away from the hidden door and seemed to be a little put out.

"Is there a reason why you're asking? If you're bored from sitting so much, we could go for a walk and talk about—"

He stepped closer and took her hand. Her cold, insensible hand that couldn't feel his touch even if she willed it.

"I would like to be your boyfriend, Ono," he said in a hushed voice. "I'm willing to live here forever if you'd like. For your sake."

"*My* sake?"

"That's right. But I don't know if we should. You seem to be more frightened and unsure of yourself with each passing day. But you don't have to worry with me here. I'm strong enough to protect you now and won't let anything bad happen to you. Even if Lucinda and her army finds me…and Master Sergei continues to disappoint you."

Although his intention was to please her, everything he said troubled her. He was developing supernatural powers when it came to intuition, which enabled him to read thoughts, and sense feelings and emotions.

"In two more months, I won't be a child any longer. We can be soulmates if we want…like my father and mother. We're physically attracted to one another anyway, are we not? And we only have ourselves to think about."

Onoskelis shook her head. "You forget, Cass, your family has always been important to you, and their opinions matter greatly. I'm sure they wouldn't approve of our bond. We have a dozen years between us, and you have so much yet to learn. Plus, we're different in other ways too—"

Cassius' lips curled but not into the charming smile she was accustomed to seeing. He was snarling. "Just because we're different doesn't mean we're incompatible."

Onoskelis shrugged. The hardest part about visiting Middle Earth was relearning emotions and how to express them. Now that she was back in Hell, her emotions were stuck on overdrive. She wanted to shut them off more than anything, but Cassius was making it difficult.

"You can love someone so much," she told him. "But you can never love them as much as you'll miss them when they're gone. That's how I feel about my best friend Yokai. She means the world to me and always will."

"So, I don't?" Cassius began pacing back and forth in front of his bedroom chamber again, like a caged animal preparing to strike. Then he halted in place and looked toward the entrance of winding tunnel, leading to a dozen dark destinations. She had brought him here to this cavernous sinkhole, as far away from Lucinda's mansion and the Gates of Hell as possible. No one in their right mind would come here. Especially Crighton Daemonium. That thought alone gave the Shapeshifter a small slice of peace. Although, lately, she was questioning her judgment and the actions that brought her here.

"How do you get over someone who was never yours?" Cassius asked. "Who do you blame when you've broken your own heart?"

When she didn't answer, he stomped childishly into his room, closing the door behind him.

The air suddenly chilled, alerting her to someone's presence. Looking up, she noticed a blue jay sitting in an alcove above her and a red squirrel chattering his shrill annoyance from a hole in the wall. These two denizens had tracked her down and would make her presence known. As she watched them, pure dread washed over her.

These Woodland Shapeshifters were nocturnal creatures, unlike Onoskelis. They relied heavily on their sharp sight and hearing. Their survivalist skills helped them while hunting in any environment. To evade the threat of predators, like Lucinda and her guards, their senses had evolved to extraordinary levels, allowing them to hear at a higher frequency than bats. They could elude their enemies and spring into action before an attack came their way. There was no doubt in Onoskelis' mind that they had come here searching for Cassius. The only questions that remained were who had sent them and how much time did they have to escape.

Before her eyes, they transformed into two ebony-haired demons, identically in every way.

One of them approached Onoskelis with his lips pulled back, exposing his pointy white teeth. His green flaring eyes were darting all over the place, just as they would in his rodent form. "My name is Sham, and this is Morph," he said. "We've been tasked with finding deserters and bringing them back into the fold. Are you Onoskelis, the Imperial Shapeshifter? Is this where you've been hiding?"

She swallowed hard and reluctantly nodded.

"And do you have a captive with you? A young demon you've been passing off as your brother?"

She hesitated before nodding again.

"We have been aware of your actions for some time now. It is difficult to avoid Hell's Intelligence in the dark," Sham told her. "You must cease this charade and follow your orders. If you don't return to basic training immediately, you'll be swimming in the Lake of Fire by nightfall."

"And what about the boy?" Onoskelis asked. "I can't leave him alone. He is my responsibility. My charge."

"You should have considered that before taking him. Now we must deal with this mess and make it all go away. If your commander learns what you've been up to, you won't be long for this world. I can promise you that."

Morph looked at Sham. "You know I never make special requests like this, but maybe we could cut her a break. As far as I can tell, no real harm has been done…aside from abandoning her post and keeping a boy away from his family."

Sham shrugged his shoulders. "I don't know. We were tasked with solving this problem. The only way I can see that happening is to claim the boy was lost. But we would need to bring him to his father and guarantee the return of this soldier to her base. Are you okay with that, Morph?"

He paused before nodding his agreement.

Sham turned back to Onoskelis. "You better get going then. We're breaking a few rules here and Queen Lucinda won't be pleased if word gets back to her. The fact is, we're putting our lives on the line for a fellow Shapeshifter. You're just lucky we have that much in common."

Onoskelis reached into a deep hole in the wall and withdrew her black bag. Inside of it was her army-issued armor and a Spartan Legions helmet. She secured the leather armor over her clothes and tucked her helmet under her arm. Then she opened the hidden rock-covered door. Behind it was a winding tunnel that branched off in three directions—one leading to Hell's Gate, the second leading to the army barracks, and the third to the corridor outside the Knight of Darkness headquarters.

"Please tell the child I'm sorry," she said. "I was trying to save my best friend...an innocent Changeling named Yokai."

Morph shook his head. "Unfortunately, we know about her. Queen Lucinda made short work of her six weeks ago. If someone told you they could bring her back to life, they'd have to be the greatest magician in the world...or God himself."

Onoskelis gasped. "It can't be true! How do you know that?"

"We know a great many things," Sham said, "including the danger you've put yourself in by being here. Master Sergei gave you up. That's how we found you. He's pretending to be a hero to up his standing in the Knights of Darkness. Word has it, he's claiming you kidnapped Cassius because you can't have children of your own."

Onoskelis looked down, feeling the weight of the world pressing down on her. "But that isn't true. I swear!"

"It doesn't matter what the truth is. You created your own agenda, and that's a serious offense. It's time you realized you're a member of a winning team. By volunteering to be a soldier in Lucinda's army, you're also a hero for Hell," Morph told her. "But if you ignore our warning and run off, mark my words, you will be found by Trackers. Your soul will be devoured by the Queen and your body turned to ash in one of her blazing furnaces."

"Then I guess I have no choice." Onoskelis stepped inside the tunnel, unaware that Cassius was watching her from the crack in his bedroom door. Within seconds, she disappeared. But the mystery remained on which way she went.

The bedroom door opened wider.

"Are you Crighton's son?" Sham asked.

Cassius remained silent. Then he opened his door all the way.

"We were sent here to find you. Your mother has been worried sick, and I believe your father is searching for you right now...in the Knights of Darkness corridor. They'll be thrilled to have you back home, exactly where you belong."

Cassius furrowed his brow. "What about Onoskelis? If we leave without asking permission, she'll be terribly upset."

The Woodland Shapeshifters looked at each other and laughed wholeheartedly. "If you're worried about disappointing your kidnapper," Sham said, "you've got bigger problems than we thought."

Morph smiled at Cassius then he turned back to his friend, keeping his voice low. "What about the Red War? This boy is a priceless commodity. It's rumored that his grandfather is leading the first wave against Hell."

"The Red War is of no concern to us. This boy is being returned to Crighton...the way we planned. Sadly, Onoskelis will be captured and taken to the Lake of Fire to suffer the consequences of her actions. And as for us, we're meeting Master Sergei at the Sand Pit to collect our reward...the large bag of sapphires for a job well done."

"But what if Master Sergei doesn't show up at the Sand Pit?" Morph asked. "What if he ditches us and reneges on his promise? What recourse will we have?"

"You and I will search him out, which shouldn't be problem. Then we'll turn ourselves into Hecate and Lucinda once again and stretch him on the rack, tearing him limb from limb. How does that sound, Bro?"

Morph rubbed his hands together, smiling. "Bloody good, I'd say. Bloody good. But what if he agrees to give up the jewels after we torture him. What do we do with him then?"

"Why, the same thing, of course," Sham answered. "As I'm sure you're aware, the dead can't cry out for justice, especially when they don't deserve it."

CHAPTER 23

LONE SURVIVOR

Lucinda's eagle-eyed soldiers were quickly becoming well-trained marksmen and expert fighting machines. She was following the guidebook of Preston Defense, demanding that her army march twenty miles a day wearing their armor, packs, and weapons. Outings included crossing rivers and bridges and using battering rams to smash their way into buildings on Middle Earth. After a long day's march, they practiced ariel fighting, using their newly acquired demon wings. Then they spent hours sharpening the swords and spears housed in the armory.

Samara passed by groups of them wearing her black-hooded jacket, masking her face in dark shadow. Several of them greeted her with a nod, believing she was a recruit on her way to the training grounds. Remarkably, she managed to slip past all of them by simply grunting and keeping her feet moving. There was something to be said about confidence and acting with purpose.

After reaching the armory, she wove around distracted soldiers and retrieved her bow and quiver. Then, on her way out, she passed by a centurion, guarding the door.

"Off to practice?" he asked, smiling.

She nodded and kept her eyes down.

"I have three committed sons like you, I'm proud to say. Keep up the good work and one day soon you'll all be strong warriors in the Red War."

Samara remained silent under her hood.

"Well, get on with it then," the centurion said. "I'm sure your instructor is waiting."

She nodded a second time and continued walking. When she reached the elevators, she removed the bow from her shoulder and locked a pentagram-engraved arrow in place, ready to fire at any given moment. Then some disparaging news reached her. A nearby soldier was relaying a story about the elevators dropping earlier that day, crushing the workers beneath them.

"You should've seen it, Ordo. Mangled bodies, and blood and gore everywhere. Guess we'll be taking the stairs and exercising in the mining tunnels for the next few days."

Damn it. Taking the fastest route to the third level prison cells was now out of the question. Begrudgingly, Samara detoured through a second tunnel and heard two guards at the end of it, arguing over their favorite succubus.

"That's not true. Vergara has the best rack."

"But Clio gives the best head."

"You're right about that!" They both chuckled and enthusiastically nodded.

Samara hung back, hoping they would move on, taking their nasty tales with them. Instead, they leaned back against the wall, lit cigarettes, and appeared to be in no hurry. She noticed a maintenance tunnel in the corner just beyond them. However, she needed a distraction to use it. Exchanging the demon arrow for a regular one and taking careful aim, she shot a wall torch a hundred yards away. It dropped with an echoing thud to the ground, sending them running towards it. With only seconds to spare, she made a mad dash for the adjacent tunnel then waited to hear if she was discovered. When no one came she moved on, keeping an eye out for any sudden movements. She reached a graveled section and cringed from the crunching sound under her boots. Eventually, she reached the end of the rocky pathway. But there was a split divide, leading in opposite directions.

Damn it! This is a maze! Which way do I go?

With no map to follow, Samara had to trust her instincts. The path inside the right tunnel slanted upward, while the left continued downward. She took a deep breath and stepped through the left opening. The air gradually warmed as she walked.

When she was much younger, Ariel told her a story about the cell her father and Tyrus had rescued her from, teetering on the edge of a cliff. "The heat inside the room was unbearable," she had said. "If not for Tyrus and your father, Lilith and I would've never gotten out."

Go toward the heat, she told herself. *That's where the cells are... that's where I'll find them.*

It was dim inside the stronghold, and the first torch she crossed that burned with black flames mesmerized her long enough to lose sight of the uneven ground. She stumbled and was about to fall when a hand grabbed her wrist, pulling her back. To her stunned disbelief, she came face to face with an armor-clad solider wearing a black Kaldor helmet.

Ah, shit! A black knight!

"Shhh!" He held a finger to her lips. "We're not alone."

"No kidding. Are there dragons in here too?"

He spun her around again, wrapped his arm around her shoulders, and covered her mouth with his hand. She struggled, trying to free herself, but it was no use. He was holding her tight against him, restricting her movements. She stomped her heel on his instep, but it had no effect on his armor-clad feet.

"Calm down" he whispered beneath his helmet. "There's no need for that. I'm here to help you."

I know that voice. I know it! Who the Hell is he?

Samara felt a jab in her neck. He released his tight hold, and she staggered before him, gazing up into brown eyes that gave every indication he could read her mind. Her vision blurred and her eyelids grew heavy, making it difficult to see. She tried to walk away from him, sliding her hand along the wall to remain upright. Yet, no matter how hard she tried, her eyes wouldn't stay open. Her legs stopped working. Her heart sank, and she dropped to the ground, knowing she was in serious trouble.

When she finally came to, pitch blackness surrounded her, and the air was hot. Her brain ached and felt as if it were swollen, pushing against her skull. The upholstery under her hands felt rough and the smell of fresh pine filled the air—a familiar scent from the logs her father split every morning. Her ankles were cinched to the legs of a chair and her wrists zip-tied to the arms. Desperate to free herself, she struggled against them, rubbing her skin raw in the process. She took a deep breath and closed her eyes, expecting to hear at least something around her. But there was nothing. It was as if she'd been dropped into a vacuum, syphoning the air and all reality from her life.

She cried out for help, but of course, no one came. Sighing, she admitted defeat, at least for the time being.

"Hi gorgeous. It's about time you woke up," a familiar voice said. His chuckle came from the other side of the room.

It couldn't be him. Could it? The last time she'd seen Damian's friend was when Lucinda transformed him into a detestable, slimy creature.

"Warwick? Is that really you?"

"None other. You have great hearing and a remarkable memory. More assets to add to my growing list."

"Why are you doing this? I've never done anything to you. I don't even know you."

He ignored her question. "Your escape ruined the lives of three demons, and now you're back again. Are you a glutton for punishment, or what?"

"I'm here for my family! Your psycho mother imprisoned my parents, and she has my little brother too."

"She must be hungry for souls again."

Fresh panic rushed through Samara's veins. She struggled harder than ever to break free. Bright lights suddenly filled the room, temporarily blinding her. When she could see again, she scanned the room, desperate to find a way out. But she saw none—only Warwick, sitting on the other side of the room, analyzing her with his large, uncertain brown eyes. He raised a glass of water to his thin lips, like he was sipping a cocktail and didn't bother to ask if she was thirsty. His armor had been replaced with a buttoned-up white shirt and ragged black jeans.

"Come on, Warwick, "she said sweetly. "Enough with the games. Let me go. You have no reason to keep me here…"

"Oh, but I do. A very good one."

"Which is?"

"I want you. That's why."

Samara could feel heat creeping up her neck and looked away, tugging desperately at the menacing ties on her wrists. When she looked back, his eyes were still on her.

"You're hurting yourself. Stop that! NOW!"

She remained still, watching him. The brash character she'd met weeks earlier had digressed into a twisted, volatile character.

"Please stop," he added softly, pushing his brown hair out of his eyes. "There's no need to struggle, Sam. The ties are only necessary until I'm sure I can trust you."

"Trust me? Are you out of your fucking mind?" She sighed and relaxed in her seat, glaring at him. "What do you want from me, Warwick?"

He stood up and began pacing in front of her. "Well, if you really must know, I'm going to use you as my personal weapon." He smiled maniacally, sending a shiver down her spine. "Your ability to teleport between worlds is remarkable and of great interest to me. With my expert knowledge and your exceptional talent, we're going to create an army of superior soldiers, destroying Arch-demons and Archangels alike. Together, we'll destroy Heaven and rule Hell."

"And just how are you going to do that?"

"By breeding, of course. I have stupendous stamina and energy. I've seen my mother's special forces…large and muscular, the kind of men suited to military training or prizefighting. They were built from your father's seed, but no time was spent on educating them. They're dumb and indecisive. They can be told to do practically anything. We could easily overtake them with an organized, unstoppable force."

Samara rolled her eyes. "You can't be serious."

"Oh, but I am…completely. I've been thinking about this for a while now…after Damian told me about your special gift."

Are you kidding me? Damian told him. Samara looked down, shaking her head.

"I'm hoping you'll train me," he continued, "and pass your knowledge on to our team—"

"I have no idea what you're talking about. I can't do anything special. I have no abilities. Isn't it obvious? If I could, I wouldn't be here right now, would I?" Then she added in a mocking voice, "Oh, and good luck on screwing yourself an army. I'm not spreading my legs for anyone, especially you."

Warwick glared at her, and she looked away, trying her best to stay strong.

"You're going to change your mind, after you see how good I am."

"Really? And who have you been practicing on? *Yourself?*" She laughed, hoping to humiliate him.

"Oh, you'd be amazed. During my one-day visit to Earth, I impregnated three married women, deflowered six virgins, raped two men, and broke up four families. And that was just a warmup exercise. When it comes to fucking, it's all about enjoying the ride. But then you wouldn't know about that, would you?" He shoved his hair back on his head and it fell into place, partially covering one eye.

Normally, she wasn't easily shocked, but his disgusting claims appalled her. "You should be really proud of yourself...harming defenseless humans."

He quirked a smile. "I was sowing my wild oats, as they say... getting ready for you, Sam."

"Come on, get real," she said. "You can't honestly believe I would give birth to soldiers to help you take over the world. I'd kill myself first. Don't flatter me with your ridiculous claims and assumptions."

Warwick jumped up and crossed the room. There was red in his eyes as he stood over her, and she realized death was staring down at her—daring her to challenge his authority. But she didn't cower. She was past all that.

"I don't know what confining me here is going to accomplish," she growled.

"We're all mentally imprisoned, whether you want to believe it or not. You live in your dream world in Middle Earth, but you can't escape from what you are."

"And just what do you think I am?"

"My perfect mate, of course."

"But what about your mother? I imagine she'd be pretty upset after hearing your plans."

Warwick roared like a wounded animal. He slammed his fists on the top of the chair then leaned in close. "My mother had me beaten!" Anger and humiliation were boiling up inside him, spilling over in a froth of rage. "Beaten brutally in my own home…here where I've lived over half my life. And after all I've done for her!"

"Hmm…seems you can know everything in the world and still make bad decisions."

He huffed. "That's your response? You disappoint me, Sam. You're no better than she is."

"Well, at least you're safe now, which is far more than I can say for myself."

Warwick furrowed his brow in frustration. "You know nothing. You are just mewling quim. I will rule Hell one way or another. And you will help me, or I will personally see to it that you endure a slow, painful death. Is that what you need to hear?"

Samara feigned a smile. "Yeah, sure…whatever."

"I mean it! I'll destroy you!"

As he towered over her, looking furtive and enraged, Samara caught a whiff of alcohol on his breath. Her first thought was he'd been drinking, though she knew the rigid code in Hell forbade it. Still, she wouldn't put it past him to break every rule, since rebellion seemed to be his sole purpose for living.

"You don't scare me, Warwick," she fumed. "You can't just grab someone and expect them to do whatever you want. It doesn't work that way. Especially with me." She could feel her whole body quaking inside, despite her brave words. "Your mother wasn't kind to me either, but do I blame you? Come on...find someone else to bear your soldiers. I am not the right demon for you."

Warwick ceased talking and continued to stare fiercely at her, as though Samara had become the embodiment of his mother. He swore bitterly under his breath. Then he drove his fist into the rock wall above her, sending stone fragments flying and blood splattering from his torn fist.

Samara was shaken to the core, but still refused to yield. After debating on a way to reach him, she attempted a new approach. "I honestly don't know why she insists on being cruel. Your mother obviously has no appreciation for the wonderful son you are."

In a dazed sort of fascination for her sympathy, Warwick stared down at her for endless seconds. Then he lowered his head, and his eyes began wandering furtively about him. Without volition, there flashed the unbidden thought in Samara's mind that he resembled a vulture—the same hideous creature she'd seen staring at her in a dream. Uttering a stifled little cry, she saw him swing his gaze toward her. She shrank back, as if anticipating a blow. But then she heard him snicker and looked up to see him shaking his head.

"You're a pathetic, manipulating cunt. I don't know why I'm wasting my time with you when you obviously have no appreciation for my plans." He placed a hand under her chin, lifting it up so she was looking directly into his eyes. "Need I remind you? You've reached an age where your emotions rule your mind. You act so strong and brave, but I know you're not. You're as weak as the arrows in your quiver. As pitiful as your antiquated bow. If I wanted to, I could tie you to my bedposts right now and fuck you day and night, filling your belly with my superior seed. But what's the point in making you miserable? I'm giving you a chance here to be part of something great. Open your ears and stop complaining. Don't reject something you're not capable of understanding." He pushed her face away from him and walked toward the archway. A raven flew out of the adjoining room, landing on the Y-shaped wood perch bolted into a nearby wall.

Samara stared wide-eyed. "What…what's that?"

Warwick turned back around. "Beautiful, isn't she? Just a little pet I acquired from a subpar creature. She used black magic to restore my body after restoring her own. Then she seduced me with her promises of love. For ten days, we fucked like rabbits, until her charms wore off. Then I saw her for what she really was. An ugly, middle-aged sexual deviant. Of course, I had no choice but to kill her." He snorted a laugh. "Anyway, take a little time to mull over my proposition. I'll expect your answer in say…two hours."

"You're crazy! I'm not going to abandon my family for you."

Warwick snorted. "Mark my words, you're going to beg me to save you from Lucifer. You're going to fall madly in love with me, Sam. When that happens, we'll rule Hell together, provided you give me what I want. And don't go thinking some white knight is going to rescue you. Damian Hunter and his band of incompetent lowlifes couldn't be bothered to help the likes of you. Believe me, I know that better than anyone."

He turned away from her and strode into the next room. The lights in the ceiling dimmed, leaving her in semi-darkness. She stayed very still for a few minutes. Filled with fear. Not frightened by Warwick, but of the unknown. She was certain he was watching her. *Very* certain. She could hear a camera in the room refocusing, delivering tight shots of her to his phone or computer, or whatever he was using to gain his information.

You'll beg me to save you from Lucifer. How could that be right? Lucifer was long gone, wasn't he? Lucinda had taken his place after his blazing demise.

You're going to fall madly in love with me. Was Warwick really that arrogant? Why would she even consider his offer? He said nothing about rescuing her family—about freeing them and allowing them to live a peaceful existence when the war was over. She wanted to scream and remind herself about the terrible things he had said. How he had yelled at her and called her an unmentionable name. But an idiotic part of her wanted to believe he was redeemable...that he deserved a second chance—she knew what it was like to be mistreated by your own mother.

Samara shook her head. *What was in that shot?* She wanted to erase Warwick's twisted conversation from her mind. Erase every thought of him. Then something occurred to her. The perfect means for escape.

"Warwick?" she called out. "I know you're watching me right now, so let's take a few minutes to discuss our options, shall we?" She sighed, waiting for a reply.

Nothing.

Samara continued anyway. "You want me to help you overthrow Lucifer, is that right? By the way, I had no idea he was still around. Talk about modern miracles..."

Still nothing.

"I'd like to know more about you and your battle plans. So, let's discuss this whole matter. You know, get to know each other better. It's not a bad idea, taking over Hell. I've never been particularly fond of Lucinda anyway, and her father...well, I've never personally met the guy, but I've heard some horrid stories. And then there's Heaven to think about, which might prove a greater

challenge. I understand God doesn't take guff from anyone…
demons or humans alike." She waited for a reply.

The sound of the door opening answered her. Warwick
strolled into the room, the lights grew brighter, and she could
see his face was completely devoid of emotion. When their eyes
met, he pushed his hair off his forehead—a habit of his apparently. "What's the point in bringing me here?" he asked. "Is this
part of a plan you've concocted to escape?"

"No. It just seems to me you're trying hard to act like a bad
guy. But honestly, I don't see it. And at the same time, I can't
even consider doing as you say, until I know who I'm dealing
with. Right now, you know very little about me. So, let's…get
acquainted." She smiled, hoping to earn his trust.

He sighed and sat down in his chair.

Samara jerked at the bands on her wrists. "Are these really
necessary? I mean…where can I possibly go?"

Warwick gave her that twisted little smile again. "I'll remove
them when I'm certain you won't escape. Now, let's forget all
that for a while. Tell me a secret that no one knows."

"A secret? What are we, seven? Like what?"

"Just share something personal, and we'll go from there."

She racked her brain. "I was in love once. When he died, I
thought my life was over. Then I met his brother and all the feelings rushed back."

"Damian Hunter, right?"

"I don't know why I'm telling you this. You obviously know
all about him."

"But do you love him, Sam? That's the big question."

"I don't know that I ever did or ever will. Damian reminded
me why I don't trust anyone."

"What about your family? Do you trust them?"

"I'm trying to."

"Why is *that* so hard?"

"My real mother couldn't bond with my father because he was tricked into becoming a soulmate with Ariel, a young guardian angel. Lucifer wanted to devour her soul, but when he discovered she was dying and my mother Lilith was protecting her, he imprisoned them. Ultimately, my mother took her own life to save my father and gave her body to Ariel to save me. She loved us that much. She loved him that much."

"That's...crazy."

"So, now that you know about my family, are you going to help me?"

"Doesn't sound like they're worth saving."

"What's that supposed to mean?"

"There's no point in driving yourself mad over them. You might as well give in and save your sanity."

Samara screamed at him and flashed the light in her eyes, but he wasn't impressed. Drawing into herself, she wished she hadn't shared anything, especially her feelings about Damian.

Warwick pulled his wristband over his wrist with a jerk. "Anything else?"

"Just help me free my father and uncle. Please..." Her eyes glistened with emotion. "They came here looking for Ariel and Cassius. If you do this for me, then I'll seriously consider your offer."

"Hmm, I don't know. I'm going to have to think about it."

"Lucinda is clearly involved, and I know how much you hate her. On top of everything else, she created clones of my father and is planning to use them against my grandfather."

"And he is?"

"Castiel."

"You're kidding, right? The leader of the Archangels is your grandfather? But he's an angel."

"And my grandmother is a demon. So what?"

"That means you're one quarter Nephilim."

"Yeah, I suppose I am. What about it?"

Warwick chuckled. "I just wanted to hear you say it."

Samara shook her head, not understanding. "Why?"

"Because that makes you no better than me. No better than any of the whores in Hell."

"I HATE YOU!" she screamed, still trying to pull her hands free. "You had no intention of letting me go. You knew all along who I was and still insisted on tormenting me. You're an asshole, Warwick! A fucking asshole!"

Warwick sat in his cushioned chair, resting a black box on his lap. "What are you going do about it, Sam? Absolutely nothing, that's what."

"You despicable piece of shit!"

"Insult me all you want. You're never leaving here. Not without me."

Angry tears filled her eyes. She turned her face away to avoid looking at him. "We'll see about that," she muttered.

Warwick cleared his throat and announced, "Time for Plan B." He flipped open the black box. Then he poked a hypodermic needle into a small bottle filled with wine-colored solution, pulled out the syringe and flicked it a few times. "Since you insist on behaving badly, you're getting a full dose of my hormone-infused elixir. It's from the witch's black arts book I managed to steal from my mother. The last female I experimented on complained about hot flashes, but that quickly passed. Then she started sweating profusely and grinding the chair she was tied to, begging me to fuck her as hard as I could.

Of course, I had to accommodate her more times than I'd care to admit. Since then, I make a practice of visiting her once a week in the Pleasure Quarters...to keep my equipment fine-tuned. I never want to be accused of inexperience or needlessly jacking off. I assure you, Sam, that has never been an issue. Not with all the horny succubae running around in Hell, begging for relief."

"So, you're turning me into a whore? Is that it?"

"Oh, it's much better than that. I'm eliminating your inhibitions and fears, along with any concerns for your family. In fact, I doubt you'll even remember them when I'm done." He tilted his head slightly and pursed his lips. "If for any reason this doesn't work and you insist on behaving badly, your head will roll just like the Goblin Witch's did. Then my search for a qualified queen will start all over again, and that's the worst of it. There's nothing more defeating than wasting time you don't have." Warwick drip-tested the needle, and his smile of satisfaction grew. "Shall we proceed?" He set the box down on a nearby table and stood up, holding the needle in plain sight.

With his words still haunting her and undeniable fear growing, the sound of thunder erupted, deafening her ears. The lights dimmed, and Warwick fell back in his seat, spell-bound and unable to move. A humongous hairy brown creature suddenly appeared on the ceiling. It had four sets of eyes, six legs and a large, crooked claw attached to its spider-like body, but she could see through it. After soundlessly crossing the wall, it leaped to the ground and crawled across the slate tiles. Warwick's eyes remained wide open, fixed on its shadowy movements. He seemed to be its main target, but this was no consolation for Samara. Having no substance indicated the maniacal being had been summoned there, and although it seemed incapable of assuming a dominating posture without specific direction from its master, the threat was real all the same.

Closer and closer the shadow approached, growing larger and larger in size. Then, in one swift, terrifying motion, Warwick was swept off the floor and thrown into a corner. He seemed to be suffocating from the shadow's claw, gripping, and squeezing his throat. All of his limbs were spread out around him, and he shrieked, "Help me, Sam! Help me!"

Samara had no idea what she was seeing, but everything was surreal. She pulled on the ties hard, wishing she would wake up and discover it had all been a nightmare.

"You got him?" A lilting voice asked—dry and airy, the like of which Samara had never encountered.

"Definitely," answered another voice, soft and feminine. "What a demented demon he is! I recommend termination in the cruelest way possible for our sister's death, and the same for his deplorable mother."

"The time will come for that, Iris. But right now, mind that he doesn't get away. Pull one of his wings off, so he won't be able to fly."

"That's not a good plan. The more life he's got in him, the more he'll fight and kick. I've got him firmly in my grip, but I can't hold on forever."

"Then what do you suggest?"

"I think I know a way to keep him from ever harming another soul."

Samara swallowed hard. Whoever had Warwick held him tight enough for the demon wings on his shoulders to crumple. His legs were crossed and squeezed painfully together, and his head was so violently pressed back against his body that it was a miracle his neck hadn't snapped. But that wasn't the worst part. While he was suffering and struggling for a breath, he was picked up and thrown through the archway. As she stared in disbelief, the wall took on a life of its own, narrowing the opening rock by rock until it was sealed shut. Warwick was now trapped inside the dark, windowless room where no one would ever find him.

"What about the other one?" The shadowy creature asked.

"Send her back to where he found her. She's an innocent in his wicked plot."

"A powerful innocent. The only innocent soul in Hell."

"The big question is how will we find her again if she remains unmarked? She doesn't have a tail or horns. Not even wings."

"Then we'll give her a few. I sense she has a connection to something powerful and ancient. We will give her the wings of a Phoenix. She's not like other immortals, Iris. So, her wings should be unique. She'll soar when the time is right. When the prophecy of Nexus comes to fruition, and her true destiny is known."

"But what if she's not the chosen one, Sister? What good will feathery wings be?"

"Feathers smeathers. This one will soar beyond everyone's imagination. Just wait and see."

Samara could still hear the Goblin Witches whispering back and forth, yet they remained hidden in the shadows. The smell of sulfur and ash permeated the air, growing stronger by the second. Not knowing what else to do, Samara pleaded for her life. "Do whatever you must, Iris, but please don't hurt me. I have a mission to complete. I won't tell anyone you were here. Not anyone…I promise."

"How did she know my name?" Iris snapped. "Did she hear us talking? Does she understand Menishe? The mother tongue of ancient languages?"

"I don't believe that's possible, Raven. Not unless she was raised by warlocks."

The smaller witch shook her head. "Not possible. Not this one. We need to leave before all our secrets are known. Before we're found here and burned at the stake. Which reminds me…"

Samara felt a burning sensation on her left shoulder, spreading down her back. She yelped and jerked from side to side, longing for it to stop. Then the cold air around her began swirling, picking up speed, until it was howling. She lowered her head and squeezed her eyes shut. The ties snapped on her wrists and ankles, and she was propelled through the air. Her feet hit the ground with a powerful jolt, yet she remained surprisingly unharmed. When she opened her eyes again, she discovered that she was standing where Warwick had found her—bow and arrow in hand, and her quiver strapped to her back.

For a few seconds, she stood trembling, debating whether to backtrack and find her way home or hide and hope for Damian's arrival.

"You blame yourself for the death of others," Raven's voice said. "Is this not true?"

She looked into the dark corner and saw nothing—not even the shape of a witch. Yet she knew Raven was there. "My friends… Legend and Adison. They would still be alive if not for me."

"Malarky! Their destinies were set long ago. If you want to know the truth, Samara, you only have to ask, and I will show you."

"But how is that possible? You weren't there, Raven."

"Oh, but I was, Samara. You see, Dainis was a self-practicing witch, evil through and through. She used a love potion on Legend, breaking the rules of the Covenant. His love for you broke her spell. That's why she was determined to kill you."

"Kill *me*?"

"That's right. Now, do you wish to see, or do you want to continue living with the guilt in your heart?"

"Please show me, Raven. I want to know the truth, even if it kills me."

On the wall above her, a soft light began to glow. Fuzzy black and white images came into focus. Then, surprisingly, Samara watched the tragic scene at the cabin unfold, as if watching a movie from a projector.

Legend opened the cabin door and stood before Dainis. She was dressed in a black-hooded cape, covering her head, and masking her face in dark shadow. But Legend knew immediately who she was, and anger reddened his face.

"What are you doing here?" he asked. "Were you following us?"

Dainis produced a wicked-looking knife and narrowed her black eyes. "Where is she? Bring her to me," she hissed. "Let's see who the best choice is for you, Legend."

"Get the fuck out of here! It's over! I know how you tricked me into screwing you. Crawl back into the dark hole you came out of and stay there. I never want to see you again. Not ever!"

With stealth movements, she jumped behind him and drew her knife across his throat. He dropped to his knees holding both hands to throat and collapsed on the floor with blood spraying and pooling around him. Then suddenly, Adison appeared in the door opening. He charged at Dainis, and they tumbled to ground. As he rolled over on top of her, she drove her knife into his side. Somehow he managed to pull it free. With her pinned beneath him, Adison reared back on his haunches and shoved the knife into her heart with both hands. Then he stood up and braced his back against the wall. He looked toward the bedroom where Samara was hiding. He grabbed his side and collapsed on the floor, whispering her name. The close-up of Adison's face faded into a soft blur and then it vanished along with Raven.

Samara covered his face with her hands and rocked back and forth in place. She held her breath and could feel the pressure of unshed tears behind her eyes. She wanted to scream, but she couldn't without drawing attention. The truth was almost too painful to bear. Then she heard a muffled sound. She saw a glimmer of light at the end of the tunnel and heard a sweet voice calling her name.

Samara rushed toward Ariel, threw her arms around her, and held her tight. Remarkably, she didn't seem surprised that her daughter was crying.

"It's okay," Ariel whispered. "It's okay."

"I'm sorry about my...dreadful behavior." Her voice broke and she wiped her tears away. "I'm so glad you're my mom. I really mean it."

Ariel smiled. "If I look back at everything I've done in life, you're easily one of the best things I've created. Now tell me the truth, Sam. Are you okay?"

She nodded a reluctant yes.

"Good. We'll share everything later...when we're all home safe and sound."

Samara stared at the mysterious stranger, hurrying through the tunnel to join them. "Who's this?" she asked Ariel.

"A Tracker demon. He teleports in a shimmer and can change into inanimate objects when threatened. But I didn't know about his talents until he shared them with me."

"Wow...and he agreed to help us?"

Before Ariel could answer, Samara extended a hand, and he reluctantly shook it. "What do I call you, other than amazing?"

"Perseus," he said. "Your mother insisted I come."

"Oh, right. I see you brought a gun and sword with you. Are you good with them?"

He nodded. "I brought pentagram bullets too."

"Great! We can't thank you enough for helping us…honestly."

He looked at Ariel then back at Samara. "You might change your mind after you find out who I am."

Samara narrowed her brow, confused. "Why is that?"

"Because I kidnapped Cassius, trapped your mother, killed your dead brother, and my sister is Lucinda's assassin."

Samara's jaw slacked, digesting his words. "Wait a minute. Killed my dead brother?" She swung her eyes back to Ariel. "Who in Hell is this? Lucifer's twin?"

"Like I said, we'll talk about it later. Perseus is here to make everything right."

"Are you crazy?" Samara glared at him. "You're a monster! Why are you here?"

Ariel put her hand on Samara's arm. "Calm down! This is getting us nowhere."

"After what he's done, how can you possibly trust this guy?"

"We have a mutual agreement."

"An *agreement?*"

"That's right." Ariel pulled the knife from her waistband. "If he refuses to help us, I won't hesitate to kill him."

Samara stared at the jagged knife in disbelief. "But you're angel. You can't kill anyone."

"Archangels have been killing demons and humans since the beginning of time. My assigned classification might only be Guardian but defending my family will always come first."

Samara nodded. "I believe you, Mom, but there's one more thing you should know that might affect what we do here.

According to Warwick, Lucinda's wretched son, Lucifer is back in Hell and eager to get even with anyone who might have wronged him. I'm afraid his anger might be directed at everyone in our family, especially you."

"And why would you say that?"

"If you hadn't become a soulmate with Dad, then Satan would have remained in power. He wouldn't be fighting against his own brother in the Red War."

"I know you believe that, but the war was predicted years ago, sweetheart. Nothing in this world will prevent it from happening, although it might be delayed a few centuries. I've had dreams for weeks now and, oddly enough, your friend Damian was in all of them. Perhaps meeting him was predestine, arranged by unseen Heavenly forces. But whatever the future holds, one thing is certain...our world will never be the same."

CHAPTER 24

PRISON BREAK

Perseus held a torch aloft, leading the way to the prison cells. Verifying it was safe, he stepped carefully over the uneven ground, while Samara and Ariel followed closely behind. The tunnel contracted to a narrow, sloping shaft the deeper they went. They slopped forward, feet sloshing along the muddy floor, no longer trying to avoid the water that oozed in rivulets down the narrow passageway. The cavern entrance was now out of sight behind them.

"There's something else I need to tell you," Samara whispered to Ariel. "I don't know how she did it, but Lucinda created replicas of Dad."

"Replicas?"

"Clones. They're all younger versions of him, but given time, they're going to mature, making it impossible to tell them apart. I don't know why they were created, although I suspect it has something to do with the Red War."

Ariel shook her head. "Lucinda. Of course she's behind it."

"I didn't know how wicked she was until I met her…until I witnessed her cruelty firsthand. Now all your negative feelings about her make sense."

Perseus stopped ahead of them and looked back. "We're here."

The putrid smell drifting in the air turned Ariel's stomach. Far worse, the ghastly scene before them left her frozen in her tracks. It seemed Lucinda had added some personalized decorating to the torch-lit entrance in her attempt to dissuade demons from rebelling against her. Two rotting corpses were mounted on the walls, holding scythe axes coated in blood, most likely their own.

"Nice touch," Samara whispered, grimacing.

"Poor creatures," Ariel said. "Lucinda's more twisted than I thought." She was beginning to wonder how they would get past the main guard when she spotted his sprawled-out body on the ground. He was asleep on a blanket with his legs crossed. Unconscious likely from consuming the entire contents the empty bottle at his side. His left hand was feebly grasping a spear and his right was resting on his bloated belly. If Lucinda saw this, Ariel was sure he would be joining his buddies on the wall.

Perseus bent over the sleeping guard and cut the leather cord around his neck. He pulled off the collection of keys and met Ariel's eyes. "Do you have any idea where they are?"

"No, but I'm sensing Crighton's presence in the last cell. I want you stay here in case anyone shows up."

He handed off the keys and pulled out his sword. "Be careful," he whispered. "I'll be here if you need me."

Samara followed Ariel to the end of the colonnade, veering off to the left. They both held their breath while Ariel inserted a skeleton key into the lock and turned it. Then it took all their strength to shove the hefty door wide enough for them to enter the dark chamber, lit by a single torch. On the floor, two bodies were curled up in opposite corners, making it difficult to see their faces. At first, Ariel thought she'd made a horrible mistake. Ram horns had grown out of their heads and long tails had sprout from their backsides. Small demon wings were fixed on their shoulders, which confused Ariel, knowing Crighton had grown beautiful black ones.

One of the chained bodies rolled over, bringing his face into view. Ariel bent down to verify his identity. He was snoozing so soundly that he wasn't even aware of their presence. Tears welled up in Ariel's eyes, blurring her vision. "Crighton, it's me. Come on, wake up. We need to get out of here." She shook his shoulder and his dull eyes slowly opened. She jumped back, realizing it wasn't him.

"Who are you?" He asked, rubbing the back of his head. "Did Lucinda send you?"

The demon chained to the wall in the opposite corner uncurled from his position on the cold, wet ground. He looked around, obviously disoriented. Then he glanced down and pulled out a syringe from his thigh, where someone had clearly stabbed him. "Did you do this?" He grumbled. Then he looked around, gathering his senses. "No...wait. It was that wolf guy. The one with the fangs. He insulted me, and I took a swing at him. Just how did I end up in here?"

"I don't know," Ariel answered, backing away. "I'll try to find out. Come on, Sam. Let's go. Lucinda is waiting..." She stepped through the open doorway, holding her daughter's arm.

"You're not going to leave us here, are you?" One of the demons asked. "The commander's going to be pissed."

Samara glanced at Ariel. "I'm sure he'll send a search party."

"You really think so?"

"Yes, of course. Just sit back and relax. They'll be here soon."

"You're going to tell them we're in here, right?"

"Of course. Why wouldn't I? Now, you need to be quiet. You don't want to disturb the other prisoners."

"We don't?"

"They might get upset and start rioting. I'm sure you don't want to be responsible for that."

"No, of course not." The first Crighton clone sat down, while the other curled back up against the wall, drawing his blanket over him.

Apparently, intelligence was not an inherited gene.

Samara and Ariel closed the door. Then they quietly hurried down the long L-shaped corridor to join Perseus. Honoring his promise, he stood between them and the entrance, anxiously waiting with his sword drawn.

"What's going on, Ariel?" he whispered. "You're not leaving them here, are you?"

"Crighton and Tyrus are gone. We have to get out of here while we still can."

The three of them moved slowly past the sleeping guard then hurried toward through the first tunnel. "Where are we going?" Perseus asked, assuming the lead again. "Back to where we started?"

"Wait. Stop here." Ariel held her hands before her and walked in a circle until she found the strongest of the energy patterns in the vicinity, and then paused before it. "Crighton and Tyrus are close by. I know it, Perseus. Regrouping with them is our only option. Then together we'll find my son and led you to your sister."

"Are you sure?" Samara asked. "You thought Dad was in that cell, but you were wrong."

"The clones are confusing my senses. Now that I know what a clone feels like, the subtle difference, I'll know my soulmate when he's near…when I see the love and concern in his eyes."

"I'm hoping that's true," Samara whispered. "In the meantime, we need to keep moving. Being caught by soldiers or Lucifer himself could turn into a living nightmare for all of us."

CHAPTER 25

REUNION

Perseus, Ariel, and Samara were approaching the antecham-
ber, three miles south of Purgatory. When they were inside
the western bank of tunnels, the sound of approaching soldiers
halted their movements. A shout and blast of gunfire echoed
ahead of them. Lights from dozens of torches were getting closer
and would soon be surrounding them on all sides—trapping
them in a circle of despair.

Ariel reached for Samara's hand and closed her eyes. "Dear
God, help us," she whispered.

Her prayer seemed pointless, and then to Samara's utter
amazement, a knight came out of the shadows wearing a Kaldor
helmet. "I've been waiting for you. This way," he softly beckoned. "There's a secret passage where we can escape up ahead."

"Wait a minute!" Samara snapped. "If you're Warwick, move
on! I've already played this game. I'm not about to do it again."

The knight stood silent for a moment. Then he lifted his helmet, revealing his blue eyes and dark shaggy hair. It was Damian,
the last Cambion Samara ever expected to see. "Tyrus sent me
to get you," he told them. "You need to stay close and remain as
quiet as possible."

Samara disregarded his warning. "Where's Cassius?" she
asked. "Where's my father?"

"Crighton is searching for Cassius and told me to find all of you. I'm sorry, but we're running out of time here. You have to trust me, Samara."

"There's that word again." She shook her head. "I don't trust *anyone* in Hell, on Earth, or anywhere in between…and especially not you. I made that mistake and won't make it again."

"Well, you'd be wise to trust me *this* time. Being found here is the last thing any of us want, believe me. If you haven't heard yet, Lucifer is back. He's determined take over Hell and destroy all his enemies…demons and angels alike. Word has it he brutalized his own daughter for taking his throne. I can't imagine what he'd do to us."

The sound of stomping feet was getting louder by the second, coming straight at them.

"So, are you coming or not?" Damian asked.

Samara looked at Ariel. She knew better than to trust deceptive creatures, but what choice did they have? "Lead the way," she told him, wishing she had another choice.

"The passage was built for escape," he said. "No ladders were built into the walls to keep Lucifer and his enemies out. We're about to enter the Knights of Darkness headquarters through a distorted entry. It can be unsettling at first, but the sensation will pass, and the opening will disappear behind us. I'll go first…just to prove it's safe for all of you."

Damian's words were still registering when he vanished before Samara's eyes. Perseus glanced back at them then stood aside. Ariel squeezed Samara's hand. "It will be fine, Sam. Just do as Damian asked. He came here to help us. Try to remember that." She disappeared through the passage, and now it was Samara's turn. She could hear the soldiers rapidly approaching and drew a deep breath before stepping through the opening.

Perseus entered last, and the wall sealed behind him, leaving all of them in a dim, torch-lit room.

Nine Master Knights were seated around the table in armchairs totally engulfed in flames, yet they remained unscathed and completely relaxed. Two guards stood behind each of them, heightening the drama in the room. Tyrus was standing next to the wall, and the strained expression on his face told Samara that their presence was being tolerated at best. Whatever request they had in mind needed to be presented quickly to avoid ire among the Knights at the table.

Three more demons walked into the room with slicked-back hair, looking remotely superior and debonair in their elegant black suits. The most attractive member in the group approached Ariel. He had a handsome chiseled face and neatly trimmed black hair with an off-center natural white streak, setting him apart from all the others. He also wore a black patch over his left eye, adding an air of mystery to his appearance.

As he walked around Ariel, he scrutinized everything about her and seemed to care less if anyone noticed. "I'm still trying to understand my niece's behavior," he said. "The sacrifice Lilith made to save you was never approved by our members. Were you even aware of that?"

"Hello, Master Sergei." Ariel met his face with cold contempt. "I never expected to see you here. One of the hardest things in life is having vile words in your mind and heart that you can't utter. Not in the presence of others."

"And why ever not, pray tell?" He cocked his head, looking for all the world like a maligning raven. "It's never stopped Crighton before, has it?"

"Not where you're concerned. I don't understand why I get the sense that you know more about my son's disappearance than anyone here. Why is that Master Sergei? Why do you hate my family so much?"

"My, my. Would you look at that." His eyes were locked on Samara. "It seems the older she gets the more she resembles Lilith. I imagine she has the same disposition as well. Headstrong and over-confident, right?"

Ariel noticed a dozen eyes watching her. "I suppose she does at times. But isn't that true of all teenagers?"

"I wouldn't know. But naming her after your rival? What were you thinking, Ariel? That's such an impulsive thing to do."

Rival? Samara turned to Ariel, stunned by his remark. Was she truly named after the Queen of Hell? Why would her parents do such a thing? Her mind was reeling but, fortunately, she had enough sense to stay quiet.

For a long moment, Ariel remained silent. Then she turned to her daughter to address her concerns. "The Queen changed her name from Samara to Lucinda when she ascended to the throne. Your father and I owed her for saving all of our lives and we honored her by naming you after her."

Ariel's malevolent eyes swung back to Sergei. "And just to clarify, Lucinda wasn't always my enemy. She sacrificed her freedom to protect our family. Her position in Hell and the pressures of her job changed her into who she is today."

Master Sergei laughed without humor. "Just keep telling yourself that. Her intention to control every aspect of Hell and every demon within it has never changed, not one iota. She and her father would love nothing more than to see the Knights of Darkness completely destroyed, though they lack the ability and fortitude to make that happen." He sat down in his chair and glanced around the room. "By the way, this is the first time we've had a sit-down with an angel in the room, though I hardly consider you one. The inner conflicts and divided loyalties you assumed by acquiring Lilith's body must be unsettling to say the least."

"Whatever I'm feeling doesn't change why I'm here. My family is—"

"Ah, yes. Your family," he interrupted. "Only it isn't entirely yours, is it? Where's the head of your household, Ariel? Where's Crighton, Lucifer's number-one soul seeker?"

"He's searching for our son as we speak," she said in a harsh tone. Her blue eyes looked around warily, searching for a co-conspirator in the room. "But you knew that, didn't you?"

"Of course, not. Why would I?"

"You have a relationship with Onoskelis. I can sense it. I can read it in your eyes. She was responsible for taking my son...for keeping him alive."

"Well, let's just hope he still is."

"Cassius better be, or you'll be counting down seconds." Ariel instinctively searched the sea of faces for a shocked expression. When she didn't see one, she lowered her voice to a whisper. "What about Onoskelis? Where is she hiding? I'm sure you know better than anyone."

"Actually, I don't. She's lived in so many places and is constantly moving. I have no idea where she's hiding, nor do I have any interest in her perverse activities."

"Interesting choice of words."

He softly chuckled. "Onoskelis isn't the problem here, Ariel. If you kept your children on leashes, they wouldn't be running off, looking for ways to escape."

"Who said anything about escaping?" she asked. "Did Cassius run off? Is Onoskelis looking for him right now?"

"He could be stone cold dead for all I care."

Ariel dropped down in a chair next to the wall. "If that's true, you'll be joining him very soon. I'll make sure of it myself."

Samara sat next to her behind Damian's chair and tried to quietly reason with her. "This isn't the way to handle this matter, not before the Knights of Darkness. It's only going to make the situation worse."

"I said hello to him and look where that got me."

Samara lowered her eyes and kept her voice low. "When is all this going to stop? This battle between the Knights of Darkness and our family?"

"As soon as Sergei admits he was wrong. I know his history, as well as everyone else's in this room. But for some reason, they've forgotten the cruelty he's capable of...the torment he proudly inflicts. He's a megalomanic. His kind of narcissism helps him blend in with the haters in Hell and the wicked souls on Earth. Believe it or not, Lucinda is the least of our worries. She might be a pathological liar and good at deceptive conversations, but I've always known where I stand with her. The same doesn't apply to Lucifer or that pantomime villain sitting over there." She glared at Sergei, obviously longing for a reason to kill him.

Samara shook her head. "We can't talk about any of this now. Someone might be listening, and your hate won't further our cause."

After taking a controlled breath, Ariel glanced at Tyrus and kept her voice low. "Remember the reason why we came here. There's someone who needs us more than anyone else."

"Cassius," he said. "He should be our only concern. There's a plot going on in this room to use him as leverage in the war, but we need to make sure who the players are before we act."

"They're all here," Damian announced.

The last three Knights stepped into the War Room, and Samara's fascination grew to epic proportion. Searching for a shadow behind every face wasn't conducive to solving their personal problems, but it was fascinating all the same. Each of the twelve members clutched a black briefcase and wore matching black ties, looking like venture capitalist super spies. Not one of them wore a trucker hat, leather jacket or pair of Royale Nero sneakers. Here in this dark, oppressive room, the bespoke gentlemen wore Gucci accessories and were part of the fascinating world of elegance, refinement, and style. Their hairstyles were well-groomed, and even their facial hair had been trimmed to a desirable length. Before arriving at their designated seats, they passed by a wall of photos featuring celebrities who had risen to success in a short period of time. It was easy to assume that their souls had been sold, yet somehow this collective group had managed to keep their distance from Lucifer and Lucinda, pledging their loyalty solely to the Grand Master and unified Knights of Darkness.

Amazing. Their presence filled Samara with awe. "I've never seen anything like this before."

Damian shushed her quickly, as though she had spoken too loudly in church. Embarrassed by his reaction, she edged closer to Tyrus and studied the vast number of books filling the shelves. After a moment or two, she found herself watching Damian again. He had removed his armor and now sat at the table in his black jeans and matching t-shirt, completely engrossed in an ancient book of some sort. She had to admit he looked hot when he wasn't correcting her. This was a guy who wasn't afraid to show how he felt, and his kisses were truly unforgettable. If he spent time kissing human girls and female demons as often as she suspected, he was probably even better in bed. But she wasn't prepared to find out. Love was an inconvenient, distracting game, and as far as she was concerned, it would never be in her playbook. They were living through a time when hate and fear were stronger, and fantasies were inconvenient. Yet somehow, Damian Hunter managed to invade her thoughts and dreams on a regular basis, leaving her wondering what might have been.

Why can't I get you out of my head? Why are you always popping up in my life?

Oddly enough, she could sense him thinking about her too. He looked up suddenly, forcing her to look away. Although she resented his overprotectiveness and insensibility, Samara now owed him a debt of gratitude. Without him, she could be sitting in a prison cell, waiting for Lucinda's judgment, along with Ariel and Perseus.

Tyrus seemed to have noticed the source of her distress. He leaned down and whispered so only she could hear. "He has twenty Black Crow assassins to rescue and countless souls waiting to be claimed, yet he made time to be here for you. That tells me that he cares more than you might believe. But, of course, not all Cambions are created equal. Some are better with words than others, and some find it hard to share their feelings."

Samara lifted a brow in silent query. Damian said he was following Tyrus' orders. Did she overreact to his belittling? He was being vigilant, while watching out for her, but his perplexing behavior and smothering left her questioning her own self-worth.

Damian shut his book and looked up. "What do you think, Sam? Should I offer some help?"

For a moment, she was transfixed on his eyes then looked away. "Of course, you should. You gave us sanctuary, so why not help us entirely?"

"I'm not sure yet. Tyrus has demonstrated his devotion and loyalty, while your father continues to ignore us. He was asked to join the Knights of Darkness before you were born and refused to accept the invitation. But the Red War is now imminent, and he can no longer remain neutral. He's either for the war or against it. He needs to make his position clear."

"And what about you Damian? As a Black Crow member, I thought you opposed the war, yet you sit there plotting battle strategies and Lucinda's takedown. I realize now that I know virtually nothing about you or what your organization stands for."

"We're all about peace, Sam. Preparing for war is one of the most effectual ways of preventing it. And just so you know, I forgive demons and humans alike, but that doesn't mean I accept their behavior or trust them. I forgive them so I can let go and move on in my life."

Samara huffed. "Just be honest with me or stay away from me. It's not that difficult."

"You can't just give up on someone because the situation's not ideal. Great relationships aren't great because they have no problems. They're great because both parties care enough about each other to make it work."

She was silent, trying to digest what he was saying.

"I'm responsible for hurting you. I admit it and honestly regret it. I'm still hoping you'll let me back into your life so I can set things right. So, I can do what I should have done instead of what I was told to do."

At the same time, another conversation was taking place on the other side of the table, stealing her attention away. "Why are you here, Tyrus?" a gray-haired Master asked. "Your intrusion was not welcome the first time and neither is this one."

"I understand, Master Hordes, but please hear me out. Perhaps Crighton will change his mind about the Knights of Darkness if you agree to act on his behalf. His son is being used as a pawn in the Red War and doesn't deserve the situation he's been thrust into. He's just an innocent child with no knowledge or experience in these matters. Surely, you can understand why Ariel and her family are upset…why they came here seeking your help. They fear for their family's safety and are asking for our protection."

"Death is part of the risk we all take by living. You know that as well as I do. Taking Ariel's son was wrong, but this matter is between Lucifer and Castiel and doesn't involve us in any way, shape, or form. But it's certainly interesting when you think about it. Don't you agree?"

"Lucifer?"

"That's right. We are silent observers in Hell's imperious dominion. Our decisions are governed by the votes of our members and the final verdict of our Grand Master. None of us act alone, not even our Grand Master's son." There was stunned silence, punctured by Master Sergei's shrill laughter. "I see by your expression Tyrus that you weren't aware of his return. Although he hasn't officially declared himself King of Hell, that leaves you and the rest of your family in a precarious situation, doesn't it? If I remember right, you and your family were responsible for his demise…for destroying his body so he could never come back. Now that I think of it, I wonder what his new skin looks like—don't you?"

Ariel's face paled, and her eyes became distant. "How is it possible? He can't be alive. He just can't!"

At the sound of footsteps approaching, everyone in the room became silent. "Bow your heads," Master Hordes directed. "The Grand Master is here."

Verity, Damian's mother, studied every face in the room before sitting down in the thirteenth chair. Her poise expressed dignity and grace, and she was unlike anyone Samara had seen before. Her shimmering eyes were the lightest shade of blue making them appear translucent. Nine thin elk-like horns grew from the top of her head, adding strength to her regal appearance. Her shoulder-length black hair framed her flawless face in feathery wisps and flowed around the pointed cartilage at the top of her elf-like ears. Her lips were the softest shade of pink—the same color as the stone in the antler-horn necklace around her throat—and she wore a silver semi-sheer gossamer gown, revealing the geometric tattoos on her upper chest and down the length of her arms.

Sensing her awe, Verity smiled at Samara. Then she leaned toward her and spoke in a near whisper—confiding like they were girlfriends at a party. "I believe I know you, although we've never met before. Legend spoke about you often. Seeing you up close provides a better understanding of his fascination. You're far prettier than I ever imagined, Samara." She swung her eyes toward her son. "Don't you agree, Damian?"

He stared at the table and solemnly nodded.

Verity turned her attention toward the Knights seated before her. "My son Legend developed an unhealthy obsession, as young demons are prone to do. He was naive and trusting...and didn't understand the ways of the world. Sadly, he didn't realize a wanton creature could easily destroy him."

"That's not true," Damian said. "Samara isn't responsible for Legend's death, and neither were the Gorgon brothers...murdered by your order."

Samara sucked in a quick breath and met his gaze steadily. *Naburus and Lestat are dead? Were they involved in Legend's death? Did Verity kill Adison too?*

Damian snorted loudly and shook his head. "Legend challenged an Arch-demon to a fight and failed to show up. The gang members that killed him will face the same fate...thanks to the Black Crows."

"Oh, my son...you couldn't be more wrong," Verity said. "I never give an order without confirming my facts first." She let out a sigh of impatience. "Legend didn't challenge gang members to a fight. He didn't insult anyone...aside from his jilted lover. If you really must know, Dainis Gorgon dared to give ear to his claims of love, fucking him night after night. Then he shifted his loyalty to Samara, infuriating this cunt. Like a female in heat, Legend was fickle and had the attention span of a rabbit. I don't blame him for his foolish male behavior. However, I hold the vixen at this table responsible for what transpired in that cabin. If she had refused Legend's affection rather than encouraging him, my son would be alive instead of buried in a grave."

Samara swallowed hard and reminded herself to stay calm. No matter what might be said, she needed to appear strong and unaffected. Her family's safety and security were at stake.

Damian was staring at her with an unreadable expression on his face, but his mother's frown said it all. She hated Samara more than anything in the world and didn't care if anyone knew it.

Not even her son.

Damian cleared his throat. "I believe you owe Sam and her family an apology," he said. "I've never known you to be so wrong about someone, especially when you know how I feel."

Verity narrowed her eyes. "And how exactly is that, might I ask?"

"You can read my thoughts and sense my emotions, so I'm sure you're aware."

"Come on, sweetheart. Here's your chance to share your little secret. I'm sure Samara would be interested in knowing. Wouldn't you, child?"

Samara kept her eyes down, squeezing her hands in her lap. She wanted to run out of the room, run back to Middle Earth, run upstairs to her room, and throw the covers over her head. But more than anything else, she wanted to avoid the possibility of ever seeing Verity again.

Sensing her fear, Damian spoke out, failing to hide the annoyance in his voice. "Why are you doing this, Mother? It's rude and completely unnecessary, especially in front of the Knights and Black Crow members."

Anger and humiliation were boiling up inside Verity, spilling over in a froth of rage. "You have no idea what love is," she told him." You're enchanted by this tempestuous creature, like your brother before you. She's got you hoodwinked into believing she cares. But don't let that pretty face fool you. She doesn't know the first thing about love and neither do you. Love is sacrificial, love is ferocious…it's not emotive. Our culture and nature don't allow us to comprehend or engage in this human experience. I thought you understood that, Damian, but obviously you don't."

His face was a kaleidoscope of emotion. "You forget, Mother. I'm a Cambion being, which means I'm half-human."

"That's far worse, my son." Verity stared straight ahead. She responded quickly to the gestures of affection, the pats of approval, the jerks of impatience, the firm motions of command, and to many other variations of feelings circling her table. She had become so expert at interpreting the unconscious range of emotions from her Knights that she was able to divine the very thoughts of everyone in the room. "As any of the Knights at this table can tell you, humans have no respect for themselves, so why would they respect or love others? They destroy lives because they are angry, incompetent, and frustrated. They cannot be as those they seek to persecute with their blatant disregard for life.

They are empty voids of original thought, lack creativity, and do not wake to the potential of their lives but solely to the destruction of others. Evil is a lazy sloth on the back of those of us who work hard to improve our demon lives. We strive to lift the burdens from downtrodden, mistreated souls, struggling to survive in Hell. But humans will suck the effort we have made and use it to their advantage. These Earthbound creatures leap from person to person acting wise and playing the fool, as they connive their next act of betrayal. They know they are worthless and cannot bear the happiness of others. But who really cares, Damian? As you say, you're only half-human. The demons in this chamber protect innocent souls while human beings on Earth destroy their spirit, individuality, and confidence. You claim to know love, but I assure you, my son, it's just a word in the human vocabulary…not a viable, heartfelt emotion. Sleep with Samara if you must, but don't for a moment believe her capable of loving you. Although her birth mother was Ariel, warrior blood runs through her veins and her heart. Lilith was admired and respected by the Knights of Darkness, but she lacked the ability and desire to maintain a monogamous relationship. I suspect her daughter is cut from the same cloth and would destroy you if given the chance." Verity sighed and shook her head. "Enough of this tedious subject. Present your case, Tyrus. We will discuss your family's dilemma and decide if our assistance is warranted."

"You're evil," Damian muttered. "Through and through."

She smiled and folded her hands on the table. "You've got a good heart, Son. Sometimes that's enough to see you safe, but mostly it's not."

With no one allowed to leave the room, Samara sank back in the chair next to Ariel, feeling guilty and utterly worthless. Thanks to Verity's lecture and her son's disturbing disclosure, she had been stripped of any possibility of happiness in her life. She stole a quick look at Damian, and he looked away, hiding the pain on his face. It seemed to her that he'd spent his life on the outside looking in, driven down until there was nothing but hopelessness, distrust, and complacency.

"Now, let's get back to the matter at hand," Verity said. During the next thirty minutes, she listened, refused, wavered, and ended their meeting by yielding. The Knights agreed to restore order, maintain peace, protect Crighton's family, and ensure the safe return of Ariel's son in a timely fashion. Though she should have been relieved by their decisions, Samara never felt so empty, confused, and miserable in her whole life. Years ago, her father told her a man could be destroyed but not defeated. Obviously, the men he was referring to hadn't faced Verity or had the misfortune of being one of her sons.

The meeting was adjourned, and the Knights of Darkness began filing out, disappearing the same way they'd arrived. Verity told her son to accompany the Daemonium family back to their home, but Samara quickly refused. She had no interest in hearing lame excuses for his mother's vicious attack or exposing herself further to Damian's defeatist attitude.

However, before she could walk away, Verity reached out a hand, grabbing hold of her wrist. "You'll be pleased to know that your father and brother have been located. They will be questioned and returned to your home by nightfall. In addition, Tyrus will be taking Perseus to see his sister. And one more thing, Samara. Don't assume what I said to you was a personal attack. I'm trying to be a good mother the only way I know how. Obviously, I'm very protective of my son and want him to make the right choices. I'm sure you'll understand when you get older and have demons of your own. Losing a child can be devastating, and drastically changes the way a leader views the world."

"I understand more than you know." Samara jerked her arm away from Verity. She stared into her eyes, refusing to look away. "We've experienced loss in our family too and faced it together. We also recognize cruelty when we see it. By insulting the human population, you insult your son. You might want to remember that the next time you give a lecture."

Samara wrapped her arm around Ariel's shoulder and kissed her cheek. Then she scowled at Verity. "By the way, I was under the impression that rules in this dark kingdom prohibited you from being a mother. It seems they were implemented for good reason."

Verity snickered at the unintentional pun. "Those ridiculous rules and regulations should have been done away with years ago. Obviously, I've chosen to ignore them. No one will ever control my life. Not ever." She smiled again, alluding to the depth of her wickedness.

Samara glanced back at Damian. His elbows were propped on the table and his chin was resting on his fists. His eyes were closed, but she was sure he heard every word.

Interesting. What Samara wouldn't give to be a fly on the wall during the next two minutes.

"Goodbye, Damian," she said softly. "Good luck with your life." *And good luck with mine.*

Closing her eyes, Samara thought about the warm kitchen in their home, about her father and Cassius, and their overdue reunion. She maintained her hold on Ariel's shoulder and within seconds they were transported back to the place where their adventure began.

In all honesty, Samara felt a little tired and a little wiser, but the guilt over contributing to needless deaths couldn't be erased or easily forgotten.

Not for as long as she lived.

CHAPTER 26

PREPARATIONS

Lucifer had grown tired of the whores in the Pleasure Quarters and was anxious to bring Samara into his fold. The first time he saw her since leaving Hell was in a Middle Earth diner with her father and young brother having lunch together. He watched her from outside as she laughed at something Crighton had said and wished he'd been in on the joke. Resting his hand on the wood siding and adjusting himself with the other, he felt like he was watching a performance through the window. He just couldn't get enough of Samara—how she smiled, licked her lips, the way she sucked on the straw in her Coke. He got lost in his own thoughts while staring at her and before he knew it, time had evaporated, and they were preparing to leave.

That's when Lucifer went back to Hell, feeling more miserable than ever. Sitting in his throne room, he studied his remodeling plans, flipping one page over the other. The dungeon was being sandblasted to remove unsightly stains, and the torture chamber was having more hooks and chains installed. His renovated bedroom suite would be double in size to accommodate his new amenities, including a walk-in closet for Samara's custom-made wardrobe. He had marble statues created in provocative poses for inspiration in his new S & M playroom and considered modeling for a few of them. But of course, his time constraints wouldn't allow that. He insisted on a hot tub with disco light-ing and a full-service bar with Johnny Walker Black on tap. His interior designer would soon be installing a rotating, circular bed with mirrors on the ceiling and a sound system with prerecorded moaning. There was so much to do and so little time. He needed a palace worthy of his new queen and the entertainment he was anxious to provide.

A winged demon walked by the open doorway, capturing his attention. The resemblance to his former soul seeker was uncanny and incredibly disturbing. He called out to one of his guards, bringing him immediately to his side. "What can I do for you, Master?" he asked.

"I just saw a clone created in Crighton Daemonium's image. How many of them are there?"

"Two dozen, I believe. Lucinda had the succubus in the Pleasure Quarters impregnated with Crighton's sperm, and they produced dozens of—"

"Get rid of them right now! Throw those abominations in the furnace. Do whatever is necessary. I never what to see another one those horrid creatures for as long as I live! Is that clear enough for you, or do I need to take care of them myself?"

"Whatever you say, Master. I'll make sure you never see a Crighton clone again."

"Good. I'm depending on you. Now send for the seamstress. I want beautiful clothes for my Queen…copies of all the latest fashions from Paris, Milan, New York, and London. My Samara is going to be the best dressed demoness in the world!"

"Yes, of course. I'm sure she'll look amazing in whatever you pick out."

Lucifer opened a fashion magazine and began flipping through pages. As weeks went by, a complete wardrobe was created using Samara's measurements, and renovations on Lucifer's palace progressed at record speed. He continued to watch her from a distance and kept her foremost in his thoughts. He even trailed after her on a hunting trip with Crighton and Cassius. More than anything, he liked spying on the fight in her—witnessing how she never quit until her arrow struck her prey. He watched her wash up, pull off her jeans, and slip into her sleeping bag in the forest. It would have been so easy to scoop her up in his arms with her weapons out of reach. With very little effort, he could be back in Hell before anyone realized she was missing. But timing was crucial to his plans and preparations were still underway. His new palace would be completed in just a matter of days. It would be a home to inspire her—to impress *all* his mistresses. But she was by far the most important. Her opinions would matter most if they were pleasing and always in his favor.

Lucifer returned to his throne room, pulled on his velvet robe, and dropped into his chair. "Soon she'll be mine. Samara won't be able to deny me. Not when she can have Legend and me at the same time."

He smiled and looked down at his new pet. The troubled creature had mistaken him for his brother and now appeared to be regretting his foolish error. "Looks can be deceiving, can't they? I bet you wish you hadn't spoken to me, huh? A word of advice, Damian. The next time you swing a punch make sure it connects."

The Cambion was on all fours chained to his throne like a dog. Lucifer kicked him in the face, leaving him hissing and splitting blood on the floor.

"What do you think, Bro?" Lucifer waved a hand around him. "Is Samara going to like the new improvements? I'm having a bed made especially for her. Not that she'll be sleeping..." Lucifer rubbed his crotch and cackled with glee.

Damian snarled. "Kidnap her and she'll fight you forever. You can offer her the world and she'll deny you. Samara is motivated by only one thing…her family. She'll never allow you to be part of hers and they won't accept you either. Not in my brother's body or anyone else's."

Lucifer leaned down and struck him with the back of his hand. Then he snapped his fingers, summoning a guard. "Put this mutt with the rest of the Crows we captured. Then pour me a glass of whiskey, the good stuff this time. And make sure there's ice."

"I'm sorry, Master, but we can't keep ice in Hell. It's the temperature, I'm afraid. It melts before it hits the glass."

Lucifer lifted his eyes towards Heaven. "MUST WE ALL SUFFER?"

The guard kept his head down, anticipating a beating. When all was quiet, he glanced up.

"Alright…make it neat," Lucifer said with a flick of his wrist.

The guard disappeared leaving Lucifer toying with his riding crop, mulling over Damian's comments. If Samara opposed his advances and insisted on keeping her distance, raping her would be his only option. But her anger and resentment over taking such action would end their amiable, unassuming relationship, leaving him more frustrated than ever. His obsession with her and irrational thinking had already resulted in torturing more whores than he could count. In fact, the screams from the last one still echoed in his brain. He had never seen anyone so composed, knowing she was going to be brutalized. Despite her youthfulness, she had quickly assessed his cunning behavior and knew he was sexually twisted. "Please don't be hard on me," she said. "I'm not experienced like the others."

Surprisingly, Lucifer remained calm. There was no frenzied rage this time, just a feeling of serenity knowing he was completely in control. While keeping his eyes shut and his arm under the female demon's head, he rolled onto his side and pretended she was Samara. He was amazed that this recruit hadn't resisted his probing fingers. She raised her hips up and down, moving against him until he managed to insert three. Then she simply moaned as her wetness increased along with the speed of his motions. After gasping and rearing back in ecstasy, she relaxed enough to share stories about herself with remarkable candor.

Apparently, she'd known young boys in her past and enjoyed rough sex with them. She had even envisaged being ravaged by a fully grown demon tearing her apart. Then he dropped his drawers, and she quickly realized she had nothing to fear from the size of his cock. However, the same didn't apply to Lucifer. With him lying down next to her, thinking about Samara, he felt his cock double in size. He smiled wickedly, spread her ass, and prepared to drive his engorged weapon into her. She tried to squirm out of his arms but felt the power of his muscles. Somehow, she managed to roll over and knee him as hard as she could in the groin. Despite being naked, the blow didn't faze him at all. In fact, it only excited him more. He kept her at arm's length and, amazingly, she got an arm up to foil his punch to her head. Then she grabbed his arm and bit his wrist hard, clenching her teeth. At that moment, she knew she had nothing to lose, but instead of trying to free herself, she stayed close, dragging her fingernails across his cheek.

For a moment, Lucifer was taken aback. He wasn't used to close fighting, especially with a desperate demoness. The pain in his wrist and his face shocked him. He was a fan of dishing out torture, but this was a new experience for his newly acquired body—a fist-swinging struggle he didn't appreciate or even like. He tried to keep her at a distance, pushing at her shoulder while bleeding from her bite. Somehow, she stayed close, thwarting his punches. But eventually, she weakened, and he felt a rush of adrenaline overtake him. He pulled back his fist and cold-cocked her, leaving her stunned and defenseless. He hooked her legs over his shoulders and thrust himself into her to the hilt. With one hand squeezing her throat, he pumped all his anger, all his rage, all his pain deep inside her, refusing to yield. He felt her inner muscles involuntarily spasm and experienced the longest climax in his life, while listening to the death rattle in her throat.

Back in his room, Lucifer showered, put a bandage on his left wrist and applied some fast-healing ointment to the deep scratches on his face. For the first time in his life, he bore unsightly marks that were difficult to hide. They resulted in jibes from his unruly mistresses and concerned looks from his guards. However, the demoness' battered body was no longer an issue. It was disposed of like all the other resistant creatures—in the new flash furnace he had installed. Her troubled soul provided a flavorless substitute for the angel his black heart preferred. But with the Red War beginning in a matter of days, his coffers would soon be filled with the tasty souls of heavenly creatures. It wouldn't be long now before he could look into Ariel's eyes, open his mouth, and devour her Divine soul. Then his hard work would *really* begin.

Ah, yes. Samara would soon be his queen and frequent bedmate, but in the meantime, his preoccupation with sex was ruining his life. He rubbed his swollen cock and groaned. Forced to deal with his persistent, painful erections, he had postponed sentencing for a record number of demons. He hadn't spoken to Lucinda since her whipping and had shelved a meeting with the commander of his military forces, which couldn't be dismissed any longer. Yet all he could think about was Samara and his overwhelming need to please her.

Fortunately, there was a new development in Hell. Something he could sink his teeth into.

Thanks to Master Cletus and his unsavory ambitions, he learned that Verity and Damian were conspiring against him. While living among the Knights of Darkness, Cletus had been spying for months, collecting information. His request for two hundred sapphires to divulge his secrets followed a recent trip to Las Vegas, where he had gambled away most of the money he had stolen. Being a weekly visitor to the City of Sin, he frequented not only the casinos but the Bunny Ranch Brothel as well. He encouraged human malfeasance and claimed there was no one he couldn't corrupt—humans and demons alike. As Lucifer sat across from him in his library, he continued to extol on his attributes, believing he was impressing the devil with his treachery. But Lucifer quickly concluded that Cletus had served his purpose and could no longer be trusted. With the wave of his hand, two guards grabbed the deceptive demon and threw him head-first into the oversized, blazing fireplace then stood back while he screamed.

With four Black Crows and Damian rotting in Lucifer's prison, there were now Verity's underhanded actions to consider. She would no doubt cry and beg for forgiveness to atone for her maligning deeds. But Lucifer decided his compassion would be like his Almighty Father's, succoring the suffering underlings without sharing in the pain.

Ah, yes. Never had a Grand Master of the Knights of Darkness been executed in the Main Arena, but there was always a first time.

CHAPTER 27

CONFINEMENT

Two guards escorted Damian to the prison level in a dimly lit elevator. It dropped at breakneck speed and abruptly stopped. Damian picked himself up from the floor and was surprised to see the guards still standing. They were holding straps bolted into the walls, chuckling at his bruised, aching body.

While standing outside the admission office, one of the guards removed the dog collar on Damian's neck and left him standing before a skeleton dressed in a black robe. He checked a big book to make sure Damian's name was listed along with the nature of his crime. As he slowly scanned the pages with his bony finger, Damian couldn't help wondering why he needed a heavy robe, since the air was extremely hot—a steamy, sulfur kind of hot that opened every pore in his body.

The skeleton found his name and nodded. Then a security guard joined Damian and walked him through a long corridor to his cell. As he passed by the fire-lit torches on the walls, they dimmed a bit and the screams from prisoners became more subdued. Most of the prison guards had retired for the night and slept in corners on the floor with their pointy tails curled around them. A plate of food was brought to Damian after the cell door closed and it tasted surprisingly good. But a few minutes after he finished eating, he doubled over in agony, realizing it was poisoned. Oddly enough, as soon as he recovered, he was compelled to dig in all over again, repeating the painful cycle. Finally, he laid down on the lumpy mattress and closed his eyes.

He was just drifting off to sleep when he heard a voice shouting, "Get up, you lazy animals! This isn't a vacation resort!"

The steel bar on the door of his cell slid open, and he was herded along with other prisoners into a long line. It separated into three lines, and then all the lines came back for no apparent reason. Damian turned to the gray-haired demon walking behind him. "What's that about?"

He just stared at him, as if he didn't understand English, and continued to march in place like a toy solider.

On day two, Damian discovered the hard way that prisoners don't like to be messed with when they're beating a fellow prisoner to death. After trying to stop them, he was ganged up on and beaten within an inch of his life. Then an angry guard dragged him back to his cell, cursing at him for getting involved.

Prison was a lonely place, even with hundreds of demons milling about. They were all caught up in their own little worlds, running to and fro, wailing and tearing their hair out. He tried to talk to several of them in the exercise area, but he could tell they weren't listening.

A malaise set in within four days of his arrival. Crow members were being kept on an upper-level floor, and he couldn't help wondering if word had reached them or his mother regarding his incarceration. He wasn't given the opportunity to defend himself against the charge of rebellion against the authority of Hell, which shouldn't have come as any surprise. After all, Lucifer was controlling the Halls of Justice and had final word in all matters.

Two weeks went by without incident, and he thought getting a job might help pass the time. It turned out he had a lot of cousins in Hell, and, using connections, he became an assistant to a demon skilled in medical procedures. It wasn't a job, per se, but more of an internship. He was eager to fill his time after walking in circles, beating prisoners, and lying awake for hours on end, and the work sounded interesting.

However, after a while, it became a tedious chore—restraining demons and removing organs without the benefit of painkillers. Damian decided that he had to get away. The screams, endless lines, constant whippings, and poisoned food were killing him. He had grown tired of trying to explain that he'd already been branded, and that something as big as a railroad spike wouldn't fit into his ear, even with a hammer.

While the guards on his block wrestled with two prisoners, Damian managed to wander off. He found a cave at the end of the prison and went inside, thinking it might be a way out. And that's when it happened, one of those rare moments, which could only occur in Hell. He saw Hecate, Lucifer's prized tormentor. She was standing on a big rock, looking up at something. He followed her line of vision and spotted a pair of boots. When his eyes adjusted to the darkness, he realized they belonged to the bearded demon dangling at the end of a rope.

Perseus.

"Ah, shit." Damian realized too late that he had vocalized his astonishment.

Hecate turned her eyes on him, and he was immediately set upon by demons, throwing painful punches. He thought he was done for then Hecate surprised him by snapping her whip. Two assailants ran off and four remained. They delivered a halfhearted attack against Damian and Hecate but were driven off with little effort.

Then she turned to him and said the unthinkable. "I need your help retrieving my brother."

Damian looked up and swallowed hard. After snapping his neck, the noose tied around Perseus' throat held his head at a fixed angle and his eyes seemed to glow with the torch light. His mouth exuded a pungent yellow mist that drifted around his head, as it swung back and forth on the rope above a dark ravine.

Well, at least *his* soul was free.

Hecate handed Damian a wicked-looking knife. "Cut through the rope, but not all the way. Give him a hard shove and I'll bring him down with my whip."

Damian climbed the rock wall in the dark, finding his way up with hidden handholds. When he reached the outcropping where the rope had been secured, he pulled the knife from his waistband and began sawing away. The rope frayed as Perseus' body continued to swing from side to side. Before Damian could climb all the way down, Hecate cracked her whip above his head, snapping the unraveling rope at the right moment. Perseus fell to the ground with a thud.

His sister stood over his body for a few seconds before crumpling beside him. She wiped her nose on her sleeve. "Damn it, Perseus. Why didn't you stay away?" She mournfully asked. "Why did you have to come here?"

"Tyrus was taking him to find you," Damian muttered. "How could this have happened? Why would anyone want to kill him?"

The answer came from an unexpected source. Lucinda stepped out of the shadows with her arms crossed over her chest, leaving Damian wondering how long she'd been standing there.

"Maybe now you'll believe me," she told Hecate. "Lucifer can't help himself. His very nature drives him to lie, cheat and destroy. He uses his sinfulness to play on our weaknesses. He's tempting us to be afraid by murdering those we love most." Lucinda sighed. "This morning, I found Serene in her bedroom with her throat cut from ear to ear. He knew how much I cared about her. And your brother Perseus…I'm so sorry, Hecate. Losing members of our family is a horrible thing."

Hecate searched Lucinda's eyes for a reason behind the distress they revealed, yet she remained silent.

"Believe it or not," Lucinda continued, "Damian is the greatest threat to my father's physical and mental well-being because of his love for Samara and her unwavering devotion to him. Yet despite how they feel, my father intends to make her his queen."

Damian shook his head in disbelief. "How do you know that? Are you involved in this?"

"Of course not," she claimed. "I'm just a fly on the wall, Damian."

"And I should believe you? What kind of game are you playing, Lucinda? What do you want from me?"

"I'm not playing games. I'm just stating facts." Lucinda's voice grew more desperate and urgent. "We can defeat my father and rescue your girlfriend before he claims victory in the Red War, but I need to retake the throne and have a strong army behind me. If you promise to support me, I will free your Cambion Crow soldiers, protect your mother from harm, and restore power to the Knights of Darkness. Without me, Lucifer will tear Hell apart, destroy Earth and annihilate Heaven. So, I ask you now. Are you both with me? Or are you against me?"

CHAPTER 28

REDEMPTION

Samara returned from a successful deer hunting trip with her father and brother only to find Verity visiting with Ariel inside their house. Her claims of being tracked by a pack of demons left Samara stoic, but at the same time inwardly happy. If not for Ariel's troubled expression, she would have insisted that the wicked creature be turned away, especially after challenging her morality and insinuating her responsibility for Legend's death. Just looking at her made Samara feel sick inside.

"I'll be in my room," she told Ariel. "Let me know when your visitor has left."

"Yes, of course. We'll talk later."

Samara turned to leave when Verity stepped in front of her, blocking her exit. "There's something you need to know. Damian and some of his Crows were thrown in prison. They're being tortured daily. I can't leave them there to die, but my own life is being threatened."

"Why?"

"For speaking out against Lucifer. Now I'm being followed all the time."

"No, not you. How long has Damian been there?"

"Only a few days, but with the brutality that goes on there, I'm sure it feels like a lifetime."

Crighton set down his backpack. "Why is he being held, Verity? What crime did he commit?"

"I know it sounds terrible, but he was plotting a revolution against Lucifer."

"Lucifer? That's not possible. I witnessed his death years ago."

"I thought you knew, Crighton. He's back in Hell. My niece Serene works for Lucinda. She said he took a new body and beat his daughter for burning his old one. Now Serene is missing, and I can't reach out to Lucinda. Not when my own life is at risk."

"Lucifer has a new body? How can that be? Are you saying his soul has been drifting around all this time?"

Verity nodded. "I'm afraid so. Lucinda was the first to be punished, and I'm sure there'll be more. But right now, my son is suffering, and I need help in setting him free."

Suddenly, the room went dark. When the light came back on again, Samara couldn't pull her eyes away from Verity's throat. Her fair complexion couldn't hide the heavy line of blackness that grew there—the string of red liquid rubies spilling from her throat, staining her expensive white dress. Her eyes rolled toward the ceiling, an expression of pain and disbelief filling her face. With her neck slit wide open, blood was pouring across her chest at a horrifying rate.

Samara staggered back and gasped. Everything in the room froze. All light, all movement, all life. Verity stood across from her bleeding profusely from her neck and drops of blood were landing on her thousand-dollar shoes. She crumpled to the floor and Samara stood by helplessly watching, gagging, and trembling.

Within seconds, all light, sound, and life were restored. There was no string of rubies, no blood on Verity's white dress, no gore on her shoes. The vision was gone as fast as it came. Samara shook her head, trying to clear her thoughts. Perhaps it was too much excitement after killing her first deer. Maybe it was the shocking news about Damian. Perhaps slitting the deer's throat before field dressing it was still on her mind. Whatever the cause, the illusion stayed with her longer than any other in her life, leaving her believing a vision of Verity's future had been delivered.

Samara looked down. She had no idea what to do with this information.

Verity's mouth twitched in a pained grimace. "Please, I beg of you, Crighton. Help my son. I wouldn't ask if it wasn't crucial."

His eyes met Ariel's before answering. "After reuniting my family, I promised myself that I would stay out of Hell. Perhaps when Tyrus returns—"

"Tyrus disappeared after the Knights of Darkness meeting, and no one in Hell has heard from him. Is he the only creature capable of helping me? You must've heard what happened to Perseus. Rumor has it Tyrus was responsible."

Crighton shook his head. "Tyrus is capable of a great many things, but murder is not one of them. I suggest convincing him to help you. If you do, you'll be damn lucky."

"Master Sergei told me that he was asking about the sandpits. Is it possible he might have gone there?"

Crighton nodded. "After discovering his mother frequents the place, Tyrus has been visiting on a regular basis, hoping to see her. I'll make a few calls and let the training director at the Mission know you're looking for him. In the meantime, you can stay in our home. If you're being tracked by demons, this is the safest place outside of Hell. No one will come here searching for you, especially after insulting my daughter."

Verity grimaced. "I honestly don't know what possessed me. I'm not normally so rude."

Crighton stared at her, astonished by her stupidity. Clearly, he had no intention of helping her, and knowing Lucifer was back in Hell plotting war against Castiel was great incentive to stay away. He made a few calls as a favor to Ariel, and then he joined Cassius in the shed to finish preparing their kill.

Meanwhile, Ariel went into the kitchen to get a cold compress for Verity's head, leaving her stretched out on the couch and Samara hovering nearby. "There's something I need to say, and it's long overdue," Samara began. "I had no part in causing your son's death, and I resent you implying otherwise. If you were as diligent about checking your facts as you say, you would know he begged me to join him at the cabin—"

"You think I don't know about this?" Verity sat up and met Samara's eyes. "Legend made bad choices and, for that alone, he paid a costly price. You were a positive influence in his life, although I didn't realize *that* until recently. So, put all your guilt to rest and bury your hatred for me. I know Dainis was sent by her brothers to kill my son because I refused to save their father from Lucifer's wraith." Verity pressed her hand on her chest. "If anyone is blame for Legend's death, it is me. But right now, I need to save my only living son. Despite what you believe, Damian is my greatest joy and accomplishment. I would do anything to for him…beg, borrow, or steal. However, I'm hoping your father will use his connections to save my son. Damian means the world to me, and I suspect you feel the same way."

Ariel returned with a bowl of water and a cloth. "What are you doing sitting up? Verity, won't you please lie down and relax? Stress will do us all in if we let it."

Samara wandered into her bedroom plagued with indecision. No matter how hard she tried, she couldn't stop thinking about Damian being tortured in prison. She knew finding Tyrus was the only answer. With his help, he could gather the scattered Crows, including Eliza, and sneak into the prison to rescue Damian. But Samara would have to stay as far away from the situation as possible. After her last trip to Hell, she'd been forbidden to return there, and her disobedience would spark a fire of anger in her father that might never go out.

Samara looked in the mirror above her sink and heaved a heavy sigh. "After this, you're going to owe me big time, Damian." She washed her face and put on a fresh pair of jeans. Then she pulled a gray sweatshirt over her head. She tied her long auburn hair back into a ponytail and secured her bangs with a bobby pin. Laying down on her bed with a sheathed hunting knife in her hand, she closed her eyes and thought about the sandpits near the mouth of Hell. Within seconds, she felt herself levitating and then she was gone.

Arriving at what appeared to be the mouth of a deep cavern, Samara shook her head at the disturbing sensation she felt. The prophetic power in her brain kept warning her of imminent danger, leaving her hesitant to continue advancing.

So weird. As Samara looked around, she couldn't help noticing the lack of sand in the sandpit. Where had it gone? Why was it taken? She knew that sand was commonly used to make glass. But all of it?

Samara arrived at a small clearing and crouched low behind large rocks to investigate the strange sounds she was hearing. She quietly approached, maintaining her cover. To her surprise, she discovered a disturbing scene. Shockingly, it seemed the rumors were true. Lucifer had a fetish for holy maidens, and this was his playground.

Seven female beings were chained up by their limbs in various configurations, all of them wearing white shirts and pants.

Two of them were dangling by their ankles, while four others were hanging by their wrists on large wooden posts. Some of them were barely conscious, others were dead in both mind and spirit. Yet, one thing was certain. They were humans on a mission and perhaps Christian as well.

Grimacing, Samara realized she couldn't leave them to suffer more than they already had. After pulling a bobby pin from her hair and bent it into a lock-picking tool. She slowly approached one of the tortured women, keeping her voice low. "Don't be afraid. I'm here to help you."

This eldest member of this group was chained to a metal spike that had been driven into the ground. She wore a t-shirt with a colorful tree branching out, denoting her affiliation with the Sacred Temple of Life. Looking up at Samara, she choked out her gratitude and appeared to be the most coherent member of her group.

"Please help them first," she said. "We were all left here to die."

After confirming they were alone, Samara crept up to the first human being. She inserted the bobby pin, rocked it back and forth slightly, and felt the inside lever lift, dropping the cuff to the ground. She repeated the same maneuver more than a dozen times, until all of them were unshackled. They began crying and hugging one another, but no was trying to escape.

"You need to go!" Samara urged. "Lucifer could return any moment and kill all of you."

"Lucifer?" A young female stepped forward. "We weren't attacked by Lucifer. This creature was far worse than the devil."

Samara shook her head. "No one is worse than Lucifer. At least, that's what I've been told."

"I'm telling you a cruel, angry demon attacked us. The meanest beast I've ever laid eyes on."

Obviously, this human didn't realize Samara was a demon as well, perhaps due to her upbringing by an angel. But regardless, she needed to get to the bottom of this crime or get out of there herself.

"Does this terrible creature have a name?" Samara asked. "A way to identify him?"

The elderly woman wiped away a single tear and spoke up. "It was my son, Tyrus. He made it possible for us to be here. We came on a purification mission, but then he showed up and didn't recognize me. He just went crazy, attacking everyone. I don't understand any of this. He was so different, so bitter, so vicious. I know he visits Hell and that he's half-demon, but what in the world would possess him to do such terrible things?"

Samara quirked a brow. "You're his mother? But how is that possible? I mean...he's half-werewolf, isn't he?"

"He was bitten when he was five-years-old and locked away for his own good. But that's beside the point. Something recently turned him into the violent monster that attacked us." She shook her head. "Although he's my son, I never want to see him again. Not after what he's done."

Samara couldn't get it into her head that Tyrus was responsible for harming anyone, especially these women. "Are you sure it was Tyrus? He's my uncle and the gentlest creature I know."

"There's no doubt in my mind," the woman claimed. "Wait a minute. Are you saying you're a demon? An underworld creature from Hell?" The brown-haired woman turned back to her friends. "She looks so normal, doesn't she? I never would have guessed."

Samara huffed. She wished she hadn't bothered helping these ungrateful beings. Her father had warned her about humans, and now she knew why. She flashed a devious smile. "That's right. I'm a demon. The absolute worst possible kind. And if you don't get your fat asses out of here right now, I'm going to eat all of you!"

They scrambled, running in circles. "Where's the amulet?" The brunette asked. "Where is it? Where is it?"

The gray-haired woman picked up a necklace from the ground. On it, a blue-jeweled amulet hung, gleaming in the sun. She dusted it off and held it up high. "I got it!"

The women suddenly became an anxious chorus. "Say the words, Georgia! Say the words!"

So that's your name, Samara said to herself. *Georgia.*

Tyrus' mother nonchalantly walked toward them and glanced back at Samara. "Demons don't usually eat humans, do they?"

Samara smiled. "Only their tasty souls, Georgia."

The old woman twisted a smile. Remarkably, there was a subtle green glow in her eyes. She turned back to her friends and gathered them close. After chanting a few indecipherable words, they all vanished into thin air.

"Good riddance!" Samara shouted. She walked toward the cave and stepped gingerly inside. There was a nauseating, musty scent in the air, like locker room sweat. It was odd, considering the nature of this place. But after encountering Tyrus' mother, nothing about this place seemed normal.

Concentrating hard, she reached out to Onoskelis with her mind, summoning her to come as soon as possible. While she didn't want to interact with her after the kidnapping and fiasco in Hell, Samara would need her to witness any atrocities to avoid raising the ire of her father. Especially after teleporting to this place.

Better to be safe than sorry, she told herself.

Samara waited a few minutes then tucked her hunting knife into her waistband. She decided to venture deeper into the cave on her own rather than wait for Onoskelis. Then to her surprise and amazement, Damian appeared from the back of the cave, walking straight toward her. But he wasn't alone. There were three demons with him, very good looking and physically fit men. By their conversation, Samara gathered they were members of the Black Crow organization that had been incarcerated with him. But how did they escape? How did they arrive here?

The demon standing next to Damian had dark red hair. His long bangs fell over one of his eyes and he wiped them away repeatedly, reminding her of Lucinda's son, sealed up in a wall by witches. She was wondering if he was still there when she noticed two small horns poking out from the demon's head.

"Fuck me," Samara mumbled, taking a step back.

The red head grinned. "Only if you ask nicely. By the way, I'm Julian, but you can call me Jules. My mother was a human with a great sense of humor…thus the name."

Samara took another step back. "This is a joke, right? Horns? You have horns? All of you?"

Damian nodded. "They grew in our prison cells. The longer you stay in Hell, the longer they grow. It's been that way every day for the past month," he said with some impatience.

"Holy shit. They're real! I can't believe it. I thought only Lucinda's soldiers had them."

"Why are you here, Sam?" The hostility in Damian's voice was unnerving. "I was under the impression you wanted nothing to do with me."

Samara drew her brows down to feign a stern look. "Your mother came to my house, frantic and scared. She said you were imprisoned by Lucifer and were being tortured. But it seems her worries were unfounded and my trip here was needless."

Damian pursed his lips and eyed her suspiciously. "I managed to escape. Lucinda freed everyone else."

"Lucinda?"

"I know. Crazy, huh?"

"Why would she do that?"

"I promised to support her in order to gain their freedom."

She looked down, otherwise her eyes might have revealed her torrid thoughts.

"I fully expected to find Tyrus here, not you. Does your father know where you are, Sam?"

For a moment, she merely stared at him, her expression unreadable. Then she silently growled. *Ungrateful bastard.*

"I didn't mean that the way it sounded. It's not that I don't appreciate you being here, Sam. It's just not safe, especially for you."

Damian was essentially a mountain of contradictions—strong and smart, passionate to the point of mania, but utterly naive and unstable, capable of developing into a saint or a monster, but incapable of knowing his own mind when it came to right or wrong. Of that, Samara was certain.

She furrowed her brows, and her gaze drifted off in thought. "Apparently, it's not safe to be around Tyrus either. Where is he anyway?" she asked. "I haven't seen him in weeks. Have you?"

Damian shrugged nonchalantly, but his gaze rested on her thoughtfully for a few moments before looking away.

Suddenly, Samara became aware of a presence at her side.

"I'm Beck," the smiling demon said. He was six feet tall, musclebound, and very pale with long black hair and eyes so dark that they seemed to be pulling Samara in. "I heard everything about you, Sam. Your father is legendary."

There was also a handsome, brooding blond creature in their group. His reputation as an anti-social instigator proceeded him.

According to Damian's sister, Seth was incredibly picky when it came to the demons that he considered friends. Jules and Beck had cemented themselves at his side, despite his half-ass rudeness. "So, you're Sam," he muttered. "I don't get it, Damian. She's cute and all that, but dumb as a box of rocks for coming here."

"Damnit, Seth! You need to shut up." Damian shoved him hard, causing him to tumble to the ground. "She's ten times smarter than you. Believe me!"

Jules and Beck exploded with mad laughter while Seth pushed himself upright. Grumbling about his sadistic and uncaring mates, he made his way towards the entrance of the cave and stood there waiting for them.

Meanwhile, Damian straightened, going into what his sister had described as his game mode. Although not the greatest strategist in their group, he preferred a more head-on type of attack, as Samara had witnessed time and again. In great contrast, she preferred using her enemies' emotions against them. But that didn't mean Damian and his pack of demons were thoughtless in every regard. Word had it they used teamwork to emphasize their strengths while backing their weaknesses.

A sound came from behind them, and Damian turned, sucking in a quick breath. Without warning, he shoved Samara behind him, and then glanced at Jules and Beck. "You're not taking her," he said. "You saw her in my mind…in my brother's thoughts. You told me all about your plans for Sam. But it's not happening. Not as long as we're standing."

Samara stared at the entity before her, disbelieving her own eyes. "Legend? Is that you?"

"Indeed, it is." An evil smile that betrayed all innocence played on his lips. "Come to me, baby. Don't be shy. Oh, what a masterpiece, the way your eyes met mine."

His warbled voice was gravelly, but his tone and his face were so familiar. Legend was back, only it clearly wasn't him. His body had been claimed by Lucifer. His red eyes were looking her up and down while he licked his lips, making her stomach painfully ache.

Damian seemed to sense her discomfort and clearly knew the source of it. "She wants no part of you, Satan. Go back to Hell where you belong."

Lucifer smirked knowing he'd already won this battle. "She'll come of her own accord, if she's smart," he said to Damian. Then his eyes dragged back to Samara, lingering on any exposed skin—her collar bone and the hem of her shirt. His roaming eyes moved to her mouth and stopped. Like a compass needle, wherever he was looking was exactly where he wanted to go. "Come with me, Sam. I have many plans for the future and need you by my side." He held out his hand, waiting for her to take it.

She took a step forward in defiance. "I'm not going anywhere with you!" Both Damian and Jules used their arms to block her from getting any closer.

Lucifer snarled. "Be smart, Samara. I'm offering you a kingdom, a title, and I'm asking you nicely. But if you want me to make your choice easier for you then witness this." He lifted his hands and pushed an invisible force away from him in opposite directions. Damian and Jules flew left and right. Jules hit the rock wall, cutting his head, while Damian skidded across the ground.

Samara stared in horror. She looked for Beck and Seth, both pinned to the ground, unable to move—unable to help her.

Lucifer growled. "You can come with me, Sam, or you can watch them suffer and die. Then I will take you anyway. Oh, did I tell you my demons also have your sweet little friend Onoskelis?" He waved a hand through the air, presenting a video of the

Shapeshifter tied to a chair with her head down, appearing to be badly beaten.

Samara looked at the Black Crows on the ground groaning in pain. While Damian was screaming for her not to go, Lucifer shut him up with a flick of his hand, leaving him choking and throwing up blood.

"So, what will it be?" Lucifer asked. "Watch them all die or come with me, my queen?" He was holding out his hand again. She thought about Onoskelis, suffering because of her. Damian was on the ground now, struggling to breath. More than anything she wanted to run to him, but Lucifer raised his eyebrows and telepathically told her to stay put. She could see the fear in Damian's face as he pushed himself upright and tried to fight the pain Lucifer was causing. But he couldn't make it more than a few steps before collapsing again.

Samara dashed over to Damian and crouched before his crumpled form. "I have to do this. I know you'll come for me," Samara told him. "You have to. Find Onoskelis and a way to get me home. I beg of you."

"Don't do this!" Damian screamed. "He'll never let you go!"

"Don't forget about me," Samara said. Then she took Lucifer's hand, glanced back at all of them and disappeared into the shadows.

CHAPTER 29

ALLEGIANCE

Samara arrived safely at the mansion Lucifer had built for her, and she had to admit it was an incredible sight to behold. Every room was filled with beautiful artwork, handwoven rugs, and expensive antique furniture. After asking her to follow him, Lucifer gave her a grand tour of what he kept calling, "*Your* new home." Somehow, he managed to keep his voice calm and soft, while still wearing his shit-eating grin.

"This will be *our* room. If you wish to redecorate it, simply say so, and I will have my servants change it to your liking."

She glanced around the large space, and her eyes froze on the giant four-poster bed with black satin sheets. A red velvet bench sat in front of the footboard. A big oak wardrobe was against the wall on the opposite side of the room, along with an elegant vanity table and red velvet chair. To Samara's right was a half-open door leading to a bathroom. On her left were French doors leading to a balcony.

Lucifer watched as she looked around the room but couldn't tell what she was thinking as she deliberately blocked every thought. "I had the wardrobe filled with clothes for you," he said. "A far better style than the lumberjack look you're going for." He pointed a finger at the bathroom door. "You'll find things inside there that most humans need and like, despite being a demon. I will leave you to freshen up, and then we can sit and eat, while I tell you what I expect from you."

He walked out of the room, securing the bedroom door behind him.

Samara ran after him and rattled the handle, even though she knew he had locked it. Groaning, she went to the balcony and tried to open the French doors. Just as she expected, they were locked too. She thought about breaking the glass panes, but after looking out from the top of the five-story structure, she realized she wouldn't escape alive.

Samara paced back and forth, and after a few minutes, she realized she had no choice but to accept her current situation. Tired and covered in dust from the cave, she decided it was time to freshen up.

The bathroom was almost as big as the bedroom, and the tub was enormous too, resembling a contemporary-designed Jacuzzi. She discovered a large waterfall shower and a wall-mounted metal rack heating two fluffy bath towels. One whole wall was covered in mirrors and two sinks were on the opposite wall. Opening a cabinet, she found it filled with assorted shower gels, bottles of bubble bath, and a large selection of bath bombs in assorted colors.

She dismissed the luxuries she'd been provided and turned on the shower, allowing steam to build up and cover the mirrors. Then she grabbed two washcloths and dropped her clothes. If Lucifer was watching her, she would make it as difficult as possible to see her nude.

After a quick shower, she opened the wardrobe looking for clean clothes. What she found was a collection of expensive dresses, each revealing parts of her body she would normally keep covered. She wasn't about to dress up as a slut, so she shook out her clothes and put them back on.

Lucifer knocked on the bedroom door and walked in, placing a tray of food on the desk. "Your dinner," he said, frowning. "I thought I told you the wardrobe was packed with clothing. You can choose anything you like." His voice was cold and close to anger.

"I don't like any of those things," she said. "I'm not going to dress like a whore because you want me to. Why can't I wear something appropriate?"

He sighed, taking the dome lid off the plate. "Eat!" he demanded.

"No!" Samara tossed the tray on the floor, sending food flying everywhere.

"You don't want to wear what I have generously given to you. Suit yourself!" He snapped his fingers and her clothes vanished, leaving her naked.

Samara used her arms and hands to cover herself and noticed that the clothes in the wardrobe were gone too.

"You foolishly tossed your dinner on the floor, so it seems you would rather starve." A female demon scurried around cleaning up the mess she had made.

"You'll change your mind soon enough," Lucifer bellowed. He strutted out of the room, leaving her cold and hungry.

Struggling to stay warm, she used the thin blanket from the bed for the next two days, but her stomach growled from hunger each night, leaving her miserable.

Lucifer returned, and for an instant, she had Legend back. The look on his face was so familiar, and when he smiled, she forgot her hunger. It was so unfair! Of all the demon skins he could take, why steal Legend's?

"Do you want to try again?" he asked sweetly. He snapped his fingers, and the wardrobe was once again full of clothes.

Samara didn't immediately answer. She stared at him with her *looks-could-kill* face. Taking food or clothing from him meant surrendering to his will. But on the other hand, she was starving and desperately wanted to hide from his lingering stare.

She nodded and slowly walked toward the wardrobe, taking out a red long-sleeve mini dress. She headed into the bathroom to change. When she came back, she saw a plate of her favorite foods waiting on the table. Part of her brain wondered how he knew what she favored, while the rest of her brain couldn't think of anything other than how good it was going to taste.

Samara sat down in the chair and began eating. Then she noticed that Lucifer was smirking as he watched her eat. He circled the table and his eyes stayed on her face.

"Now, isn't this so much easier?" he said, sitting across from her. "Ready to hear your rules, Sweetheart?"

His list wasn't extreme, but it meant giving up any pride she had left.

She half-listened while eating, keeping her opinions to herself.

"Rule number one. Show me the respect of a King, and I'll treat you like a Queen. Rule number two. Misbehaving will result in punishment, as you've already witnessed. Rule three. You are mine and only mine. You will always sit at my side and show your loyalty as my Queen. Rule four. No fighting with any demons. I don't want to kill off my subjects to please you." He continued his list of demands, while she finished the last bite on her plate.

"I believe that's everything."

Samara snickered and shook her head.

"Is something funny?" he asked, raising his brows.

As far as she was concerned, this whole situation was ridiculous. If she didn't laugh, surely she would cry. And for some unknown reason, she knew weakness would *not* be tolerated. "No, Your Majesty," she said mockingly. "Nothing is funny. Please continue."

Lucifer dismissed her arrogance and stood up. He studied her face with narrow eyes for several seconds. Then he continued his demands, walking around the room. "Your role as my Queen is to be present for everything...punishments, meetings, and announcements. You will represent the authority and symbol of my power." At this point, he was standing right behind her, his height intimidating her a bit. "You will support me as your King, unconditionally. Even if you disagree with my thoughts and ideas, you will never show it. In exchange for your loyalty and devotion, you will not need to fear any demons in Hell. They will be told to respect and honor you as their Queen. Any harm inflicted by a demon will be punishable by death." He leaned over her, lowering his voice to a near-whisper. "Finally, you will be available for me to have whenever or however I choose." He ran his fingers lightly across her right shoulder and down her spine where the new dress allowed him access.

"By the way, interesting tattoo," he said. "I never took you for the type of demon to have one. It seems there's a naughty side to you, Samara."

She abruptly stood up, moving away from him. "Do you ever shut up?" She faced him, trying to stand tall and straight, ready to give the devil a piece of her mind. "Listen to me and listen good, Lucifer. I came here to save my friends, and I imagine my family as well. I agreed to stay, but I'm not going to sit here surrounded by demon scum, bowing down to you while you destroy Heaven, Archangels, and the whole human race!" She was shouting in his face. "There's no way I'm ever going to be your fuck buddy, so get that out of your head right now. I will never sleep with you, understand?"

Lucifer grabbed her by the throat and slammed her against the wall, leaving her gasping for air. "You need to watch your tone with me, little girl, or do I need to teach you manners now?" He ran the back of his hand along her cheek, soft and gentle. "I've always imagined how fun it would be to break you…kill that feisty spirit of yours," he said.

His smile terrified her more than his anger. She didn't know what he was thinking or what he was preparing to do next, despite her ability to probe thoughts. Before she had a chance to find out, a knock on the door came. Lucifer snapped his fingers and the door opened. A demon walked in looking confused by what he saw. The King of Hell was holding a young demoness by the throat a few inches off the floor. From the look on his face, he knew he had interrupted something important.

His eyes dropped quickly. "Sir…we have a problem," he said.

Lucifer growled and his eyes became black as night.

Samara felt his grip tighten as he pulled her from the wall and threw her onto the bed.

"You're lucky, Sweetheart. Our kingdom needs me. While I'm gone, I want you to think about what I said, and when I return, you will obey all my rules. Is that clear?"

Without waiting for an answer, he walked out of the room, slamming, and locking the door behind him. Samara raced around the room, checking every door and window for a means to escape. But it was pointless. She climbed onto the bed and curled into a ball and thought about her family. If her father found out what she had done, he would either disown her or put his own life at risk in a rash attempt to save her.

What was wrong with her? Why didn't she listen? Why had she disobeyed him? She started to believe that she was more trouble than she was worth and convinced herself that no one in their right mind would love or trust her again.

Misery left her crying, but soon she closed her eyes and drifted off to sleep.

Something startled her awake. Lucifer was back, throwing open the door and making her jump. "I was going to wait but no longer." His voice was like thunder. His eyes ran over her body, lingering on her uncovered legs. She found herself wishing the dress was longer.

Anger was melting from his face, as he stepped closer to the bed. "Now, this is what I need after a stressful day. A beautiful creature waiting patiently to be devoured." He ran his hands possessively along her legs. She flinched and attempted to pull away from him, but he grabbed her ankles and held tight.

"Ah, ah, ah. The rules, Sweetheart."

She froze, debating on what to do next.

Lucifer smirked then he leaned in closer to kiss her, thinking she was surrendering to his demands. His cold lips touched hers, sickening her once again. She bit his lip hard enough to taste blood. He stumbled back hissing in pain. The opening gave her a chance to jump off the bed and run out of the room. But she didn't get far. As she turned the corner in the hallway, looking behind her to see how close he was, she ran into something solid. She looked up and discovered it was Lucifer. His arms held her tight, making it impossible to run away.

"I'm going to teach you manners, little bitch." He smacked her cheek, sending a lightning bolt of pain into her jaw. After hitting the floor, he grabbed her hair and dragged her down the hallway to a small cell, cursing her all the way.

Four days later, he returned. She was allowed to shower, which had never felt so good. Then a tray of food was brought to her by a servant girl who went by the name of Nadine. She reminded Samara of a younger version of herself, so trusting and naive.

"I was told you might enjoy some wine with your meal. Do you mind if I pour?"

Samara nodded, thinking it would dull the anxiety she felt. But before she knew it, she had finished off the whole bottle, leaving her mind dazed and her vision slightly blurred.

She scampered out when Lucifer arrived, asking why she was still wearing her white bathrobe.. "Do I need to help you out of that?"

Samara stood and the world tilted. Holding her hands before her, she backed up out of his reach. "Please, leave me alone. I haven't done anything to you."

"Nor have I. Thus, my reason for coming here. Shall we begin with lesson one?"

Lucifer scooped her up in his arms and Samara felt the warmth of his skin under her cheek. In her mind, she wanted to believe this was Legend, the demon she still loved, and the wine was making him appear all too real.

Gently laying her on the bed, Lucifer opened her robe and spread her legs wide. His cock was rock hard and throbbing, but he would save that for another time. "I'm here to please you... only you," he told her.

Dropping his head between her legs, he began flicking his tongue repeatedly on her clit. Then he inserted a finger and slowly pumped it in and out of her. "I love the way your pussy looks...the way it smells and tastes," he half-whispered, inserting a second finger. "Feels good, doesn't it? So good, Sweetheart. Can you feel the tingling sensation growing inside you? The warmth spreading and growing stronger by the second? Lift your hips, Baby. Match my strokes. That's it…that's it. Keep going. Keep going. You're so wet. So ready. You're going to come for me, Samara. The way you would for Legend. He's here with you now, wanting more than anything to please you. To know he's making you happy."

Her hips were in constant motion. "Legend…I missed you," she murmured. "So much…"

"I missed you too, Baby," Lucifer whispered. He inserted a third finger, causing her to wince. "Relax, Sweetheart. You can handle it. Just relax and enjoy the feeling." He started out slow, pumping his fingers in and out of her, increasing her wetness. Then he increased his tempo, leaving her moaning and twisting on the bed.

"You're so hot, Sam. So ready. You can do this…I know you can."

Her breathing grew heavy, and then before she knew it, she was practically panting.

Lucifer licked and nibbled his way back up her neck, landing a passionate kiss on her lips. Instinctively, she began rocking her hips, matching the rhythm of his pumping fingers. Sensing her eagerness, he increased his speed, causing her whole body to buck.

"That's it…that's it," he whispered against her skin. "Almost there…almost there."

"Oh, yes," she moaned. "Yes, yes, yes…"

Gripping her left buttock, he deftly penetrated her deeper than before and continued pumping away. Within seconds, he triggered a cataclysmic reaction. She felt her whole being converging into one point and then exploding.

"Legend!" she cried out. A wave of pleasure swept up and over her. Then essence seeped out of her, dampening the sheets beneath her. The whole experience was Earth-shattering to Samara—unlike anything she'd experienced before.

Lucifer cleared his throat, breaking the magic. "That's just the beginning," he warned her. "Let's proceed to lesson two." Before she could react, his tongue intertwined with hers, massaging it before exploring the rest of her mouth. His fingers were between her legs again, aggressively pumping away. When he determined she was wet enough, he tried to enter her with his cock, but she was too tight, and he was too large. After four attempts, he realized it was too painful for her, and despite the red wine, she just couldn't relax.

Reaching into the nightstand, he took out a small gold case. "Take this!" He demanded, placing a blue pill on the palm of her hand.

"What is it?" she asked, woozy after drinking so much wine. "You're not trying to poison me, are you?"

"Would you prefer that I rip you apart?" What little patience he had was waning fast. "It's your choice, Sam. Take the sedative or feel the pain. Or would you prefer going back into the cell in the hallway to think about it?"

She barely hesitated before popping the pill into her mouth and washed it back with the last of her wine. Surprisingly, the effects took hold within seconds. Her limbs and eyelids became heavy, and a strange numbness spread throughout her body. She found herself wondering why anyone in their right mind would accommodate the devil, especially after being physically threatened. And yet, there was a part of her that was eager to learn, believing these so-called lessons could prove useful one day.

With her legs spread apart before him, he checked her wetness and smiled. "Perfect," he said. Once again, he attempted to jam his cock inside her. She was trembling and whimpering, but somehow, he managed to insert himself halfway. Then he resorted to painful thrusting and rocking his hips from side to side.

"Isn't this good?" he whispered against her neck. "Soon you'll be craving every inch…begging to ride my cock night and day."

Samara thought about Damian, bringing tears to her eyes. He would never touch her again, knowing what Lucifer had done to her—fucking her in every way possible. She bit her lip to keep silent, wishing she had never agreed to come here. But then, what choice did she have?

Gripping her hips in his hands, Lucifer thrust into her harder than before, and her eyes squeeze shut. She tilted her head to side as he pumped in and out of her, keeping a steady rhythm. To her utter amazement, each inward thrust became a sensuous jolt, lifting her heels from the bed. Once again, she was panting and sweating, pushing back at him instinctively, bringing every sensation to a crescendo. The sound of their repeated impacts of flesh embarrassed and excited her at the same time. She realized there was nothing she could do about any of it. Any hope of control was lost. So, she might as well learn to enjoy it.

One of his hands slid to the triangle between her thighs, caressing her pulsing flesh, while the other went to her left breast, clamping her nipple between his thumb and first finger. That was all she needed. She clenched the sheets on the mattress and cried out, more in anguish than in pleasure. Ecstasy rushed and ebbed back and forth in heavy waves that soon broke into shudders. But Lucifer wasn't done with her yet—not by a long shot. He continued thrusting, almost savagely now, reaching beneath her hips to pull her up into each plunge.

"That's it, that's it. Feel the heat, Sam. Feel it growing stronger…"

Her mind swam. This wasn't Legend, this was the devil, exuding his power over her. But her mind had tricked her into believing it was him, the first demon she had ever kissed.

Lucifer held her hips in a vise grip, forcing himself deeper inside her. Then he began systematically tormenting her, pumping slow at first then manically thrusting hard. In. Out. Back and forth. Touching every part of her with his cock. Touching her very soul. As his eyes darkened, his momentum built until the bed was creaking, threatening to fall apart around them. His breaths came quicker, like a racehorse approaching the finish line. He threw his head back as he moved inside her, faster and faster and faster. Pounding out a painful, yet exhilarating rhythm. He looked down at her, seeing the excitement in her eyes. Holding himself with one arm, he reached down and gently stroked her. That was all it took for her to soar over the top again. But he wasn't done yet. Lucifer resumed his rhythm, harder and faster than she ever thought possible. Her nails dug into the mattress as his endless assault continued for fifteen minutes or more.

Then he rolled over, taking her with him. With her now on top, he coached her to keep moving. "That's it. Ride it, Baby. Ride it good." His hands cupped her hips as he helped move her back and forth. The friction was driving her nuts, making her wetter than ever. "Now bounce on me," he told her. "Up and down, like a pogo stick. That's right. Oh, yes…faster, faster, faster. Yes, yes, yes!"

Her climax was so strong that she pressed her hands against his chest to keep her from slumping against him. She continued rocking, feeling another orgasm building within her. She arched her back moaning, as the next wave hit. Again, he helped her move when the strength of her climax threatened to overwhelm her.

"I'm sorry," she murmured. "I was supposed to wait for you..."

"What for? Watching you come is the hottest thing I've ever seen."

"Whatever."

"It's the truth. You have no idea."

"Prove it."

"If you talk to me like that, I will never last."

"Good. Finish what you started. I want this to end."

"Somehow I doubt that. Your body was made for this, Sam."

"Suit yourself." With her hips held down, Samara rode him faster than ever. Then she shifted gears and began gyrating up and down with him deep inside her. She squeezed her inner muscles, clamping down tight, and continued to enthusiastically bounce. Her movements sent currents racing through her body, igniting her core over and over again. If this was sex, she was all for it. But with the right soulmate, of course.

Then two wicked thoughts occurred to her, bringing a smile to her lips. How many times could she come before passing out? Before killing this creature beneath her?

Lucifer moaned and slapped her butt. "Relax, damn it! I'm in charge here, not you." He pushed her onto her back and started finger fucking her as fast as he could, caressing her G spot by hooking his fingers backwards and forwards deep inside her. If anything, her moans got louder with this, leaving her body uncontrollably shaking.

He seemed rather pleased with himself by making her come so hard. But he wasn't about to let her rest, not until he was satisfied to the fullest. He mounted her again and rocked from side to side, settling in for a long, trailblazing ride.

Bam, bam, bam, bam! The headboard slammed into the wall, threatening to knock it down. He seemed tireless in his mission to have the greatest climax of his life. "I've been waiting for you… my whole life," he breathlessly said. "You fit me…perfectly."

Samara bit her bottom lip, refusing to cry out. *Not yet!* Her mind shouted. Legend's cock was huge, touching so many places, and his fingers were constantly moving. It was too much—all too much to take in.

"Oh no, oh no…OH NO!" she kept repeating.

"Fuck, yeah," Lucifer yelled, squeezing her hips as he relentlessly rammed in and out of her at a supernatural pace, making her orgasm skyrocket.

"AHHH!!" she screamed, as this orgasm ripped through her even stronger than any of the others, leaving her breathless and nearly passing out.

"Look at me," he demanded. She locked eyes with Lucifer as he groaned heavily, his gaze never leaving hers. "I adore you," he said breathlessly. "Do you hear me? I fucking love you! Fuuuuuck!"

She felt his seed exploding inside her as his body jerked repeatedly. Grabbing her face, he kissed her hard then collapsed against the headboard, bringing her with him. She didn't know how long they lay there, trying to catch their breath. But they were still locked together when they fell asleep.

Hours later, Lucifer rolled to Samara's side of the bed. He drew her closer, tucking her into his warm, familiar arms. This is what she'd been searching for her whole life, waiting for, craving. Tears welled up in her eyes and she willed them back. Her body ached for what might have been, because now that her imagination had experienced what she wanted more than anything, she had to let it go. And honestly, it would be the hardest thing she'd ever done. She'd given her love first to Legend and then to his brother Damian. A future without them meant living with holes in her heart. But if this was how Lucifer was planning to treat her, she might be willing to accept her fate—might be able to forget that he was the devil and the root of all evil.

As if reading her mind, he climbed off the bed. "Well, well. I might be the most wicked creature in the universe, but it seems you saved yourself for me. That makes you wicked too, doesn't it?"

Unable to come up with an answer, Samara looked around her. There was blood smeared all over the sheets, and they'd been wrapped in them for hours. Her mind was filled with a confusing range of emotions: fear, anger, humiliation, and sadness. She hugged her knees to her chest, distancing herself from him. Staring down at the red stain on the mattress, she realized she'd been forced to take a step further away from her youth, while accepting her alliance to the evilest creature in the world. He was a deadly weapon, a ruthless killer, and her beguiling kidnapper.

She needed to remember that.

After pulling on his black leather pants and silk shirt, Lucifer stood up and tousled her hair with one hand. A familiar dimple appeared below his right eye. He walked toward the carved wooden door with the key to her room dangling from his neck. Then he turned and ran his fingers through his long hair. He twisted a wry smile, reminding her that the Legend she knew was merely an illusion. Lucifer's dark side had completely devoured his mind and body, burying all remnants of her former boyfriend.

"So, how about it?" His dark eyes held a trace of humor. "Same time tomorrow, my dear?"

"Absolutely not!" Samara grabbed a pillow and threw it as hard as she could, hitting the door on his way out of the room.

CHAPTER 30

BROKEN

It had been a full month since Samara had arrived in Hell, and as the days went by, she found it increasingly harder to remember her former self. Her long auburn hair was now slicked back in a braided ponytail, reaching down the middle of her back. There were gold hoops fastened to her earlobes and heavy makeup had been applied to her face, accentuating her hazel eyes. The black sultry dress selected for her to wear featured a sleeveless V-neck, spaghetti straps, dual waist cutouts leading to an open back, and a mini-length, curve-hugging silhouette. After slipping on python stilettos, she stood back, appraising her looks in the full-length mirror.

"I look like a call-girl," she told Venus, her newly appointed stylist. Lucifer had insisted on using the demon's services, claiming she had great taste and would educate Samara about the finer things in life.

"You look amazing!" she roared. "Just believe it! I worked in Hollywood for twenty-eight years. Not only did those self-serving starlets look horrid without makeup, but many of their famous assets were also enhanced by the techniques I used."

Samara stared at her reflection. "Are you sure? I don't want to give the wrong impression."

"Abso-fucking-lutely."

"Really? I mean…just look at me!"

"You're going to knock their socks off. Believe me."

"Socks?"

"Just an old-fashion human saying. By the way, there's a buzz going round that Lucifer can't get enough of you. I didn't think he was capable of love, but maybe you've changed him."

Love? Samara didn't think so. But his obsession with her was obvious, and his cruelty was undeniable.

There was a rap on the door again. Samara heard a click in the lock and the sound of the door opening. Ruby had arrived right on time. She was Lucifer's former lover and Samara's new watchdog. Lucifer had instructed her to escort his Queen to the throne room to witness his proclamations.

"Wonderful," she muttered to herself. "Just what I've been waiting for."

Down the long hallway Samara went with Ruby trailing behind her. When they entered the half-filled room, Samara couldn't take her eyes off the goat-horned demons and red-eyed monsters awaiting proclamations, announcements, and final judgments. They openly returned her stare from head to foot, while Ruby moved to her position behind the Queen's throne.

As one might expect, Lucifer stood up with a leering smile. "Ah, my Queen. You're looking extremely sexy today. How nice of you to join us," he said, holding out his hand.

Samara bowed her head slightly before taking his hand. "My King," she said, feigning a smile. She let him kiss her on the cheek before guiding her to the impressive chair next to his.

It had taken Lucifer just under four weeks, but he did it. He broke her mentally, physically, and emotionally. At first, she tried to fight back, tried to yell, and scream, believing she could escape if given the chance. But he crushed her hopes and spirit, turning her into his little puppet. She hated it, but after suffering for weeks, she would do anything he asked and would basically let him do whatever he wanted to her. Samara's parents weren't wrong when they said there were things in Hell unimaginable and unspeakable. During her time locked up in that dark cell, she had experienced them all.

The heavy doors in the throne room opened again, and three demons in chains were dragged inside. "Well, I guess it's time to get back to business," Lucifer said, returning to his throne. The menacing expression on his face told her that he had something special planned—something evil he hoped would impress her. However, Samara kept her eyes down, trying not to be part of this. Demons around her broke out in whispers, as they watched prisoners of all shapes and sizes being lined up along the walls.

"Those demons are traitors," Ruby whispered to her. "Death is too good for them."

Lucifer narrowed his eyes and asked the three demons kneeling before him, "Who did you defy? From whom are you seeking forgiveness?"

"You, Lord," came their answer in unison.

"Exactly." With a snap of his fingers, the demons on the floor in front of him exploded. Their blood and flesh flew everywhere, coating Samara in blood. She seen death before but nothing like this. She felt sick inside and her head was throbbing. Leaning to the side, she emptied the contents of her stomach on the floor then cringed at what she had done.

Lucifer snapped his fingers again and the room became instantly clean. The blood on Samara's face and hair was gone and her dress had changed from red to gold. She was stunned, disgusted, and scared, unable to control her shaking hands.

Lucifer stood up and moved next to her chair. Turning to Ruby, he barked an order. "Escort the Queen back to her room. I have a more than a dozen executions to complete, and she doesn't seem to have the stomach for them."

After reaching her quarters, Samara stepped inside, and Ruby locked the door behind her. She took a hot shower and wrapped herself up in a warm robe. Her hatred for Lucifer grew greater with each passing day, despite the amenities he had provided, until she found herself longing to kill him. But she knew when to pick her battles and when to let him do as he wished. The time would come when his guard would come down, allowing her the chance to strike. Until then, he frequently visited the Pleasure Quarters and enjoyed the company of his whores. When he wasn't with them, he slept in his private chambers with the doors locked. However, occasionally, he would visit her unexpectedly, promising to educate her sexually when the time was right. In the meanwhile, with no weapons at her disposal, Samara kept her strong fingernails sharp and long.

To her dismay, Lucifer showed up in her room that night and stood over her bed with an unreadable expression on his face. "I thought you were a kick-ass hunter," he said.

She remained silent.

"You looked weak before my subjects, and that's not acceptable. You're the Queen of my kingdom. You should be able to handle a simple execution." Clearly, he was angry and had no problem letting her know.

"You don't see the problem?" she snapped. "It's sickening for me to watch executions. Your actions were gross and disgusting!"

Lucifer smiled. "There's that fire I like seeing. I was afraid I'd broken you completely." He stepped closer and cupped her chin with his hand. Then he leaned down and kissed her hard. "You're so damn tempting, Sam," he murmured. "You have no idea how much I want to fuck you right now. Harder than ever before. On the other hand, I want to pretend it's our first time together. How would like to do some play acting, Sam?"

"What's play acting?"

"You're going to love this." Lucifer chuckled darkly. "Let's pretend you're Red Riding Hood delivering your goodies. And lo and behold, there's a horny wolf in grandma's bed eager you eat you up. What do you think of my idea? It could be really fun for both of us."

He pulled off his shirt and cozied up beside her. Samara would have rolled off the side of the bed if it hadn't been jammed so tight against the wall.

"Come here!" he demanded. "It's storybook time, Sam."

She pretended not to hear.

"Okay. Have it your way. Tomorrow is the anniversary of my crowning in Hell., after being cruelly thrown out of Heaven. As a special bonus, I'd like to proclaim our love for one another before the Council members and Knights of Darkness. Until then, I intend to fuck you every chance I get, if you don't mind too much."

"Oh, but I do. I'm not interested in sex at all and never will be. So, I recommend you visit your female friends in the Pleasure Quarters as much as possible or stay there permanently, for all I care."

Lucifer howled with laughter. "You'll change your mind soon enough." He covered her with his body, holding her down flat on the bed. With his hands holding her wrists and his weight preventing her from moving, he kissed her neck and throat. Her reaction was to mindlessly turn her head in the opposite direction, leaving her neck more exposed. She realized too late what had happened. After trailing kisses down her neck, his tongue licked at the pulse beating wildly in her throat and across the top of her breasts.

Samara's mouth released a deep guttural sound that she had never made before. Despite mentally blocking her thoughts, he seemed to know her weaknesses and where she was most vulnerable. He delivered a light bite on her earlobe and blew a warm breath across her skin. Goosebumps rose all over her body, and she couldn't think straight. Without even knowing it, she was moaning the whole time.

Holy shit! Her reaction to his touch made her angry. Lucifer was behaving so passionately, so lusty. She had to control this—had to make him stop before it went too far. She pulled her arms free and ferociously dug in her nails into his upper arms, going deep enough to penetrate his skin. He howled and she let go as he reared back on his knees. Both of them watched as small beads of blood formed in the middle of the crescent-shaped marks on his skin. His eyes lifted from the wounds to hers. She caught her breath at the stunned look in them. Anger lay on the surface, but beneath that she could still sense blazing heat.

His voice was hard and dispassionate. "For one who purports to hate torture, you seem terribly good at drawing blood," he said ironically.

"After hurting my friends and threatening my family, I would rip you apart if I could!"

Lucifer's eyes darkened. "As I would you if you ever tried to leave me. I don't see how you could ever be anything but mine."

Before she could deliver another verbal attack, he bent down over her, planting a kiss on her navel. The skin there twitched, and she sucked in a startled breath. His hands and lips explored her thoroughly, leaving not an inch of skin untouched. Soon his pants joined hers on the floor. She tried to crawl away from his advances but two hands on her hips stopped her cold. Squirming in his grasp, she realized she couldn't outmaneuver his touches.

Much to her horror, his fingers trailed downward on her body. Figuring out where he was headed, she moved her hands to block him. But with a flick of his hand, he shoved her protests away. She was left with no other choice than to watch him touch her in places she never thought possible—never even explored herself.

His lips found her most private spot again and she arched off the bed in response. Tears fell from her eyes as he continued his ardent assault. That he took no heed of her feelings was obvious. Her hands fisted in his hair, pulling roughly at the long black strands, but he refused to stop—refused to relinquish his possession of her body.

He licked and nipped at the sensitive bud above her opening. Moans forced their way past her clenched teeth. Kissing his way southward, his fingers opened her to his perusal. When his tongue pushed inside, her entire body shuddered.

The feeling was once again foreign, yet surprisingly exhilarating, as if it was the most natural thing in the world. Instinctively, her legs wound their way around his upper back. Her heels pressed against him, bringing him closer or shoving him away. She couldn't tell which, just that her body seemed to have a mind of its own and was instinctively craving the tingling sensation he was causing. With every swipe of his tongue, she found herself being drawn into the passion he aroused. She couldn't stop squirming, her muscles tensing, straining away from his touch. At the same time, her limbs felt curiously heavy, as if she'd been drugged and was incapable of escaping his hold, even if she wanted to.

"Mmm…" He began sucking and biting her neck, sounding so animal like, so barbaric. The pain he was inflicting stimulated her body in a strange way, and she cried out as her warm blood flowed into his mouth. He sucked hard again, swallowed, and licked her gently, until she stopped bleeding.

Panting, she peeked at him from beneath her eyelids. With his eyes closed and a clear sign of enjoyment on his face, he was obviously relishing her scent, her taste, and the reactions he was invoking. He moved lower on her body and spread her labia with his fingers. Thrusting his tongue faster and faster inside, Samara arched her back again, relishing this new sensation.

"Yes, yes, yes…Legend…so good…ah, ah, AH!"

He circled every angle, sending her into orbit, as the surge of her orgasm overcame her, jolting her core. Every nerve in her body was alive, leaving her shaking and gasping for air.

Seconds later, Lucifer shimmied up her body and rested his chin on one fist. He stared down at her face, licking her wetness from his mouth. "I've been longing to do that forever. To taste every bit of you…inside and out."

Samara narrowed her eyes. "My blood too? Are you a vampire as well, Lucifer?"

"Only for you, my dear. A big, full-bodied type is excellent before dinner, as my whores have taught me. So sweet and aromatic. But delving into the most sensitive places on your body and lingering there until your eyes roll back in your head is now my mission in life. However, next time we do this make sure you call out my name or you'll be speaking in tongues."

"Tongues?"

"If you still have one. Now, how about some red wine, my beauty? A little fruit of the Gods?"

She ardently shook her head. Alcohol would only weaken her mental fortitude, and as it was, her discovery that sex was her greatest physical weakness was shocking. But worse than that was knowing how much he wanted her. He couldn't be who she thought he was. He couldn't be the Cambion she believed she saw deep in his eyes, behind the thick layers of hatred that 175 years had pent up. He couldn't be good—not even for her. Not even if the world was on fire.

Lucifer stood and moved to the small table in the corner of the room. After pouring a large serving of wine from a jeweled pitcher, he drank heartily from a goblet, dribbling a good portion down his chest. He licked his lips again and smiled at her. "Ready for round two?"

"What?"

Lucifer sprang on the bed like a cat. Samara began to inch backwards, as he moved toward her. He reached out one hand and grabbed an ankle, halting her progress. She kicked her other foot against his chest, but he quickly turned, dodging the blow. He shot forward with both hands, sliding them up her legs as he advanced on her. His hips settled between her legs, keeping them spread apart as his grip fixed firmly on her hips.

"Please, I beg of you. Don't do this to me."

Lucifer began shushing her in a soothing voice, but she was so absorbed in her misery that it made little difference. He inserted one finger then two between her legs, keeping them in constant motion. Her wetness increased and soon her body was responding to the rhythm of his strokes. He inserted a third finger and paused for a second, trying to read her expression. She felt herself stretching and let out a small gasp, as a jolt of pain shot between her legs. He paused for a moment, allowing the pain to subside. Then his fingers began moving in and out of her again, slowly increasing in speed.

"That's it," he whispered against her skin. "Move your hips. Fuck every inch. I need you to be ready for me, baby. I'll be filling you up soon enough." He moved his mouth downward and captured her hard nipple between his soft lips, sucking as she moaned below him. He was surprisingly gentle, and it felt amazing, moving his lips from one breast to the other. She couldn't help but run her hands through his soft hair, believing Legend's spirit had taken over, guiding his actions, keeping him tame.

She gasped as another jolt flashed through her body. His eyes lit up, and he took the initiative to begin moving more aggressively inside her. He was determined to have her climax a third time, maybe even a fourth, and there was nothing she could do but hold on to his shoulders, riding the wildness born within her.

"Scream for me!" he yelled. "Scream!"

She did as she was told, screaming at the top of her lungs for him to end this—to put her out of her misery. He laughed, believing she was thoroughly enjoying herself. After a rough round of thrusting fingers, tongue licking, sucking and crude whispers, she was pushed over an invisible edge again, leaving her crying out as the room spun out of control and her vision blurred. It was several minutes before she recovered consciousness.

When she opened her eyes again, a slow smile worked its way across his face and into his eyes.

"I feel like I'm on a carousel that won't stop. We have to slow down, or I'll die."

"No, you won't. I haven't begun to show you the pleasure your body's capable of."

"I don't understand," she said, seriously perplexed. "Why do you insist on doing this to me…over and over again?"

"I'm preparing you for what's to come. Next week will be all about us. The covenant will come together, witnessing our union."

"Union?"

"Fucking, if you prefer."

"They watch us?" Samara stared at him in disbelief.

"Of course, they do." Lucifer tilted his head to the side. "You don't mind faking it for them, do you?"

"Faking it?" Samara furrowed her brow. If it weren't for the unmistakable soreness between her legs, she would have deemed this all a nightmare.

"As far as your virginity goes, I've already taken that with gusto. However, they come for the blood ceremony and expect a good show. I'm expecting you to give them one."

Samara was stunned by his reveal. "What if I refuse? What if I resist the whole time?"

"Then I suppose I'll have to rape you again."

"You wouldn't dare!"

"Oh, but I would. You're more like your mother that you might want to believe. Lilith spread her legs for Crighton on a regular basis, and every demon in Hell knew it. But what they didn't know is she also spread them for me."

No way! Snapping out of her trance, she sat up and tied her robe more securely around her.

Lucifer laughed and bounded off the bed, revealing the most shocking thing she'd ever seen. Blushing, she buried her face in her pillow.

"What's wrong with you? Haven't you ever seen a male erection before?"

"I close my eyes whenever we're together. I have no interest in seeing your damn cock!"

Lucifer stroked it and smiled proudly. "A nice gift from your boyfriend, Legend. Who would've known?"

"I would. That's why we never made love."

"His loss. Tonight, you're going to discover the meaning of mutual satisfaction. A little sixty-nine action, as humans like to say." Lucifer waved his cock around like a rope, leaving her cringing. "The whores in the Pleasure Quarters told me that cucumbers are a great place to start. But I don't see the point in wasting time. Not when there's *so much* to enjoy."

"I'll kill myself before doing that!"

"What did you say?"

"I'll kill myself first."

"KILL YOURSELF?" The walls shook from his thunderous voice. "I WON'T ALLOW IT! DO YOU HEAR ME? I FORBID IT!"

Samara looked down gritting her teeth, hoping Lucifer wouldn't notice her fear. She glanced up in time to see him jerking his leather pants on and tucking his huge cock back inside them before zipping up. Then he grabbed his black shirt off the bed. Scowling, he strode across the room, slamming the door behind him. The key turned in the lock, trapping her inside once more.

Sick bastard. Samara would never be free of him and slitting her wrists would be a rather extreme solution. Lucifer had some very drastic methods for dealing with those who disobeyed him or refused to honor his wishes. As she mulled over a solution, she realized that rebellion might remove her from her position as his Queen, but it might also permanently remove her from the face of the planet.

There seemed to be no escape from this furious, all-seeing, all-knowing creature. She didn't think any of the demons in Hell would help her, but what was keeping her from helping herself? If she had wings like her father, like Ariel, she could find the closest escape route, dodge soldiers, and fly away where no one would find her. But unfortunately, she lacked the feathery appendages. In addition, her teleporting powers were non-existent with being kept so far underground. Despite her acrimony where Lucifer was concerned, she had to accept her fate to keep her family and friends alive. Yet what reassurance did she have that they hadn't already been harmed or wouldn't be in due time? By demanding proof of their wellbeing in exchange for her cooperation, she might be opening an avenue for escape that no one would see coming. It was worth a try anyway, because other than a cruel death or being forced to fuck four times a day, what choice did she have?

CHAPTER 31

ESCAPE PLAN

Early the next morning, Ruby knocked on Samara's bedroom door before opening it with her key. "He must really care for you," she said, looking her up and down.

Samara slipped on her black heels and walked through the open doorway. "Why do you say that?"

"You're not dead yet." Ruby marched behind her, grumbling about being her nursemaid.

"What's your problem?" Samara asked, looking over her shoulder.

"You are," was her only answer.

As directed, Samara took her seat next to the King, dreading what she might witness in his courtroom of injustice. Fortunately, the sentencing of prisoners Lucifer performed wasn't as graphic as before. Anyone he wanted to kill had been sent out of the room to be dealt with at a designated time and place. Samara and every demon in the room knew he had made this adjustment for her.

The meetings that followed were boring for the most part. Members of the council discussed the overwhelming number of human souls arriving daily and recommended more severe discipline for rebellious demons. They argued over the mishandling of angels and shared their unorthodox recruitment methods on

Earth. Surprisingly, Lucifer had a male Archangel at his side, giving him inside information on what was happening in Heaven.

Every now and then, Samara felt a pang of hope when a demon would mention the Black Crows or her family—how their efforts to find her hadn't stopped. But that hope was crushed when Lucifer announced that anyone looking for her was being led on a wild goose chase by his army, leaving the whole congregation laughing.

Much to her chagrin, the chamber meetings went on for days and she was expected to attend, despite her lack of interest. For the most part, she would sit quietly observing. But occasionally, Lucifer would turn to her and ask, "Wouldn't you agree, my Queen?"

She merely nodded and closed her eyes to think of happier places.

When new human souls arrived, awaiting their eternal fate, he would turn to her and always ask the same question. "What should their punishment be, my dear?"

She would turn to him and tonelessly answer, "I'm sure you know best."

By now, her heartbreak at seeing souls crying out and begging for forgiveness was gone. She numbly watched a man standing in front of her, as he was kicked to his knees. "Bow in front of the King and Queen," the guard demanded.

The human stayed on the marble floor with his head down, and Samara could clearly see the bullet hole in his head. "This is Henry Field," the prosecutor announced. "During his life, he got drunk and killed his former girlfriend. After that, he robbed a bank with a group of other men and killed a hostage…a mere child. He was shot by the police, as you can clearly see." The demon closed his file and waited for the man's defending attorney to make a statement.

"Without a doubt…guilty as charged," he said, nodding his head.

Lucifer looked at Samara. "So, my Queen, what should we do with him?"

She looked at the man, feeling no pity whatsoever. "Give him to Hecate and Lucinda. I think this one deserves their special treatment," she said coldly.

"Well, you heard the Queen," Lucifer said. "Send them away!"

The man was dragged out of the throne room and soon a mass of demons piled in. Samara had been in the throne room for hours and had become bored, hungry, and tired. She turned to Lucifer, giving him puppy dog eyes. "I'm starving. Do I really have to listen to this?"

He chuckled and called out for Ruby. The female demon growled and rolled her eyes, but Samara simply smiled. Lucifer stood up and kissed the top of the Samara's head before she left.

After walking into the formal dining room, another demon immediately brought her food and left the room, leaving her with Ruby. While she slowly ate, the ill-mannered creature stood behind her, crossing her arms.

"Will you just hurry up? Lucifer wants me to escort you back to your room." She ranted quietly to herself. "Stupid creature can't even walk around Hell on her own."

"I wish I could," Samara mumbled.

She finished her dinner and stood up. Ruby had her shoe off, shaking tiny pebbles on the floor.

It's now or never, Samara told herself. Grabbing the saltshaker, she quickly unscrewed the lid. "Are we going, or would you prefer to stay here complaining?"

Ruby snarled and yanked the door open. Samara stepped ahead of her, faking a fall in the hallway. After hitting the ground, she spun around, making a line out of salt across the threshold.

The demon put one foot over the line and pulled it back howling. "You burned me! You fucking bitch!"

Scrambling to her feet, Samara bolted down the hallway and could hear Ruby screaming out her name. She wouldn't be trapped for long with guards milling about, which meant finding a place to hide as quickly as possible. To her amazement, she found an unlocked room at the end of the hallway and ducked inside. Placing an ear to the door, she heard Ruby run by, cursing, and yelling her name.

The sound of heavy breathing and a chain rattling made her jump and turn around.

"Hello, Sam." A harsh, raspy voice whispered in the dark—so familiar yet so different.

"Ty...Tyrus? Is that you?" She noticed the thick chains wrapped around his chest, arms, and wrists, securing him to the metal chair, welded to the floor. There were cuts and ugly bruises all over his face, and his clothes were covered in dirt. "How long have you been here?" she asked.

"I don't know. How long has it been?"

"A month ago, I came to the sandpit looking for you. I found your mother there instead. She and her friends were shocked by your behavior."

"What are you talking about? What behavior?"

"Raping and brutalizing her friends."

"I don't understand. Why would I do such a thing? Sam, you know I'm not capable of that!"

"Well, she claimed it was you. According to her, there was no doubt in her mind."

He was quiet for long moment. Then he said only one word, "Lucinda."

"What do you mean?"

"Lucinda's been absorbing Shapeshifters and devouring their souls. She can change into any creature, human or demon alike. I was with Perseus, taking him to his sister, and that's when I saw her change into Onoskelis. After seeing me, she threw a screaming fit and transformed into a huge gorilla. I fought back as hard as I could, but I was no match for that bitch. She dragged me through a tunnel, and when I woke up, I was here…covered in chains."

Samara had never seen him like this—looking so broken, so defeated.

"Why are you here?" he asked quietly. "It's dangerous… especially dressed like that. What's going on, Sam? What aren't you telling me?"

"It's a long story, Uncle Tyrus. One I prefer not to go into right now."

"If your father and mother saw you looking like that…" He shook his head.

"Let's not worry about them. We need to find a way to get you out of here. Where's the key for these chains?" Samara lifted the padlock and looked around. She spotted a box filled with keys on a shelf near the door and began sorting through them. "One of these have to work. Otherwise, they wouldn't be here." She set the box on Tyrus' lap and tested a half-dozen keys. None of them seemed to work. "Is Lucifer keeping you here?" she asked.

He didn't get a chance to answer. The door opened and she felt a pair of arms around her waist, pulling her into a tight embrace. Without looking back, she knew who it was.

Oh, shit.

The frightened look on Tyrus' face scared her. He had never showed fear, not around her. So, why was he doing it now?

"Well, well…look who I found," Lucifer said with a snort. "What are you two doing in here? Cavorting without me?"

Tyrus' eyes dropped to the floor, and that's where they stayed.

"Lucinda told you to remain silent, Tyrus. Do I need to cut out that wagging tongue of yours?"

Samara couldn't believe how helpless he'd become, but then wasn't she just as weak?

Lucifer turned loose a dry laugh, raising the tiny hairs on her neck. "This is my Queen puppy, though I'm not sure why she insists on keeping company with dogs."

Tyrus didn't say a word. He kept his head down, breathing hard, obviously, trying to control his anger.

"What am I going to do with you, dearest? "Lucifer asked. "If you insist on behaving badly, then so must I."

Samara tried to swallow the lump that insisted on staying in her throat. "I got lost and wound up in here," she managed to say. "It was an innocent mistake, I assure you."

"There's nothing innocent about you. Not anymore. Let's get you back where you belong, so I can come up with a suitable punishment."

He slammed the door behind them and followed her back to her room. Then he pinned her against the wall. His fingers dug painfully into her arms. "What do you think you were doing? TRYING TO RUN AWAY FROM ME?" he screamed.

"I got lost," she repeated. "It was a mistake."

"That's why you have an escort," he snapped.

Samara rolled her eyes. "I hate Ruby. It's true, I ran away from her, but that's only because I didn't want to sit in this room any longer. I've only been allowed in three rooms in your mansion and it's boring in Hell. I was exploring when I found Tyrus. We were just talking. THAT'S ALL!" she shouted at Lucifer.

He responded with a growl. "If you're so bored, then let me entertain you." He tore her dress off and then her panties. At that precise moment, the door cracked open revealing Venus' gaping mouth.

"GET THE FUCK OUT OF HERE!" he yelled. Then he threw Samara face down on the bed. He pulled off his belt and used it to bind her hands behind her back. Then he jammed two fingers into her repeatedly, preparing her for what was to come. Putting his large cock between her hands, he commanded her to stroke it. When he was rock hard, he forced her legs apart and brutally raped her, covering her mouth as she screamed. He dragged her into the bathroom bleeding, demanding she wash herself off. Then he bent her over a chair and raped her again.

"Isn't this good?" he whispered against her neck. "We should do this more often. It's so invigorating…and it's only going to get better, I assure you."

He shoved Samara, bound and naked, into a dark closet where she dropped to her knees, shivering, and silently crying. Ten minutes passed and she thought it was over. But he was still enraged, as evidenced by his glowing orange-red eyes. He dragged her by the hair to his adjoining chamber and threw her face down on his bed. He was suddenly quiet, and, after a few seconds, she tested him by shifting an elbow. He was on her in an instant, whispering hurtful things in her ear. "Move an inch and I'll kill your family. Your baby brother will be first on my list."

"Please…I beg of you…" she whimpered. "Don't do this."

His response was to flip her over and slap her face hard, twice. She had reached a point where she thought she could endure no more—that suicide was the only way out. Reading her thoughts, he raped her again and again, despite her crying out for him to stop. Bruises now covered most of her body. His sharp nails and painful assault drew blood, dripping down her thighs and onto the bed.

"Do anything foolish and you'll regret it," he warned. "My patience with you is gone! DO YOU HEAR ME? GONE!"

Scooping her up, he carried her wounded body into her room and tossed her onto the mattress. "If you don't stay put, we'll do it all over again. Which reminds me….my need to satisfy you tore your hymen. I might need to repair that and allow you a few days to heal, so I can officially fuck you with everyone watching."

Samara waited until there was silence then broke down into tears. After turning gingerly onto her right side, she begged God to kill the heartless beast that had claimed to love her.

CHAPTER 32

UTTER MADNESS

For the next three days, Samara remained in her room, traumatized by Lucifer's extreme physical, verbal, and emotional abuse. Trays of food were brought to her and returned untouched. When an attendant found her hysterical and unresponsive, a doctor was sent for, but Samara wouldn't allow anyone near her. Word soon reached Lucifer and he responded by sending Venus to her room to calm her down. She found Lucifer's Queen curled up on her bed, shaking uncontrollably.

"What can I do?" she asked, taking a step closer.

Her advance drove Samara scrambling against the wall. She raised her hands before her in a defensive move.

"It's okay, Sweetheart. I came to help you." Venus' eyes clouded with belated concern. She was noticeably concerned for Samara's well-being. "I can help you relax, if you are willing to try, but I can't alter your situation. We are all forced to endure the journey Lucifer puts in front of us. But I'm truly sorry that your journey is harder than most. Would you allow me to help you?"

Samara's lower lip trembled, but then she bit it and looked away. "There is nothing you can do to help me. Calming down will not make matters better. Unless you are willing to help me escape, I don't know why you're here."

"I wish I could. Honestly, I do. Lucifer would tear me apart and force my son to watch." She closed her eyes briefly and drew a deep breath. "All I can say is be careful. Don't do anything to anger him. Learning patience and acceptance will be difficult, but once conquered, you will discover life is easier."

Venus patted one of Samara's hands and then she was gone.

Four more days went by without Lucifer visiting, thus four days without incident. However, Samara's internal torment was causing her to wither away physically and mentally, craving death to end the anguish she felt. Her days were filled with tears and hopeless hours staring at the ceiling. She slept in fitful, nightmare-filled bursts around the clock. Her sadness was all-encompassing. If she ended it all, Lucifer would haunt her forever, refusing to allow her spirit the calm she craved. And what about her family? Would he kill them in retaliation? Once again, she had let her imagination carry her into misery.

Samara was pulled from her stupor when she heard a key in the lock and the door opened forcibly. Lucifer strode in and sat on the edge of her bed. She curled into a ball, cringing from his presence, however she didn't have the energy to scurry away. Her body was failing. He lifted her chin with two fingers, while fear clutched her heart. She slowly turned her face away and looked over his shoulder at the mirror on the wall. She barely recognized herself. Her face was unnaturally pale, and her eyes were sunken and dark. Her cheek bones and jaw line were sharp and pronounced. She could even see the shape of her teeth through her thin cheeks. Maybe this place was turning her into a skeleton. Even her hair looked like a wig haphazardly resting on her head. Her long hair, once a feature to be proud of, was dull and lifeless.

She stared at her ghostly image without emotion. Time passed so slowly in that prison of a room. Her thoughts went all over the place these days and it was hard to tell the difference between wakefulness and sleep. However, when her gaze drifted back to Lucifer, her eyes focused on him and brought her back to the present with a flinch. Her hollow eyes grew large and fearful but quickly squinted into an angry glare.

Lucifer could clearly sense her hostility, hating him with the red-hot passion of a thousand suns. He touched her shoulder and she limply rolled to her back. "My anger got the best of me. I'm truly sorry, Sam. I'll never do it again. I'll never hurt you like that."

Samara stared up at him, struggling to find her voice. "I always thought that I could handle any situation, except for rape. For whatever reason, I felt like that kind of violation would be too much for me to handle. I was right. I cannot believe you did that to me."

"Seeing you with Tyrus awoke the monster within me…the fear of losing you."

She gave a silent snort. "Fucking unbelievable," she muttered. "You've always been evil, but I never knew how deep it went."

"Sweetheart, you knew who you were dancing with the moment you arrived. You just chose to see the good and deny the bad. I personally don't think you should change that about yourself. It's possible, when you think about it, that your energy and eternal optimism could even bring out the best in me."

Shaking her head, she laughed without humor. "I greatly doubt that."

"No matter. I made a horrible mistake and for that I'm sorry. I know you can't forget what happened and I don't expect you to, but you *must* forgive me. You *must* know I wasn't in my right mind. You *must* believe I won't hurt you again…not like that. Unless you deliberately provoke me. Then there's no telling how far I will go."

"So next time, you're going to kill me…"

"Must there be a next time? You're not that foolish, are you?"

Samara's dark eyes reflected her pent-up emotions. They showed the depth of the aggression in her hate and the fire burning inside her heart.

"Just consider this, my dear," Lucifer said. "As long as there are disobedient creatures in this world for me to destroy, the joy of my existence will not vanish, and neither will you."

"Fuck you! Get out of my room! Just let me die in peace."

"You can scream all you want, but I'm not about to let you die. I'll do whatever it takes to keep you breathing. To keep you by my side…where you belong."

"Then promise me you won't harm them…my family and friends. Prove to me that they're still alive. Until you do that, you'll get no cooperation from me. I'll never give you what you want. I will fight you at every turn. I will kill myself."

"There's no need for that, Sam. The proof you asked for will be provided soon."

"Not good enough. I don't trust you and never will. They are probably already dead." Samara deflated even more.

"You know nothing. What leverage would I have if I played all my cards? Do you have to be so cynical about everything?"

"When it comes to you…yes!"

"Well, let's put all that aside for now. It's time to get presentable. There's someone I need you to see."

"Who?"

"It's a surprise. Something that might change your attitude… along with other things."

"My attitude?"

He clapped his hands and two female demons arrived. One carried fresh towels and lavender oil. The other set down a covered tray on a nearby table. She lifted the dome, revealing assorted cheeses, meats, dried fruits, and nuts. Then she poured a large glass of red wine and bowed before stepping away.

Lucifer cleared his throat, drawing Samara's attention. "Freshen up and for Pete's sake eat something. Venus is going to help you dress appropriately, something befitting the occasion." Standing up, he moved to her wardrobe. He shuffled through her dresses and selected a long sleeve, blue shimmering, low-back gown. "Until you put some weight back on your bones, we'll have to resort to dresses that…cover you more than usual." Then he reached into his pocket and pulled out a blue sapphire necklace and matching pair of earrings. He spread them out on the bed and met her pensive eyes. "Let me know if you need anything else."

"I don't trust you, Lucifer."

He nodded earnestly. "Duly noted. I'll be back for you in forty minutes."

Samara was extremely troubled by it all. She hesitated before agreeing and snatched her hand away when he tried to touch it.

Immediately after Lucifer left, a bath was drawn, but Samara thought she'd feel vulnerable in the tub. She dropped her long t-shirt on the floor and opened the frosted glass door. Taking a shower that started hot and ended cold proved to be quite invigorating. It woke her up and added a pep to her step as she prepared herself for what was to come. Venus assisted with her hair, securing it with hairpins in a French twist updo—smooth, polished, and classic. Her elegant makeup was applied with great care, hiding the dark shadows under her eyes and telltale bruises around her throat. She elected not to wear Lucifer's token jewelry, believing it was given with false promises and erroneous intent in mind.

Venus attempted a smile. "You look incredible, Your Majesty. No one will ever know what transpired."

Samara considered arguing the point but realized there was nothing to be gained.

Bowing politely, Venus left the room and closed the door softly behind her. Seconds later, Lucifer arrived and smiled after surveying Samara's vastly improved appearance. As far as she was concerned, this meant two things. He had a fear of her taking her life and was now determined to stay on her good side.

"Ready?" He asked, gesturing toward the door.

She glanced in mirror a final time and tucked a strand of hair behind her ear. Then she nodded slightly. While walking to the throne room side by side, Lucifer promised to give her more freedom, starting with no escort.

"Really? You mean it?" she asked.

"There's no need, my dear. I'll be escorting you myself from now on."

He smiled, though it was so brief that she questioned whether she had imagined it.

Upon entering the room, a gasp of horror left her lips. Tyrus was on his hands and knees with fresh cuts and bruises on his face. Seeing her, he dropped his head immediately, not daring to look up.

"Why did this happen?" she asked, reaching out to him. "Are you okay?"

"Don't!" he said, turning away before she could touch him.

The sound of shouting and fighting outside the room erupted. Lucifer moaned. "Can't these demons do anything right?"

Tyrus hissed. "They're morons. What do you expect?"

Lucifer grabbed a crop and struck Tyrus across the face. "I warned you not to speak, you filthy mutt." He watched Samara lower herself into her chair then he disappeared outside to see what the commotion was about.

After seeing the door close, Samara hurried to Tyrus' side. "I have to get you out of here before he kills you. Before he kills both of us."

"Don't risk yourself to save me. I'm not worth it," Tyrus said, turning away before she could touch him.

Lucifer was back in the room in an instant. "Sweetheart, I really wish you wouldn't pet the mutt. Please return to your seat. The show is about to begin."

Tyrus closed his eyes and bowed his head, breaking her heart. What had happened to her strong, brave uncle? To the remarkable creature that protected their family for years? They had laughed and joked, despite their differences in age. He would never say that he loved Ariel, but he felt happier in her presence. And as for her father, they were closer than brothers. Where in Hell were they? How could they allow this to happen?

The whole meeting turned into a session of punishment directed at Tyrus. While demons watched, Lucifer humiliated him by forcing him to walk on all fours at the end of a leash, bark like a dog, then roll over and beg for a treat. He was forced to run in circles chasing his tail, while the audience cheered and laughed.

Samara felt sick watching the humiliating acts unfold before her eyes. She wanted to scream at Lucifer, but then two armor-clad demons charged into the room, coming to an abrupt stop before him. They were completely out of breath, looking wild eyed and worn out. Upon seeing Tyrus, they both dropped to all fours, increasing Lucifer's angst.

"Get up!" he yelled. "You're not dogs! What is it? Why are you here?"

"I'm sorry to disturb you, My Lord," one of them said. "We thought you should know that Imperial angels were meeting with Archangels last night. They're stockpiling weapons on Earth and making plans to attack our military force in a matter of days."

Lucifer stood up and jammed his hands on his hips. "Looks like I'm making a road trip to Earth." He waved a hand, dismissing his soldiers. Then he looked at Samara frowning and swung his eyes to Ruby. "Your Queen and my advisors will be in charge while I'm away. I would ask for Lucinda's assistance, but you can see by my altered appearance and the ashes in the furnace where that got me."

Samara silently watched as he unfastened Tyrus' chain from his throne, handing it to Ruby. Her face was so badly bruised and swollen that she was barely recognizable. Word had it that her beating was the result of Samara's escape attempt, which shouldn't have come as any surprise. For days, Ruby had been avoiding her like the plague, but there was no telling what would happen with Lucifer away.

"Sorry, Sweetheart. I won't be bringing you with me," he told Samara. "Can't risk you bolting off on Earth, joining your friends. While I'm away, you will stay here and get a feel for running our Kingdom." He offered his hand, but she refused to take it. She followed him out of the Throne Room, her eyes scanning the hallway, now empty in both directions.

"What's happening across America right now is about wickedness," he told her, as they walked side by side. "It's a war with our forces of darkness. You might say evil versus good. The politicians and pundits would have their people believing that it's not about God or even about me. It's about politics, mental illness, and gun control. But we both know better, don't we? Power doesn't corrupt humans. Humans corrupt power. And the souls of the most corrupt taste divine."

He smiled at her, leaving her heart racing, her breath catching, and her palms sweating.

"Don't worry," Lucifer told her. "I won't lay a hand on you… at least, not until you agree to forgive me. According to Venus, that could take a few more days or a week at the most. In the meantime, I have plenty to keep me busy and so will you…in my absence."

When they arrived outside her room, a well-groomed, dark-eyed demon was waiting to greet them. From his shoulders to his chest to his flat midsection, every part of him looked as if he'd been carefully carved from stone. Lucifer introduced him as Cyrus, his second in command and most trusted advisor. But there was something vaguely familiar about him, leaving Samara wondering if she had met him before. Perhaps at school or the archery range, or a neighboring city in Middle Earth.

Lucifer leered at Samara, arched his eyebrows with a lascivious grin, then stretched his arms with great exaggeration. He told Cyrus to keep her safe and comfortable. Then he added, "If she runs away while I'm gone, you'll find your head on a pike."

"You needn't worry, Master," he answered quickly. "She'll be carefully looked after."

The two creatures continued down the hallway, chatting quietly among themselves, leaving Samara to her own devices.

Hours later, on her first night alone, she snuck out of her room, looking for an escape route. But her plans didn't last long. She got lost and found herself wandering about in dark, frightening corridors, leading to various prison levels. Within the walls were crude, barred cells filled with human beings who must have been mentally ill. They were pathetically crying out—talking gibberish to their invisible cellmates.

"Well, looky here!" One of them called out. "Got us a special guest. A tasty delicacy, I'd say." The deplorable creature behind the bars ogled her with his gray, filmy eyes and licked his lips with his long, saliva-dripping tongue.

She backed up and a hand grabbed her from behind, pulling her against the bars of the opposite cell. "I'll kill you, bitch. Tear you to pieces and eat you for dinner." His strong hand was on her throat, choking the life out of her. Now panicking, she back kicked the bars, leaving them humming. He loosened his grip and she screamed as loud as she could. Regaining his hold, he held her throat tighter and cackled in delight.

Samara's vision was graying, and she could feel her body going limp. Then suddenly, she felt another set of hands pulling her away. Opening her eyes, she saw Cyrus holding her at bay, surveying her for injuries from head to foot.

"Are you okay?" he asked.

She nodded and he helped guide her to safety.

"You shouldn't be wandering around at night. There's no telling what could happen…"

She stared at him, still trying to catch her breath. "I was just exploring…familiarizing myself with the Kingdom. I guess I got lost," she lied.

Unlike Lucifer, he seemed to believe whatever she told him.

"Next time you want to look around, I suggest you wait for me. I'll be more than happy to give you a tour. Though I can't guarantee it will be memorable." For a demon, Cyrus seemed almost human in his mannerisms and the way he spoke. He led her to a room filled with overstuffed chairs, chandeliers, and dark wood paneling. "Please wait here, Miss. I'll get you something to calm your nerves. That must have been a shock for you." He walked toward a large cabinet and extracted a large bottle filled with dark gold liquid. "Whiskey from Lucifer's private stock. Under the circumstances, I'm sure he won't mind," he said with a smile, walking back toward her. "I have other jobs I need to address tonight, but if you need me for any reason at all, just call out. No matter where in Hell you are, I'll hear you call my name," he said, leaving the room.

Samara sat there, taking small sips of the throat-warming liquid. It trailed deep down in her chest, igniting a fire. The feeling slowly became soothing. It was mindless pleasure—unlike anything she'd experienced before. She felt giddy and a little guilty for drinking Lucifer's best whiskey. But the liquor was a confidence-booster, and, at that moment, she needed confidence more than anything in this world.

Rising to her feet, she returned to her unlocked room. She showered and rummaged through her wardrobe. To her amazement, she found the items she was wearing when she first arrived, freshly washed and folded. Without hesitation, she changed into her jeans and sweatshirt, relishing the feel the familiar fabric. She found a bag under her bed and filled it with necessities before leaving her room again. Following the route to the Throne Room, she approached the formal dining area where she had trapped Ruby. She froze as two male demons walked around the corner talking about the deals they had made with Lucifer. They both looked at her with quizzical expressions on their faces. She was ready to fight, if need be, but then they surprised her by politely nodding. "My Queen," one of them mumbled as they quickly walked away.

Samara was confused at first. This treatment wasn't what she expected. She continued walking, searching for the room where Tyrus was being held. The door was unlocked when she arrived, providing easy access. She stepped inside and closed the heavy door behind her. Tyrus was back in his chair, mumbling to himself. He looked up and said, "You shouldn't be in here, Sam. You need to go!" He turned his face from her, refusing to acknowledge her presence.

It would have been wise to listen, but she refused to go. Walking further into the room, she reached into her bag and pulled out a water bottle and clean towel.

Tyrus turned to see what she was doing. "Why are you here? It's dangerous for both of us."

"I'm here to clean you up."

She smiled, but Tyrus didn't react. Instead, he grumbled, "I don't want you near me. Your position in Hell prohibits you from doing menial tasks."

"Position?"

"You're the Queen of Hell, aren't you?"

Samara huffed. "Not by choice, Tyrus. And I'm not asking. I'm telling you that I'm doing it. Then we're finding a way to get you out of here. Understand?"

Tyrus snorted a laugh. "So, you're making this is an official order," he said sarcastically.

Samara grimaced. She didn't feel like a Queen. Yes, the demons called her by that name, but she could read hatred in their eyes and in their minds, believing her unfit for the job.

She cocked her head to the side. "Are you going to say no to me, Tyrus?"

"I guess not," he mumbled.

She took a knee and held his face in one hand, using the other to wipe his face clean.

He reached up, holding her hand. "I'm not one to follow orders, Samara," he said, smiling again. "I'm usually the one barking them. Remember?"

"Exactly. But I love you all the same."

After finishing her task, she stood up and returned the bottle and soiled towel to her bag. Then she grabbed the padlock holding the chains around his body and wrists. She gave it a hard jerk, but quickly realized the gesture was pointless.

Tyrus frowned. "This is only temporary, I assure you. Your father would never let me rot in this place." Doubt was evident in his voice and on his face. "You know that don't you? He's going to come for both of us. Right?"

Samara feigned a smile. "Of course. But in the meantime, I can make you a bit more comfortable." She reached into her bag and pulled out the bottle of whiskey she had absconded with after leaving Lucifer's den.

"Is that the Devil's brew?"

"Indeed, it is." She found a metal cup and poured a healthy serving.

"I guess I should be thankful. It's not every day a prisoner gets to escape his confines."

"It won't be long. I promise. I'll do whatever I can to get you out of here."

Samara stayed with him for a few hours, bringing the drink to his lips, allowing him to savor every drop. It had always been easy to talk to Tyrus, whether it was something important or complete nonsense. He knew how to make her laugh and, for the first time since she arrived in Hell, she felt happy, relaxed and content.

"It's not that I haven't enjoyed the drink and throwback moments, doll, but you need to leave while you still can. Lucifer might not be in Hell, but I'm sure sooner or later his demons will be looking for you. If they find you here, they'll beat me just to torment you, and I don't want you blaming yourself for my carelessness. Not ever!"

Samara knew he was right. She wanted to get Tyrus out of here in the worst way possible. But the only keys to the padlock were dangling from Lucifer's neck. He always kept them with him, along with the key to her room.

"I'll be back tomorrow" she told Tyrus. Throwing her arms around his neck, she hugged him hard. Then she headed back to her room, feeling guilty over leaving him alone. If she could find a way to get the keys from Lucifer, maybe they could escape together. But avoiding recapture could prove to be the greatest challenge of all.

Then a strange feeling came over her. Her neck began to stiffen and tense, and a tingling sensation began to spread throughout her body. She couldn't explain how she knew it, but she was sure someone was watching her. She looked toward the end of the hallway and, sure enough, a dark figure was standing in the recessed alcove staring at her. Their eyes met briefly, then she looked away, slightly spooked. She felt too uncomfortable to check again—to see if the stranger was still there, staring at her intently. Samara's body told her that he was. Her neck continued to tingle, as if his eyes were brushing it up and down. When it stopped, she ventured a look and discovered he was gone.

Who was he? Was he following her everywhere? Did he know about her visit with Tyrus? The thought kept her awake for hours, worrying over what Lucifer would do if this spy reported his findings.

CHAPTER 33

COMPLETE MAYHEM

Samara had just shut her eyes when Cyrus knocked at her door, bringing her upright in bed. "The first meeting of the day is starting in thirty minutes, Your Majesty," he said in a sing-song voice.

Groaning, she swung her legs to the floor, feeling tired from another sleepless night. After showering and changing into her seductive attire, she walked to the Throne Room at Cyrus' side. Somehow, it seemed different without Lucifer being there, even a little unnerving. The demons in the room were arguing, threatening to kill one another, and Samara couldn't care less.

Cyrus stood behind her chair, providing advice and constructive criticism. "You need to sort this out, Your Majesty. It's important that you intercede on Lucifer behalf. After all, you are their Queen, and they obviously need direction."

This is pointless, she thought to herself. *They'll never listen to me.*

After watching her drum her fingers on the table for three minutes, Cyrus sighed and rose from the chair behind her. Clearly, she wasn't interested in ruling in Hell, and he knew it. "You need to apply logic to the situation," he told her. "Raise your voice and let them know you mean business. You're far stronger than you believe."

Samara grimaced. "I'm just a female…a meek substitute for Lucifer. The council members and vast majority of the population in Hell view me as an invader…a rebel without a cause. Whatever rules or judgments I implement won't be followed, honored or appreciated."

"You must remember that Lucinda ruled in Hell, quite efficiently I might add. Gender has nothing to do with power when you rule with an iron fist."

"If she was so wonderful at this job, then why isn't she here? Why isn't she ruling in her father's stead?"

"Are you not familiar with their history? Lucinda tried to kill him. If not for the strong spirit he possesses, he would be lost to Hell."

"And if not for Legend's body, he might be occupying yours. No one is safe from him, especially me."

"Perhaps it would be best if I took over for a while. You seemed distracted, My Queen."

Samara stood and the congregation in the room watched her with interest. "I'm feeling a bit under the weather," she told everyone. "Lucifer's chief advisor will be assuming my duties today. Please abide by his decisions as if they were mine."

She left the room with no pomp and circumstance, just a lot of eye-rolling. After making her way to Tyrus' room, she was happy to find the door still unlocked.

"We have to stop meeting like this, kitten," he said when she entered.

Samara blushed at the nickname. Sure, he always called her sweetheart or doll, but he frequently called other females by those names too. She retrieved the whiskey bottle and tin cup from the dark corner in the room. Then she poured a generous serving and tipped the cup to his lips. She sat on the floor in front of him and they chatted about nothing, just randomness, while avoiding what was currently happening.

Tyrus smiled. "You should play your role as Queen to the hilt while Lucifer is away. All the soldiers in Hell have been trained to obey their supreme leader, and right now, that's you, kitten."

"I never considered the possibility. Do you think they would follow all my commands?"

"Within reason, I'm sure."

"What if I could arrange to have you freed? You could find Damian and the Cambion Crows. Tell them how to sneak into this place and save me."

Tyrus frowned. "Unfortunately, I don't think even you have that power. The demons in this place might be idiots, but they know Lucifer would never allow you to free me."

Samara grumbled under her breath.

"I'm serious," Tyrus told her. "Take on your role as Queen. Be the old you and lead them."

She stiffened her back. "What do you mean, the old me?"

"The you I knew before Lucifer broke you. I see traces of that spirited girl when we're alone. The tough little archery pro. Feisty, sarcastic and strong," he said smiling. "But you've become withdrawn, unsure of yourself. You accept what others want from you. Lucifer may have gotten only one thing right in all his years on the throne and that was making you his Queen. I have never met another woman more capable, more worthy of that honor. But you just need to find that powerful person inside. That warrior with a killer instinct."

Samara nodded, realizing he was right. For too long, she had allowed herself to be a victim—a plaything for Lucifer. It was time to stand up and be strong. To take back her life.

"And one more thing," Tyrus told her. "If for any reason I don't survive, you need to run, Sam. Find the portal under the prison. It will lead you to the cave near the sandpits. From there, you can teleport back to your family...where you'll be safe."

Samara frowned. "You're not going to die here," she told him. "I won't allow it. I just won't."

"Sweetheart, I know you mean well, and I love you for caring. But you need to start thinking about yourself. Lucifer will lose interest in you the same way he did with your grandmother. You must know that he only wanted Acadia after she escaped with your father and reconnected with Castiel. Now, with his brother leading the Archangels against him, Lucifer will use whatever tool he has at his disposal. And that might include you. Believe me...there's a time to accept your unfortunate circumstance and there's a time to say enough is enough. You need to grow up and move on, kitten. You need to stop worrying about me."

Samara kissed his cheek. Then she left the room and went to bed, thinking about his words.

The next morning, she was up before Cyrus came to wake her. After dressing in black leather pants and a black sheer mesh blouse, she styled her hair in a slicked-back ponytail and stepped into a pair of shiny black stilettos. Now ready for battle, she was going to take charge, applying her logic, know-how and untested negotiating skills.

She looked in the mirror and lowered her chin. *It's now or never*, she told herself.

Cyrus walked behind her through the hallway and threw open the door to the Throne Room. She walked inside, watching demons roll their eyes. Taking her place at the long table, she listened intently as a story regarding a lost relic was told. As it turned out, a pack of Woodland Hunters were guarding it with their lives and two soldiers from Lucifer's army had been killed, trying to recover it. The table of demons talked over one another, suggesting what should be done.

Samara watched them for almost a minute. Then she grabbed Cyrus' arm when he was about to stand, halting his movement. She stood and glanced at the group of angry faces in the room. Then she coughed to get everyone's attention, but arguments continued, dismissing her presence. Taking a deep breath, she yelled, "STOP!"

Instantly, every council member sat down and stared at her.

"This is a huge problem. We've lost two men and, unfortunately, made the hunters aware of our interest in the relic. How do you suppose we fix this mess?" she asked the three men seated before her. None of them responded. They just looked at each other for answers. She snorted a laugh and continued. "Okay, tell me this. What do you know about the hunters who are hiding it?"

One of the council members asked, "What do you mean? Are you asking what kind of information we have?"

Bloody morons. "What are their names? How many are there? How is the relic protected? What experience do they have with demons? Do they have any family?" She looked at their perplexed faces, grumbling inside. "You can jump in any time, if you know the answers."

None of them spoke. She wasn't sure if it was because she was female and a former hunter, or if they were truly scared. She pointed at the noisiest demon in the group. "I'd like to hear from you, Tinkerbell," she said.

He growled and looked at her frowning, refusing to speak.

"Well, seeing as you all lack respect and don't know how to address your Queen properly, I'll give you silly names, until you earn your real ones. Now, Tinkerbell, you said the hunters saw you in the woods."

The blond demon leaned forward. "Yes, I managed to escape," he said. "But the hunters know I was there."

"So, that makes you useless to me. Cyrus, please eliminate this useless demon. He no longer has value in Hell."

Cyrus did as he was asked, turning Tinkerbell into dust.

Another demon leaned forward. "Please, your highness, may I speak?"

She nodded at the tall, dark-haired creature. "Go ahead, Sweet Pea," she said.

"Most feared and beautiful Queen, my name is Jadyn. Please don't hurt me, Your Majesty." He bowed his head. "There were four hunters and now there are three. They used Holy water and salt to kill demons and had weapons for killing vampires. One of them has twin daughters. I saw them at a dinner together in the forest."

Samara smiled. "Very good. Now that's what I call knowing your enemy. Jadyn, take two guards with you and find the twins. Capture one of them and keep them hidden away. Then claim the relic and bring it back safely. Should there be any reprisals or more deaths by the hunters, you have a bargaining chip, namely their child."

Other demons in the room nodded and talked among themselves. They seemed impressed with how Samara handled the situation.

Cyrus smiled. "Very good, your highness. That matter will be handled as soon as possible."

By the end of the day, the council members were eating out her hand. She took a break from their meetings to sneak off and visit Tyrus for a few hours.

After hearing her report, he told her, "I'm so proud of you, kitten. I would've loved to see you in action."

The week went by in similar fashion. Samara attended meetings during daylight hours and visited Tyrus at night before returning to her room. And Jadyn did exactly as he was told. He left the female twin in the care of the whores in the Pleasure Quarters and presented the lost relic to the council. On closer inspection, it turned out to be a hand-carved gold box resembling a small coffin. Samara opened the lid and found a devil doll inside. She wanted to scream. The lack of significance for such a thing was unfathomable, especially considering the loss of life surrounding it.

Surprisingly, Cyrus seemed delighted with the strange object and when questioned told her why. "Many years ago, the witches of the Gnarly Forest created that doll with cuttings from Lucifer's hair and ripped pockets from his shirt. They were planning to trap his soul inside the doll and destroy it in their communal fire. But they were frightened away by the hunters in the woods and left their treasure behind on an altar. Lucifer has been desperate to find it after learning that the colony of hunters possessed it."

Interesting. "Are the Gnarly witches capable of accessing the tunnels?"

"I...don't really know. But I doubt they will attempt to enter Hell."

"Well, believe it or not, I encountered two of them while being held captive by Warwick, Lucinda's son. They trapped him inside a wall and set me free in the tunnels. I wouldn't be surprised if he's still there."

Cyrus shook his head. "Lucinda isn't the best mother in the world, but I doubt she would allow him to suffer. They have a unique bond, those two. If he's in trouble, he'll reach out her."

Samara rubbed the back of her neck. "Is it possible that Warwick is watching us in the shadows? Reporting back to his mother?"

"It wouldn't surprise me at all. When he's in Lucinda's favor and not acting out, those two are thick as thieves."

"But doesn't it worry you that they're hiding out? They could be plotting against Lucifer. Waiting for the right moment to assume power again."

"That's not my concern," Cyrus said. "I follow whoever is on the throne and right now that happens to be you. But tomorrow is another story. Lucifer will be back, and everything will return to normal."

Samara felt sick inside. She wanted to escape from the madness, taking Tyrus with her. With no loyalty in the Kingdom, word of her disobedience was sure to reach Lucifer. Then all Hell would break loose. She would be tossed into the Pit of Despair, never to be found again.

Cyrus cleared his throat. "Would you like me to escort you to your room?"

Samara feigned a smile. "If I don't know where it is by now, then I'm definitely in trouble. Aren't I?"

"I know it's not easy for you, living this life," he said, "but always try to remember, you're not the only one with problems in Hell. You're one of many, along with Lucinda. In a hundred ways, she isn't deserving of sympathy, but I still think of her as a tragic figure, stuck in Hell with the rest of us with no way out."

CHAPTER 34

NIGHT TERRORS

Samara went to bed and had the most frightening nightmare of her life. Demonic faces were surrounding her, leering at her while stretched out on the ground, stripped bare from head to foot. She was then yanked off the ground and forced into a cell where the mad humans were kept. Staring between the bars, she witnessed her father chained to a wall with her young brother beside him. Hecate was cracking her whip, ripping into their bodies, while Ariel kneeled before them, praying to her almighty God. Suddenly, Ariel was jerked to her feet by a hooded villain and shoved into a different cell with an insane creature. Then Lucifer arrived, observing the scene, and grinning from ear to ear. Ariel's cries for help left tears streaming down Samara's face.

"I have a gift for you, Sam," he said. He held out his arm producing the most horrifying sight imaginable. Tyrus' head dangled from his clenched hand, dripping blood onto the ground.

Her gut wrenched and she squeezed her eyes shut, willing it not to be true.

"Too much?" Lucifer chuckled. "He asked for my pardon for all of you and received my answer in the Court of Justice. There's nothing to forgive, I told him. Dogs instinctively crave affection, even from the wrong demons. Your Queen betrayed you, and she betrayed me. Her family will suffer for her mistakes, I said. Then I cut off his head and burned his body. He was a man devoid of hope anyway, so it seemed befitting to end his torment."

Samara screamed bloody murder, rattling the bars. "I HATE YOU, I HATE YOU, I HATE YOU!"

Cyrus charged into Samara's room followed by two guards. He found her in the corner of her room, curled up in a ball, covered in sweat and shivering from fear. Calling out for assistance, a female demon arrived. She guided Samara into the bathroom. After carefully washing her off and changing her into a fresh nightgown, the demon helped her into bed and followed Cyrus and his men out of the room.

The door remained cracked open, allowing Samara to hear Cyrus' voice. "Must have been the whiskey she drank. The bottle I gave her was found in the trash a few hours ago. Looks like I'm going to pay big time for this."

Within hours of his arrival, Lucifer burst into her room. He called her an ingrate, lush and raging alcoholic. After pitching a glass full of wine against the wall, he insisted that she get dressed immediately and join him in the Throne Room.

Samara's hands shook while dressing in a provocative gold gown. She styled her hair the way Lucifer liked it—long wavy tendrils around her shoulders and down her back. She secured his sapphire necklace around her throat and attached the dangling sapphire earrings to her earlobes. Clearly, they were token gifts to ease his conscience after raping her for hours—a way to seek her forgiveness. But it couldn't be bought, and she refused to forget, despite wearing his jewelry.

Taking a deep breath, Samara started down the hallway, counting her steps. She arrived in the Throne Room, regretting she hadn't left Hell before now.

It seemed Lucifer had been waiting for her arrival. He disappeared briefly then kicked Tyrus into the room. Her uncle was covered with fresh cuts and bruises, and the culprit behind his injuries was grinning. The whole episode seemed like a bad dream that she would never wake up from.

"Stop it!" she yelled, then quickly regretted her words.

Lucifer raised his brows. "Do you have a problem, my love?" he asked, daring her to defend her uncle.

Thinking quick on her feet, she answered, "I don't want blood all over the place. And I don't want to witness you putting it there." She looked at Tyrus, more worried than she had a right to be. In Hell, he was her only friend, her only ally.

Lucifer smiled, accepting her answer. But the look in his eyes told her it wouldn't be the end of this. The rest of the meeting felt forced and uneasy. The tension in the room grew and was so thick at one point, that it could almost be cut with a knife. Lucifer said he was happy about the demons retrieving the relic, though he failed to show it. Then he claimed he could use it to stop his brother, though Samara had no idea how. After that, things went downhill fast. He was unhappy with the condition of his mansion, with battle plans involving Archangels, with the lack of sand in the pits, limiting the production of food, wine, toothpaste, glass, paper, paint, and plastics. His temper was constantly flaring, leaving demons walking around on eggshells, unsure how to please him or what to say. By lunchtime, four of them were reduced to dust.

Then things got even worse. Demons were arguing over selling souls. "I think we should shorten the time limit for making deals," one trader said. "The price points for the most wicked souls are going up fast. We stand to make a killing in the market if we play our cards right."

Tyrus surprised Samara by mumbling under his breath, "With converts multiplying, soul trade is being reduced around the world."

"What did you say?" Lucifer asked him, narrowing his eyes.

"He just clarifying, Your Majesty," the trader answered. "I'm sure he meant no harm."

Lucifer growled. "Who do you think you're talking to? The village bumpkin?" Before he could answer, Lucifer snapped his fingers, reducing the trader to dust. "Does anyone else need advice from this mutt? Raise your hand if you want it chopped off!"

When no one responded, Lucifer jumped out of his chair and smashed Tyrus' head on the floor. Samara winced and stared at Lucifer in horror. All the demons in the room kept their eyes down, afraid to move, afraid to breathe.

Tyrus was now bleeding profusely, bringing tears to Samara's eyes. She needed to do something to stop the abuse but was too afraid to act. For the first time since Lucifer began his sick games, she felt genuine fear trickle through her, believing it was only a matter of time before she would face a similar fate.

Tyrus mopped his forehead and stared down at the blood on his hand. Then he looked up at Samara, grimacing.

Lucifer stepped back a few feet, following his line of vision, and openly displayed a beastly snarl. "My Queen doesn't like blood on the floor. Clean it up!" he yelled.

"If you could just provide a towel…"

One of Lucifer's guards tossed him a toothbrush.

"Not with that!" Lucifer shouted. "With your tongue, you mangy mutt!"

Samara stood up, anger and hatred bubbling within her. "Enough! This meeting will last all night if you allow these constant interruptions." She looked at one of the traders. "I believe we were discussing the current market price for souls. Isn't that right?"

Her plan worked. Lucifer pointed at the toothbrush and Tyrus began scrubbing the floor, wiping his blood on his filthy pants.

"Would you remind us of the current rate?" she asked.

Lucifer snarled. "Who gave you the right to run this meeting?"

"If you allow me to help, there will be fewer deaths in this room."

"My, my. Give you power for a week, and you think you can overthrow me. Imagine that."

"I'm not overthrowing anyone. I'm doing the right thing. If you weren't behaving so bloody childish, you'd recognize that!"

The face of every demon in the room paled, and Lucifer instantly became angrier than she had ever seen him before. Her life was over—there was no doubt about it. She had pushed too far and now found herself regretting her actions. But then to her surprise, Lucifer smiled, throwing her completely off guard.

"I've always admired strong female leaders. But there are limits to my patience. You need to remember that My Queen."

"What kind of limits?" Samara looked confused, so Lucifer attempted to further explain.

"Take Lucinda, for instance. She's been rubbing demons the wrong way lately. She showed up in Middle Earth a few days ago with Hecate. They caused a scene in the hot springs and in the hotel. It was highly inappropriate. She has offended more than a few demons and council members. And quite honestly, I'm ashamed to call her my daughter."

"Well, whatever she's done, I'm sure it was just to make a point. Women should be able to make their own choices and stand up for themselves when they're mistreated."

He picked up his crop and smacked it across his palm, looking angry enough to use it on her. "I hope you weren't referring to yourself," he growled.

"Actually, I was referring to women in general. Their intelligence and points of view could be beneficial. You might even consider adding a few to your council."

"Why would I do that?" he yelled. "I have my hands full with my daughter. I don't need to hear about female ideas, beliefs, or practices. Lucinda's methods are intrusive, and her opinions are disturbing. Surely, you can't agree that she should be spreading such ideas. I mean, not even her son can condone what happened between her and Hecate."

"I don't understand. What happened?"

"They spent the night together!"

"Well, that doesn't mean anything," she stated obstinately, determined to keep the focus away from Tyrus. "How could it? Lucinda was severely beaten by Hecate. I would assume they're enemies now, not lovers."

"I want to believe that, but it's not the first time Lucinda's warped mind has produced biased opinions and poor judgment. For months, I've heard rumors about her bisexuality in the Pleasure Quarters. However, she's never been so open about being…uh…well…intimate with a female," Lucifer said uncomfortably.

"If something did happen," Samara started, "then they must really care about each other. And if they do, why wouldn't you accept it?"

"And what if I refuse? Those two conniving bitches are up to something…I can feel it. They could be plotting against me right now, for all I know." Lucifer stood up and rambled on, pacing back and forth in front of his throne. "They're angry at me for punishing Lucinda…over torturing her. It's ridiculous! She destroyed my body! She's lucky to be alive."

Samara tried to hide her annoyance. "Somehow I doubt there's anything to worry about. They're probably in their private quarters right now, making plans for the future."

Lucifer stomped his foot. "EXACTLY! They're plotting my assassination right now!"

Cyrus butted in. "Don't you think you're being paranoid, Your Majesty? I'm sure there's nothing to worry about. Didn't you say Lucinda's son was back? It's possible they're with him, engaged in some innocent activity."

"INNOCENT?" Lucifer let out a huff. "They're conspiring against me. I'm sure of it. I can feel it in my bones."

"They would be fools to collude against you, My Lord. No one will follow Lucinda. She has no army, no loyal supporters. No power in your kingdom. However, there are other important matters that do require your attention and—"

"REALLY?" Lucifer retorted, huffing. "Lucinda hates me more than any creature has a right to. That's why she's keeping her distance, why she's scheming against me. I want you to find out what she's been up to. Why I've heard nothing out of her for the last month. If she refuses to cooperate, then bring her son to me. The threat of torturing a loved one works every time."

Cyrus silently nodded.

"And tell the guards to put that Hybrid back in his room. His smell is beginning to annoy me. And you know what happens to mutts when I'm annoyed."

Samara looked at him, the furrow between her eyes turned from concern to confusion.

"They're reduced to dust, that's what!" He answered his own question.

She clenched the arms of her chair hard enough for her knuckles to turn white. "Do I have your permission to return to my room? I have a terrible headache and need to lie down."

"I bet you do…after finishing off my favorite bottle of whiskey." The frustration in his voice and on his face was undeniable.

"If only I knew that anything besides humiliation would come of it," she said coldly.

Lucifer sighed and shook his head. "Goddamn it! Cut back on your drinking and keep your opinions to yourself. You're either on my side, by my side, or in my fucking way. So, choose wisely, my Queen. Push my patience too far and—"

"You don't need to remind me."

He looked at her solemn face and snorted. "Fine, fine. Leave if you must. Cyrus will accompany you. But if you're found wandering around in the hallways again, I'll have you stripped, whipped, and caged. Is that understood?"

Samara nodded and slowly came to her feet. How many ways could he break her? She had lost track and was now reduced to a sack of broken glass in the shape of a woman. Her edges stuck out at hard, invisible angles, waiting for an unwary hand to snag them and recoil. So, she kept her eyes down, following Cyrus to her room, looking like a chastened child.

When he offered to bring her a bottle of fresh water, she answered, "No, thank you." He nodded and quickly turned on his heel, eager to leave her presence. She considered apologizing for the whiskey she'd consumed, but then decided against it.

Nothing would be gained by revealing the trust she had broken, while visiting Tyrus every day.

Sitting down on the edge of her bed, she wiped angry tears away. Her heart was heavy with feelings that she didn't have the strength to uncover—that she preferred to ignore.

Cyrus' hand was on the doorknob when he turned around and faced her. "I want you to know that I sit back and observe every demon in Purgatory, whether we talk or not," he said. "I know Lucifer's strengths and his hidden weaknesses. I also know mine. I keep track of who talks about me and smiles in my face. I know who I can trust and who to keep my distance from. When I watch you pretend to be normal, I see the pain in your eyes. I know the ache in your heart. And just to clarify, I took the blame for the whiskey and was punished for it. You were being tested by Lucifer and failed because honesty is your greatest failing. Knowing this, I wish I could help you escape from here. But as I'm sure you're aware, there's no forgiveness in Hell. My son would suffer greatly for my actions. With his mother gone, he's all I have."

Samara nodded in reluctant agreement.

"Thank you anyway, Cyrus," she said. "I appreciate your kind words."

Surprisingly, he crossed the room quickly and sank to his knees, hugging her like he would never let her go. Then he stood up, avoiding her eyes, appearing to be slightly embarrassed. "Bye, Samara. I mean…good night, My Queen." His simple, earnest response and the conviction on his face floored her.

Immediately after closing the door behind him, it dawned on her that nearly two months had passed with no word from her father, Ariel, Damian, or the Black Crows. It seemed they had all forgotten about her. After being raped, tormented, and humiliated by Lucifer, there was nothing he could do to her that hadn't already been done. The only thing she dreaded was the thought of never leaving here again—that at some point, her usefulness would end, and he would turn her into dust. Until that time, she had no choice but to drown her misery in wine.

It suddenly occurred to her that her reawakened instincts were near the surface now. She had experienced them with the stranger in the shadows. Her powers weren't waning. They were simply waiting for the right moment—for Lucifer to slip up so she could escape and take Tyrus with her. But she needed to be patient and observant. She needed to convince Lucifer that she had resigned herself from rebellion and was willing to be his Queen and soulmate—that she was willing to dismiss his abuse.

It won't be easy, she told herself. *But it's only a matter of time before he fucks up by trusting me again. He'll fall asleep and I'll steal his keys. Then Tyrus and I will be out of here for good.*

That night, she was desperate for sleep but feared the nightmares that plagued her. Rummaging through her nightstand, she found two overlooked sedatives. Apparently, Lucifer had pocketed the rest of them during his last visit, fearing she would off herself after his repeated attacks. Looking around the room, she spotted a large glass of wine on the circular table, along with an assorted cheese sampler. After indulging herself in the tasty selections, she swallowed the sedatives and washed them down with a full glass of wine. Then she laid her head down on her soft pillow and closed her eyes, hoping an escape plan would come to her, if she could just get a decent night's rest.

An hour later, she woke up a little drowsy, wondering where she was and why her hands were tied behind her back. She was blindfolded as well. Then a series of clouded events washed over her, causing her heart to race. She shook her head and realized too late that the combination of cheese, sedatives and alcohol was a mistake. She rolled over and emptied her stomach. When her body finally relaxed, she struggled against whatever was tied around her wrists and pushed herself upright. The ground was rocking and jostling. That is why she was so nauseas. She was in the back of some sort of vehicle, and they were traveling somewhere fast. She wondered who had kidnapped her and tried to listen for clues.

A sudden stop made her lurch forward. She heard the back of the vehicle open and fresh air filled the space. A male voice yelled, "Take her out!"

Then a second voice yelled, "Ah, crap! Look at the mess she made!"

Large hands grabbed hold of her and jerked her onto the hard ground. She could feel the warmth of sunlight washing over her, but with a blindfold over her eyes, she couldn't see her surroundings.

"Hurry up!" Another voice yelled. "Get her inside before someone sees her!"

Hands went under her arms and Samara was quickly carried across some distance and could sense that they entered a building. Whoever carried her came to a quick stop and set her down roughly.

"You know who she is, don't you?" A third voice asked.

"Yep," the first voice answered. "Lucifer's Queen Bee, that's who. He's going to shit his pants when he finds out we have her. I absolutely guarantee it!"

CHAPTER 35

STOLEN PROPERTY

Cyrus stood between two guards in the Throne Room, his inscrutable face incapable of disguising his sense of expectation. "It's official, My Lord. Samara is gone."

"What do you mean...she's gone?" Lucifer's voice echoed throughout the chamber. His dark eyes narrowed, and his nostrils flared. "First you lose her in the mansion and now you can't find her anywhere? As my second in command, I hold you solely responsible."

"I understand, Master, but we're doing everything we can to locate her, and we may have a lead."

"You are obviously worthless!"

"I've got soldiers searching everywhere for clues. We're trying to determine how they were able to enter Hell and escape unseen with the Queen."

Lucifer growled. "What an incompetent fool you've turned out to be. Must I break your son's neck for you to have answers?"

"No, Master," Cyrus replied stiffly. "One of our scouts just reported back. It seems Samara was taken to Earth by members of the Black Crows. However, their world isn't like ours. There are millions of human beings and so many places to hide."

"They're Cambions!" Lucifer exploded. The Hellhound at his side gave an indignant growl, and Cyrus eyed the saliva-dripping creature warily. "They're half-breeds. They have limited powers and no beasts to protect them. And yet you cannot find my Queen?" He stepped closer to Cyrus and kept his face inches away. "Make me understand," he hissed, his eyes never leaving his face. "Tell me why your searches have failed...why I shouldn't demote you right now. Why I shouldn't crush you under my heel."

Before he could answer, Lucifer ordered everyone out of the room. Then he turned back to Cyrus, staring at him with glowing red eyes. "If you tell me the truth, I'm going to be mad, but I'll get over it. If you lie to me, I'm never going to be able to trust you again. Your choice."

"I would never lie to you, Master. I swear!"

"Then tell me, Cyrus. Why haven't you found her? Is it because you still care for her? Did you let her flee...on purpose?" His amber eyes bore into Cyrus' black ones.

"I stopped caring for Samara years ago. She doesn't even remember me." Cyrus set his jaw and challenged Lucifer with a stern look.

"Then stop wasting my time and find her. Make her trust you," he hissed. "Then bring her to me."

Cyrus swallowed hard. "What if she doesn't trust me?"

"Then kill her. Samara is a great fuck, but she's become more trouble than she's worth."

"What about her parents? When they get word—"

"If they show up in Hell, I want them brought to me right away. It's about time I settled old scores."

"There's one more thing...you should know," Cyrus sounded nervous and kept hesitating as he spoke. "Tyrus is missing too."

"HOW IS THAT POSSIBLE?" Lucifer yelled. "ARE YOU TRYING TO DRIVE ME INSANE?"

Cyrus kept his eyes down. "No, Master. The padlock on his chains was snapped by the invaders. But he didn't leave with them. He was spotted near the sandpit cave, heading into the woods."

"Interesting. So, he saved himself. That worthless piece of shit…"

"It appears that way."

Lucifer shook his head, still frowning. "Enough talking. Send patrols to Earth immediately. I want the heads of every Black Crow and especially Damian Hunter's. I should've destroyed him when I had the chance."

Cyrus nodded and turned away, his footsteps echoing on the damp stone floor.

Lucifer remained on his throne, stroking the neck of his Hellhound. "Time to shed this skin, Rhino," he said. "I just picked out the perfect replacement, and you're going to love it. Cocky, clever, and delightfully devious. And he's rather good looking too. No one will even know it's me, except for you and the rest of the pack. Your sense of smell is amazing. So we're going to be apart for a while. Cyrus will oversee your care, and he's going to take all of you hunting. If you happen to find Tyrus, I want you to rip him to pieces. No more mercy for that beast or for anyone protecting him. Is that clear?"

Saliva was dripping from the Hellhound's mouth. His beady eyes were glowing bright red, and steam was rising from his nostrils. It had been a while since any of the hounds had eaten in preparation for the hunt. They were hungry for fresh meat and, more than anything, they were eager to please their master.

CHAPTER 36

TIED & TESTED

Samara had been tied to a metal chair, preventing her from escaping. She shook her head hard, loosening the scarf over her eyes. It dropped to her neck and stayed there. The lights were off. A few seconds passed before they were turned on, blinding her briefly. Gray metal cabinets lined two walls on either side of her. Directly before her was a stone-covered wall and in the center of it was a large black door. With no windows or ceiling vents, it seemed to be only way out of the room.

The smell in the air became nauseating, reminding her of damp, moldy food, or possibly rancid meat. Samara heard a rustling sound and realized that something—no, someone—was in the room with her. The drooling creature slowly circled the chair, leaning close to sniff her. It was a male demon with black matted hair and a sallow complexion. His black sunken eyes were constantly moving from her face to the door, like an animal longing for permission to eat.

"All mine?" He asked no one as far as she could tell, while reaching for her shirt. Then he cocked his head to the side in quizzical fashion. "Thorn eats now?"

"Leave me alone!" Samara yelled. "Don't touch me! Stay back!"

He ignored her demands and lifted her shirt up, revealing her stomach. Meeting her eyes, he grinned playfully. His mouth was filled with pointy teeth and all of them were covered in blood. She turned away, not wanting to know the source. He touched her stomach with a single finger, and she recoiled, wanting to slap it away.

"Nice," he whispered. "So fresh. So soft." He placed his ear above her chest, completely unnerving her. Then he ran a sharp nail across her belly causing her to wince. His action drew a fine line of blood, leaving her shaking. He bent down and licked tentatively at the trail of blood as she squirmed in her seat, screaming for him to stop.

Raising his head, he licked his lips and said, "Thorn wants liver. Can Thorn open the belly now? Get liver out?"

"Get away from me, you sick bastard," she hissed.

Her body was freezing, her hands were shaking, and her thoughts were so scattered that she couldn't think straight.

"Thorn likes liver first. Always good first," he mused. "Then heart and kidney. Save brain for last."

She sat paralyzed with horror, unable to scream. Had she been brought here for this creature's next meal?

The black door flew open. "Thorn! Get away from her!" A man's voice tore through the room, jarring Samara in her chair.

Thorn jumped, scratching her stomach again in the process. He looked hurt and angry. "We're not happy today, Blade. Thorn was having alone time...when...when this *thing* showed up." He pouted like a child and threw himself onto the ground in what she perceived to be a full out tantrum. "Make it go away!" He yelled, curling into a ball. "I want to rip it apart, but Thorn won't let me. He wants to play games with it. Keep it in his file cabinet with his dead rat."

Within a few seconds, Thorn's facial expression relaxed, and he appeared almost serene. "Blade! You're here! I missed you."

It seemed Thorn had split personalities, both disturbing.

"Go back to your hole!" Blade yelled.

"Thorn good. We're having fun, aren't we?" he asked Samara. The maniac glint was back in his eyes and his smile slowly spread, revealing his sharp teeth again.

"I...I don't like games," she stuttered, not sure what to say.

The creature rolled his eyes and scrambled away on all fours, disappearing into a hole in the wall.

Blade leaned back against the stone wall a few feet from her, arms crossed and cold blue eyes on her. "So, you're the Queen of Hell. Why would you allow yourself to be used as a tool, a mere instrument to satisfy others? Your potential is limitless. The volume of possibilities that you have is void of restriction. What has been driving you? Lust or insanity? Or can you no longer discriminate one from the other? Have the months of abuse by Lucifer impaired your vision? Dulled your mind and your innate skills? The boundary line between strength of character and submission doesn't exist for you anymore. You must walk, run even. Allow your feet to transport you to a place where the lines begin to form. You need to find clarity through the separation of unsightly and malevolent bonds. Only then can you find yourself again."

"I don't understand! Why am I here? Are you a demonic philosopher? I thought the Black Crows took me, but you're not part of their group. You're just a villain...no different than Lucifer!" she screamed.

Blade snorted and shook his head. "I was a Black Crow once, but they became political, and I'm far from it. My organization is built on honesty, trust, and alliance. You have value but don't know it yet, Samara. You need to rediscover your worth." He untied her from the chair, but kept her hands cuffed. "After a simple test, your freedom will come...if you have the right answers."

He put his hand under her arm, and she pulled away. "I don't need your help or anyone else's," she growled. She walked beside him through the open doorway and into another room. There was a bright overhead light and wires and plugs everywhere. On the closest wall was a blinking control panel, like something out of a Frankenstein movie.

"Relax," Blade told her. "This test won't take long."

"Why is this necessary? Why are you doing this to me?"

He shoved her into a chair unnecessarily hard and sat down across from her. She straightened in her seat and looked around, noting the walls were white except for one. There were blood stains on it, raising her anxiety level.

There was a knock on the white door and Blade got up to answer it. "Doctor Ashe," he said. "Thank you for coming on short notice."

Samara knew immediately this doctor was human. She wore a white lab coat, and her brown hair was pulled back in a bun. Her brown eyes looked large behind her thick spectacles, and Samara could smell her vanilla hair conditioner.

"You know the routine," she told Blade. "I need your assistance with plugging her in."

Despite desperately struggling to get away, they managed to put needles into Samara's arms with wires leading to the control panel.

Doctor Ashe cleared her throat. "All right. I'm going to run the system check now. If she has the blood in her that Dante has been talking about, then we will know soon enough."

She typed keys on the computer, and before Samara had time to figure out what she meant, she felt a jolt. White-hot pain radiated from the tip of her toes to the top of her head, temporarily blinding her. It took a few second to realize that the agonizing scream was coming from her.

Then everything went dark. Samara realized it wasn't because she had passed out but because all power in the room had shut down.

"What the fuck happened?" Blade asked, obviously annoyed.

"Some kind of reaction in our system," the doctor replied.

"We need to check the main circuit."

They left the room and Samara was more in the dark than ever. When they returned, a needle was stuck in her arm and blood was taken, leaving her feeling lightheaded. She didn't know what they had done to her, but the urge to vomit returned. Taking a deep breath, she tried to steady herself. Maybe this wasn't real. Maybe if she closed her eyes and fell asleep, she would wake up and discover it was all a bad dream. But a growl from Thorn in the next room made it all too real—too frightening for her mind to accept.

CHAPTER 37

SELECTED

Samara heard a muffled conversation outside the white door. "I honestly think she's the one," the doctor said. "Yeah, it seems Dante was right," Blade added. "We'll explain it to her in due time, but right now we need to get moving."

The door swung open. "We're going," Blade growled, unfastening Samara from her chair.

She wanted to ask where, but instead stared straight ahead, allowing him to lead her wherever he wanted, if it was far away from this place.

He guided her through a long hallway with concrete floors, their steps echoing as they walked. She heard a distant scream pierce the air and stopped abruptly. "Keep going," Blade hissed and pushed her forward again.

"Keep your hands off me!" She snapped.

"What are you going to do about it?"

"If I wasn't cuffed, I'd show you."

Blade snorted a laugh. "You've got a lot of guts for a girl. You know that?"

"I've been told," she said. "Listen, I don't want to be here anymore than you want me here. So, just lay off. I'm not going to move any faster by you shoving me."

He chortled and spit at her feet. "I see why Lucifer made you his bride."

"Bride? Are you kidding? I was his prisoner in Hell, the same as here."

Blade nodded. "I get it. Let me get you situated, and we'll go from there. Okay?"

They passed by a dozen doors she assumed were offices or private rooms. Then they went up a set of stairs to the fourth floor where the walls had been painted a dark maroon color. The carpet on the floor matched the walls and, fortunately, the air was considerably warmer.

After reaching the door at the end of the hallway, she heard some fumbling behind her and a jangle of keys. Blade unlocked the room and directed her inside.

"This is your room for the time being," he said.

"For how long?" she asked. "I don't understand. Why am I here? Who's Dante?"

"I'll answer all your questions when the time is right."

"And when will that be?"

"Soon." Blade closed the door and locked it behind him.

Standing in place, she looked around her at the bleak accommodations. It was a stark difference from the elegant bedroom Lucifer had created. There were folded sheets and tan blankets on the foot of a small mattress, a simple nightstand, a wooden chair, and small metal lamp. The only window in the room was high on the wall, and the bars on it were held in place by a thick wood frame.

Samara immediately began to think of ways to escape. She pushed the chair under the window and scanned the room for something to break the frame. If she could manage to do that, she could break the windowpanes and climb out onto the ledge, making her way to freedom.

Picking up the lamp, she swung with all her might, hitting the wood frame. It only cracked the frame and now the lamp was broken.

The door clicked open.

She spun around, jumping off the chair with the broken lamp still in her hand.

Blade filled the opening of the doorway. "Trying to escape is pointless," he told her.

"How did you—"

"There's a camera." He pointed to the corner of the ceiling where a small camera was mounted. He smirked and she glared at him defiantly.

"Sit down." He pointed to the chair, and she refused to obey. "Do you want answers?" he asked. "Then sit down."

Reluctantly, she sat on the edge of the bed and eyed him warily. He pulled up the chair and sat across from her. "I suppose you're wondering why you're here." Pausing, he stared into her eyes, waiting for a response. When she failed to react, he added, "You may ask anything you'd like."

Samara narrowed her eyes and blurted out, "Why did you kidnap me? Who are you? Where am I?" She wanted answers and wanted them now.

"You're where you need to be. We took you because this is where you belong."

She glared at him. "What kind of answer is that? Just tell me where this is and why I'm here."

"You are here to escape your emotional bonds. To free yourself from Lucifer's hold and the reach of outsiders."

Samara exploded, jumping to her feet. "What gives you the right to control my life? Did you rescue my uncle Tyrus? I want him here! Right now!!"

"That's impossible. Your relationship with your uncle will only corrupt you, leaving you useless to anyone. Now sit down!"

It took all her self-control not to throw herself at him. More than anything in the world, she wanted to pound her fists on his insolent face—to find a way to channel her powers and transport herself out of this place. Samara heaved a sigh. It hurt her to think about Tyrus in Hell, no doubt being punished for her escape. Her fertile imagination showed her all the horrible ways Lucifer would make him suffer. Maybe even kill him out of anger.

"Well?" he asked.

Begrudgingly, she sat down but refused to look at him. A few seconds passed, then he cleared his throat. "You're here because we believe you're one of us. We believe that you—"

"I can't be one of you. I can't!"

He crossed his arms over his chest. "Don't interrupt me, Samara," he growled.

She remained silent, watching him with hatred filling her thoughts.

"We believe you're one of us," he continued. "Not only just one of us, but the girl Dante has been talking about for the past month. The girl he saw in his dreams."

Recognizing her confusion, he attempted to clarify. "Dante is our tracker. He finds demons that have gifts and the potential to join us. He told us that our target was in Lucifer's mansion. That's why we went there…to bring you back."

Samara huffed. "Who are you, Blade?" She blurted out, unable to restrain herself any longer. "You claimed to be a Black Crow but aren't any longer. Is Damian your enemy now? Are you planning to fight against him? If so, I have no interest being part of anything you're planning to do."

Blade eyed her dangerously and snarled. "Our plans will be told to you soon enough."

Samara turned away. "Don't expect any cooperation from me. If my father finds out I'm here, he will—"

"Do nothing. The same way he did nothing to save you from Lucifer. If you haven't figured it out yet, your family washed their hands of you months ago. The same way my family disowned me. And as for Damian and the Black Crows, they're weak and worthless. Why didn't they go to Hell to rescue you when you were so willing to save them? Why didn't they find Tyrus and free both of you when Lucifer was gone, and they clearly had the chance? It's because they were afraid of being captured again… afraid to risk their lives to save you."

Samara felt the heat of her temper growing. "How do you know all that? Were you spying on me? Were you watching me from the shadows in the corridors of Hell?"

"You'll never know for sure, will you?" He rose from the chair and crossed the room, glancing back at her with a wicked grin. Then he locked the door behind him, leaving her to seethe in anger and confusion.

CHAPTER 38

BEAST BLOOD

Samara stood back against the wall, imagining what it would feel like to flee through her unlocked door at the end of the long hallway. Heading in a northerly direction, she would eventually reach the metal staircase leading to the basement where Thorn was eagerly awaiting her liver. The only other choice she considered involved sure-footing her way down the steep-sloping roof outside her barred window, and then rock-climbing her way off the five-story building. After risking life and limb, and possibly a kidney, the last obstacle in her mental toolbox remained solid. Even if her teleporting skills miraculously returned, it would be impossible for her to pass through the mortal plane within the realms of Heaven and Hell, reaching her home on the doomed planet called Earth. Only a spiritual guide like Ariel knew the location of all living things in the Universe—the home to the four galaxies and their planets. But with Samara's mind channeling powers being blocked, communicating with her surrogate mother was out of the question.

A new visitor arrived at Samara's door, holding the key to her room in his hand. "My name is Dante. I'm the tracker who found you." He had coal-black hair reaching his shoulders and a dark shadow around his jaw. His light gray-green eyes made him appear less threatening than his counterpart, Blade, though it was too early to make that call.

"My name is Samara," she offered.

"I know who you are." Dante leaned forward, keeping his voice low. "I assume Blade told you everything about us."

"Very little, actually," she muttered, refusing to hide her anger.

His brow creased. "Is something wrong? Are you being mistreated?"

Samara dropped down on the chair, fuming over his ignorant questions. "If mistreatment includes keeping me in this place against my will, then I'd say yes and be done with you."

Dante's eyes hardened. "You were selected for an important mission. It's an honor you should be proud to accept."

"You're saying I have a choice in this matter?"

"Actually, no."

"Well, I'm saying no to keeping me away from my family and friends. I thought I made that clear to Blade. Didn't he tell you?"

"You're sacrificing a little inconvenience to save the world. Your answer should be yes, absolutely!"

"So, you're telling me that my isolation will turn me into a superhero who saves the world? What kind of crock of shit is that?"

"Not this world. My world. *Our* world."

"Demons don't have a world of their own. And even if we did, I don't understand how keeping me away from my family is going to help save it."

"Samara, listen. If I tell you everything I know, will you at least try to understand?"

She shrugged her shoulders. "Fine...tell me. What else can I do?"

Dante took a deep breath and began. "Your family and friends are limiting your potential. They restrict your powers on Earth and limit your future growth. Emotional bonds are damaging to everyone, Samara. By cutting your ties, you become stronger… more capable of accomplishing great things."

"That's how you're planning to survive? By alienating yourselves from everyone. And just how lonely is that?"

"It's best to cut all bonds before we cut them for you."

Samara sprang to her feet. "What does that mean? Are you planning to kill everyone I care about? Is that your great plan?"

"Sit down!" He shouted. "You haven't heard the whole story."

"I refuse to sit down. I don't want to hear anything you have to say."

"Please listen to me! Samara, they aren't even your parents."

She dropped into her chair. "You're lying. You're a treasonous demon, no better than that creature in the basement file room."

"I'm not lying," Dante said softly.

"It can't be true. It just can't!"

"Why do you say that?"

"Because they've taken care of me my entire life. I think I would know if they weren't my parents. If Ariel didn't give birth to me and Crighton wasn't my father."

"Believe me, they were never your parents. Lilith mated with a human being, producing a daughter…a Cambion with the ability to teleport and channel her thoughts to other living beings. Ariel gave birth to you using Lilith's body, but your father wasn't Crighton. Your real father was a warrior in Lucifer's army. He goes by the name of Roman King. Years ago, he sold his soul to Lucifer in exchange for his wealth and noble position. Both are enemies of The Tribe, our 200-member faction, fighting corruption and injustice in the world…dedicated to saving our planet."

"I…I don't believe it," she said flatly. He had to be lying to her. This could *not* be the truth.

"According to the prophecy, you're the only living being that can kill Lucifer and his commanding officers."

Her eyes widened. "Look, I don't know who you think I am, but I don't kill unless absolutely necessary. And that means shooting woodland animals with a bow and arrow, not two-legged devils."

"Well, if you had witnessed the horrible things your father and Lucifer did, then you would jump at the chance," he insisted.

"Jump at killing?" She huffed. "We're talking about murder, right? If I'm truly their greatest threat, then why didn't Roman kill me after I was born? Why didn't Lucifer turn me into dust?"

"Perhaps they didn't know your true identity…the threat you pose to both of them."

Samara snorted a laugh. "I'm finding all of this too convenient and extremely hard to swallow. If you knew how I grew up on Middle Earth, then you would find it difficult too."

"Memories can sometimes be pure fantasy, rather than actual recollections."

"Wow, that's priceless. You might also consider that sometimes we keep our feelings to ourselves because we prefer it over pouring our hearts out to the wrong demons."

"I'm not wrong, Samara. You need to know that it would've been easy for your *so-called* parents to hand you over to Lucifer, making him their ally instead of an enemy. When you think about it, isn't that what they basically did…leave you in Hell to fend for yourself?"

Samara was left speechless. She had no words to describe what she was feeling. Inside, she was broken and hurt, crushed by his callous words. But at the same time, she refused to believe that the home she'd built with her family was non-existent. She'd been alienated far too long and trusting anything Dante was telling her was dubious at best.

"Just answer two questions for me," he said. "Why didn't Ariel and Crighton come looking for you? Why didn't they rescue you when it was so easy for us to grab you?"

She shrugged a shoulder. "I was told that Lucifer's army led them on a wild goose chase. I could see that being a problem, can't you?" Meeting his eyes, she asked a question that had been troubling her for hours. "How did you find me? I'm one in seven billion when it comes to Cambions if your story proves right."

"I'm a Tracker. That's my power," Dante said with conviction. "I can locate demons that have the same blood type as me. Their vibrations and auras are unique."

"Really? What kind of blood do you have?"

"Beast blood," he answered, his brown eyes burning with intensity.

Samara remained silent for a few moments. His words caused a strange sensation in the pit of her stomach. "Beast blood, you say?"

"That's right. Our planet, Nexus, exists in the Twelfth Dimension. It's a shadow realm inhabited by powerful residents and colorful creatures invisible to the human eye. When an atmospheric quake destroyed the caves where the four Phoenixes and Nexus Dragons lived, only one of each species survived. They mated and created Wiverns. These magnificent creatures can fly and breathe fire. They were given the powers of rebirth, healing, and destruction. Their only weakness is being controlled by demons possessing Beast Blood."

Fascinating. Samara listened with the interest of a child hearing a fairy tale for the first time.

"If you're born with this blood, you're gifted with extraordinary powers. The only thing that separates us from other demons and Cambions is the concentration of this blood in our veins, which determines the strength of our talents. And just so it's clear, this is not a skill that demons acquire, it is the unique capability you're born with."

Samara thoughtfully nodded. "Before going to Hell, I was able to teleport around the world and channel telepathic thoughts. But I seem to have lost my abilities, which would make me useless to you and your Wiverns."

"If I'm correct, you just turned eighteen. Hence, your gifts are inconsistent and erratic. But they will grow stronger and more reliable now that you're no longer in Hell. Soon you'll discover an immense power within you, unlike any you've witnessed before."

"That's...crazy!" She frowned at him suspiciously. "I don't understand my part in any of this, or why I would be given this... power."

"In our world, there is a Mother Beast. She is the strongest, most spectacular creature that has ever existed. She resides in the bowels of Nexus and is the size of twenty elephants. She has the power of thirty beasts within her body, and no one has been able to rule her. Not for centuries. That is until Lucifer found his new body and set his sights on controlling her." Staring straight ahead, Dante cast black looks at the cracks in the wall. "He's going down a destructive path and is taking our world with him. As his only living cousin, I've chosen a path to rebellion that will see him dead before long," he said darkly.

Samara met his eyes. "You're his cousin?"

"Our world was peaceful. There were beautiful forests and greenery everywhere. Nobody was afraid to go out into the open without five others coming along for protection. Then suddenly, everything changed. Lucifer said he wanted to make our world a better place. *How?* I asked him. He told me that he needed the Mother Beast. I told him it was impossible. He said that if he could have her, then he could control the rest of the underworld creatures and prevent them from destroying Nexus."

Dante shook his head. "It's frightening to know the destruction of your world is imminent.. With Lucifer controlling the Mother Beast, complete darkness will soon cover our planet. And Earth will be next, I promise you. But now there's a ray of hope." A look of awe crept into his face. "You, Samara."

Her jaw dropped. "Me?"

"That's right. The prophecy foretold that you—"

"Prophecies don't exist. No one knows what the future holds. Least of all, you and your lunatic crew."

"Come on, Sam. You've already learned about Beast Blood, secret powers, and our hidden world. Don't tell me what is and what isn't possible. Prophecies do exist. This one came from a very special monk who had the gift of vision for past and future lives." He handed her a scroll and instructed her to open it. "If you don't believe me now, perhaps you will after you read that."

She unrolled the parchment and began reading to herself:

Born to one of two mothers in the month of June, a female demon will grow to adulthood in a place between two worlds. First named by an angel, this guardian bears a noble surname, yet rules no realm. She possesses a warrior's heart yet was thwarted in battle. Her human father, Roman King, sold his soul to the devil, yet her soul remains pure. Among all others, she is the chosen one, for she bears the mark of the phoenix, rising from the ashes. She will be the hero to Nexus and her people, and her name will be Samara King.

Could it be true? Samara asked herself. *Am I truly the Guardian? Does Beast Blood flow through my veins? Am I a Cambion...like Damian, his sister, and the Black Crows?*

It all seemed so unlikely, and yet she matched the description in the prophecy to a T. Her birthday was June 15th. Technically, she'd been born to two mothers. Lilith and Ariel. She grew up on Middle Earth, a place between two worlds. Her first name, Samara, was given to her by an angel and, according to Ariel, translated into Guardian. She'd been trained in archery, yet never went to battle. And the phoenix that miraculously appeared on her shoulder blade couldn't be explained away, not even by Ariel. However, after being raped by Lucifer repeatedly, the state of her soul was in question. She also refused to believe that Crighton wasn't her father. He had raised and protected her, while Roman King was merely a name on a piece of paper—a corrupt human being she had zero interest in knowing.

Dante peered into her face, breaking her concentration. "So what's the verdict, Samara? After reading the words in the prophecy, you can understand why we were so excited to find you... why you were taken from Hell and brought here. You're the hero we've been hoping for...the answer to all our problems."

Samara shook her head. "If I'm the answer, you have bigger problems than you thought. I've only trained with bow and arrows, and you need an experienced leader. Someone who isn't afraid to go toe to toe with Lucifer. Forewarned is forearmed," she quoted under her breath. "In order to find the right person for this job, you need to ignore what's on this parchment and find ways to evaluate important intangibles, like weapon skills and leadership abilities."

Dante was smiling.

"What's so funny?" Samara asked him.

"You're a natural-born leader and don't even know it. It's in your blood…in your DNA."

"I'm…I'm no leader," she claimed, but his eyes told her differently. His eyes told her that he was eager to follow her lead, backing her up as she plunged headlong into an impossible mission.

"We all know what we know," he said. "I bet if you'd stuck around on Middle Earth, you would've made it a better place. A place where evil doesn't even exist."

"You're a dreamer, Dante. I want to help…you know I do." She was suddenly choked up with emotion and tears welling in her eyes. "But I don't know how." A single, hot tear escaped and trailed down her cheek.

Dante wiped it away with his thumb. His eyes clouded with concern and his voice lost its edge. "I want you to know that I would never deliberately upset you."

Damn it. She was shedding unwanted tears, making herself look weak. It was going to be harder to say no than she had thought. Once upon a time, she was psyched to travel into the great beyond, to join the battle against Lucinda and take her place in line in the cosmic revolution. But now, she was plagued with doubts and fears. What if being a Beast meant being nobody, nothing? What if instead of meeting up with all those who'd gone before her—dying bravely for a just cause, she landed on some deserted planet devoid of anything? She had no way of knowing what was going to happen, and her apprehension was growing by leaps and bounds.

Samara looked at Dante. He was staring at the ground, preparing to launch into another speech, no doubt.

"Thanks for helping me believe about...you know...the future," he said quietly. "We would be lost without you. I swear!"

When she looked up at him, it was suddenly easy for her to imagine that her fears were pointless. That he would trust and protect her no matter what.

"Let me ask you something," he said, looking almost compassionately at the beautiful face before him. "Do you believe in magic?"

Under the circumstances, it seemed like a strange question to ask. "I've witnessed some strange phenomena, but I don't know if I'd call it magic."

Dante quirked a brief smile. "Well, I believe in you. And you're the closest thing to magic I've ever seen."

A flush crept up her neck and moisture filled her eyes. She turned away from Dante and erased her tears in one swift movement. This clever demon had somehow wormed his way into her affections with his good looks and sweet words. She told herself that it didn't matter. Her heart belonged to another, and she needed to remind him as well.

"You seem to have forgotten why I'm here in the first place, Dante. Perhaps, a recap is necessary. I was kidnapped and brought here against my will, not that I preferred Hell and Lucifer's company. But for future reference, there's no need for you to act like my friend. Don't ask me questions relating to my personal life and don't try to get close to me. I don't like you for a number of reasons, and I most assuredly won't like you in a few months."

A crazy chuckle escaped his lips, as he tried his best not to look disappointed. "I'll definitely keep that in mind, Samara. From now on, it's all business between us and nothing more. I promise."

CHAPTER 39

THE PROPHECY

After Dante left Samara's room, Blade walked in with a scowl on his face and a napkin-covered tray. "Let me warn you right now. You're not getting anything fancy here," he said, handing her the tray. "We live on rations and bare essentials, not wine, filet mignon and caviar."

Smart ass. Samara set the tray on the edge of the bed next to her and lifted the napkin, revealing a tuna fish sandwich and warm bottle of water. *How quaint.*

Blade leaned back against the wall with his arms folded over his chest, keeping his eyes locked on her.

Samara glared. "Are you really going to stand there and watch me eat?" Refusing to be intimidated, she started to take a bite of her sandwich then stopped to ask a legitimate question that deserved a reasonable answer. "If I'm your shining ray of hope, then why must I remain a prisoner in this place?"

"Because I'd hate to feel like I made a mistake by trusting you."

Samara's eyes narrowed into slits. "I don't trust you either," she shot back. "And one more thing. If you ever push or threaten me again, make sure you're ready to fight. I might be a female demon, but I'm not a coward."

The door opened again and in walked a medium height, blond-haired demon, looking physically fit and extremely self-confident. He had an oval face and large green eyes with long lashes, reminding her of a younger version of Damian. "Good morning," he said brightly. His smile lit up his face and brought a dimple to his right cheek.

Blade moved away from the wall. "Thank you for coming," he told him.

Dismissing the stranger's presence, Samara kept her eyes on Blade. "According to Dante, I'm one of your team members now. So, what's the problem?" she said hotly. "Don't tell me you have something against female demons..."

Blade's eyes said it all. Rather than address her remarks, he gave her a cold, bleak look. Then he glanced back at the handsome stranger in the room. "This is Aryan," he told her. "Don't cause any trouble or disrespect him in any way. If you do, I guarantee you'll regret it."

Blade nodded at his comrade and walked out the room, leaving him alone with Samara. Taking large bites out of her sandwich, she stared at Aryan, sizing him up. The collar of his red shirt flapped around as he stepped toward the vacant chair. The small buttons just sat there on his shirt, sad and unused, making his outfit look undone. He wore a fine gold chain and small medallion around his neck. A set of blue Buddhist prayer beads hung off a belt loop on his gray, well-worn jeans, and below them were grungy combat boots.

Interesting.

While subjecting himself to her scrutiny, he ruffled his messy hair and gave her a lopsided grin. She looked away quickly, finishing her meal.

"It's all right," he said. "I get that a lot."

"Get what?" she asked.

"I mean...I *am* rather handsome, aren't I?" he teased.

"Humble too."

Aryan stepped closer and placed his cool hands on her shoulders. "I can read minds, silly." He smirked. "That's my ability or power, as you might call it."

She leaned back, distancing herself from him. "Would you mind keeping your hands to yourself?"

Her comment left him chuckling. "Relax, kitten. I can be a bit forward, but there's no need to be rude."

Kitten? Only Tyrus called her that. "Keep your eyes out of my head too," she added.

Damian was the only Cambion who left her heart racing, so why was this creature having the same effect on her?

Memories flooded her brain. *Damian.* Where was he now? She missed everything about him. His perfect smile, his perfect kiss. How he held her, making her believe he loved her. But she had been separated from him for so long. It had been two months since she'd seen him—since she came to his rescue and failed. A lot had happened to her in those two months. Her heart ached thinking about how worried he must have been, after disappearing with Lucifer. And yet here she sat, comparing the love of her life to a demon she just met.

"Samara?" Aryan looked worried, his arms were reaching out, ready to catch her if she lost consciousness.

"I'm fine," she mumbled.

"You're looking pale." He forced her to lie down on the bed. "What's wrong? Is there anything I can do?"

When she didn't reply, Aryan stared directly into her eyes. In that split second, he stole all her memories and sat back analyzing them.

"Don't do that again," she growled. "You have no right to look into my thoughts."

"He's still alive? Damian? Your boyfriend?" The look on his face revealed shock and utter disbelief. "You know you can't have emotional bonds tying you to Earth," he said harshly. "You need to sever them right away. You must be pure of heart and mind when you cross over into the twelfth dimension of Nexus. Otherwise, you'll die."

"I don't understand. How will I die?"

"Twelfth-dimension particles attach themselves to lingering ties and emotions and erase them. If you try to carry them with you, they will explode in your heart and mind, sending you into oblivion."

"It's not my fault! You can hardly blame me. Think about what you're forcing me to do. I'm supposed to shut down my emotions…ignore the love I have for everyone in my life. That's crazy! That's impossible for me!"

"It's the only way to survive."

"And what if I don't want to come with you? Then what will you and your friends do?"

Aryan shook his head. "You have no choice. Nexus is dying, and you saw the prophecy with your own eyes. You need to understand, Samara. It's very real. You can't refuse."

She hesitated, gritting her teeth. "Make me understand this is real," she said quietly. "Make me believe it's true."

He paused before answering. "Mother Beast, our most powerful being, has been peaceful for centuries. She controls smaller beasts, keeping them harmless. She even aided humans in their environments by maintaining the perfect balance between air, land, and waterways. But then *he* came along and disrupted everything," Aryan growled. "I don't know how Lucifer did it, but somehow he has managed to assume control over the

Mother Beast. With his powers and hers, he's become virtually unstoppable."

"What do these powers consist of?"

"Electrical currents in the atmosphere, sending shock waves around the world. The mega storms that result will destroy entire continents and millions of lives. The planet with suffer. He will do the same thing to Earth with his blackmail scheme against Heaven."

Samara drew a sharp indrawn breath. "I had no idea."

"But that's not all. Lucifer's most frightening power is annihilation. You don't need knives, spears or firearms when you can turn your enemies to dust with the wave of a hand."

Samara sighed. "I'm afraid I've witnessed his verdicts more times than I can count. Lucifer destroyed soldiers and council members for insubordination and bias opinions." Although she would never admit it, she regretted turning Tinkerbell to dust to earn the respect of the council members. Looking back now, she never considered his mistress' feelings at the time, only her black eyes and vicious beatings.

Aryan cleared his throat, drawing her attention. "It's even worse when Lucifer feels threatened. You see, my sister refused to reveal the hiding place of the prophecy scroll and was brought before his tribunal. He stared at her with his evil red eyes and squeezed his throat with one hand, forcing her to choke herself with his mind control."

"What a horrible way to die," Samara said quietly. "I'm so sorry."

"Believe it or not, she's very much alive." Aryan's eyes were filled with bitterness and hate. "But Lucifer likes to play with his toys for hours. After she refused to cooperate, he drilled into her mind with his piercing stare and saw the prophecy in her thoughts. His scribe copied it down word for word on parchment paper. As a result, my sister was driven stark-raving mad and doesn't remember anything, which in many ways is a blessing."

Samara instinctively pressed her hand to her throat. "I don't know why, but somehow I feel responsible."

Aryan shook his head. "You shouldn't. You had no way of knowing what he's capable of or what the future would hold. But Roman is a whole different story. He was secretly hiding when the Holistic Seer met with a Patronymic Monk. After witnessing the prophecy being shared, he kept it a secret. Weeks later, word reached Lucifer, and he killed every Seer he could get his hands on. Then he stripped Roman of his title and eliminated his voting rights on his council."

Samara shook her head.

"But that isn't all. We're now in a constant state of fear and distress. Thousands of families in Middle Earth are being separated from their children. They're being kept in cages and fed to the Mother Beast. She's never done this before, I swear. Lucifer's evil influence has changed her drastically, turning her into a fire-breathing, flesh-eating monster." Aryan blew out a breath. "Samara, it is of utmost importance that you come with us. Your help is desperately needed."

"I…I don't know if I'm capable. Just…just give me some time to think about it," she mumbled.

Aryan nodded curtly. "You have three days and no more," he said. "Lives are depending on us…and especially you."

He stood up to leave and Samara reached for his arm. "I need to ask a favor."

"Yes? What is it?"

"Don't tell anyone about Damian. Especially not Blade."

"I will try, Samara. But you know what must ultimately be done, don't you?"

She nodded slowly and released a tight-lipped exhale. She swallowed hard, remembering the trouble she'd taken in Hell to get her lipstick just right. To get everything just right. But now everything was going wrong, and she was powerless to stop it.

CHAPTER 40

POWER HUNGRY

Samara read the parchment scroll a third time, looking for a loophole in her distressing dilemma. Clearly, the prophecy was intended for her, though she wished wholeheartedly it wasn't. The words were so specific, from the month of her birth to the phoenix birthmark on her shoulder. The only sticking point was her last name, which still gave her pause.

The door to her room suddenly swung open, lifting her eyes. Dressed in black, Blade cut an imposing figure, even in the cavernous room. "Good morning, Samara. Did you sleep well?"

Since when did Blade care about her sleeping habits? What was this character up to? Those were the questions she wanted answered.

"I'm here to escort you to The Tribe meeting," he stated, devoid of emotion. "Your presence has been requested." He stood before the door, waiting for her to join him.

She tilted her head curiously and followed him through the door. They turned right and walked down the dark hallway, not saying a word. Then Samara broke the silence.

"Can you explain the team member's abilities?" she asked him, as they exited another tunnel.

He gave her a sideways look. "What did you say?"

"Nothing."

"Tell me. Your questions seem to mean a great deal to you."

Samara smiled. "That's the best thing about me," she told him earnestly. "My inquisitive mind."

"Really? What about your eyes? They're so…expressive."

Did Blade just give her a compliment? With his serious expression, it was hard to know for sure.

"So, are you going to explain their abilities, or not? Your team members, I mean."

"Sure." Blade motioned that they should turn left, and she obediently followed.

"If you have Beast Blood, then you have one unique power… the exception being Lucifer, as you already know. Regarding abilities, there are seven good, four neutral, three evil and two rare. The seven good powers include mind-reading, tracking, growing, healing, divination, light bending and age-shifting. The four neutrals are invisibility, levitation, electricity, and speed. The three evil powers are illusion casting, torture, and fire. The two rare types are rebirth and soul-stealing."

Samara nodded her head, snagging whatever information that she could.

"Dante possesses a talent for tracking. He feels a natural pull towards demons with Beast Blood. Aryan was born with the gift of mind reading, which is self-explanatory. You met Doctor Ashe once. She controls healing."

"I had the ability to teleport, but I guess lots of demons do. It will be interesting to discover what power I've been awarded. With my luck, it will be growing plants."

Blade laughed. "No offense to you if your skill is planting. Although my ability hasn't been tested yet, I'm able to mold and bend light."

"Wow. That's incredible. Invisibility would be good too. By the way, I met someone when I first arrived. I think his name is Thorn. What is *his* power?" she asked out of curiosity. "He was craving my liver and kidneys."

Blade laughed again. "Thorn is not what he seems. In our world, dragon hybrids are Shapeshifters. They can take on the form of a demon then turn back into dragons whenever they want. His shapeshifting skills are a bit rusty. He's been stuck as a human for the last three days. He also won't be a threat now that he knows who you are."

"Why would you bring a dragon here?"

Blade shrugged. "We brought him for self-defense. A dragon can be useful when a threat arises."

"Who would have thought that?" She snickered despite her situation. "So, you came here to visit and never left, right?"

"Correct," Blade replied.

"Why, of all places, did you choose this place? I get the strangest vibrations here."

"No surprise. It was an insane asylum and the only abandoned place available, so we had no choice. I really don't think it's that bad. In fact, it's real quiet and peaceful like."

She snorted and shook her head. "An insane asylum? How fitting for your crazy crew."

Her comment drew another laugh from Blade. "I don't know if crazy is the right word for them, but they're definitely committed."

They came to a stop in front of a gray metal door and Samara was nervous about going inside. "So, aside from my teleporting ability, will I be given a new talent at this meeting? Something impressive?"

"That's why we're here, Samara. You're about to find out what your superpower is, and I promise you, it will be unique to everyone else's."

"Can I ask you one small favor?"

"Sure. What is it?"

"Since I'll be learning new names at this meeting, would you mind calling me Sam? I seem to respond better to that name."

"Of course. By the way, my real name is Dagon. When I was nine years old, everyone in my neighborhood started calling me special. I was rambunctious, hyperactive, and overly enthusiastic. I received my moniker at twelve when a bully wanted to fight me. Everyone crowded around, eager to see what would happen. The bully pulled out a knife, and although he was much bigger and stronger, it didn't matter to me. I attacked the bully with the fanaticism of an angry dog, turned his knife on him, and easily won the fight. From that day forward, I was known as Crazy Blade. Everyone in my circle of friends got to choose their name, and I liked the name Crazy. But when I got older, I realized that everyone was getting the wrong impression about me. So, I decided to go by the name Blade."

Samara smiled. She liked the musical twang to his speech and the way he wrinkled his nose when he spoke. He was handsome and confident, and made a striking impression in his black, snug-fitting shirt and slacks, although she told herself she shouldn't notice.

He stepped back, holding up his hand in a halting motion. "So, what's your honest opinion? About the name, I mean." He seemed genuinely interested in what she had to say, which surprised her.

After pushing her long bangs out of her eyes, she looked up at him under her lashes. "It's unconventional and macho at the same time. I guess the best word to describe it is threatening."

Blade nodded curtly. "You're not the first to tell me that." He began walking with purpose again and glanced quickly in her direction, as if he wanted to say more.

"Do I make you uncomfortable?" she asked. "Or was it the bluntness of my answer?"

"Both." He frowned and kept his eyes on the ground ahead of him. Clearly, he was beginning to wish that someone else had been chosen to look after her.

"Why is that?" She leaned forward, prodding him with the language of her body, the fierceness of her eyes, and the tone of her words.

"You ask too many questions," he said roughly. He came to a stop in front of a white metal door. "We're here."

Samara stood in place, hesitant to go inside. "I could never sit still when I was a child," she told him. "Especially when I was given lessons on etiquette. I know how to behave properly, of course, yet sometimes I made the conscientious decision not to. How fortunate for you that I've chosen to behave myself today. Otherwise, you'd have your hands full. But I assure you that can change in an instant." She looked up at him and smirked.

For a moment, he stared at her in disbelief then his eyes flared with fury. "What are you saying, Sam?"

The door opened and Aryan was standing before them. "Are you coming or not?" he asked. "Everyone's waiting."

Samara walked into the room and stood before the assembly of diverse individuals. "Thank you for your patience," she told them. "It was a bit of a walk to get here."

"Welcome." The greeting reverberated around the table. She spotted a few soft smiles and noticed a few scrutinizing stares fixed on her.

"Er…hi," she nervously replied, lowering herself into a black high-back chair.

Blade, Dante, Aryan, Esther, and Dr. Ashe were among the group of eight. Samara looked beyond their faces, familiarizing herself with the room. It was completely incased in stone and gray tile. Black notebooks were neatly lined up on a white laminate shelf on one wall above a dark gray credenza. The light fixture suspended above the matching gray table was modern in design but somehow managed to soften the sterile atmosphere.

Blade cleared his throat, drawing everyone's attention. "This is Samara or Sam, as she likes to be called."

A curly-haired boy nodded in her direction. "I'm Milo. That's Fox." He pointed to a haughty-looking girl with long black hair. "Situs," he added, gesturing towards a purple-haired male who gave a small wave, which Samara nervously returned. "This is Esther, our mama bear, and I guess you know the rest of us."

Aryan's lopsided grin turned into a smirk when Samara turned away. Flirting with anyone was out of the question, especially with her heart longing for Damian. She stared at the center of the table and kept her voice even. "So, I guess I'm here to learn the scope of my abilities."

Dante nodded. "That's right. After voting and arriving at a unanimous decision, we're going to offer you a choice. Ready to listen and learn?"

She drew a deep breath and slowly released it. "Ready as I'll ever be, I guess."

"Good. Let's get started then," he said, rubbing his hands together. "So, I don't know if anyone has told you about all the abilities we have in this group. Do we need to go over the individual classifications?"

"Blade already informed me," she replied quickly.

"Great. That will save time. The first seven are classified as superior and include mind reading, tracking, harvesting, healing, divination, light bending and age-shifting. The four neutrals are invisibility, levitation, electricity, and speed. The three evils are illusion casting, torture, and fire. And lastly, the two rare talents are rebirthing and soul stealing."

"Wow, so much to consider," she murmured. Samara couldn't help wondering what everyone could do and what her great talent would be.

"The first three gifts are the easiest to determine. Tracking, mind reading and divination. If you have any of these, then you would have shown signs already. If you were a tracker, then you would have felt a natural affinity towards us. However, you showed an obvious aversion at first."

Blade smirked at those words and Samara narrowed her eyes at him.

"If you're a mind reader," Dante added, "then you wouldn't have asked so many questions. And if you were a Seer or your ability was Divination, then you would not appear to be as stable as you are since Seers are constantly being pelted with new and sometimes frightening visions."

Esther stood up and shoved her gray hair behind her shoulder. "We're going to test you for some other powers now. These talents require a bit more space." She nodded toward the far side of the room, which was absent of any furniture.

Samara was half-afraid to speak, fearful that a quake in her voice would expose her trepidation. What would she be expected to do?

"Relax," Esther said, reading the distress in Samara's eyes. "You've got nothing to worry about. We're just going to test you for speed, levitation, electricity and fire."

Samara tensed at the word fire. She remembered it being listed in the evil category and hoped with all her heart she would not get it. She also wished there weren't so many eyes focused on her.

"So, for speed you need to step onto the treadmill we have set up. I just want you to run as fast as you possibly can and will yourself to go faster. Got it?" Esther smiled.

"Er…yeah." Samara imagined how stupid she was going to look, running aimlessly in place, like a horse with nowhere to go. Obviously, the others had the same thought. Aryan leaned back in his seat and let out a loud snort of amusement, while Blade openly smirked. She shot daggers with her eyes and clenched her fists. "Okay, let's do this," she said, taking a deep breath. She began running in place. After a few minutes, no newfound power came to her, no sudden burst of speed. She only felt her heart rate increasing along with her pulse.

"Definitely not," Aryan called out. "I've seen snails run faster."

Samara slowed down and glared at him, receiving a grin in reply.

"Okay, he's right," Esther said. "Let try levitation. It's easy. Just imagine yourself lifting off the floor. I'm a levitator myself and I find that closing your eyes helps a lot."

After a few seconds with her eyes closed, Samara decided that enough time had passed.

"Nope, definitely not," Esther concluded, looking slightly disappointed. "Let's move on to the next power. Electricity is the same. You just will it to make it happen. Point to the light fixture above the table and let's see if you can turn it on and off by willing it."

Samara did as she was told, feeling extremely foolish. But nothing happened, disappointing her further.

"Last skill in the category is fire. Turn toward the far wall and hold your palms up. Just think about the word heat. If fire is your skill, our specially treated wall will ignite."

A sense of foreboding crept into Samara's body. She didn't want an evil power, especially fire. After following Esther's instructions, she was relieved that nothing happened and quickly brought her hands to her side.

"Okay, well that's settled then," Esther announced. She walked back to the table and Samara followed. She resumed her seat and Blade stood up.

"I'll take care of this one," he said. He withdrew a small flashlight from his pocket and turned it on. Then he set it on end in the center of table. He instructed Samara to lift her hands, keeping her palms toward the flashlight. He moved behind her and placed his hands over hers, forcing Samara to lean back against his body. Then he spoke softly in her ear. "Concentrate, Sam. You can do this. Turn it off, and then turn it on again."

From the corner of her eye, she caught Aryan staring hard at Blade's hands. Then his eyes shifted to their bodies, measuring the distance between them. A frown formed on his face, telling her that he wasn't happy with the current situation.

Samara lowered her hands. "I can do this myself," she said.

"Just let me demonstrate how it's done." Blade moved away from her and put his hand above the top of the flashlight. Then he directed the light toward her. The beam of light instantly bent, shining directly into her eyes.

"Show-off," she muttered. "Now, let me try." Despite her best effort, she kept producing fruitless results. "How do you do that?" she helplessly asked.

Blade smiled and pulled her in closer. "I'm sorry to say it's not your talent. Some of us were just born lucky I guess."

Oh, shit. Samara wished she could talk to him without butterflies in her stomach. He was standing too close, and she was afraid everyone would notice the blush in her cheeks.

Then Blade chuckled and she sensed he was reading her mind. "You'll probably get something lame…like harvesting," he said. Then he leaned down and whispered in her ear, "I bet you've got a talent for growing things."

The sexual innuendo wasn't missed on her. "Hey!" Samara punched his shoulder. He grabbed her arm, pulling her close. Their faces were mere inches apart, and she could see the heat in his amber eyes.

Aryan hit the table. "Let's try to remember why we're here."

Looking around, Samara realized that everyone else was staring at them with amusement while Aryan was glaring. She immediately stepped back again, feeling her face warming.

What am I doing? Aryan was right. There were talented demons present, and she needed to focus on staying loyal to Damian, whether he appreciated it or not.

"I don't think light is my power," she hastily said, avoiding Aryan's eyes.

During the next twenty minutes, she failed all the tests for age-shifting, healing, and invisibility. Then Milo got up from the table. "Let's see if harvesting is your gift. I know everyone thinks it's not a worthwhile power to have, but it can be useful when you need it. For one, you'll have a lifetime supply of food," he said, as if sensing her negative thoughts. He pulled a packet of seeds from his pocket and directed her to hold out her hand. After staring at the collection of seeds on her palm, she closed her eyes and imagined them sprouting. She gave it an honest try and opened her eyes again. "Um, it's not working, Milo. So, I guess this isn't my power."

She noticed that the whole table looked uneasy and were exchanging subtle glances.

Dante took a deep breath, and then spoke. "We only have a few more powers left to test. Rebirth, soul-stealing, illusion casting and...torture." With the last word said, there was a ripple of restless murmur at the table. "We can't test rebirth," he said, "as we would have to kill you to find out whether or not you're capable of being reborn. And we can't test soul-stealing, as you'd have to steal one of ours, ending a life."

Samara's heart hammered in her chest. She didn't want either of those powers, especially after hearing about her father's past, which included delivering souls to Lucifer. "There must have been a mistake," she said. "Can't I retry the other ones first?"

Blade stepped forward and took her hand in his. "Powers come naturally, Sam. And we need to know yours...to better understand what we're up against."

"Wait a minute. I can teleport anywhere and channel thoughts. Doesn't that count?"

"All of us can, Sam. It's a given. And since we need a test subject, the responsibility falls on me."

"Blade!" she protested, shaking her head. "You can't do this!"

"I'll be fine," he insisted. "You've got nothing to worry about...not where I'm concerned."

Her hands trembled and her breath caught. "So...which one am I expected to do first?" she half-whispered.

"Illusion casting," he answered.

"What...what's that?"

Dante spoke up. "Illusion casting is the ability to create realistic, dark hallucinations. If this is your talent, Blade will witness a vision that's real enough to touch. It's in the same category as torture because it can be a painful experience. Nobody in this room knows how it works, so you'll have to try it by yourself."

Samara froze. She had no interest in frightening Blade with life-like visions that could leave him mentally scarred or even worse. "I'm not trying this on you!" She told him. "It's not worth it."

"Just do it!" Blade snapped. "I'm stronger than you think. It's the only way we're going to find out for sure."

"But I—" She looked at the others for support, and each of them nodded for her to proceed. "What if something goes wrong? What if I hurt him?"

"Dammit!" Blade shouted. "Get on with it, would you?"

"Alright! Fine! If that's how you feel, I'll do it," she huffed.

Samara took her position before Blade and stared directly into his amber eyes, apologizing silently before testing this evil power. At first, it was hard to imagine a horrible, monstrous thing. Her brain wasn't wired for it. But then she began digging deep into her subconscious fears. She recalled her experiences in Hell—the sense of loneliness in being locked away in a cell. How Lucifer brutally raped her, leaving her broken inside. She rocked back and forth in place, reliving the pain and agony. Then the nightmare re-entered her brain and her imagination went wild. Blade replaced her father in the torture chamber, and she had replaced Hecate wielding the whip, slashing his skin to pieces. In that moment, a cold, calm sensation swept over her, chilling her to the bone. She had no purpose in life other than inflicting as much pain as possible to the subject in front of her. In the recesses of her heart, a strange brew was stirring—a vile mixture of hate, cruelty, and madness. More than anything, she wanted to lash out, to cause as much pain as possible.

Her ego and sense of dominance wouldn't allow Blade to be the one walking away. *Take as much skin as possible,* her mind told her. *No mercy, no hesitation, no pity.* The more he cried out, the more determined she became to destroy him. To leave him as broken as she felt inside.

Blade's knees buckled, and he fell to the ground screaming at the top of his lungs. His face was twisted in agony. In stark contrast, Samara was almost giddy with excitement. In her mind, he was a small bug she could crush under the heel of her boot—he was nothing. That's when the satisfied look came to her face. She was in control and proud of it. No one would ever abuse her again. Not Lucifer or anyone else. She'd kill them first. Gut them like a deer and eat their heart for dinner.

Then she heard a sound, a distant rumbling in the room. Voices were calling her name and hands were reaching out, trying to hold her back.

"STOP IT, SAM! YOU'RE KILLING HIM!"

Samara shrugged off their hands, spun around and snarled at the giant rats in the room. The power was growing within her, stronger by the second. No one was going to keep her from killing this freak of nature—this anomaly kneeling before her.

"Back off!" she yelled. "Take one more step and I'll destroy all of you!"

While she continued to torment Blade with visions of Hell, his terrified screams continued. It seemed she was determined to kill him, then a familiar voice broke into her thoughts.

"Sam, it's over," Aryan calmly said. "You need to stop now. Draw back your power."

Samara turned to her left. She saw a distorted image of the young man with golden eyes and strawberry-blond hair. Was he real or just a figment of her imagination? She blinked repeatedly then stared harder at the face breaking through the fog.

"Aryan? Is that you? "Samara slowed the power inside her by listening to his soothing voice—by believing in his kindness and undying compassion. But then the muted light in the room turned to darkness once more. Slivers of horrifying visions came to her in quick flashes—images of what she'd put in Blade's mind. Her body trembled and her heart raced. She gripped the back of a chair to keep from collapsing. Her ears caught the sound of a terrified scream filling the air. It was Blade, thrashing around on the ground, fighting off his invisible foes. Hands were grabbing his arms, pulling him close, guiding him back onto his feet. Voices were assuring him it was over and that no one would harm him. At the same time, Aryan rested a hand on Samara's arm, startling her.

"Can you hear me?" he asked. "Are you okay?" Samara heard his questions, but she was incapable of answering. Her body was locked in place, and her eyes were staring blindly at Blade. He was sobbing and retching, grabbing his gut while several members of their group were trying to hold him up.

Then Samara slowly came to her senses. "No!" She screamed. "Not torture! Please Dante…I beg of you…take this power away. I don't want to hurt anyone. Not ever again!"

She hated herself for what she had done to Blade. The thought of permanently injuring him left her heart aching. *Why me?* She asked herself. *Why am I cursed?*

After dropping down into her chair, she lowered her head, feeling the weight of the world on her shoulders. Aryan laid a cold compress on the back of her neck and seemed more concerned about her than Blade. "Are you okay? Would you like a glass of water?"

Samara shook her head and noticed that the room seemed unusually quiet. Everyone had returned to their seats at the table and were staring at her. And their expressions weren't hard to figure out. They feared her and the daunting power she possessed, but more than anything else, they feared what she could do to them.

CHAPTER 41

JUST REWARDS

Lucifer sat on his impressive stone-carved throne, blowing smoke rings into the air, filling the room with cigar smoke. He was surveying his new, enormous trophy room. Circling the space were life-sized bronze sculptures of charging animals secured to white marble slabs and pedestals. Sixty animal heads had been mounted on the dark-paneled walls above the gray and white checkered granite floor. One of the most prized possessions in Lucifer's collection was the oversized blue area rug spread out before him. It was created from the feathers of the two powerful phoenixes he had personally slain. But as he had discovered in recent days, killing a phoenix was no easy task. They were born with the power of rebirth and healing. Yet these mighty birds couldn't escape his wrath, especially with thoughts of Samara filling his brain.

Designed and built to his specifications, the room had sixty-foot ceilings and was large enough to comfortably hold the Mother Beast. It had taken months to build trust in the creature and lure her to this remote place. But now that Circe was here, the fear Lucifer instilled in all the demons in Hell had been magnified tenfold. Her feedings proved to be a challenge, as she'd grown accustomed to devouring human flesh. Fifty demons had met their demise while serving her leafy greens, yet Lucifer claimed their carelessness was to blame. The fact that the length of her chain was never revealed added excitement to Lucifer's drop-and-run game.

Next to his throne was a unique floor lamp created from a life-size mermaid skeleton holding a silver candelabra with six lit candles. Lucifer unrolled the parchment scroll he had kept under lock and key for the last nineteen years and stared at the name on the bottom of the page. While Samara was confined in his mansion, he had failed to recognize her role in the prediction, especially with Crighton being her father. Then a few days ago, during one of Roman King's binge-drinking episodes, he unwittingly confessed to fathering an 18-year-old daughter. Although he had no clue as to her identity or how to find the twin demons involved, Roman raved about taking part in the eight-hour orgy inside the infamous Pleasure Quarters.

"I wonder if she's a whore too?" He asked his demon friend.

"Babies get switched all the time by Shapeshifters, especially in Middle Earth. She might be a goddess or someone important, for all you know."

"Now, that's a thought. Nineteen years ago, I was jamming my cock into anything that moved. Who knows...I might have fathered a few heifers too."

They both laughed cheerfully, finished their drinks, and wandered back to their rooms. When word about their exchange reached Lucifer, he called Roman into his private chamber. He offered him a snifter of brandy then watched him throw it back, while reflecting on his great misadventure.

Focusing on the error of his ways, Lucifer lashed out without warning, jamming his lit cigar into Roman's left eye. "You're so stupid!" He screamed. "You should have told me! I had her here, under my roof, and now she's gone, gone...GONE!"

Of course, Lucifer realized that this could lead to his ultimate downfall—the only way he could be defeated, and he refused to allow this to happen. Ultimately, he could choose one of two solutions. He could either kill Samara or convince her to come back to him. If he killed her, all threats would be eliminated, or so he hoped. However, if he could convince her to join forces with him in his battle against Heaven, then together, with Circe, they would be unstoppable. But unfortunately, Lucifer didn't have the luxury of deciding because Samara was still proving impossible to find.

There were so many questions clouding his brain. How did she escape? Why couldn't his army find her? Did she already know about the future of this world and the one beyond it? If she did, then how did she become so well informed?

Another thing that was keeping him up late at night was Samara's ability to remain so well hidden. No mere demon or human being possessed the ability to completely disappear, not off the face of the planet anyway. This led Lucifer to one foregone conclusion. He wasn't alone in his attempt to convince Samara King to join a side in the battle of Arch-demons against Archangels—of unalloyed evil against namby-pamby good. Lucifer with his superpowers and his obedient Mother Beast would easily defeat his brother Castiel and his Almighty God. But in the meantime, who was blocking his efforts to get Samara back? Perhaps an opposing force was setting up an ambush right now, waiting patiently for him to arrive. He would make short work of his enemies without hardly lifting a finger. Even so, it was annoying to think about undisciplined beings running around challenging his authority.

The tension in Lucifer's body was back and he longed for a release. Sitting on his sofa in his red velvet robe, he grinned wickedly at Clio. He placed his hand on her thigh and squeezed, though a little harder than before.

"Ouch! Please be gentle."

"You're right, Clio. I'll try to abide by your wishes. But right now, you need to address mine." He moved his legs apart and shoved her head down between them. She clamped her mouth around his cock and went to work, pleasing him the only way she knew how.

"How dare they challenge me with their primitive skills?" Lucifer huffed, shifting in his seat. "I'm the most ruthless conqueror there has ever been. It's ludicrous to imagine that mere mortals would attempt to dismantle my realm. Their pathetic cries will leave me laughing. I can promise you that." His cock was moving like a piston in Clio's mouth, driving him over the edge. Before long, he was bouncing in his seat, rearing back, and struggling to catch a breath. This went on for five minutes, then he blurted out, "I'm coming!" After emptying his balls, Clio dropped to the floor and skittered away to the toilet room to drop his load.

When she returned, Lucifer asked her if his special guest was ready for him. She nodded and asked politely if she could be excused. He reluctantly agreed, then he added, "Same time tomorrow...and bring a few of your friends with you."

As Clio was leaving the room, a servant delivered a silver-domed tray and set it on the table next to Lucifer's throne. He lifted the cover and smiled at the dozen raw oysters his chef had secretly prepared to address his waning vigor. They were rich in zinc, essential for testosterone production and the maintenance of healthy sperm. "Perfect. I need fortification for this next go round. If this doesn't work, nothing will," he told himself.

After washing them down with a chilled glass of vodka, Lucifer wiped his mouth on a cloth napkin and rose from his chair. He strode down the long hallway toward his bedroom where Master Sergei was waiting in a white terrycloth robe and matching slippers.

Lucifer opened the door and feigned his surprise. "Well, well…what do we have here? A Knight of Darkness inside my boudoir? How exciting!"

Sergei's face paled at seeing Lucifer's new body. "Did Chancellor Knox offend you in some way? I thought you were satisfied with Legend's skin. Why would you take the Chancellor's body when yours was perfect in every way?"

Lucifer huffed. "You have no idea what you're talking about. You're such a kiss ass—and a Master Knight too! You don't deserve the title. If Crighton hadn't blinded you in one eye, I would've taken your head instead. After all, you tormented and raped one of my premium whores and my best soul-seeker's lover. I'm honestly surprised you're still breathing right now, especially after kidnapping his son."

Master Sergei cleared his throat, giving Lucifer the impression that he had something important to tell him, and that he would be wise to pipe down and pay attention. If it was one of those stories that piqued his ever-vigilant sense of outrage, there was likely to be eye-rolling, deep sighs, and even some headshaking at the ridiculousness of it all. However, Lucifer had arranged this strange meeting and speaking out of turn could result in cruel punishment. Or even worse, death.

"You and Onoskelis went to great lengths to plot your kidnapping schemes. If they were so well thought out, why didn't you bring Cassius to me? I could have used him against my brother in the Red War. Torturing his grandson would've brought him to his knees. Instead, you and that twit fucked up everything. Now that brat is back with Crighton and his mouthwatering angel, and I've got you to thank." Lucifer snorted and shook his head. "Onoskelis will be found soon and served for breakfast. I'm going to enjoy every tasty bite, while I devour her soul and absorb her powers. But what am I going to do with you, Sergei? Hmm…that's a puzzling dilemma, isn't it?"

"Please, I need to explain, My Lord. Just give me a moment to—"

"Shut the fuck up! I put a lot of thought into my new, improved look and you haven't even bothered to compliment me. Not once! Maybe I should've taken your skin instead. What do you think, Sergei? Stealing it would've meant one less eye, but I seem to adapt well. Don't you agree?"

Master Sergei swallowed hard and forced a worried nod.

Lucifer smiled and rubbed his gray beard. He stepped into his bathroom and left the door open, welcoming Sergei's prying eyes. After removing his alligator boots, black shirt, and leather pants, he laid them neatly on the counter. Then he tied on a red velvet cloak around his neck and raised a razor-sharp sword into the air.

"Don't you just love it?" he said, turning around in place. "I was tired of dreaming about Samara, and those constant hard-ons were keeping me awake at night. After throwing that ridiculous skin into one of my instant incinerators, I honestly considered taking yours, but Milton's was so much nicer. He loves a good cigar, has nicely trimmed brown hair and, according to my daughter, to-die-for blue eyes. Plus, his skin is so supple, soft, and surprisingly blemish-free." He smoothed his hand across his stomach. "And the toned abs are especially nice. Don't you agree?"

Sergei nervously looked away. "Is this really necessary?" He murmured. "I've never intentionally harmed or violated anyone. Well, not for the last twenty years, at least."

Lucifer angled his head, sizing up the demon standing before him. "I hate the Knights of Darkness and anyone who defends them. You above everyone else should know that I detest anyone micromanaging my kingdom, especially that uppity bitch, Verity. No one kidnaps, rapes or pillages Middle Earth without my approval. And they certainly don't sneak around in corridors, spying on my daughter, unless they're a demented pervert…or far worse." Lucifer pursed his lips and continued to stare at him. "Is that what you are, Sergei? A fucking pervert?"

"No, of course not! I only wanted to speak to her. I didn't know you were officially back, or that Lucinda was involved with Hecate. I knocked on her door, and when she answered, I opened it at the wrong moment. It was an innocent mistake, and I sincerely apologized for it."

"Well, my daughter insisted that the punishment befit the crime. And that's why you're here, Sergei. I'm trying to be a good father by earning Lucinda's trust back. But I hate raising a whip when another course of action is befitting and so easily implemented."

"Why are you doing this to me? I'll do anything, but not this. I beg of you…"

"Are you wearing them?" Lucifer asked. "Clio's sexy pink panties? I know how much you've admired them. If you're not wearing them under that robe, I fully intend to use this sword, and I promise you, Sergei, you're not going to like the results."

He dropped the robe on the floor and stood before Lucifer wearing panties and nothing else.

"Turn around and let me admire you," Lucifer said. "That's right. Ah, so nice. Such a tight, sweet ass you have, Sergei. Oh, pray tell, why have you been hiding it from me?" Lucifer was licking his lips and stoking his cock at the same time, preparing himself for the fantasy he'd been dreaming about all day—a Knight of Darkness kneeling before him, trembling in fear.

"I won't forget this," Sergei muttered. "I promise you. Not ever!"

"You won't have to, my darling. You're going to be my sex slave from this night forward. Call me sir or baby when we're alone together. And don't avoid me or resist my advances, Sergei. Your only purpose in Hell is to please me and nobody else. Is that clear? Now, assume the position you made famous in the Pleasure Quarters. Who knows? You might actually find this enjoyable."

Sergei stood motionless at the end of the bed, refusing to cooperate.

"Well? What are you waiting for? An invitation to die?" Lucifer poked the tip of his sword into Sergei's side, leaving a trail of blood dripping down his thigh and onto the marble floor. "Defy me and it will only get worse. I can promise you that."

The Master Knight crawled into the center of the bed on his hands and knees. Then he braced himself on his elbows and closed his eyes. He let out a small squeak when he felt a pinch on his ass. Looking over his shoulder, he spied Lucifer standing behind him, throwing open his cloak while balancing the sword in his left hand.

"Don't worry, sweetheart," Lucifer told him. "I'll be gentle. Well, as gentle as I can be anyway." He stared at the large mirror across from him, admiring his new physique. There were two things about Milton Knox's body that he could attest to with definite certainty. He had rock-hard abs and a cock to match. For the past three days, it had been tested on hustlers like Sergei and, surprisingly, there hadn't been a single complaint. But then Lucifer's motley mind wouldn't have allowed it. The prince-of-darkness and Chancellor Milton Knox were more alike than they knew. They loved good cigars and had become great fans of pain and pleasure, delivered in equal increments, particularly while training male playmates.

CHAPTER 42

LIVING NIGHTMARE

D amian took a long drag on his cigarette while sitting near the window on the roof level of an old hospital, twenty miles away from Samara's house. After recalling his shocking visit with her father, he blew out the smoke slowly and felt it curl around his face before wafting away in the crisp evening air. It seemed Crighton Daemonium had washed his hands of his daughter for good. He would never forgive her for deliberately disobeying him. To make matters worse, she had volunteered to stay with Lucifer, albeit to protect everyone she loves, and didn't leave when she had the chance. The disclosures by Tyrus explained away his incarceration and the dilemma Samara had found herself in, but this bit of information only infuriated Crighton further.

"I don't know why you even bothered coming here," he told Damian, shaking his head. Standing outside his home, he claimed Samara was more trouble than she was worth, though Damian doubted the sincerity of his words. The break in his voice and unshed tears spoke volumes, attesting to his undying love for his daughter. Yet he refused any assistance from the Black Crows regarding the endless search for her.

As Damian stood back watching in disbelief, Crighton faced off with Ariel in a screaming match, resulting in them going separate ways. More than anything, he wanted to fix their problems and bring Samara home safely. However, his greatest mistake was listening to his sister's boyfriend when he suggested using the map he had been gifted with. According to him and his lovesick sister, it was like a treasure map, pinpointing Sam's exact location on Earth.

"The guy is a reliable source," Eliza claimed. "Shit Damian, we've been following you for months with no results. When are you going to listen? If you really want Sam back, take a chance on us, would you?"

After arriving in the township of Casper, Damian knew right away they'd been misled, like all the other false leads they had followed. To make matters worse, a strange plague was rapidly spreading everywhere, turning residents into flesh-eating zombies.

To Damian's utter disbelief, Eliza and her idiot boyfriend still had faith in the map they'd acquired. But, of course, they were wrong. Damian's warnings and his pleas for them to stay together were disregarded. Foolishly, they wandered off, each on their own, in search of Samara and were never seen again.

Three days later, Damian surveyed the scene around him and began assessing his situation. He was stuck smack dab in the middle of Casper, low on ammunition, low on supplies, and surrounded by insane creatures of every shape and size. After barricading the stairwell that led him to roof, he was safe for the time being. But unfortunately, he was locked in a stalemate with two major problems. No water and rising temperatures, he was going to die of either dehydration or starvation. Those seemed to be the biggest problems though, along with no longer having backup support and constantly worrying about Samara.

All the planning, patience, and raw willpower by the Black Crows had gone to waste because of one stupid mistake. He never should have come back to this town. The fact is, he wouldn't have, if he had stuck to his guns and refused to listen to his sister. He'd spent the last four months avoiding this town completely, especially with Legend's body missing from here. In all truth, it held too many memories for him—memories cloaked in darkness and despair.

While attempting to distract himself, Damian thought about the peaceful countryside on Earth with its rolling green hills, mountain streams, and heavily wooded forest. That was his true home, not this horrible, sick town. Besides all the quasi-romantic bullshit he'd experienced in his life before meeting Samara, it was much safer in the country than in the city, especially with the Red War looming and Archangels arriving at his house. But with this horrible disease spreading and his inability to escape roaming zombies, how long would he truly survive?

Damian didn't know what the township had officially called it. Hell, he didn't know if anyone else was left out there to give the disease a name. All he knew was that the residents in this town had been affected by the deadly virus Lucifer had no doubt created after discovering he and his crew were heading here. If you were unfortunate enough to catch it by breathing air in an enclosed space, it was only a matter of time before you went mad. The high fever was a sure sign of infection. Within hours, it went straight to the brain.

Sadly, he watched his Black Crows—Cambions he thought he thought of as family, turn into wild-eyed beasts, taking chunks out of each other before coming after him. As far as he knew, the entire population of Casper had become predatory. But that wasn't the worst of it. Should a carrier of this godawful disease be brought down with a gun, a blunt instrument, electrocution or whatever, within minutes that same dead body would stand up and attack again, although a bit slower each time.

Damian figured something else out too. Shoot them in the head with a demon bullet and they would go down permanently. It became a rule with him—head shots or no shots. But ammo was precious, particularly pentagram bullets. That thought served to remind him of his current, untenable situation. With no food or water, trapped on a roof with only six bullets to his name, time was running out fast and no one was coming to save him.

Damian took a final pull on the cigarette between his fingers then flicked it over the edge of the roof. He watched as it spiraled end over end before finally landing in a tiny shower of sparks in the courtyard below. Unfortunately, the thoughtless action drew attention. Dozens of sets of eyes turned skyward, picking Damian out against the backdrop of the evening sky. Voices drifted to his ears, but they were no longer Cambions or residents in this town. Feral growls and piteous moans rose in the air all around him. Rotting hands reached skyward, directing the masses to his location.

Damian leaned over and looked down. The zombies were three stories down, and he was safe from them, but only temporarily. He estimated at least fifty of the walking dead creatures in the courtyard, and he was certain more were now inside the vacant hospital. On the other hand, their living brethren could prove to be a bigger problem. Breathing carriers weren't hampered by postmortem concerns, like decay and rigor mortis. They moved as fast as he did and were just as strong. He knew for a fact that two of them were searching for a way to bring down the fire escape ladder and ascend the roof.

Yet Damian remained confident that he could get past the zombies in the courtyard, even on foot. A decent jog was twice as fast as any of the rotting freaks could go. But then he would have to deal with the living carriers. They could chase him down faster than Lucifer's pack of Hell Hounds. Not that it mattered. With the zombies as support, the carriers downstairs had an almost certain chance of killing him before exiting the main door. He felt the frown on his face and the lines in his forehead. Since when was he so fatalistic? Or maybe, he was being realistic.

He spun on his heels and walked briskly away from the edge of the hospital's roof. He had to leave his rucksack and half his gear downstairs near the access door he'd taken to get up here, but he still had his weapon. He picked up the rifle—a nice lever-action Winchester 30-30, and jammed a round into the chamber. Action was better than inaction, he decided. He'd be damned if he was going to sit up on the roof and slowly die of dehydration. He'd be damned if he let them win that easily.

"You're going to have to work for it, fuckers." He took a deep breath and cradled his rifle in his arms. The sun was sinking lower behind the green hills to the west. It was going to be dark inside the building soon. He had an old, chipped Army-issue crookneck flashlight clipped to the epaulette on his shirt, and he flicked it on. Dancing beams of light swayed in front of him. It would have to do. He had nothing else. While pulling the rusty metal door open slowly, the hinges cried out with raspy, grating sound. Noise had gotten him into this mess in the first place, sending him to the roof.

He left the door standing open. Twilight cast a bit of illumination into the darkened stairwell, and he was thankful for that much. His eyes swept the roof. Likely, this would be the last time he would be outdoors, at least alive. He inhaled deeply, breathing in the scent of autumn. It seemed a shame. Autumn was always his favorite time of year. Halloween would be soon, and the thought made his eyes narrow. This year, the monsters were real.

With one last look around, he turned and stepped into the stairwell. His boots rang out on the hollow metal stairs as he began his descent, rifle held out in front of him. The creatures could be anywhere inside the sprawling three-story structure. He had to be on guard. After arriving on the third-floor landing, he stepped onto a concrete base and halted in place. There would be a throng of bloodthirsty creatures waiting for him at the door on the ground level. He would only hasten his inevitable death going that way. He wracked his brain for an alternate route. *Elevators.* The hospital was undergoing renovations, and during his harried ascent, Damian had noticed two of three elevator shafts were hanging open. Apparently, they were undergoing some maintenance just before the ungodly plague hit. There might be a way to climb down that way. It would put him across from the building with the greatest concentration of zombies.

He turned his back on the stairs and reached out to grab the doorknob. Turning it, he discovered it was unlocked but he didn't open it. Now came a moment of indecision—anything could be waiting on the other side. He took a quick breath, primed himself, and swung the door open, snapping his rifle up. The beam from his flashlight sliced through the darkness, illuminating the empty, sterile corridor beyond. He lowered the barrel of the Winchester but kept it ready for any sudden movement. He stepped forward onto the white tiles of the ward and scanned the corridor as he slowly advanced. There were signs of violence here. An empty wheelchair lay at his feet, tipped up on its side A bloody smear led away from it. He leveled his light over it and watched the beam taper off to nothingness a few feet away. The silence was unnerving. It must have been sound proofed. He could have company on this level without even knowing it.

Hesitating, he slowly moved the chair out of the way with his boot, sliding it across the floor slowly to make as little noise as possible. Then he moved on. Every room was inspected with his flashlight dancing through the empty patients' room where disheveled beds and discarded clothes showed the haste in which everyone left. Forgotten cards and pictures of families were taped to walls. A forgotten rose in a dried-out vase caught his attention. The dried petals were scattered on the table and floor.

Damian reached the nurse's station near the center of the level, resting the rifle on his shoulder and reaching up with his free hand to grasp the flashlight. He panned the beam across the walls, lighting up the signs, and the mural painted on the wall behind them. It was an eerily happy scene drawn in bright pastels of a park in the sunlight. People were having a picnic and a boy was throwing a Frisbee to a badly drawn dog. Beneath it, in shaky black paint was written: **Painted by our favorite little patients, 2013.**

Holy shit! He was in the children's ward. The plague had obviously spread throughout the ward, just as it had everywhere else. Damian shuddered at the thought, trying to avoid picturing the small children enduring the grotesqueness of this zombie pandemic Whatever had happened here seems to have occurred many days earlier. A sign on the wall indicated the elevators were up ahead. He was walking in the right direction, but unfortunately, the end of the hallway had been blocked to seal off the rest of the hospital. Rolling beds, mattresses, crutches, gurneys, and IV trolleys had been thrusted together in a giant heap. Damian surmised it was the last stand on the third floor. There was a gap through the middle of the blockage. It wasn't much, but he knew it was large enough for a living carrier to infiltrate the ward. No doubt they had pulled themselves through the opening, one after the other like sand through an hourglass. Whoever had been hiding behind that barricade would not have survived.

Taking great care to keep the noise of his movements down, Damian padded quietly up to the blockade. He slung his rifle over his shoulder and propped his foot up on a bed frame, reaching out his arms to pull himself up. For the briefest moment, his flashlight's beam flitted across the gap in the obstacle. Shrouded in the darkness of the hallway, it took less than a second for the carriers beyond to react to the stimuli. A hissing face with bloodshot eyes flew into the gap with bared, glistering teeth shaped into a feral growl. Damian yelped and fell of the side of the barricade, landing with a grunt on his back. The rifle dug painfully into his shoulder blade. He rolled onto his side and pushed himself back onto his feet. Before him stood a carrier, a living host of the virus. She was maybe ten years old and was spasming frantically as she tried to pull herself through the gap. Her arm was tangled in the debris, and she had lacerations up and down her face. Damian knew those marks. They were caused by demonic fingernails rending flesh. She had been infected by a living carrier, and now she, in turn, was eager to infect him.

Damian backed away slowly, rifle trained on her little form. He was breathing heavily, adrenaline coursing through his system. His vision swam and his trigger finger itched. But then he reminded himself about the ammunition situation, and slowly realized that she wasn't going anywhere. The young girl had mired herself in the obstacle. She growled and gibbered, foam built up at the corners of her mouth as she tried to get at him, throwing herself forward again and again, rattling and shaking the entire barricade. But her arm held her back. The pure, unsullied hatred in her eyes drove an invisible stake through his heart.

She was corrupted, body and soul She was the enemy—Lucifer's creation.

"Bastard," Damian whispered. "You bastard." He stepped towards her, raising the rifle above his head slowly. In the last moment before he brought it down, he thought he saw a flicker of comprehension in the little girl's eyes. Perhaps, he thought, even a hint of humanity, just like his sister and her boyfriend, before they vanished off the face of the Earth. Then the rifle butt smashed into her forehead, snapping her head back. She squawked once, a pitiful sound, and then fell limp and silent. The light went out of her eyes. As he watched, rivulets of blood ran down her now-peaceful face, dripping onto the white tile floor. Knowing she would come back to life in mere hours, he adjusted her arm and pulled her through the opening enough to have clear access to her neck. After removing her head from her body, he took a long, shaky breath and wiped the blood off the rifle butt and knife on one of the mattresses in the pile. Then he turned to go and felt his knees go weak. He kneeled quickly, reaching out a hand to the floor to steady himself. Why was this happening to him? To the world even? What point was there in going on?

He let himself slump into a seated position, back against the barricade and leaned his head back. His eyes drifted to the right, where the limp arm of the infected girl hung. He watched her blood pooling on the floor. Soon, he thought, he would be like her. At peace or perhaps in Hell. Maybe, he thought, he should save one of the bullets for himself. He furrowed his brow, glancing around the dim corridor from his spot on the floor. What was he thinking? When the world was dead and society was stripped away, all he had left were his fortitude and thoughts of Samara. Despair was not one of his defining principles, he reminded himself. He needed those bullets for a more constructive use than suicide. Rage, however, was always one of his vices. But even vices had their uses.

He pulled himself to his feet and dusted off his jeans as he stood. He turned to see the face of the infected girl. Her eyes were staring at nothing, across the large space, through the nurse's station. Away from her filthy damaged body, she looked at peace "I don't what kind of life you had before all this happened, but you didn't deserve this. No one deserves to go out this way. I'm going downstairs right now and I'm going to kill as many of those monsters as I can before they get me. You'll have your revenge and so will I."

Fuck the elevators, he thought. "I want them to know I'm coming." He strode back through the ward, kicking the fallen wheelchair he had passed earlier. It clattered into the stairwell and crashed down half a flight, landing in a bent and useless pile of chrome and plastic. He was right behind it, slamming his booted heels on the metal stairs and dragging his rifle barrel along the railing, making each step an exercise in making noise. Even if the creatures were two floors away, they would hear him coming. He had nothing to lose with Samara out of his life, but it would have been nice to have more bullets. To go out in a blaze of glory.

How many would he take with him before the bullets ran out? Five? Ten? Twenty? He rounded the final flight in stairwell and stopped in his tracks. He was facing the door to the lobby and could hear pounding on it from the other side. From an upper window, he could see that the sky was dim and blue—it was twilight. That was fortunate. The fading light would help him. He reached into his pocket, pulling out his crumpled pack of cigarettes, and opened the top. Only one left. He stuck it between his lips and lit it, watching the reflection of the burning coal as it glowed brightly in the glass panel of the Emergency Use Only steel case. Then he smashed through it with the butt of his rifle, sending glass shards crashing to the ground. He swept the rim of the case with the rifle butt, clearing away the shards still hanging there, and driving the zombies on the other side of the door into a frenzy. Their pounding increased as he reached into the red box and pulled out the heavy axe, cradling it in his hands.

"Alright," he said, walking back to the front of the door. He leaned the axe against the wall by his feet and brought the rifle stock to his shoulder. "Time to die." He took a drag on the cigarette between his lips, blowing smoke to the side, and then he flicked it away. Before he had time to dwell on the what ifs in his life, he reached out a hand, turned the knob and kicked the door with as much strength as he could muster. To his stunned amazement, the hallway was empty. He could see the swaying trees outside on the grounds through the building's wide windows, and the open front doors were no more than a dozen feet away. There was absolutely no one in sight. In fact, he could hear a pin hit the ground if he had one.

"Where the fuck are they? Where in the hell did they go?" Damian ran to the window. He had anticipated going down with a fight—in a blaze of glory. All the Black Crows had been drawn into the fight before disappearing between buildings. And yet here he stood, physically unscathed. There was no evidence that the apocalypse had even occurred, no grotesque bodies or even traces of blood.

Damian stood quaking in his boots. He dropped to his knees, disbelieving his own eyes. If not for the souls that had been taken, he might have believed it was a horrible dream, a fantasy of fear, an epic mistake. But in that moment, as he looked all around him at the undisturbed setting, he realized that Lucifer was behind it all. He set the stage, created the mind-shattering drama, and brought the curtain down, destroying everyone Damian cared about except for Samara. She was the key to all of this—the glass figurine Lucifer couldn't bring himself to break.

Not yet anyway.

Damian had to find her. He had to protect Samara from the evil that Lucifer would unleash if he discovered her whereabouts on Earth. Reaching out to members of the Magic High Commission might be the only solution. But the witches from the Gnarly Forest were unpredictable and were prone to doing their own thing, earning them contempt from other powerful beings, like Lucinda.

But Lucinda was a possible option. With her on-the-outs with her father and her rumored relationship with Hecate, together they could be the answer to finding Samara. After all, they had helped him once before. But if he didn't act soon, the nightmare he had suffered could be just the beginning and a swift ending to all of humanity.

CHAPTER 43

SAD REGRETS

Crighton paused at the door to Samara's room, before stepping inside. It felt foreign without her there, heavy and looming. All of it looked impersonal. Her bathroom and overflowing closet didn't smell like her perfume or makeup, it was tidy because Ariel wanted it to be perfect for her return. Colorful photographs adorned the cream-colored walls, and the lilac drapes matched her bedding. Crighton felt like he was invading her privacy as he opened the closet door and spotted all the toys stashed and out of sight. She had trouble getting rid of old things and collected over the years. Dolls, teddy bears, her fluffy purple elephant.

Taking out the elephant, Crighton stared at it. He had bought Sam this for Christmas years ago when she insisted on celebrating the human holiday. It used to be on her bed. Why wasn't it there now? Was it because she had grown up? Shit…was he so blind that he had missed that? But she was still smaller than him, so young. And she needed him, but he was afraid. He was, quite honestly, a coward.

Crighton swallowed hard, gripping the elephant in his arms. Then he spotted something glinting in the bottom of her closet, under a pair of shoes. A trophy? Was this the trophy in the picture on her wall? The one she had tried to tell him about when he had cruelly brushed her aside? It was no wonder she had shot the deer, despite her love of animals. She was always trying to please him, trying to gain his approval. After Caleb's death, he put Cassius on a pedestal that his daughter had no chance of reaching. He even risked his life in Hell to find him.

Damnit Crighton, when did you turn into your father? he muttered to himself under his breath.

He set the trophy on her dresser and sat on her pink stool facing the mirror. Who was this pitiful demon? Who was the guy in the mirror that let his daughter go? That refused to save Samara from harm, even when his heart told him that saving her was the right thing to do?

Photographs adorned the dresser, many of which he hadn't noticed before. And they were mainly pictures of him and Samara from years ago. One picture frame caught his attention. It had been laid face down, which drove him to pick it up. It was one of those cheap magazine frames, an Iron Man one. It seemed Sam had added a sketched picture of her own. It wasn't an image of her or her father. Not Ariel or even her brother. It was a picture of Spiderman.

Iron Man and Spiderman were her forever heroes.

Samara's curly writing was underneath the sketch. *If I was Spiderman, maybe Daddy would love me as much as Cass...as much as Ariel.*

"Here you are," Ariel said.

Crighton dropped the picture and almost fell off the stool. "Christ, baby, if you want to kill me off, try a more conventional way!" He chuckled and picked up the picture from the floor. Then he placed it back on the dresser upright this time. Tyrus was in the doorway, leaning against the frame with his arms folded.

"What are you doing here?" Crighton asked.

Tyrus stared at him. "Why would you ask that? Are we not family anymore?"

"Because this isn't your usual haunt, is it?" There was a hint of menace in his voice.

"If your aim is to make me feel shitty, it worked, Captain High Ground! I never claimed to be the best uncle in the world, you know!"

"It's not a competition. But obviously, Samara thinks it is and has for a very long time."

Tyrus pushed himself away from the doorframe and came into the room. He picked up the picture Crighton had just been looking at. "You should talk, sounds like you haven't been the best father, right?"

Crighton snatched the picture back and set it face down on the dresser, just as Samara had left it. "What the hell do you know? I don't need a lecture on how to raise my daughter!" It wasn't his best response, but a voice in the back of his head was agreeing with Tyrus, and Crighton didn't like it one little bit.

"I know that your daughter is in desperate need of her father, who brushed her aside when someone else came along. Cass is a great kid and all, but so is Sam. You won't like hearing this, but you know who I see? Castiel, our heavenly father. You whine and moan about what a crap example he was, but you need to only look in the mirror to see him." Tyrus shook his head and didn't hang around to elaborate further. He knew that his point was made, even if his half-brother rejected it.

Crighton growled. He hated being proved wrong. He would argue that hot was cold if he felt he was being challenged.

Ariel was in the doorway and Cassius had joined her. By the frowns on their faces and downturned eyes, it was clear to see they were miserable. "Dad, you told me that families always stick together," Cassius said. "If that's true, then where is Sam?"

Ariel smiled at her son. "You're right. We always have...until recently. If we don't find your sister, we won't be whole again, and I can't accept that. What do you say, Crighton? Are we going to rescue our daughter, or forget she ever existed?"

Crighton heaved a heavy sigh. "Alright, alright. Grab a change of clothes, personal effects, and some food. I don't know how long this is going to take, but we're not coming home without her. Not without our Sam."

Ariel flew at Crighton and threw her arms around his neck. She kissed all over his face and whispered tearful words into his ear, in an emotional embrace. At the same time, Cassius stood in the doorway smiling. "I knew you wouldn't leave Sam behind. I told mom this morning that you're too good of a father for that."

Crighton smiled cautiously. "Okay, both of you get ready. We need to leave here as soon as possible."

"No problem," Cassius said.

Ariel pulled out a bag from under the bed, opened it and was preparing to pack when she heard a series of knocks on the front door. She hurried across the living room to answer them, puzzled why anyone would be at their house at such a late hour.

"Ah...it's me again," Tyrus said. He was standing on the stoop wearing a sheepish grin, carrying his sword and a fully packed bag. "Thought you could use some help with Sam."

"Since when do *you* knock?" Ariel asked, shaking her head.

He stepped away from the entry, revealing the faces of two surprising guests. It was Verity and Hecate, the last demons Ariel ever expected to see.

"Um...Crighton! I think you need to come here!" she called out. "Right now!"

He leaned into Cassius' room and told him to pack light before joining Ariel at the front door. Then he experienced the same shock as his wife.

"I don't understand," he grumbled, uncomfortable in their presence. "Why are you here, Hecate? And you, Verity? What do you want from us?"

"Holy shit, Crighton," Hecate said. "You look more horrified than surprised."

"Do you blame me? I heard you were whipping demons in the torture chambers, thoroughly enjoying your job. I never expected to see you here without Lucinda on your arm. Should we be expecting her too?"

"Believe it or not, I didn't come here to harm you. Verity and I came to help find your daughter."

"And just why would do that? You have no love for her. Why even pretend to care?"

Hecate glanced at Verity. "I don't need to remind you, Crighton, that Lucifer is the most wicked, abominable creature that's ever existed. But his daughter Lucinda is becoming far worse. As they say, stay close to your enemies, and that's exactly what I've been doing. You might not know this, being isolated on Middle Earth, but after absorbing all the gifted beings in Hell, she's now capable of turning into anyone and anything she desires. That includes your good friend and half-brother, Tyrus."

Tyrus stepped out of the shadows. "I knew it!" he yelled. "Lucinda attacked my mother and allowed her and her friends to believe it was me. How perverted and cruel is that?"

Hecate nodded. "That's right. Lucinda is determined to destroy the reputation and lives of anyone challenging her authority. But worse yet, her goal is to take back her crown and destroy Heaven using her father's trained army. She's planning to kill him, but with the Mother Beast protecting him, none of us are safe any longer."

"The Mother Beast?" Ariel asked, furrowing her brow. "What is the Mother Beast?"

Verity glanced at Hecate before answering. "A huge monster trained to obey his every command. It will cause the end of the world as we know it."

"But that's not all," Hecate added. "An ancient scroll was discovered nineteen years ago. It predicted the return of the Phoenix, the guardian that will save our planet from the beast. We came here to share the identity of the chosen one and felt it important for you to know."

"And why's that?" Crighton asked.

"Because the guardian is your daughter...Samara."

"That's crazy!" Crighton yelled. "She just a demon...a female demon. There is no way she is a guardian. She is not the Phoenix. I won't allow it! I won't!"

Ariel laid a hand on Crighton's arm, silencing him. "I always knew there was something special about her. Samara has so much love to give and has the strongest soul and disposition I've ever encountered. That's why Lilith sacrificed her life to keep Sam alive. She knew what was coming and saving the world was her gift." Ariel looked around her—at family and unlikely companions willing to offer their help. "We have to find her before Lucifer does," Ariel told them. "He will kill our daughter because he knows the truth about her. But let me assure all of you, he doesn't. My dreams and visions are filled with my daughter. She possesses more power than any creature on this planet, but she hasn't been trained to use it. Although it can be an evil power and can bring death and destruction, it's truly a gift from above that will save all of us." Ariel reached for Crighton's hand. "We need to believe it's not too late to turn Sam away from the darkness, from the evil pushing her toward Hell and into Lucifer's waiting arms. But time is of the essence, and we need to act quickly."

Crighton agreed. "We never know how strong we are until strength is our only choice. Right, Tyrus?"

"Exactly. Let's sit down and make a real battle plan. Then we'll deal with whatever comes next. Beast or no beast, I'll grab everyone when the world starts shaking. You don't have to worry, Crighton. Our family will be safe."

"But what about everyone else?" Ariel asked. A short distance away, Cassius stood before Hecate and Verity, assuring them that he knew every tunnel in Hell.

"I don't know if it's the right thing to do," Crighton said, "but I'm personally taking everyone in and out of Hell. If we all survive, as I trust we will, just remember when it came down saving my family we were in this together...no matter what methods were used or what rules were broken. It's all about rescuing Sam and reuniting our family. Nothing else matters. Is that clear?"

Crighton and Tyrus exchanged knowing glances, and Ariel nodded, willing to agree to anything if it meant she could see Samara again.

CHAPTER 44

NORMALITY

E sther took out pots and pans from a kitchen cabinet and began preparing breakfast, just as she had done every morning for the past two weeks. Within minutes, the smell of sizzling steaks, fried eggs, hash browns, biscuits and coffee wafted through the air. Samara arrived shortly after eight and noticed that everyone was already seated at the table. They were all busy, either reading newspapers, typing phone messages, or making notes while eating.

Esther's gray hair was pinned back in a severe bun and her gray eyes were surprisingly tense. Her apron was loosely tied around her waist and was covered with flour from the biscuits she'd been making. Everyone referred to her as Mother Bear, and for good reason. She seemed to control all the "youngsters" in the room, including what they ate every day. The only problem was she had the tendency to overcook everything, turning a perfectly good piece of meat into leather.

Samara stepped behind her to get a glass of water and noticed a fresh steak on the grill. Picking up a fork, she stabbed the meat and slapped it onto a plate.

"What do you think you're doing with that?" Esther asked, frowning.

"Why eating it, of course."

"But that's not even cooked yet. It's bloody."

"It looks perfectly fine to me." She pointed at the charred lines on the steak. "Rare. Just the way I like it."

"Suit yourself," Esther huffed. "You'll end up with worms in your belly."

Samara chuckled. "Even better." She brought her plate to the table and cut a half-dozen pieces before taking a few bites.

Dante was seated next to her, sketching away on a piece of paper. Angling her head, she peered over his slumped shoulder, adding a comment to his progress. "Ooh, nice. So detailed for an architect rendering. What's it for?"

"It's our escape plan," he replied briskly. "A map that everyone can follow."

"Wow…you've gone to so much trouble. It's so elaborate."

"Don't be silly. Your safety is our number one concern." He noticed the blood from Samara's steak on her plate. "Now that's a surprise. All this time I thought you were a vegetarian like me. Not a friggin' vampire."

"It's better than eating leather."

Esther bustled towards them. "You need hash browns and scrambled eggs to go with that undercooked steak." She used a metal spatula to shovel more food on Samara's plate, covering the meat beneath.

Samara mouth sagged. "That much?" Her plate was piled high with food, more than she could possibly eat.

Esther jammed a hand on her hip. "You should have said something sooner. Now, it's on your plate and we don't waste food here." She hovered nearby, waiting for Samara to shovel food into her mouth.

"It's not that I don't appreciate it—"

"Did you hear me? We don't waste food…so eat up!"

"Okay. I'll try my best." Samara's stomach had been upset since she had arrived, which she attributed to nerves and anxiety. It didn't help that Esther fried everything in lard and used cream and butter in all her recipes.

"I went to a lot of trouble this morning when I could have slept in," Esther grumbled, loud enough for everyone to hear. "If you don't like my cooking, then maybe you should be doing it."

Aryan was flinging his arms around and spilled his orange juice on the table. "Oh, sorry, Esther. Clumsy me." He smiled sheepishly and stole a glance at Samara.

Esther came back to the table with a cloth, looking exasperated. "You shouldn't set your glass so close to the edge. Next time, you'll be cleaning up your own mess."

Meanwhile, Milo and Situs were having a raucous fight at the opposite end of the table. A glass crashed to the floor and food began flying.

"Milo! Situs! NO!" Esther yelled. "Spill another drink and you'll be mopping it up!"

Situs leaned back in his chair, kicking the table, sending a colorful drink onto the ground, and shattering the glass.

Esther completely lost it. "You're both pigs!" she screamed. "As if I don't have enough to worry about. Here I'm cooking meals all day, cleaning dishes, and putting them away. Now, there's glass all over the floor and you two will be the ones cleaning it up! You better hope the drinks you spilled don't stain the carpet. Otherwise, you'll be cleaning that too!"

Situs looked worried. "Sorry, Esther." He picked up a washcloth and Milo did the same.

"Yeah, sorry," Milo echoed, then softly chuckled.

Esther's face was filled with fury. She stormed away, cursing under her breath.

When Samara looked around the table, she realized that none of the others must have noticed, or if they did, they simply didn't care.

Aryan shrugged when her eyes fell on him. He knocked over a container of utensils, sending them crashing to the floor. "Shoot!" he yelled. When he bent down to get them, Samara couldn't help but laugh. After all, he hadn't lied. He really was incredibly clumsy.

"So, does this happen often?" Samara asked.

Blade answered from the right side of the table. "Yep, basically. But don't worry about it. Esther likes you best because you don't cause problems and use good manners. It seems those pricey etiquette lessons paid off."

"You could've used them too," Aryan told him. "Remember when she totally whooped your ass for trampling on her garden?"

Esther re-entered the room in time to hear the conversation. "It was richly deserved," she said sharply. "Do you know how hard it is to raise vegetables on Nexus?"

The room erupted in laughter, leaving Blade scowling. He turned his attention to Dr. Ashe, as she rose from her seat, adjusting the red bun on the back of her head.

"Done already?" he asked.

"That's right. I need to get back to the lab. I'm running a second blood test. The last one had strange results." Clearly, she was all about work, as she seemed to lack social skills.

"You're always in the lab," Milo called out from the floor, still moping the carpet with Situs.

"Oh, I agree. I foresee that staying at this breakfast any longer may be hazardous to my health." She pointed at the two troublemakers.

"That's stupid," Situs scoffed. "And so is your lab work."

"As I've mentioned before, laboratory work is complicated. It's not always fun, but it's necessary."

Samara put her chin onto her fists and asked curiously, "Does this test involve me, Dr. Ashe?"

"I'm not at liberty to say," she replied, holding an impatient hand in the air. "And, of course, it can't wait. So, if you don't mind…" She pushed her chair away from the table and walked briskly away.

Samara glanced at Aryan. "Dr. Ashe is very busy, isn't she? What is she currently working on?"

"No one seems to know. But feel free to call her Ashe."

"She introduced herself as Dr. Ashe, so I believe she wants me to call her by her professional name."

Milo mischievously grinned. "Of course. That's the reason why I don't."

Samara glanced at Fox. She was sitting alone and hadn't said a single word during the entire meal. Her full attention seemed to be focused on the celebrity magazine in her hands—the kind young human females enjoyed reading. Samara had to admit there was a time when she couldn't get enough of Brad Pitt. After watching *Legends of the Fall*, she fell in love with his dreamy eyes and perfect shoulder-length hair. But then a magazine story came out exposing his relationship problems, ending her crush.

Deciding she didn't want to interrupt Fox, Samara turned back to Esther. The Mother Bear in the group was attempting to spoon a third serving onto Blade's plate, which he was profusely refusing. Their interaction brought a bubble of laughter to Samara's throat. Esther was now trying to force-feed him, like an overgrown baby, and Blade wasn't having any of it.

As she looked around the room, Samara was surprised that she was beginning to enjoy her stay with these entertaining, complicated individuals. She realized at that moment everyone's life was different from hers and no matter how good they may have had it they experienced some level of difficulty along the way. While a few read books and magazines to forget about personal issues, other members were willing to insert themselves in deep conversations—unfamiliar territories in their attempts to make the world better.

For the most part, they shared what they were thinking, what they might have been feeling at a particular moment. Whether they responded or not to her presence, Samara just wanted to absorb the vibrations in the room, until she felt comfortable with interacting. Most of her words came out as half-whispers or soft-spoken words, but they all came out. And although some heaviness had been lifted from her shoulders by being there, it came back again—the fear of being judged, being ignored, being inferior even within her own family. But there was no ridicule in this group, no steps back, not a single insult delivered.

Oddly, for the first time in her life, Samara felt genuine warmth. While the most confident members in the group went in for a hug, she assumed the rest were hesitant because they lacked information about her identity—about what she was willing to bring to the table. Of course, they allowed her to take her time, explaining whatever she found interesting. But little by little, they had gotten it. They understood what it meant to be united for a common cause, for the future they all wanted to witness.

CHAPTER 45

DECISIONS, DECISIONS

Samara secretly followed Dante, Blade and Aryan to the cave next to the mental institution, and now stood outside debating whether to go inside. There would be an angry confrontation for leaving her room at midnight, and she honestly didn't know if she was prepared for that on a dark, rainy night. She had to bolster her confidence with self-talk for a few minutes but ended up tiptoeing in. If only to eavesdrop enough to discover what this clandestine meeting was about, she was determined to do it. She followed the sound of voices though pitch black tunnels until she saw a flickering light and the sound of voices nearby.

"Lucifer's army is closing in," Blade said, keeping his voice low. "We've got to get moving or it will be the end of all of us!"

The sound of a fist hitting a wood table jolted her. "I'm telling you she's not ready!" Aryan shouted. "We need to prepare her...to make sure we covered every issue."

"What isn't she ready for?" Blade asked. "We're cutting her emotional ties. She knows everything about our world, and she possesses the ultimate power. Why can't we leave now?"

"Because she doesn't know how to use it properly, and because we gave her three days to decide," Aryan reminded them. "We need to honor our promise and allow her the time she needs to sever all ties. We all know what will happen if she doesn't."

"We don't have three days!" Dante yelled. "Lucifer knows about the institute. It's just a matter of time before we're discovered."

What's stopping me? Samara asked herself. The sand was running out, and they needed an answer. But cutting off everyone in her life to save a planet? She wasn't ready to make that commitment...but it was a whole planet. She needed more facts.

Sighing, she turned back around. The walls in the cave were damp and musty with bits of moss growing on the walls. As she retraced her steps, every movement echoed in the dark, and it was getting harder to see. She went into the tunnels following voices but heading out she only had voices behind her and silent darkness ahead. It took a few tries, after coming to a dead end or two, but she found her way out and hurried back to her room.

She had so much to think about. She didn't have much time to make a final decision before Lucifer arrived. She sat on her bed feeling sorry for herself. Why was this happening to her? What if she just simply refused to help them? What if she didn't care enough about saving the entire planet? Shame filled her heart, leaving her miserable. Terrible things were happening on Nexus, and she was pouting over losing her boyfriend—over never seeing Damian again.

Well, he is your boyfriend. The guy you can't go ten minutes without thinking about. You deserve to have a happy life with him. Right? But that doesn't mean all those families should suffer because of your selfishness. You were chosen for this—and yet you argue with destiny?

The argument with herself went on for almost an hour, driving her crazy.

Damian was handsome, kind and loving. And more than anything, he deserved a second chance. If she gave in and followed her heart, The Tribe would label her an insensitive bitch for allowing their families to die. But dismissing her own family members seemed so unfair. She was trapped in a horrible dilemma either way. Sacrificing her happiness and love for Damian to save others from a terrible wrath was a noble gesture. Yet despite the prophecy, is it what she wanted for herself?

Samara needed the chance to decide, even if her heart told her she was being foolish. Seeing Damian one final time was a reasonable request, and it would help her make up her mind. "I've got to do it," she said aloud. "I simply must."

"You know, the first sign of craziness is talking to yourself." Blade was standing at the open doorway.

"Oh, it's you," Samara mumbled.

"Yeah, only me. Do you mind?"

She shook her head.

Blade entered the room and sat down next to her. He looked around at their surroundings before speaking again. "Out of all the nice rooms in this place, you ended up with this one?"

"You put me here, remember?"

"I guess I did."

"Is that all you came here for? To lament over your room choices?"

Blade's face held a serious expression. "Unfortunately, I've got bad news to share. Lucifer's spies are in the area. They're using a Tracker to find you. But lucky for us, we have decoys moving around trying to confuse them."

"Nice." She kept her eyes down, fearing he would read the indecision in them.

"I wish it was. They found our area much quicker than we anticipated. Along with that, we think they may have brought a beast with them."

"Into this world?" Samara's fear heightened, and she struggled to not show it on her face or in her mind.

"Yeah, but we don't know for sure yet. Fortunately, we have enough time to change your looks. If you don't mind cutting your hair and dying it black, it will be easier to smuggle you out of here. Esther is waiting outside to help you."

"So, you're here to tell me that we have leave soon," she said glumly.

Blade turned toward her, determination in his eyes. "Yes, that's exactly what we have to do. Staying here not only risks your life but everyone else's too. After we get you back to Nexus, we can implement better security and keep you safe until the time is right."

"The time is right?"

"Until we can direct your power where it needs to go. But I can't go into that right now. We need to get you ready."

"I'm scared. There are so many unknowns, and I hate to say this, but my heart is aching."

Blade put an arm around her back and drew her close. She tried to ignore the butterflies in her stomach and continued to stare down at the ground. Fearless now, his awe for her turning to tenderness, he lifted her chin, looked straight into her eyes, and smiled. But she sensed his courage was slipping. He wanted to run and hide, to protect himself from the approaching forces.

She lifted her eyes. "Blade, I can't…"

"Join us." He brushed a strand of hair from her face. "You belong with us…and you know it. I've never been so sure of anything in my life."

For a fleeting second, she felt a longing in her heart, but then it hardened. "I…I can't."

"Why can't you?" He dropped his arm. Disappointment darkened his brow.

"I...I'm still..." She cleared her throat. "Damian."

His brow furrowed, and he abruptly stood. "What does that mean?"

"It means I still have an emotional bond on this planet...on Earth. Damian is my boyfriend, and I care deeply for him."

"So, you lied," he said quietly.

"No, I didn't." She stared into his eyes, beseeching his understanding.

There was complete silence, and then Blade huffed. "Aryan knows, doesn't he?"

"Yes, but..." At seeing the harsh look on his face, she immediately changed tactics. "Blade, I promise. I will let Damian go—"

"Let him go?" He let out a hollow laugh.

"Just give me a chance," she desperately pleaded. "I promise...I will! I just need to see him one more time. That's all."

"So, seeing him is going to help?" he sarcastically asked. "That's going to be the first step to bring an end to this...rebellion? You seeing your boyfriend one last time."

"Yes, it will. Please..."

Blade turned away. "Fine. If you see him again and you honor your promise, then good for you. But if you see him again and can't let go, then I will take care of him myself."

With those words said, Blade slammed the door. She could hear him in the hallway talking loudly to Esther. "Put your hair dye and supplies away. She's going to screw all of us before she's done."

CHAPTER 46

FINAL GOODBYE

Samara rubbed her sore arm after getting a climate shot and vaccine for Nexus. The only thing left to do was cut her emotional tie to Damian and, as far as she was concerned, that wasn't going to be easy. She believed that her family had written her off already, so severing that connection had been done for her. Seeing them again would have painful anyway. They never would've agreed or understood her motives for going to Hell. But Damian had witnessed it all. She had saved his life while protecting her family's, and in the process ruined her own.

Dr. Ashe tapped Samara's shoulder, drawing her attention. "You might experience a few dizzy spells, which is perfectly normal," she said. "But at least you'll be protected from the atmospheric bacteria floating around in Nexus. We experienced a strange virus a few years ago, the source of which was never determined. So, the second shot should protect you just fine."

Samara thanked her and headed out of the building as quickly as possible. She slid into the back seat of a brown station wagon, now fully packed with five Tribe members and unmarked boxes in the rear compartment. When she asked Dante what the boxes contained, he replied, "Weapons."

She looked around at the passengers in the car. Aryan, Fox, Milo, Situs and Dante were apparently joining her on the three-hour journey. According to Dante, Blade had refused to come for personal reasons. She could only assume he was angry over her lack of commitment and emotional baggage.

Several guns had been handed out and were resting on laps. Small boxes containing bullets were on the dash.

"All this so I can see my boyfriend?" Samara asked, nervously laughing.

Dante nodded. "Your safety is our priority. By the way, you won't believe what Blade went through to find your boyfriend. He said he wouldn't do it for anyone else."

"Well, I really appreciate him understanding."

"I don't know about understanding, but maybe you could thank him when we get back," Dante said. He checked his mirror and glanced toward the backseat. "Get ready for a long ride, everyone. And try to keep the car clean. There's nothing worse than smelly trash everywhere."

The wheels rolled across the asphalt and onto the empty highway. After five minutes of loud music blasting over the radio and chatter reverberating throughout the car, the group finally settled down and soft conversation ensued. They munched on bags of chips and carrot sticks, and sipped water from plastic bottles. While Dante drove the miles it would take to reach Hollymead, Samara fell into a relaxed state of mind and kept struggling to stay awake.

Milo bit into an apple and began chewing loudly. "Did you guys know that my first kiss was on a battlefield?"

Aryan snorted. "What did you do? Kiss a corpse?"

Milo grunted. "And what about your first kiss?" He asked Aryan.

"Mine was totally sad. She didn't know how to kiss, plus it was weird with her crying the whole time." A revolting look went around the car.

"Females are always crying," Situs sagely added. "They're just too sensitive."

Fox bolted upright and glared at him. "Says the guy who sulked for an hour because a waitress didn't laugh at his stupid why-did-the-phoenix-crossed-the-road joke.'"

Samara smiled half-heartedly. She needed a distraction, and the carload was providing it.

Fox huffed. "And what the fuck, Aryan. Don't you dare tell me the girl was a poor kisser. I've seen you kiss with your eyes wide open." The carload roared with laughter. "Mama didn't raise a dumb bunny, so don't try to hoodwink me," she said, smirking. Noticing Samara's feverish daze, she crossed her arms over her chest. "These little boys need someone to shape them up," she murmured before sitting back in her seat.

The car quieted down, and time melted away. Then Dante called out from the driver's seat, "Looks like we are getting close, right?"

Fox looked at her map and checked their surroundings. "Yeah," she called back. "Fifteen minutes."

Samara took deep breaths, trying to control her racing heart. They drove down familiar streets and arrived at an apartment building a short distance from Damian's house.

"This can't be right," she told Dante. "He lives in a house, not an apartment."

"Perhaps he moved, and you weren't aware of it. According to our information, this is where he drops his boots."

Samara's heart fluttered with joy at the thought of seeing Damian again, especially after so many months apart. Then she reminded herself that she was here to let him go.

"Sam, remember," Dante cautioned her, "when you talk to him, don't reveal anything about us. Nothing at all, understand?"

"Yes, I know. I know!" she impatiently said.

Fox opened the door so they could get out. "I'll come with you," she said.

Samara's feet felt light and pure happiness was pulsing through her veins. This was it, the moment she'd been waiting for—a chance to see Damian! She couldn't stop thinking about his powerful kisses throughout the three-hour drive. Her cheeks were positively glowing, and she couldn't keep the smile off her face. At the same time, Fox looked extremely unhappy.

"The sooner we get out of here the better," she muttered darkly. "Just try to remember why we're here."

Samara told herself that she needed to be unhappy. After all, this was a final goodbye. But just the thought of seeing Damian again left her heart soaring.

Fox walked up to the large mailbox listing the names of the occupants in the beige-painted building. She traced her finger from Damian Hunter's name to his apartment number, while Samara gazed up at the balconies.

"It's 4C," Fox announced. They stepped into the elevator together, and it opened on the fourth floor. They rounded the hallway, and as they approached Damian's apartment, Samara noticed that the door was sitting wide open. Popular music was blaring, and bodies were crowded inside. Cocktails and beer bottles were everywhere, indicating a party was going on, but none of the faces were familiar.

What the hell?

Samara squeezed around and between guests in the room, until she arrived at the back of Damian's long, black sofa. He was sitting with a curly redhead, sharing his near-death experience.

"I'm so glad you survived!" she gushed. "Otherwise, you wouldn't be here. Now, would you?" She giggled and wrapped her arms around him, kissing his neck. "It's not good to be alone...not at a difficult time like this. I'll leave my number on the kitchen counter for you."

"Ah...no need to do that," he said in a casual tone. "I've got it etched in my memory."

"Really?" she asked, leaning back to look into his eyes. "You don't want me to write it down?"

"Not necessary. You're unforgettable, don't you know that?" He chuckled with friends seated across from him, leaving Samara deflated. A tiny part of her heart was so happy to see him safe and laughing. But the other part was a black pit that threatened to suck her into it.

He's happy without me, she told herself. *He's laughing without me.*

"Is that your boyfriend?" Fox asked. "I never would've guessed that was him."

While Samara stood back watching, the bimbo next to him patted his knee. "If you get lonely tonight, remember you can always call me. I don't even need to leave."

Unbelievable! Without realizing what was happening, Samara began circling the couch with Fox trailing after her.

"Sam, we need to be careful," Fox whispered. "Stay calm..."

"Hey Damian" Samara said, disregarding Fox's warning.

His expression of shock left her mind reeling. He pushed the girl away and quickly stood up. "I can't believe you're actually here..." He took a step forward and raised his arms out to her and she quickly stepped back.

"So, this is what you do when I'm gone," she said. "And to think I came here expecting you to be excited to see me."

"I am! This party isn't a real party, Sam. It's a celebration of life."

"Right. And who is *she*?" Samara nodded her head towards the girl. "Entertainment?"

"No, that's Mika…a classmate from high school." Seeing the matching frowns on their faces, Damian abruptly changed the subject. "Sam, I don't know if you're aware that El died four days ago. So did her boyfriend and most of the Black Crows. We went to Casper to find you and—"

"I see. So, I'm responsible for their deaths. Is that what you're saying?"

"Of course not! Why would you even say that?"

"Who else can you blame, but me?"

"Lucifer, that's who! He set us up to fail with a fake map, pinpointing your exact location. Then he infected the entire town with a horrible virus, turning humans into zombies. They attacked us and killed everyone, including my sister." Damian sighed. "I know it sounds ludicrous, but I swear it's true."

"Wow. I guess you're lucky to be alive then. By the way, interesting name for that town, isn't it? Casper? Like the ghost? And flesh-eating zombies? Seems my old pal is channeling his torture in a new direction."

The girl got up from the couch, flipped off Samara and called her a cunt. A switch in Samara's brain turned on and rage poured into her body. She drew back her fist and punched Mika in the jaw as hard as she could, snapping her head to the side. She fell to the ground, completely unconscious. Mika's friends started screaming and threatening to beat her up. Samara turned to leave and motioned for Fox to join her.

Damian hurried across the floor and stood before Samara, blocking her exit. "Why are you so angry?" he asked. "What did Lucifer do to you?"

She snorted a laugh. "Believe me, you don't want to know." Then she looked at Fox. "Come on, let's go. This party's over."

Damian held up his hand. "Wait a minute. You can't leave like this, Sam. I'm worried about you. Please stay…"

"Why? Clearly, I don't belong here. I'm an outsider now and can never come back."

"How can you say that? You have to know how much I care…"

Samara looked down. "I'm not capable of loving anyone. Not anymore."

Fox stepped closer. "We have to go, Sam. Everyone's waiting."

"Everyone?" Damian asked.

"Yeah…my new family," Samara answered.

"But you already have one. I know they're worried about you. Don't you miss them at all?"

"They wrote me off months ago. The same way you should."

"I don't understand!" he yelled. "Why are you doing this, Sam? Where are you going? How can I find you?"

"I'm following my destiny, taking charge of my future. And I strongly suggest you do the same. Goodbye, Damian. It was nice knowing you."

Damian followed her to the open doorway and stood there, watching her leave. "I'm not going to give up on you, Sam!" he yelled. "I love you! Do you hear me? And I know you love me too!"

After reaching the first floor, they scurried across the parking lot. Fox opened the car door and Samara slid inside. As they sped away, everyone was anxious to know what they had missed. "Come on!" Dante shouted. "Fill us in! We want to hear everything."

While Samara stared straight ahead at the passing scenery, Fox twisted halfway around in her seat grinning, her multi-hued eyes glowing. Her voice raised an octave as she launched into a dramatic account, capturing everyone's imagination. "After she flipped her off and called her a cunt, Sam totally creamed that bitch!" Roars and cheers of approval erupted in the car. "No doubt she'd do again if she could. Pow!"

Samara was dimly aware of the conversation going on around her. Still numb and heartsick inside, all she knew for certain was her relationship with Damian was over, just as she promised it would be. Yet more than anything, she hoped she wouldn't live to regret her painful decision.

CHAPTER 47

COMPLICATIONS

After the car arrived at the institute and the riders got out, Samara felt a wave of nausea suddenly hit. She rushed to the closest bathroom and leaned over the sink as dry heaves racked her body. Then her nose began bleeding. It was all over her face and down her neck. Leaning forward, she pinched the soft bit at the bottom of her nose, and the bleeding stopped after a few minutes. It was a trick Ariel had showed her when she was eight years old. It happened after waking up from a nightmare.

Funny how that just popped into my brain.

"It's no big deal," Fox told Dante. "Just trauma over ditching her boyfriend. I'm sure she'll get over it. Plus driving on those winding roads was enough to make anyone sick."

Samara could hear their voices through the closed window, which was crazy. She discovered that her magnified hearing was selective too. She could tune into conversations throughout the building, through solid concrete walls. Even listen to an exchange between Aryan and Esther in the kitchen at the far end of the building.

What the hell? What is happening to me?

Sweat was oozing from every pore. Samara's shirt and jeans were clinging to her body. She splashed cold water on her face and drew in deep breaths. When her body stopped shaking and she could stand without bracing herself, she stared at the square mirror above the sink. Her complexion was pale and dark circles were under her eyes. Plus, her arm was aching so bad she could hardly lift it.

Why do I feel so horrible? What kind of poison was in that shot?

As she made her way upstairs to her room, holding onto the metal rail, Dr. Ashe stepped out of her lab and called out to her. "Samara! I need to speak to you right away. I ran a second blood test while you were gone, and there's something you should know. Something that affects all of us."

No kidding, you fucking bitch! Samara shook her head. Did she say that out loud or was it only in her mind?

"I am so sick. I need to take a shower. Maybe that will help," she mumbled. "We can talk later…."

Blade was standing outside her bedroom door. The blank look on his face was as disturbing as she felt. "What is it?" she snapped. "I'm sure you can see that I'm not feeling well. Those damn shots—"

Blade shook his head. "The shots aren't the problem. It's something else."

"Goddamn it! What aren't you telling me? Why are you acting like such a pussy?"

"Are you hearing yourself, Sam?" He asked. "Really hearing yourself?"

"I'm hearing everything! More than I want to! Now, would you mind getting out of my way? I packed before we left. Are you going to tell me I can't bring anything now? Not even my toothbrush?"

Blade was avoiding her eyes. He seemed to be struggling with staying calm. "Sam, you need to know what happened while you were gone. It's crazy! All of it! I can't believe it myself. I really can't!"

The sound of approaching footsteps in the connecting corridor pulled their attention away from one another. Samara blinked and rubbed her eyes, disbelieving what she was seeing. Standing before her was the true Phoenix—the curly-haired brunette she'd been mistaken for, despite matching every description in the prophecy. Her purple aura was unlike anything Samara had witnessed before, and her face was so angelic, so flawless that she didn't seem real. She smiled softly, batted her blue eyes, and unfurled her gold, glowing Phoenix wings, causing Samara to stumble backwards a few steps. She simply couldn't take her eyes off the vision before her. Everything about this freak of nature was mind blowing, beyond mesmerizing.

To think that a Phoenix tattoo on Samara's shoulder had qualified her for this creature's job was almost laughable.

Blade cleared his throat and kept his voice low. "I'd like to introduce Shamara King, the Guardian and Phoenix from the prophecy, and the true battle-ready warrior of Nexus."

Dr. Ashe rushed up the stairs, calling out Samara's name. Then she halted in place on the top landing. Seeing the Phoenix, she bowed her head in respect and refused to look up. It wasn't until Blade cleared his throat that she was brought back to her senses.

"What's the problem, Dr. Ashe?" he asked. "Sam's right here. What do you need?"

She turned to Samara and spoke in a half-whisper. "Would you like to come downstairs with me? There's something private I need to share with you."

"Oh, let me guess. You're going to tell me that you stuck me with the wrong needle? Right? Because, obviously, your wonderful Nexus crew has a habit of making huge mistakes. HUGE!"

Dr. Ashe couldn't seem to make eye contact. Perhaps her nerves were jarred, or she was frightened for some reason or other. It mattered little to Samara. She was angry over everything that had been done to her, and intimidating this bitch was just part of the game.

"I...I think it would best if we spoke in private," she said. "Come downstairs to my office and we'll go over a few options."

"Options? What are you talking about? What did you do to me? I don't care if anyone hears this. You need to come clean. What's wrong with me, Ashe? Goddamn it! Just say it!"

The doctor put up both hands. "Alright, alright. If you insist on making this public, I have no choice but to tell you right here. You're pregnant, Sam, and farther along than you might believe. Judging by the power you demonstrated three days ago, nearly killing Blade, there's no doubt in my mind you're carrying Lucifer's son. But, fortunately, there's good news in all of this."

"Good news?" Samara choked out.

"The evil power he allowed you to share is his alone."

Samara tried to swallow but couldn't. She tried to speak, but the words just wouldn't come. She held back her feelings on the edges of moistening eyes and bit her lip hard enough to draw blood.

Blade shook his head. "I'm so sorry. This couldn't have come at a worse time. It seems you're cursed, Sam. Undeniably cursed." He kept talking, but his words became garbled noise, an irritating hum in her brain.

Then it was gone, thankfully silent.

Samara looked up at Blade, the inferior being she had come so close to loving.

What a waste of time...a waste of skin.

The smile Samara summoned was tentative and thin. "Cursed, you say?" Something twisted in her middle. Something blooming, climbing up through her bones. Something growing at an alarming rate. She rested her hand on her belly, stilling the movement inside.

"Don't degrade your souls to the extent of believing in curses," Samara told them. "Nobody can curse you except your maker, and mine is patiently waiting for our return inside the Gates of Hell." She moved closer to Blade and gave him a wicked smile. "Oh, my goodness," she said, "I can't tell you how excited Lucifer is going to be after hearing my remarkable news. The talent his son has shown while still in my belly tells me you've got more to worry about than my wretched soulmate and his trained Mother Beast. *We* know who our enemies are, and your name is on the top of our list...along with every self-serving Nexus creature on this planet. My son will burn your phoenix alive because, as we all know, fowl tastes better cooked to perfection."

Samara winked at Dr. Ashe and vanished into thin air. Where she ended up, no one was certain. However, two weeks later, boot prints on a wooded trail led Onoskelis to the location of a familiar demon, sitting under the bough of a snow-covered tree.

Inspiration behind Annihilation

The apocalypse was supposed to happen on October 21, 2011. American radio host Harold Camping had arrived at this prescribed date through a series of calculations that he claimed were based on Jewish feast days and the lunar calendar. In addition to his claims about the end of the world, he also predicted that on May 21, 2011, at precisely 6:00 p.m., God's elect people would be assumed into heaven, in an event he called the Rapture. Those who were not raptured, he said, would have to remain on Earth to wait for their doom five months later. According to media reports, some of his followers quit their jobs, sold their homes, and invested large amounts of money in publicizing Camping's predictions. When the Rapture did not occur, Camping re-evaluated his predictions saying that the event would take place simultaneously with the end of the world. After October 21, 2011, the self-proclaimed prophet stated that "nobody could know exactly when the time of the apocalypse would come."

Exactly. So, why do we continue to dwell on the end of time when we're enjoying the best years of our lives now? When the world stops spinning, hopefully not for at least 5,000 years, we can only pray that future generations appreciate the sacrifices made by past generations, and that the beauty that surrounds them continues to thrive. The creations and inventions that brilliant minds develop on a daily basis will someday surpass anything we've imagined possible. In my younger years, there were no cell phones, personal computers, or flat-screen televisions. Now, everything seems to be designed around comfort, flexibility, beauty, and affordability. However, while I'm living and breathing on this planet, poking fun at our "normal" existence and expectations by producing colorful, off-the-wall literature will remain to be my greatest pleasure.

Isn't it fun to believe that a demonic community, based on the normality of our human existence, resides in some weird twelfth-dimension universe, welcoming demons, and angels into their fold? This is why I write...simply to stretch the imagination and to thoroughly entertain.

—*Kaylin McFarren*

Author's Biography

Kaylin McFarren has received more than sixty national literary awards, in addition to a prestigious RWA Golden Heart Award nomination for *Flaherty's Crossing*—a book she and her oldest daughter, New York Times/USA Today best-selling author Kristina McMorris, co-wrote in 2008.

Prior to embarking on her writing journey and developing her popular *Threads* psychological thriller series, she poured her passion for creativity into her work as the director of a fine art gallery in the Pearl District in Portland, Oregon; she also served as a governor-appointed member of the Oregon Arts Commission and currently oversees interior design projects for the Yoshida Group of Companies.

Her self-published books are written in multiple genres and include award-winning romantic thrillers, mysteries, a time-travel adventure, and now, a paranormal fantasy series. She hopes that her stories are entertaining and that they linger in the minds of readers long after her final twists are revealed.

In addition to writing, when she's not traveling between homes in San Diego and Portland or spoiling her two pups and three grandsons, she enjoys giving back to her community through participation and support of various charitable, medical, and educational organizations, and encourages others to do the same.

Made in United States
North Haven, CT
27 January 2022

15358861R00285